Seth Margolis currently lives in New York City with his wife and two children. His previous bestselling novel, *The Other Mother* ('outstandingly well written . . . compelling' *Publishing News*; 'well observed . . . sympathetic' *OK!*; controversial . . . gripping' *Company*), went on to become a film entitled *Losing Isaiah*.

GW00707780

Also by Seth Margolis

The Other Mother
False Faces
Vanishing Act

The Hypnotist

Seth Margolis

HEADLINE
FEATURE

First published in Great Britain in 1996
by HEADLINE BOOK PUBLISHING

First published in paperback in 1997
by HEADLINE BOOK PUBLISHING

A HEADLINE FEATURE paperback

The Hypnotist is published in the USA under the title *Perfect Angel*

10 9 8 7 6 5 4 3 2 1

ISBN 0 7472 5469 9

Typeset by CBS, Felixstowe, Suffolk
Printed and bound in Great Britain by
Mackays of Chatham PLC, Chatham, Kent

HEADLINE BOOK PUBLISHING
A division of Hodder Headline PLC
338 Euston Road, London NW1 3BH

For Carole

Acknowledgments

The author would like to thank Assistant Chief of Detectives, John J. Hill of the New York City Police Department for his priceless insights into investigative procedures. Mark P. Goodman, an Assistant U.S. Attorney, and Gilbert 'Sonny' Hight, a criminal investigator, both of the U.S. Attorney's Office, provided invaluable legal background.

Renni Browne repeatedly sent me back to the word processor to dig deeper, and for this I am deeply grateful. Thanks also to Peter Cooper for clever advice that only seemed over-the-top at first.

Howard Koch, Jr. and Kimberly Brent saw the possibilities in this book long before it was completed, and helped guide my thinking in several critical areas. Warm thanks to my agent, Jean Naggar, who never wavered in her faith in this book and this author, and to Lou Aronica, a shrewd editor and enthusiastic supporter.

Finally, deep appreciation to my loyal friends at Headline Book Publishing in London – Clare Going, Sue Fletcher, Marion Donaldson, Jane Morpeth and Sarah Thomson – all of them as friendly as they are capable.

January 1963

From a distance they resembled two tiny astronauts, swaddled in bulky down coats, ski masks covering their faces, steam puffing from their mouths. They moved stiffly across a field of luminous snow, the smaller one clutching a doll of some kind, walking backward, the older one advancing with outstretched arms.

'It's *mine*.'

The smaller child hugged the tattered doll tight. 'No!'

The word was nearly swallowed by the whistling wind that swept curls of dusty powder from the snow's surface.

'Give it to me.'

The two children faced each other, neither moving, one a head shorter than the other. Even beneath the layers of puffy down, even from a distance, it wasn't hard to tell that both were girding for battle.

'Now.' The taller child stepped forward. 'Give it to me now. You know it's mine.' The voice was high-pitched, reedy, but with the carefully enunciated staccato of a child imitating a reproachful parent.

Still clutching the doll, the smaller child stepped back, hesitated, then turned and ran.

'Give it back!' The other child set chase.

They lumbered across the white field, plunging forward more

than running as their boots pierced the crisp shell of frozen snow.

What exactly were they fighting over? A doll, yes, but even viewed from a distance it was clearly not the cuddly kind that was popular with little girls and even some boys. This doll-of-contention wore a red, pointed cap. Its face had the exaggerated features and expression of a clown, yet it wasn't exactly a clown – too gaunt, almost menacing. And one of its hands grasped something long and thin. A cane? No. Although the doll was clutched in the smaller child's arms, it was evident that the object in its hand was being held aloft, brandished like a wand.

The smaller child reached a chain-link fence at the far edge of the field and stopped for just a second, looking in either direction then back toward the other child. The fence was seven or eight feet high, each link encased in shimmering ice. Climbing would be hard enough even without the ice. Impossible, holding the doll.

The smaller child scampered along the barrier, eyes focused on the ground to the left where the fence met the snow crust. The taller child cut diagonally across the snow before reaching the fence, gaining a few feet.

Suddenly the smaller child collapsed – no, the movement was more deliberate, like sliding head-first into second base. A moment later, safely on the other side, the opening in the fence almost invisible against the snow, the child turned.

'Leave me alone!' The high-pitched voice sounded tinny over the still whistling wind.

The taller child found the opening in the fence and shimmied through, though with greater difficulty.

The landscape on the other side was scrubby, forcing both children to dodge squat, snow-laden bushes. Puffs of breath hovered above the two of them, as if they were powered by miniature steam engines.

4

The smaller child reached the crest of a gentle hill and turned to shout. 'Go – away!' Panting out the words between breaths. 'Leave – me – alone.'

Crunching through the crusty top-snow, the taller child was closing the gap between them.

'Give it to me. It's mine!'

The smaller child charged down the hill, sinking into a waist-high drift before clawing back to the surface and plunging down again. The pursuing child also sank – there had to be a depression under the snow, or a ridge – but quickly managed to get back on track.

The lower half of the hill was protected from the sun by a stand of trees to the west. The snow crust was harder there, and both children were able to run on its surface without puncturing it. In fact they practically slid down the hill, skating on the shimmering, treacherous veneer.

A sharp whistle pierced the air. At the sound the first child tried to stop, but continued sliding and fell to one side, perhaps deliberately, to gain some purchase on the slippery slope. Even the taller child hesitated a moment.

A second whistle, louder. The smaller child looked toward the bottom of the hill at the dark gash that ran across the otherwise all-white landscape, disappearing to the north around a bend lined with pine trees. Train tracks, kept clear of snow from frequent use.

'It's mine!'

The smaller child started at the voice, and looked up into the angry eyes peering out from the slit in the ski mask.

Another whistle, nearly deafening. Both children turned toward the noise, captivated by the awesome spectacle of the approaching freight train. Within moments it was passing by, car after car, endless. The earth trembled beneath them. The smaller child – perhaps frightened, perhaps simply cold from

5

sitting on the snow – stood up and stared open-mouthed as the cars passed: boxcars, tank cars, flat cars piled with lumber.

The taller one reached out to grab the doll, but the smaller child cradled it just in time.

'No!' The protest was all but drowned by the passing train.

Again a mittened hand reached for the doll, now practically engulfed in the small child's down jacket.

'It's mine!' the tall one shouted.

'You said I could have it. You *said* I could.'

The small child turned to face the red, snow-topped boxcars whizzing by. The taller one raised both hands in front and paused for a split second, then shoved hard, sending the other child sprawling, propelled across the snow, tumbling head-first down the hill.

The taller child looked up just in time to see a blur of blue snow jacket . . . whirling black wheels, one after another . . . swirling gusts of white snow . . . patches of red here and there, where . . .

It was as if the smaller child had vanished.

The taller child sat on top of the icy snow, as if waiting for the other to reappear, doll in hand, from beneath the train. Minutes went by. Boxcars and tank cars and flat cars passed by the dozen. Quiet finally returned as the train receded down the track.

The taller child stood up and slid down the hill, eyes averted from the flattened jacket and blue jeans on the track, staring instead at the tail of the train as it disappeared around the distant bend.

At the edge of the track the child finally glanced down, then quickly away, and started up the hill, panting, slipping, falling back. Three feet up, two feet back down again. Eyes red, tears welling up. *I didn't mean it, I didn't mean it.*

'Mama!'

The child stopped half-way up and listened. The tinny notes were faint, muted by the snow. Had the minute music box inside the doll been on all along? No. Then why was it on now? The music was irresistible, hypnotic, its very faintness drawing the child back down the hill.

Eyes averted, as before, the child approached the track, crouched, felt around the body . . . looked squarely at it for one brief second, then grasped the doll and stood up.

The child stared at the doll, fresh splotches of red dotting its slender body, the music sharper now, more precise. 'Somewhere, over the . . .' The child switched off the music and turned to address the mangled heap on the track.

'He's *my* wizard.' A step back, breath puffing from the mouth hole in the ski mask. '*My* wizard.'

Hugging the doll, the child began the slippery climb to the top of the hill.

Saturday 28 January

1

Julia Mallet leaned over the bed and gently stroked her daughter's forehead.

'Want a song, honey?'

Emily nodded.

'Which one?'

'*You* know, Mommy. I'll start. "Somewhere, over the rainbow . . ."' Emily had inherited her mother's throaty voice; on the phone, she was often mistaken for a child much older than her four years.

By the time they got to 'troubles melt like lemon drops' Emily's eyes were starting to close. Julia sang 'Why, oh why can't I?' solo, and had turned to go when a burst of laughter from the party on the other side of the closed door got through to Emily.

'You look silly, Mommy. Everybody looks silly tonight.'

'That's because I told them to dress silly,' Julia said.

'Why?'

'Because it's my thirty-fifth birthday, and I asked everybody to dress the way they looked seventeen years ago, in nineteen seventy-seven.'

'Why?'

'Because that's the year I started college, and a lot of my college friends are here. It's a come-as-you-were party.'

11

'Why?'

'Because I'm silly, okay?' She bent to give her daughter a kiss, and Emily slipped an arm around her neck to keep her close a minute longer.

'I love you . . .'

Emily's eyelids were drooping. Her blonde curls fanned out on the pillow.

Julia stood up. 'How much do I love you, Em?'

Her daughter spread her arms wide. 'Much as the Empire State Building,' she mumbled before her arms dropped and her eyes closed.

Julia shut the door to Emily's room and heard Steely Dan's 'Hey Nineteen' over the roar of twenty conversations. 'Way back when . . . in sixty-seven . . .' She made her way through the apartment to the far corner of the living room and surveyed her guests. Emily was right, they did look silly: bellbottoms, peasant blouses, granny glasses, beads – lots of beads. Midtown Manhattan sparkled beyond the large window that almost entirely formed one wall of the room.

'Julia, you look fabulous. I love your hair – Pocahontas, right?' Gail Severance looked especially silly in a flowing, lushly floral dashiki.

Julia kissed her on the cheek. 'What kept you?'

Gail touched one of her earrings, a dangling silver peace sign. 'You think it's easy to pull a look like this together?'

She placed her hands on Julia's shoulders and turned her around to face a small decorative mirror.

'We haven't changed a bit since Madison. Except for the better.'

Julia studied their images. Gail overstated everything, but she had a point. The fifteen pounds Julia had dropped somewhere along the way since '77 had added definition to her face, accentuating her full lips, long slender nose, and the big green-brown eyes that were still her most striking feature. And Gail, once a chubby freshman who by graduation had seemed too thin, now looked chic rather than anorexic, with her sunken cheeks, flat chest and bony shoulders.

'I see Jared's on the prowl,' Gail said. 'He should wear a sign around his neck: "Warning, one-night stand ahead".'

Julia looked over the crowd and quickly spotted Jared DeSantis. He was easily the most attractive man in the room. Jared was *always* the most attractive man in the room.

'Marianne's here,' she said. 'She flew up from DC.'

'I saw Paula and Martin on the way in.'

'Separate rooms, no doubt.'

'Richard's here too.' Gail glanced at her friend and arched her eyebrows. 'Alone.'

'Forget it, Gail.'

'His separation became official last week. He announced it the minute he saw me, like a credential.'

'He's put on weight, hasn't he?' Julia said. 'Poor guy must be eating his heart out since Kim gave him his walking papers.'

'Heavy or not, it wouldn't hurt you to go out on a date once in a while.'

'Don't start, *please.*'

A glass shattered somewhere in the apartment, followed by a burst of giddy laughter. Julia started to move toward the hallway but Gail took her arm.

'Ever since Emily was born – make that conceived – you've been practically celibate.'

Julia sighed. *Completely* celibate – and so what?

'It's okay to have a daughter *and* a sex life, you know.'

'But a sex life is so . . . time-consuming.'

'If you didn't spend every spare minute boxing at that seedy gym you like so much—'

13

'Boxing is great exercise. Aerobically, it's better than the Stair-Master, the—'

'It's a substitute for sex, Julia. You know I always tell you the truth.'

'Well, in my opinion honesty is way overrated. And I need another drink.'

Julia turned and headed for the bedroom bar, snaking through the crowd, stopping every few feet to talk, still a bit disoriented by the unlikely tangle of old friends, recent acquaintances, colleagues, neighbors . . .

Julia Mallet. This is your life.

'Great party, sweetheart.' Jared DeSantis slipped an arm around her waist and pulled her toward him. 'I never knew you were so popular.'

'The drinks are free.' Julia gently extricated herself from Jared's arm. 'And half of the guests work for me.'

'Well, you *are* Madison Avenue's Top Woman Executive.'

Julia rolled her eyes. Would she ever stop taking flak over that Madison alumni magazine article, which had seriously exaggerated her importance?

'I'm the top woman executive at Todman DiLorenzo. There are plenty more senior women on Madison Avenue, thank God.'

'You'd never know it to look at that bunch.' He nodded at the agency group huddled in the hallway. 'All of them drinking white wine or club soda like good little scouts. Bet they'd wax the floors if you asked them to.'

Jared pointed his beer at Gail, standing in front of the living-room window, eyes darting nervously around the packed room. 'Is Gail planning to jump or what?'

Julia glanced at Gail. She was glued to the spot where Julia had left her, shielded by a gloomy expression that warded off all advances.

'Why don't you talk to her, Jared? For old times' sake.'

14

'The old college try?'

Julia looked back at Gail. 'Parties bring out her armor. It's like she won't let anyone but her closest friends get past it.'

'I wouldn't worry about Gail. She exudes something . . .' Jared stared at her a few moments. 'I don't think she wants people to get past the armor. She doesn't need anyone else. There's nothing really . . . hungry about Gail Severance.'

'She's a cookbook writer.'

'Ha ha. I look at Gail Severance and I sense a woman who's satisfied. Contained, anyway.'

Julia glanced at him. If anyone was qualified to appraise a woman's hunger it was Jared. But Gail, satisfied? She might needle Julia about her social life, but Gail seldom dated and had never had a long-term relationship with a man.

'I don't know, Jared. *I* look at Gail and I'm happy the windows are shut.'

Jared took a hot mozzarella canapé from a tray. 'Classy party,' he said.

'It's a lot of work. I don't know why I bother. Except that it's my thirty-fifth birthday and there are so many people I want—'

'I know why you do it.' Jared popped the canapé into his mouth. 'Throwing a party puts you in control.'

'In control of what? Three waitresses and a finger-food chef?'

'Your whole life is about control. Perfect job, perfect apartment, perfect daughter. And no husband to complicate things.'

'You make it all sound selfish.'

'Not selfish. But I'd love to be around the day Julia Mallet lets go of her control. *That* would be worth waiting for.'

'I'll send you an invitation.'

Jared lightly ran a hand over her cheek. 'Remember, back at Madison . . .'

Julia swallowed hard. He wasn't going to bring up their one night together, second semester freshman year? Surely it had faded into a forest of such encounters, vivid though it remained in her own memory.

'Those nights in your dorm room when you used to hypnotize us?'

'Oh, right,' she said, remembering. They'd get together, get high, and at some point Julia would hypnotize them, using a technique she'd learned from a psychology professor. Sometimes she'd manage to hypnotize nearly everyone in the room. Then she and anyone else not in a trance would think up complicated scenarios for the others to act out.

'That was fun,' Julia said.

'That was control. Ultimate control.'

Julia started to turn away but Jared took her arm.

'We all have only one, maybe two real strengths, Julia. Yours is your determination, the power you have. You might as well accept it, make the most of it.'

'I keep forgetting you were a Psych major.'

'It's the whole point of you, really, this authority of yours.'

Julia sighed. Jared was probably right. His most appealing quality to women wasn't his looks, splendid as they were. It was his way of making a woman feel understood – completely, profoundly understood – that made his focused attention thrilling and scary and incredibly erotic.

'What's *your* one strength, then?' she asked, wondering if he knew.

He closed his eyes for a few seconds, and when he opened them his whole face lit up in a brilliant smile.

'This,' he said with a shrug.

Julia felt a catch in her throat and put her arms around him. How long could he survive on that smile? At thirty-five, Jared had never held a job longer than it took to qualify for unemployment benefits. None of his friends, Julia included, could quite figure out how he supported himself, and he parried inquiries by mentioning the occasional acting or modeling job, his rent-controlled apartment, his meager wardrobe. No one pushed him too far on this; everyone who cared about Jared wanted him to be as perfect as he looked.

'Love you,' she said.

He revved up the smile and squinted engagingly. 'It's mutual.'

Julia turned and saw the rest of the Madison group walking toward them.

'This feels like a conspiracy.'

Gail handed her a gift-wrapped box.

'The invitation specified no present,' Julia said as she tore off the wrapping paper and removed a silver photo frame from a Tiffany's box. The picture . . .

She closed her eyes for a moment, tried to speak, then looked from one friend to the next.

A nurse had photographed the seven – no, eight of them – in front of Lenox Hill Hospital four years ago. They'd all come to escort her home, her six oldest friends – and someone new. Only the day before she'd thought nothing could top giving birth to Emily.

'I . . . you know what this means—'

'A simple thank you will do,' Gail said.

'Thank you. *All* of you.' Julia took a deep breath. 'Now I *really* need another drink.'

But she was waylaid on her way to the bar by the agency gang, who gushed over the apartment, the canapés, Emily's blonde curls, Julia's appliquéd bellbottoms. Even her boss, Max Altman, managed a compliment.

'You look terrific,' he said. 'The seventies become you.' He touched her shoulder with his right hand and left it there. Max

17

regarded her having a child out of wedlock as an invitation of sorts, a license. She was fair game.

Julia was about to remove the offending hand when Marianne tapped her shoulder and asked to 'borrow' her for a moment.

Borrowing people was Marianne Wilson's forte. As chief of staff to the chairman of the Senate Finance Committee, she maintained a precise double-entry bookkeeping of favors owed, favors dispensed, chits outstanding, chits ready to be called in.

'Jared just had the most wonderful idea.' Marianne looked the part of a high-level behind-the-scenes DC Rolodexer: soothingly handsome, smartly dressed – even in a peasant blouse and bellbottoms she exuded sophistication – tall, broad-shouldered, with a strong athletic figure.

'Jared's ideas usually pose a health risk.'

Marianne smiled. 'Not this one. Remember at Madison, how we used to get together in your dorm room and you'd—'

'Hypnotize everyone? Forget it.'

'Why not?'

'There are forty-five people here, Marianne. You want me to hypnotize the whole lot of them, make them think they're the Vienna Boys Choir?'

'God, I'd forgotten that one. I can still hear Martin's falsetto.'

They spotted Martin in the kitchen doorway, talking to an attractive woman who lived across the hall from Julia. His wife, Paula, was several feet away, resolutely scrutinizing a framed print.

'Not the whole group. Just us, the Madison crowd, after everyone's left.'

'But why?'

'Because it was fun. Remember *fun*? Anyway, Jared's come up with the perfect scenario. You'll bring us back to Madison, senior year, nineteen eighty-one.'

'What?'

'Look, you're the one who dreamed up the come-as-you-were theme. You can help us really relive it.'

'Why the hell would we want to relive Madison?'

'Because those were the best years of—'

'Bullshit. I was twenty pounds overweight and a compulsive grind.'

'They were the best years, Julia. You could screw without worrying about dying from it. We thought herpes was the end of the world.'

Julia smiled and was glad she'd persuaded Marianne to fly up for the party. Her decisiveness was always bracing. If the caterers went on strike, Marianne would step in to cook, serve, and clean up.

'Remember our pact?' Julia said. 'If Ronald Reagan got into the White House we were moving to Australia?'

'Yeah, well, Reagan was good for some of us. Martin over there socked away, what, ten million? You think he's still a Democrat?'

'Was he ever?' Julia said. 'I had a hard time believing he was majoring in Economics. I thought you went to college so you wouldn't have to worry about things like economics.'

'See what I mean? Those were innocent times. Even getting arrested together over spring break was a lark.'

'It didn't feel that way at the time. Martin had a fit when he got pulled over outside of Daytona. When the cop saw the marijuana in the ash tray I thought my life was over.'

'That night – you, me, Gail and Paula in one cell – it was magical somehow.'

Julia had felt so close to all of them that night, convinced that their fates were inextricably intertwined, and comforted by that conviction. Now, nearly two decades later, those six friendships were still the ballast that kept her stable and on course.

'I'll never forget Martin's wailing on the other side of the jail, demanding to see a lawyer.'

'But they let us go in the morning. Things were easier then. A few soothing commands from you later on and we'll all be there again.'

'All except me.'

'Mesmer himself couldn't hypnotize you, Julia. You need to be in control.'

'I wish people would quit saying that.' She stopped a passing waiter and asked for a glass of white wine from the bedroom bar. 'Anyway, I'm out of practice, and you've all changed. Who says I can get you all under?'

'It's worth a try. There's Richard! Has he put on weight? Poor guy. I wonder if he's heard of this new herbal diet half of Congress is on. I'll see if he's interested.'

'In the diet?'

'In *hypnosis*.'

Marianne left Julia and charged into the living room.

The party had thinned out by twelve-thirty. A few couples danced to a scratchy Led Zeppelin album – 'Carry me back, carry me back, carry me back . . .' – but otherwise a desultory end-of-the-party languor had descended on the apartment. Julia wrote a check for the caterers, poured herself a glass of wine, and hoped the remaining guests would leave soon.

Paula Freemason approached her in the hallway. 'Martin's calling our sitter to see if she can stay with the boys a little longer. I think Jared's hypnosis idea is brilliant.'

At Madison Paula had never been hard to hypnotize. Judging by her voice, not to mention the alcohol on her breath, she'd be even less of a challenge tonight. She wore a Madison College sweatshirt and denim bellbottoms; she fitted in well, but then Paula's wardrobe hadn't changed much since the seventies.

'Do you really want to go back to Madison?' Julia said. 'Does Martin?'

'I don't think he ever wanted to leave – he took five years to graduate.'

'Wasn't he on academic probation half the time?'

'The entire time. And I was Phi Beta Kappa and valedictorian. So now he's a millionaire commodities dealer and I'm a housewife and mother of two.' Paula sighed. 'Christ, I sound like a contestant on *Jeopardy*.'

Julia checked her watch. 'I have about an hour left in my energy tank. If the party winds down soon, I'll think about hypnotizing.' She headed for the front door, where a cluster of people were leaving.

Fifteen minutes later she fielded a moist kiss from Max, shook hands with his beleaguered-looking wife, and returned to the living room, where she was greeted by six expectant faces.

'I might have known you'd be the last to leave.'

'I'm feeling drowsy just looking at you,' Jared said.

'How flattering.' Julia faked a frown but felt a rush of warmth. These were her oldest friends, and the bond of shared history was still strong and reassuring.

'I loved it when you had me pretend to be Judy Garland,' Marianne said.

The other five groaned.

'God, that was *wonderful*. When you brought me out I could still feel what it was like to *be* Judy, with all those adoring fans.'

'I never understood your fixation with Judy Garland,' Richard said. 'I mean, she was dead by the time you were, what, ten?'

'So was Beethoven,' Marianne said. 'That doesn't mean I can't enjoy the *Moonlight* sonata.'

'Still . . .'

Marianne turned to Julia. 'Could you do that again, make me Judy?'

Jared sat up. 'Hey, I thought we were going back to nineteen eighty-one. And I have the perfect accessory.' He took out a joint and a matchbook from his shirt pocket and waved them in front of him. 'Mind if I smoke?' He put the joint in his mouth and lit it.

'How about the time you hypnotized us back to our childhoods?' Gail said.

'Yeah, didn't you set the curtains in Julia's dorm room on fire that time?' Jared blew out a stream of smoke.

Gail rolled her eyes. 'It was amazing. I'd forgotten all about it. When I was a kid I used to play with matches at my grandparents' house. Once I actually set fire to the living-room drapes.' She took the joint from Jared, inhaled, and handed it to Richard. 'I must have suppressed it – until that night when you brought it back.' She turned to Julia.

'Some things are better left undredged,' Julia said with exaggerated primness.

But in fact she felt a shiver of anxiety. It was one thing to play with memory in 1981, when they'd had no secrets, when candor was worn like a badge of honor. But adulthood brought with it all sorts of compromises, big and small – and worse, the deceptions and subterfuges required to succeed in a world oversupplied with bright, ambitious college graduates.

'Maybe we should call it a night,' Julia said.

'She's right,' Martin said. 'Maybe this isn't the time.' He looked to his wife for confirmation, but Paula was already teetering around the room, turning off the lights.

'Nineteen eighty-one, here we come!' Paula took a hit from the joint and handed it to Julia, who examined the soggy tip with a decidedly un-studenty squeamishness.

'I haven't gotten high in years.' She inhaled, struggled not to cough, and looked around the room at the six eager faces – nearly twenty years older than when they'd all met, but still, somehow, the most reliable mirrors of her own self.

She fought back a yawning reluctance. 'It's just that . . .' She exhaled the smoke. 'Well, I love you all . . .' She shook her head as if to clear it. 'God, one toke and I'm already a mess.'

'We love you too, Julia,' Marianne said.

'Seeing everyone together here, after all these years . . .' She picked up the silver-framed photograph. All seven of them beamed proudly at Emily, there outside Lenox Hill, as if the group itself had spawned this eight-pound-three-ounce miracle. 'I don't want to risk losing what we have.'

'What risk?' Jared said. 'We're family.'

'It's just that you can't know for sure what's going to happen with hypnosis,' Julia said.

'That's the fun of it,' Marianne said.

'Please, Julia,' Paula said. She looked almost desperate.

Julia took another hit and handed the joint to Martin, who immediately passed it to Marianne.

'All right, I'll do it. But don't say I didn't warn you.'

2

'Is everybody comfortable?'

Julia scanned the room. Her six 'subjects' reclined on the floor, backs against sofas and chairs. She sat at the end of the room, nearest the door. Nervous light from the Manhattan skyline outside her twenty-seventh-floor window flickered across the room. The ceiling fixture in the foyer provided the only other illumination.

'Excellent.'

She lowered her voice and concentrated on keeping out all inflection. *A deep, throaty voice like yours is an asset in hypnotic induction*, Alan Reiger had told her.

'Now take a deep, cleansing breath. Breathe in . . .' All six inhaled. 'Slooowly breathe out. As you exhale, feel the stress leaving your body. Feel the tension leaving your body. Once again, breathe in . . . Now let the tension out in a long, slooow exhale.' She saw Paula's head loll to one side. Already under? 'Listen to your breathing as you take deep, deep breaths. Pay no attention to any sounds from outside your own body. They are not important. They are not important at all. Feel your body relax as you breathe in . . . and breathe out. Breathe in . . . breathe out.'

Alan Reiger – a tenured professor, forty years old, married with three kids – swore he'd never once been attracted to a student until he met Julia. They became lovers midway through her first semester at Madison, screwing on the floor of his tiny book-crammed office nearly every weekday afternoon, Julia thrilled and frightened when he held her fast, lying next to him, while student after student knocked on the door . . .

'. . . Let your whole body ease on to the floor. Concentrate on your feet. Feel the tension drift out of them. Feel them relax. Feel the relaxation move up your legs. Now your shins, your calves are completely relaxed. Feeel the tension leave your legs . . .'

Can you teach me to do that? she had asked. The book on hypnosis and pain relief was on a floor-level shelf in his office.

Why do you want to learn hypnosis?

So she had told him about her father's bone cancer, the contorting agony that was destroying both her parents. *Hypnosis is a potent tool, a dangerous tool,* he'd said. But he could refuse her nothing.

'. . . the muscles in your stomach relax. Tension is floating from your torso, drifting away. Listen to my voice; nothing else matters. All you can hear is your own breathing and my voice. Listen to my voice. Your shoulders, feel them start to relax, feeel the tension rise . . .'

He had taught her how to achieve induction using nothing more than a soothing, repetitive monologue, how to gauge how deeply under the subject was. When Gail Severance recited the alphabet – omitting the letter D at Julia's suggestion – Julia had felt a shiver race down her spine, perhaps her earliest moment of total, self-consummated pleasure.

'. . . rising from your neck as it leaves your body, drifts away from you. Focus on my voice, on my voice alone. You are completely relaxed now. Your body is so relaxed you feel nothing, nothing at all. You are floating on warm air, floating without tension. Focus on my voice only . . .'

She'd induced her father quickly over Christmas vacation, told him that his cancer-ravaged legs were cooling, healing, that the pain was leaving him, draining away. He was to drift into a deep sleep, and when he awoke the pain would still be outside him, where it could not touch him.

'. . . lighter, much lighter. Your arms are so light you can't keep them down by your side. Feel the weight drain away from your arms. Your arms are lighter than air; they're floating. Floating . . .'

Paula's arms were the first to rise, Martin's the last. Julia smiled. Susceptibility to hypnosis was in direct proportion to the subject's responsiveness to authoritarian power. Paula took orders, Martin gave them.

Now six adults, eyes closed, held their arms in front of them like B-movie zombies.

She'd missed this, she really had.

Two days before returning to college she'd given her father a post-hypnotic suggestion: whenever he counted back from five, he would enter a light trance, sufficiently conscious to make pain-relieving suggestions to his subjective mind, from which he could awaken himself by counting to ten. He never said anything, but Julia's mother, suspicious as she was of the 'whole business' as she called it, marveled that his last months were far more comfortable for him than any other phase of the illness.

'The coin in your hand is so heavy now you can't hold up your arm any longer. It's so heavy . . . too heavy.'

Six pairs of arms sank to the floor. They were probably under, but it was always interesting to see just how far.

'Now, when I say "alphabet", I want all of you to recite the alphabet. When I say "stop", you'll stop.' Julia paused. 'Alphabet.'

They chanted in unison. She let them get as far as H before ordering them to stop.

'Now, after I clap my hands, the letters . . .' Julia paused to select two letters close enough to the beginning of the alphabet to keep the exercise from getting tedious. '. . . the letters D and H will disappear completely. You will erase the letters D and H from your memory. They will be obliterated. You won't be able to think of them, nor will you be able to say them.'

Julia waited just a second before clapping, then said, 'Alphabet.'

All six recited the alphabet. Gail and Paula charged right from C to E and G to I without hesitating. The others paused for just a second before the omitted letters – but all of them left out D and H.

'Stop.'

Sudden silence.

'Now, I'll ask you one at a time to recite the alphabet. Start reciting when you hear your own name and the word "alphabet". Jared, alphabet.'

His eyes still closed, he spoke slowly, his voice thick. 'A, B, C . . .' Pause. '. . . E, F, G . . .' Pause. '. . . I, J—'

'Stop.' He needed more work. 'Jared, the letters D and H have left your mind. They're . . . they're floating out the window toward the Hudson. You can see them drifting away from you. When I clap my hands, you won't be able to say the letters D or H, you won't be able to think about the letters D or H. They will be gone.'

She clapped. 'Jared, alphabet.'

'A, B, C, E, F, G, I, J—'

'Stop.' Enough. It was virtually impossible to skip two letters without hesitating, unless those letters had been erased from memory.

Three down, three to go. Suddenly she wasn't the least bit tired.

* * *

27

The age regression to 1981 was even easier. She just talked them back gradually, ordering them in a calm, steady voice to go back in time to Madison College, Haydenville, New York, senior year.

'When I count to ten you will wake up. It will be early May, you'll be sitting on the grass in the main quad. The sun is bright, the air is warm. One, two, three . . .'

Their eyes opened slowly and smiles broke out on all six faces. They glanced around, almost shyly.

'Finals are coming up,' Julia said. They turned to her, looking almost but not quite normal; their movements were on the slow side, eyes just a bit wider than usual, the grins on their faces vacuous. 'What's everybody doing after exams?'

'Getting trashed,' Jared said.

'My friend's father,' Martin said, 'he's this dentist or something. My friend says he can get us a whole fucking cylinder of laughing gas for the party.'

'Far out,' Gail said.

'Is that stuff safe?'

Paula began an earnest recitation of the merits and hazards of nitrous oxide. Julia recalled that Martin had in fact acquired the gas for a graduation party. She vaguely remembered a giddy night tinged with a last-hurrah hysteria, all of them strenuously trying to have the best night of their lives, though few of them, herself included, would remember much of it.

'He's got this, like, fifty-dollar-an-ounce shit,' Martin said. 'But I can get it for forty, forty-five max.'

Julia smiled. Martin may have been a lousy student, but it was easy to see how he'd made millions in commodities.

The conversation droned on for several minutes. Had they really wasted so much talk on drugs? Were they really, like so, like, inarticulate?

This is what they'd all wanted to relive?

Then the craziness started.

Julia didn't see it right away. Eyes slightly glazed, they were all talking finals, job interviews, the Grateful Dead, and the one inexhaustible topic – recreational drugs. Then Julia, on the verge of bringing them out of the trance, saw Gail staring at Martin Freemason as if he were Jerry Garcia in the flesh. Was she seeing him as he had looked in 1981? He'd been one of the cuter boys in the Madison senior class, cute being the highest of accolades back then. If anything, his looks had improved over the years, his features acquiring definition if not authority.

Still, Gail wasn't the type to moon over a boy, never had been. Julia saw Martin glance at her, then quickly turn away. A moment later he looked back, as if to confirm that Gail was still watching him, then turned away again.

The conversation buzzed along. Julia was about to get their attention and bring them out when Gail started crawling across the living-room floor toward Martin. He shot her a warning look, alternately glaring at her and at the others – especially Paula, who'd been his girlfriend for years before they got married.

Gail slid her arm around Martin's shoulder and began nuzzling him.

'Stop it,' Martin whispered.

All eyes turned to them.

Gail rubbed her shoulder against Martin. Any minute now, she'd be purring.

'Get away from me,' he said, louder this time.

When Gail ignored him he shoved his elbow into her side. She rocked back on her haunches and stared at him, her eyes filled with tears that threatened to spill over.

'Gail, please.'

'You said . . . you said you would *tell* her.'

Martin glanced at Paula.

'You told me you were *tired* of her,' Gail said. 'You told me she was boring, a lousy—'

'Why are you saying these things?' Martin was still whispering, as if the entire room couldn't see and hear exactly what was going on. 'Why don't you go back to—'

'What is she talking about, Martin?'

All heads turned to Paula, whose face had gone white.

'She's stoned,' he said. 'Fucked up.'

'I am *not*.' Gail slithered toward him again, but he blocked her with an elbow. She stared intently at his arm for a moment, as if it held the key to their misunderstanding. Then she glanced up at his face.

'You fucked me – hard – and now you're just, like, saying it never happened?'

'Martin, what is she *talking* about?' Paula said.

'Just bullshit,' Martin said. 'I told you, she's wrecked—'

'NOT bullshit.' Gail started pummeling Martin with both fists. 'It wasn't. Wasn't.'

Julia clapped her hands. Enough with the time-tripping. For a minute there she'd neglected her responsibility as impresario.

'Okay, everybody, listen up. When I say—'

'NO!' Paula lurched across the room at Gail and Martin, flailing at the two of them in such a flurry of movement it was hard to tell which one was the target.

'Listen up! I'm going to count to . . .'

But it was no use. Now Jared was trying to pull the three brawlers apart. Marianne hovered to one side, gazing fascinated at the unlikely trio. Richard Portland was staring into his lap, moaning 'Truckin'.' She'd have to deal with them one at a time.

'Paula. Paula!' Julia managed to get her arms on Paula's shoulders and locked eyes with her. 'Paula, when I count to ten I want you to—'

Wait a minute. Was it wise to bring Paula back to the present while leaving the others in 1981? Julia had already decided that when this soap opera was over she'd order all six of them to forget everything that had gone on. Maybe Paula had never known about her husband and Gail. Or maybe she knew but had forgiven him.

She let go of Paula, who immediately rejoined the brawl, and glanced around the room. There was no way she'd be able to bring them out *en masse*; she'd have to start with Paula, get her out of the fray as soon as possible. But what would she do with her while she worked on the others? She didn't want to risk having Paula witness – from a contemporary perspective – what was going on in their little circle.

Shit. She'd done this dozens of times and it had never gotten out of control.

Think, Julia! She wouldn't bring Paula out of her hypnotic trance; she'd move her to another place. Another mental place.

'Paula!' She took her friend by the shoulders. 'Paula, I'm going to count back from five. When I reach *one* you will close your eyes. Then I'll count up to five, and when you wake . . .' Julia paused. What year should she pick? Something safely distant, when they were children. But not too early, when they were just babies – that could get messy. She'd make them four, Emily's age. All of them had been born in 1959, so she'd add a few years . . .

'When you wake it will be nineteen sixty-three. You will be four, four and a half years old. Paula, when I count back to one you will close your eyes and sleep. When I count up to five you will awaken as yourself, but the year will be nineteen sixty-three. Five, four, three, two, one.'

Paula's eyes closed slowly. So far, so good.

'One, two, three, four, five.'

Paula opened her eyes, blinked, looked around. 'Mommy?'

Julia had to smile at the childish inflection. 'Be a good little girl and I'll be right with you.'

Now for the others. She'd take them all back to 1963, which would serve as a kind of buffer zone between the débâcle of 1981 and the present. Surely there were no sexual peccadilloes in 1963! She'd start with Gail, then Martin. And once the three most agitated people were safely in their childhoods, she'd be able to mass-hypnotize the remaining three.

Then, after a few calming minutes, she'd bring them all out.

Light-headed with exhaustion, the grass having long since worn off, Julia surveyed her six friends and found their antics anything but amusing. She was just too damn tired – and scared. Losing control as a hypnotist was dangerous. What if she hadn't been able to bring them out of the Madison trance? It would have worn off eventually – hypnotic states are never permanent, horror movies notwithstanding – but before that happened things could have gotten even more unpleasant.

At the moment they were all moving around the living room, inspecting every piece of furniture, every object, with childlike fascination. There wasn't much interaction, though. Just like Emily with her friends – parallel play, it was called, and it perfectly described what she was witnessing: six adults who thought they were children, moving close to each other but having little or no contact.

Richard walked across the room and curled up next to Julia on the sofa, leaning his head against her shoulder.

Oh, Lord. Julia shimmied a few inches down the couch but he followed her. He was nuzzling his cheek against her arm when a shout distracted them both.

'That's *mine*!'

It was Marianne, holding the framed photograph.

'I had it first,' Gail said in a whiny voice.

The other 'children' turned to watch.

'Give it to me,' Gail said.

Marianne pulled the photo to her chest. Gail's hand shot out and grabbed for it. Even without sex, things could get ugly.

'Children!' Julia shouted.

Marianne and Gail froze.

'Put the frame back on the table.'

Marianne looked defiant.

'*Now.*'

Marianne replaced the photo.

Julia cleared her throat and summoned a last surge of energy. 'Thank you. Now, everyone pay attention. When I count to ten, you'll . . .'

Paula lunged across the room, hurling herself against her husband. Martin, caught by surprise, toppled to the floor, Paula on top of him. The others stood gaping, except for Jared, who took several steps back, practically flattening himself against the window. His eyes were wide with terror; his hands, balled into fists, thumped against his hips.

As Paula pummelled her husband, Gail sank slowly to her knees, drawling out some sort of song, tears overspilling her eyes.

This was bad. Some vestige of hostility from 1981 must have remained in their subconscious minds.

'Okay, listen up. I want everyone to . . . I want everyone to sing a song. Together. How about . . .' It took her only a second to come up with a tune they'd all know. '"Somewhere, over the rainbow, way up high . . ."'

Jared joined in first, then Paula, and finally the others. Now the room was a cacophony of scratchy, tired voices.

Saved by the Wizard of Oz. Julia waited a moment, then crossed the room and grabbed Paula by the shoulders.

'When I count to five, you will—'

The doorbell.

Julia cursed as she left the six choristers in the living room. She hurried to the front door, peered through the peephole, and felt her spirits sink even lower.

Max Altman.

She opened the door just a crack.

'Sorry to bother you, I left my raincoat.' His words were slurred, but there was nothing fuzzy about the leer on his face.

'I didn't see it,' Julia said.

'Oh.' He teetered to the left, then pushed against the door, barging right past her. 'How about a drink, Julia? I came all the way over . . .'

'You live three blocks away, Max, and I'm tired.'

'We can . . . discuss the media . . . the media plan for . . . whatever the hell product you're working on.' He grinned as he slapped a hand on her shoulder and let it slide down her arm. 'You're the one . . . you never stop talking about fucking business.'

He took two steps into the apartment and stopped short. 'What the hell . . . ?'

The Madison crowd huddled in the center of the living room, intently if dissonantly singing '. . . that's where you'll find me . . .'

'Max, you have to leave. Now.'

He glanced at her, then back at the chorus. 'Weird,' he said, then tottered past her and out of the door.

Julia returned to the living room, and Paula.

'When I count to five, you will fall into a deep sleep. When I count back to one, you will wake up with no memory of what has happened.'

Paula stopped singing and looked over at her husband, who was dutifully belting out the song. Julia repeated the instruction, then pushed Paula on to a chair and counted to five. Paula's eyes finally closed.

Thank God.

'Sit down, all of you,' she said.

Only Jared failed to obey. Julia led him by the elbow to the couch, pushed him down, and practically shouted her instructions.

'You will have no memory of what has happened under hypnosis. No memory at all.'

She counted to five and scanned the room. All six were out. She counted from five down; six pairs of eyes opened slowly and blinked.

Richard was the first to speak. 'I thought you were going to hypnotize us.'

Gail nodded. 'You were going to take us to nineteen eighty-one.'

Julia shrugged. 'I tried,' she said. 'A few of you went under, but not everybody. It didn't seem fair to—'

'But it's almost two o'clock,' Martin said. 'I could swear it wasn't even one when we started.'

'It took forever to get just a few of you in a trance, then I tried for a half-hour to get the rest of you under. Now it's late, and I hate to be a lousy host but I'm dead on my feet . . .'

Only Martin looked dubious as they all left the living room. Julia saw him place a hand on Paula's shoulder, but she squirmed out from under it.

Julia hugged Gail at the door. 'Did you have a good time?'

'Wonderful,' Gail said. 'Great party.'

Julia's only other concern was Jared. She kissed him on the cheek; he put his arms around her, letting one hand fall on to her ass. She needn't have worried about him.

She said goodbye to the last of the guests and slumped against the door. Disaster had been averted, if narrowly.

She walked into Emily's room, leaned over the bed and kissed her warm forehead. She went to her own bedroom and undressed, trying to shake the picture of Paula hurling herself at Martin and Gail . . .

Shit! She'd forgotten to renormalize them after the alphabet test, and that kind of induced amnesia could linger for several days. What if one of them had trouble with the newspaper tomorrow morning, or wrote a memo on Monday omitting all Ds and Hs?

Julia yawned and climbed into bed. Emily woke up at seven-fifteen on the dot no matter what time she went to sleep. Worry about the missing letters would have to wait until morning.

Sunday 29 January

3

In Manhattan, the heavy mid-January snowfall covers a multitude of urban sins: garbage, potholes, the pitiful flimsiness of the acacia trees – more often referred to as ghetto palms – that line the streets. Even the noise level is muffled by the dense snow.

West 73rd is a fairy-tale street. Fresh powder gilds the orderly rows of hundred-year-old brownstones. Few people venture out in the blizzard; when they do their footsteps crunch heavily as they make their way carefully down the precipitous stoops to the sidewalks.

Snow has even begun to accumulate on the head and arms of the Wizard, huddled between two stairways near the Columbus Avenue end of the street. How long has it been? One hour? Two? The cold penetrated the thick parka after fifteen minutes; now it is starting to infiltrate the body, reaching deeper and deeper, numbing muscle and bone – no, not numbing, or there wouldn't be that droning pain. Behind a wool ski mask the Wizard's eyes are red and ridged with cold-tears. A leather glove bats a glaze of snow from the top of the mask. The Wizard glances right, left.

Where is she? Where is the monster?

The tall, thin woman left her building at eight-fifteen, carrying a satchel. The Wizard followed her to a health club on Columbus. How long can anybody stay at a gym on a Sunday night, with children at home? Earlier that day, when the Wizard saw her with the children . . .

A figure turns on to the street from Columbus. The Wizard hears the crunching, peeks out. No, it's a man, hands in pockets, head bowed against the driving snow.

Ten minutes pass. Fifteen. Shivers have intensified into shudders, a near-constant physical humming, like an idling engine. But the Wizard isn't even close to giving up. Pain is familiar – not welcome, exactly, but reassuring in a way. Pain is a reminder.

Concentrate, concentrate. *Remember*. Eyes closed, it all comes back: the darkness, the smell of coats – the sweet, sharp smells were mother's, the musky ones *his* – the bed a nest of shoes and boots and hangers that fell when the front door slammed for the second time and it became clear that there would be no release until morning. It was safe inside, even though the sound of the key turning in the closet lock meant soiled pants more often than not.

Memory is fuel now, the kindling of motivation, long dormant until it returned without warning to—

Someone has turned the corner. The Wizard steps from behind the stoop, looks.

It's her. Walking down the street, stepping carefully through the accumulating snow. Her chin-length hair is tucked up inside her wool cap, but there's no mistaking who she is. Or what she is. *Monster*.

The Wizard steps from behind the stoop, crosses the street, walks swiftly toward the woman, stops just ten feet away. Heart pumping, body now warm with anticipation. *Now*.

'Which way is Broadway?'

The words are almost swallowed by the wind, but the woman hears, stops, turns to answer. Sees the gun.

'Oh, no. Oh, please God—'

'In there.' The Wizard gestures to a recess formed by two stoops situated fifteen feet apart.

'Please, no. I only have ten, maybe fifteen dollars. I'll give you everything I—'

'*Now.*'

The woman steps into the dark alcove. She continues to plead, but her words have no impact. *Remember*. Smell his musky presence, looming in the closet door. Let memory be the guide.

'Please, I have two small children – they need me, please don't—'

'I know all about your children.'

The first bullet misses the woman, setting off a mini avalanche of plaster and snow.

'Oh no please no please no I beg—'

Monster.

The second bullet explodes just above her nose, throwing her back against the stoop then down to the ground, leaving a lurid red trail.

A surge of warmth, a pleasurable tensing down below. Yes, this is right, there was no mistake. Breathing heavily, trembling – but not from the cold.

Hide the gun now! In the right pocket, not the left. In the left is the paint. Yes, here it is. The cap pops off. Shake it first. *Click click click* – the agitator ball. The Wizard smiles at the notion: the agitator ball. Now cover the face. Cover it! The Wizard brought the paint without really knowing why. But deep impulses are in control now; the Wizard merely obeys. Shiny, runny black paint coats the woman's face, covers the blood, the dusting of snow.

Now the wall. The Wizard shakes the can again, aims it at the wall.

Damn. The wall is already defiled with graffiti. Seven deft strokes with the can and the signature is complete.

No time now. The Wizard replaces the can in the left pocket, peers out from the recess, finds the street empty but turns back to the woman.

Even covered with paint and blood, the monster's face endures. The Wizard takes out the gun, fires again. And again.

The face is gone.

Monday 30 January

4

The doorbell rang just as Julia was wrestling Emily into her winter coat.

'Who is it?' she shouted through the closed door.

'Detective Bettalini, Police Department.'

Police Department? She unlocked the door. Detective Bettalini – heavy-set, with dark skin and thick silver hair – flashed his badge and stepped into the apartment.

'Mind if I come in?' he said.

Julia was about to close the door behind him when she heard a commotion from the hallway. She glanced out and saw a policeman in front of apartment 15D, talking to the tenant. Another cop was just leaving 15F.

'What's going on?'

Emily grabbed a handful of Julia's skirt, staring wide-eyed at Bettalini, who was looking around the foyer through squinting eyes, as if he expected to find a body slumped in a corner.

'*Hello*?' Julia said. 'I asked you what's—'

'You are Mrs . . . ?'

'Ms Mallet. Julia Mallet.'

He wrote her name on a small pad of paper.

'Do you know Jessica Forrester, lives in 12C?'

'I've met her . . . why?'

'When was the last time you saw her?'

Julia shook her head slowly. 'I see her in the elevator occasionally on the way home from work.'

'How recently?'

'I really don't know – a week ago, two? Has something happened to her?'

'She was . . .' He looked down at Emily. 'Don't you have something to do in your room, sweetheart?'

Emily stepped behind Julia, still clinging to her skirt.

Bettalini shrugged. 'She was killed a few blocks from here, last night.'

'Oh my God. How—'

'What were you doing last night, *Mizz* Mallet?'

'I was home with my daughter the entire . . . Why in the world are you asking *me*?'

'We're doing a door-to-door, the entire building. Anyone see you at home? Your husband?'

'I'm not married. Emily was here with me.'

'What time did Emily go to sleep last night?'

'Eight-thirty, nine. As usual.'

He noted this in his pad, snapped it shut, and fished a card from his coat pocket.

'You think of anything, here's my number.'

She took the card. 'I'm sure there's—'

'*Anything*. A conversation with the deceased, something you heard in the laundry room. Call me.'

He let himself out. Julia stood in the foyer for a few moments, deaf to Emily's breathless questions. A doorbell chimed across the hall, and Julia heard Bettalini announcing himself a few seconds later.

'*Mommy*, how come he's not wearing a uniform? Is he a real police?'

'What? Oh, yes, he's . . . We have to hurry, Em. We're late

for school.' She grabbed her keys and left the apartment. At the end of the hallway two police officers conferred in hushed voices. The elevator was empty, but the lobby was unusually crowded for this time of day, as residents huddled in small groups to discuss the news. People who had barely acknowledged each other in the past were eagerly exchanging information, acting . . . neighborly. Even murder had its positive side.

'I don't *want* you to go.'

Emily buried her face in her mother's skirt. Julia glanced around the pre-school classroom, found Emily's teacher, and mouthed, 'Help me.'

'The Monday morning syndrome,' she said, as Robin Lane placed a hand on Emily's shoulder. The visit from the detective hadn't helped matters. Emily was uncanny at picking up on Julia's mood.

'Your friends are playing house in the corner, Emily. Don't you want to join them?'

Emily shook her head in Julia's skirt.

'We're having a special snack today. Graham crackers and—'

'I hate graham crackers.'

Robin looked at Julia. 'It's your choice, as always: stay for a while, or let me handle it.'

Some choice. The eight-thirty client meeting had already been rescheduled twice. She crouched and talked softly into Emily's ear.

'Darling, I have to go now.'

'I don't *want* you to go.'

'Robin will take good care of you, Em. I wish I could stay, but—'

'NO!'

Julia stood and nodded to Robin, who held Emily by the

arms as Julia extricated her skirt from her daughter's fists. She turned and walked toward the door.

'She'll be fine in a few minutes,' Robin said. 'She always is.'

Out in the hallway, Julia leaned her forehead against the wall and took deep breaths. Blowing off the meeting would have meant shortchanging her job. Leaving Emily in tears meant shortchanging her daughter.

Mondays.

Emily's crying stopped a minute later, right on schedule. Julia glanced back into the classroom and saw her daughter in the play kitchen, taking a saucepan out of the miniature oven and giggling as she and two other little girls pretended to eat something. Blonde hair, pale blue eyes, rosy complexion – could everyone see Emily's radiance, or was it just her?

Julia sighed and started down the hall. One minute of gut-wrenching trauma and Emily had all but forgotten her.

'It still says quality when we're looking for value.' Frank McGuire slammed a fist on the conference table.

Julia collected the storyboards to stop any further scrutiny. The creatives had done good work on the laundry soap and fabric softener re-positions. If McGuire had actually *earned* his job as head of marketing for Able Brands he'd recognize this. But the Nephew had the taste of a chimpanzee – without the intelligence.

'Able Brands has spent millions of dollars to establish a quality image for its products,' Julia said.

'No one cares about quality any more. Consumers want value. Wake up and smell the nineties, Julia.'

She stared at the chandelier for a few moments, willing it to come crashing down on the Nephew. All six glass globes would shatter on his bald head, cutting him in a hundred—

48

'Can I see the revisions next week?' McGuire stood up, uninjured, and grabbed his briefcase.

'That shouldn't be a problem,' Julia said. 'I'll walk you to the elevators.'

Five minutes later she was arranging the pink message slips on her desk in descending order of anxiety. All morning she'd tried without success to conjure up Jessica Forrester's face. They'd crossed paths a hundred times in the elevator and lobby, exchanged pleasantries now and then, and yet Julia couldn't bring the woman's face into focus. She sighed, put the messages aside, phoned the gym to confirm her appointment with Carlos, then called home as usual to make sure that Pamela had picked up Emily and brought her safely back.

'Benjamin has chicken-pops,' Emily said when Pamela put her on the phone.

'Chicken-*pox*,' Julia said. 'That's too bad.'

'We made him a card. Bye, Mommy.'

Julia hung up and saw Max Altman standing in the doorway, decked out in his dark grey meeting-the-client suit and a red power tie. He'd put on weight recently, the new pounds obscuring what was once a rather handsome, sharp-featured face.

'Great party,' he said.

'Thanks.'

'Great food.'

He was looking for absolution for the after-party visit, but he wasn't going to get it from her.

'I'm glad you enjoyed it.'

She grabbed her gym bag and headed for the door. Max had touched her just once at the office – on her left breast, in the elevator, shortly after her maternity leave. She'd shoved him away and threatened to report him to the agency's chairman.

She could have sued, might have won – and would have

been forever known as the woman who took Todman DiLorenzo to court. That one fact would have obscured everything else she'd accomplished. So she'd turned the incident to her advantage, making it clear to Max that she'd tolerate no further groping, and that she'd never, ever forget the first incident.

'Enjoy your lunch,' she said as he stepped aside to let her pass.

'Remember your manners, Julia. I don't know why I let you get away with—'

'I think you do, Max.'

He cleared his throat. 'How did it go with McGuire?'

'He hated the new concept. Too *quality* for the Nephew's down-market sensibilities.'

'Value is the watchword of the nineties.'

'Where have I heard that before?'

'You may be senior vice president of this agency . . .' Max cleared his throat again. He'd have to mention his own title now. '. . . and I may be executive VP, but if Able Brands walks, we walk with them.'

'I'll keep that in mind. Now, I have an appointment . . .'

Max glanced at her gym bag. 'Oh, Julia?'

She turned.

'I read in the *Times* this morning about that woman in your building. Did you know her?'

'Not really.'

'No one's safe today,' he said, shaking his head. 'No one.'

Gleason's Gym was a short crosstown cab ride from Julia's office. Just west of Tenth Avenue on 48th Street, it occupied an entire floor above an auto body shop. Julia climbed the steep, dingy staircase, opened the door with 'Gleason's' stenciled on its frosted glass window, went in, heard the muffled *pop* of gloves making contact, and felt the tension already starting to ease.

She waved to Jose Gutierrez in the center ring. She didn't recognize his sparring partner but he had to be good – Jose was a Golden Gloves contender. Around the periphery of the ring, men pounded the heavy bag, tossed a medicine ball, skipped rope, cooled down on peeling wood benches.

'The Mallet!'

Julia turned and saw Carlos Negron walking toward her. 'Hey, Los. How come you're not in the center ring?'

'With Gutierrez? He's young enough I could be his father.'

'He doesn't have your left hook, though. And he never won the Golden Gloves.'

'That was before he was born.' Carlos smiled, revealing two missing teeth.

'I only have a half-hour today,' she said.

He trotted over to Gleason's sole locker room and disappeared inside. A minute later the door opened. Out came a teenage boy still pulling his shirt over his head, Carlos following.

'All clear,' Carlos said.

Julia changed quickly into a T-shirt and shorts and tied back her hair. Her health club uptown had started offering boxing lessons, but the trainers there never really worked you hard – at least, not if you were a woman. Besides, she never could throw a real punch wearing spandex and makeup.

She joined Carlos at the bag. He helped her wrap her hands, then she squeezed them into her gloves, balling her fists. Carlos put on flat focus gloves as they walked over to a corner of the room equipped with mats on the floor. He activated a timer on a small shelf.

'Okay, now, three-minute rounds. Start with ten combinations.'

Julia assumed the stance, left foot forward, right foot back and angled out. She flexed her knees, raised the gloves to her chin. Left jab first, always start with the jab.

She landed a left in the center of his focus glove, then powered a right. Left, right, left, right. Ten times.

Her punches felt a little tentative. Carlos leaned into them, she noticed, as if to heighten the impact. She squinted and visualized Max Altman's face on Carlos's left glove, then landed a solid hook on Max's fat nose. Another left, a right. The bastard. How dare he even mention the party, let alone hover in her office waiting for some sort of . . . pardon? Christ, she could get his ass kicked out of the agency if she wanted to.

'Let's see some hooks.'

She fired a left hook, then a right. Ten times. Carlos called for other combinations: hooks, jabs, uppercuts, feints.

Sex substitute? She hooked a left and felt Carlos's glove give a little. Gail was full of shit. Julia had been celibate since Emily was born because she hadn't met a man who was worth forfeiting time with her daughter.

'From the legs, Julia,' Carlos said. 'Your power's in your legs. Otherwise you're just slapping me.'

She landed an uppercut smack in the middle of Carlos's glove, which ricocheted lightly off his chin. More like it. Her arms felt looser; she was bouncing on the balls of her feet, juiced.

'You're leaving your left side open,' Carlos said. 'Keep your hands up.'

Okay, so she wasn't exactly on the prowl for men, but Gail was no Cosmo girl either. Who was she to comment on how Julia spent her free time? She fired an uppercut, a left hook, another uppercut, now a right. POW. Carlos lost his balance, took a few steps back.

'Fuckin' A, Mallet! Don't let me get away, now. Come after me.'

She charged at him, blasting combinations, hitting the focus gloves dead center. She put her entire body behind her fists, striking at him in a surge of power that began in her feet and shot up through her legs and torso into her arms. She drove Carlos back toward the ropes, saw in his eyes that she was connecting, she was *on*.

Sex substitute? Not a chance. She pummelled him with uppercuts, hooks, jabs, everything she had.

Sex never felt *this* good.

The cab hit traffic heading back to the office. The workout had done the trick: Julia felt mentally primed for a long, meeting-clogged afternoon. She noticed a *New York Post* on the front passenger seat and asked the driver if she could borrow it.

The *New York Times* had buried the murder in the Metro section, but Jessica Forrester's picture had made the front page of the *Post*, under the headline WALL STREET HONCHO GUNNED DOWN.

Julia recognized her at once: pretty in a spare, nervous way – pale complexion, narrow nose, thin lips. She didn't look like a honcho of anything. Or a murder victim, for that matter.

Julia turned to page four for the full story. She studied a photograph of what looked like a recess between two brownstone staircases. Several bouquets of flowers had been placed in front of a graffiti-splattered wall. The city was full of such instant shrines.

She read the caption: 'The body of a thirty-two-year-old woman was found on West 73rd Street late Sunday night.'

Julia shivered – New York was undeniably dangerous, but murder had never struck this close to home before – and read the article.

The body of a thirty-two-year-old woman was discovered today in a brownstone recess on West 73rd Street between

Columbus Avenue and Central Park West. Police are trying to determine a motive in the shooting death of the mother of two small boys.

According to Detective Stanley Bettalini, the woman's pocketbook, which contained over a hundred dollars in cash, was not taken.

The victim has been identified as Jessica Forrester, 32, of 234 West 68th Street. According to her husband, Roger Forrester, she was returning from an aerobics class at a local health club when the attack occurred.

Ms Forrester was killed by three bullets to her head. Detective Bettalini declined to specify the type of weapon used.

The victim was a vice president of Blount & Reeves, a private money-management firm headquartered in downtown Manhattan.

The Upper West Side is one of the safest areas in the city. According to officials at the 20th Precinct, there was only one homicide in the area last year.

Julia finished the article and quickly retreated to the sports pages. At least the Knicks were back on track. Too bad she'd given Saturday's court-side tickets to a client . . .

She turned back to page four and studied the photo. She held it close to her, then, squinting, at arm's length.

'I changed my mind,' she told the driver. 'Seventy-third, please, between Columbus and Central Park West.'

Ten minutes later the driver started to turn on to West 73rd, then stopped.

'There's something going on up there, looks like it's blocked off. You want me to . . . Hey, isn't this where that lady got herself killed?'

Julia paid him, got out and started down the street. Five-story brownstones lined the block, most of them divided into small apartments, a few still single-family homes. Steep staircases provided access to most of the buildings, with ground-floor apartments accessible through doorways underneath the stoops.

Ahead, Julia saw a police car double-parked and two patrolmen facing a small crowd of photographers, reporters and rubberneckers. Her pace slackened as she got near the scene. The *Post* photo was grainy and heavily shadowed. She was probably wrong, in which case she'd feel like an idiot for wasting what would surely amount to her only free half-hour of the day. On the other hand . . .

She slowed down further. Yellow scene-of-the-crime tape was still strung across the two stairways. Two cops stood in front, arms crossed against their chests. A teary-eyed woman held out a bunch of red roses; one of the cops took it, stepped over the tape, and placed it on top of a pile of bouquets.

Julia inched through the crowd, half longing to turn away before her worst fears were confirmed, half dying of curiosity.

'Excuse *me*,' a woman said as Julia tried to move around her.

'Wait your turn,' an elderly man said without taking his eyes off the murder scene.

Finally she was close enough to see. She looked at the steps and sidewalk just in front, swept free of snow; no doubt the footprints had been analyzed, the snow sifted for clues. She looked at the flowers; the pile had grown since the *Post* photo. Gradually she let her eyes drift to the wall formed by the side of the steep staircase, cream-colored except for the plump, oversized letters of the graffiti artists – and the black letters she'd seen in the paper.

For a moment she simply stood and stared at the wall. Then

she whispered the letters, one at a time, as if to convince her brain of what her eyes saw. T. E. W . . .

'Oh God,' she said.

'Yes, such a tragedy.' The woman next to her shook her head. 'We live across the street, at number twenty-one.'

'The Wizard,' Julia said.

The woman glanced from the wall to Julia. 'The who?'

Julia pointed to the letters, crudely sprayed just above where the body had been. 'The Wizard.'

'You're reading it wrong. There's no H and no D.'

Julia gaped at the two words, hardly blinking.

'This lady thinks she knows what the graffiti means,' the woman said loud enough for most of the crowd to hear. 'Must be one of those fortune tellers.'

This garnered a few laughs. One of the police officers, grim faced, walked over to Julia.

'Something you want to tell us?' he said.

But Julia couldn't respond, her eyes riveted to the black letters on the wall.

TE WIZAR.

The Wizard. Minus the D. Minus the H.

5

'Let me get this straight. You told . . . no, you *ordered* your friends to *forget* the letters D and H?' Detective Third Grade Stanley Bettalini's right fist was kneading his face. 'This is what you're telling me?'

Julia sighed. 'It's all in the report I gave to the crime-scene police. They were in a trance, they—'

'A hypnotic trance, which you put them in.'

'They *asked* me to. Okay? It was a party game.'

'And you didn't hypnotize anybody else that night – didn't ask anybody else on the Upper West Side to forget D, forget H. So what you're telling us is, the perp has to be one of the people who stayed late at your apartment Saturday night. Now have I got it right, Miss Mallet?'

'Yes – I mean, no. I just . . .' She swallowed hard. One of her friends, a *killer*? Not possible. If only that woman hadn't overheard her at the crime scene, then blabbed about it loud enough for the cop to hear. Now she was stuck at Manhattan North Detective Bureau while a meeting she'd called was happening without her and a mountain of pink message slips . . .

Te Wizar. How else to explain *that* message?

'It could be a coincidence. Or one of my friends could have written those words before . . . before the killing.'

One of her friends, a graffiti artist? Easier to imagine one of them killing someone than spraying paint on . . .

'I'd say it's a coincidence,' she said. 'Definitely.'

Bettalini shifted his bulky frame in his chair.

'You see, I've known these friends half my life. They're not the type.'

'What type aren't they?'

Julia heard the hiss of steam from outside the Plexiglas-walled office and felt the early barbs of an incipient headache. 'They're not killers,' she said.

'And what makes you so sure?'

Was he taunting her? 'Marianne Wilson works for Ruth Rinaldi. Senator Rinaldi – it's in the report. And Martin Freemason, he's the head of Excell Commodities. You may have heard of them – they're huge, the biggest in—'

'So what you're telling me is, these friends of yours are rich and successful and therefore can't be murderers.'

God, she must have sounded—

'And this girl – excuse me, this woman who put the moves on the other guy . . .' Bettalini looked down at the report on his desk. 'Gail Severance. What does she do?'

'She writes cookbooks.'

'She ever been in any kind of trouble?'

'Of course not. Though that . . . incident does appear to make her seem more guilty than the others.'

'*More* guilty?'

Christ, she'd been more articulate in shouting matches with the president of Able Brands.

'She didn't do it. None of them did.'

'And yet you live in the victim's building; you think you spotted a connection between her and you and your friends.'

Julia stood up. 'May I go now?'

'One more thing. About the writing on the wall . . .' He

58

shrugged. 'Shit, the *writing on the wall*. We didn't mention it to the press. We'd appreciate your following suit.'

'But anybody can see it. It's still there, on the wall.'

'Along with a lot of other graffiti. The only people who know it's significant – who know it *may be* significant – are you and the killer.' He gave her a sour grin. 'Do I have that right, Miss Mallet?'

'Was the paint still wet when you found her?'

'The cops who caught the job didn't check. But the crime scene unit did some tests maybe an hour later. The paint was fresh.'

'One or two of my friends might have experienced some difficulty with the missing letters,' Julia said, 'but I doubt they'd connect it with the photo in the *Post*. And by tonight they should all have recovered the letters.'

'Including the killer?'

Julia started for the door.

'Like I said, keep this Wizard business to yourself. If the press asks you—'

'The press?'

'Wall Street types don't get nailed every day of the week, now do they? You think we do a door-to-door for anybody?'

She turned and left.

Julia found a line forming outside her office. First in was the account executive for Puff Fabric Softener.

'Able's marketing people want to scrap daytime TV and replace it with all-print,' she told him while she rummaged in a desk drawer for aspirin.

'Julia, that's, like, half our billings down the toilet.'

And most of your clout. She swallowed two Advils with the cold dregs of morning coffee.

'You went way over budget on the last shoot,' she said.

'But—'

'The only reason you went to LA was to make sure the producer shot the boards.' She held up her hand to stifle his defense. 'Those storyboards were approved by Moses himself; we didn't need all that extra footage, particularly the shot of the actress sailing through the ozone.'

'Her dress was so soft, she—'

'Spare me,' Julia said. 'The client wants all-print, the client gets all-print. End of discussion.'

He left.

'Next!'

'Julia, there's no way I can deliver an entire print campaign in two weeks.' The art director leaned on Julia's desk, thrusting his face close to hers. 'Why is it that detergent gets months, literally months, to bang out fucking boilerplate, and scouring cleanser – which involves far more creativity, everyone knows it does – scouring cleanser gets a lousy two weeks?'

And so it went for the better part of an hour, followed by another hour of the paperwork that sprouted like weeds whenever she was out of the office more than a few hours. When the phone rang at six, her secretary long gone, she let her voicemail take it, then retrieved the message a minute later.

'You have . . . one . . . new message,' the electronic voice informed her. She pressed the star button to hear it.

'Hello, Julia.'

Hello, Mother – oh, that's right, first you have to introduce yourself.

'It's Mother.'

Now say something about the message.

'Is that a new message? You sound like you have a cold. I tried you at home, but Pamela said you were still working, surprise surprise. Did you know that woman in your building,

60

the one who was killed? I almost had a heart attack when I saw her address.'

And now the real point of the call – something about Emily.

'I was hoping I could have Emily some night this week.'

HAVE Emily?

'I saw the most darling little sweater and skirt set at a shop on Madison and I thought I'd take Emily over there after school, then we could have dinner together. Please try to call back tonight. I know how exhausted you are after working all day . . .'

Get ready for the coup de grâce.

'I don't know how you have any energy left for Emily, putting in the hours you work, I really don't.'

Neither do I, Mother. And something else I've always wondered about – do all indifferent mothers grow into such energetic grandmothers, as if they've hoarded their maternal enthusiasm until they can apply it for maximum return? Or is it something specific about you and me?

She erased the message, read a few memos, and picked up the phone when it rang fifteen minutes later. At least she was safe from her mother.

'Julia Mallet,' she said before the receiver was half-way to her face.

'Can you meet me for a drink?'

Only one person never introduced herself, didn't need to.

'Gail, you never drink.'

'I've never been *grilled* by the cops either. I felt like Ethel Rosenberg.'

Julia smiled. 'Detective Bettalini?'

'You too?'

'Let me call Pamela, see if she can sit tonight.'

Julia rushed home at seven and played a few rounds of hide-

and-seek with Emily. She was almost out the door when Emily came flying out of her room, Pamela Richardson right behind her.

'Don't go, Mommy!'

Julia scooped up her daughter. Some days all she did was say goodbye to Emily – at least, that was how it felt.

'Am I a terrible mother, Em?'

Emily nodded solemnly.

'Really terrible?'

Another nod.

'Really, *really* terrible?'

Emily started to nod, then broke into a smile and shook her head. Julia let out a long, slow breath, kissed Emily, hugged her a third time, and handed her to Pamela.

'Don't worry about us, Mrs M,' Pamela said in her rich Jamaican accent. Julia had given up correcting the Mrs part. 'Just have fun.'

Julia took the seat across from Gail at one of Piero's quieter tables, in the back, away from the crowded bar. 'You look wonderful,' she said.

Gail had the kind of face a camera loved, all sharp angles and shadowed planes. A long, slender nose, high forehead, wide, thin lips – the type of severe beauty that women envy but men, Julia guessed, were put off by.

Julia looked at the half-filled glass in front of Gail. 'Is that *Scotch*?'

'I needed a lift.' Gail drained her glass and signalled for the waiter, who appeared instantly and inclined his sultry, unshaven face toward Julia.

'*Ciao, bella.*'

Piero's was one of those high-concept West Side pasta joints where the fusilli cost as much as an East Side steak and was laced with Latin sexuality. Sometimes the mixture could be bracing; tonight Julia wished she'd chosen a less challenging spot. She ordered a glass of Soave. Gail nodded at the waiter's 'Another whisky for the signorina?'

'So – confess,' she said as soon as he was gone. 'Why is that policeman interested in us?'

'I don't know much more than you do,' Julia said.

The waiter returned with their drinks and began reeling off the night's specials. Gail waved him away before he'd finished with the appetizers.

'All he told me,' she said, 'is that he was questioning people who were at your party.'

Julia took a sip of wine. 'That's basically what he told me.'

The lie sent a chill through her. She'd already betrayed her friends on Saturday night by not letting them remember what had happened under hypnosis. Now she was withholding information from her oldest friend.

'But *why*? What could they possibly have to link us with that horrible murder, other than that we happened to attend a party in her building the night before? You didn't know the woman, did you?'

Julia shook her head.

'God, isn't this exciting?' Gail said. She must have caught Julia's disapproving frown. 'In a tragic way, I mean.'

'What kind of questions did Bettalini ask you?'

'He wanted to know where I was Sunday night,' Gail said. 'It was like a bad movie.'

'Where *were* you?' Julia took a sip of wine. 'Sunday night.'

'At home – where did you think I was? Alone, as usual.'

Julia didn't return Gail's smile.

She doesn't need anyone else. There's nothing really . . . hungry about Gail Severance.

'My editor called last week. If the cilantro manuscript isn't in by April, they may cancel my contract. Apparently cilantro is even hotter than anyone realized. When it was plain old coriander no one cared; now it's called cilantro and people can't eat enough of it. My editor wants to put the book on the fall list. The last Mrs G book didn't sell as well as the one before it – *I* say because it was on zucchini, *they* say because of the spring pub date.'

Mrs G was Gail's *nom de cookbook*. Every title in the series had an elderly *hausfrau* on its cover, standing over a big pot or chopping up the target vegetable or tasting a spoonful of something clearly delectable.

'Is that what you told the police?' Julia said. 'You were testing cilantro recipes at eleven at night?'

'I didn't know I'd need an alibi.' Gail squeezed a piece of bread until bits of it were forced out between her clenched fingers.

'Gail, what's wrong?'

She dropped the wadded bread on her plate and signalled for the waiter. 'I just hate having my life . . . exposed. I mean, who is this cop to come into my apartment and . . . Oh, yes, I'll have another Scotch. Julia?'

'Shouldn't we order?'

'I'm not really hungry. You go ahead.'

Julia ordered the pappardelle with Parma ham and some sort of funghi.

'I know I'm over-reacting,' Gail said. 'It's just . . . I've just never been – interrogated before. Well, there was that time in Florida over spring break . . .'

'The police didn't *interrogate* us,' Julia said. 'They just wanted to know who bought the grass they found in the dashboard.'

'But they couldn't break us.'

Julia laughed out loud.

'Seriously,' Gail said. 'We stuck together. I felt so close to you and Paula and Marianne that night – safe. I mean, we were in a jail cell, for God's sake, but I knew nothing bad could happen to any of us if we stuck together.'

Julia picked up a piece of bread and dipped it in a shallow dish of basil-flavored olive oil. She could still feel the damp chill of that cell; she and Gail had fallen asleep in each other's arms to keep warm. Marianne and Paula had done likewise.

'Back at Madison, did you and Martin ever fool around?'

'Where on God's earth did you come up with *that* idea?'

'I was thinking of him, how he'd handle the cops. They probably questioned him, since he was at the party. Anyway, did you?'

'Maybe we sucked face once, senior year. I was so drunk at the time I hardly remember. He and Paula were pretty much inseparable.'

'I always got the impression he fooled around.'

'Martin? Maybe it would have been better for all concerned if he had. I always felt those two stopped growing emotionally the day they found each other. Sleeping around, blind dates, dealing with rejection – it's all character building, if you ask me.' Gail smiled warmly at the Scotch glass the waiter placed in front of her.

'Paula peaked at Madison.' Gail took a sip. 'I don't care how many kids she has.'

'Two.'

'Our valedictorian. Complete with a speech about nurturing children for the future. What a load of bull! And Martin, he's still the Marijuana Maven or whatever it was he called himself back then. Only now he deals in hog bellies and corn futures and—'

'Gail, what's *wrong*?'

Gail looked down at her glass, twirled her index finger in

65

her Scotch, then took the finger out and touched it to her tongue. 'Do you ever have those moments that somehow crystallize everything for you?'

'I guess so,' Julia said.

'That detective coming to my apartment this afternoon, it was kind of an epiphany for me. It put everything in place, you know? "What were you doing Sunday night?" Same as I do every night. Testing recipes for dishes I wouldn't feed my cat, if I had a cat, which I don't. Suddenly I saw my whole fucking life . . . and I didn't like what I saw.'

'You're more successful than any of us, except maybe Martin. Your books—'

'Please, I don't need a pep talk. I'm late with a deadline for the first time in my life and I've already spent the advance renovating my kitchen. Which I may have to pay back.'

The arrival of Julia's order saved her from having to respond.

'That looks great,' Gail said, suddenly animated. 'Mind?' She speared some pasta. 'I think I'd enjoy shoe leather as long as it wasn't seasoned with cilantro.'

'I forget – what's the name of this pasta?' Julia asked.

'Pappardelle.'

'Delicious.' She fished in her purse for a pen and paper. 'Would you mind writing that down? I may want to make it sometime.'

Gail looked puzzled – Julia had the cleanest stove on the West Side, practically a virgin – but she jotted down the name of the pasta anyway.

'Thanks.' Julia took the paper, heart pounding. 'Pappardelle,' she read from the paper.

With the D present and accounted for.

In front of Piero's the two women hugged each other and headed in opposite directions, Gail a few blocks north to the crosstown bus stop, Julia west to her apartment.

The night was painfully cold, a stiff wind gusting off the Hudson River. Julia checked her watch. Nearly ten-thirty, and she'd planned on an early night. She should have taped the Knicks–Celtics game, which was probably over already.

She turned off Columbus on to West 65th Street. Not a bad block, almost charming if you overlooked the patches of blackened snow and the piles of garbage awaiting morning pickup.

God, what a day. The police at her door first thing, those missing graffiti letters, Gail's strangeness at dinner – obviously the visit by the detective had unhinged her. She hadn't left the D out of pappardelle, but she could well have left out the two letters on that wall, and later regained . . .

Gail Severance, a killer? She'd have a moral crisis over the graffiti alone. So she'd lied about her and Martin. So what?

She heard footsteps clopping on the sidewalk almost in time with her own. She turned without stopping, and thought she saw someone disappear behind the front steps of a brownstone.

Probably a tenant heading into a basement apartment. Still, she picked up her pace. Poor Jessica Forrester had probably . . .

Footsteps again, closer this time. How could anyone have gotten closer without her hearing? She waited a few seconds before turning.

Nothing. No one.

She turned back, nearly jogging now. Twenty yards to Broadway. If only 65th Street weren't so dark. Not to mention deserted. Fifteen yards to go. Ten. Then the footsteps again. Now she was positive. Someone was following her. Again she turned. Again she saw nobody.

'Julia.'

The whispered name was almost swallowed by the wind blowing into her face. Perhaps it *was* the wind, conspiring with her own paranoia and exhaustion.

'Julia.'

A faint, hoarse voice. A man's? She wasn't sure.

She stopped and turned. The sidewalk was empty. Who had called her? Why?

A long, hushed silence, then a soft rustling from behind a stoop not ten feet away.

The Post *had said Ms Forrester was killed by a bullet to her head.*

Julia ran to the corner. Once safe on the crowded Broadway sidewalk, she turned and approached a couple heading uptown.

'Please, I need . . . I . . .'

'Is something wrong?' the man asked.

'There was someone following me, on Sixty-fifth. Could you just . . . look and see if . . .'

The man, elegantly turned out in a long black coat, glanced at his companion and trotted to the corner.

'Nobody there,' he called back.

Julia walked to the corner and looked for herself. Empty.

'Are you sure you're all right?' the woman asked. 'Maybe we could hail you a cab.'

Julia shook her head. 'I live just a few blocks from here. Thanks.'

She hurried on. Once inside her lobby she returned the doorman's greeting and called for the elevator. Only in her apartment, both locks engaged, did she admit to herself that she *had* heard a voice. She had.

Tuesday 31 January

6

'Julia Mallet? Detective Raphael Burgess, Manhattan North. I'm here about the Jessica Forrester murder.'

She frowned and cursed under her breath. She had just left a budget meeting and needed the rest of the morning in her office, alone. She pointed to a chair and sat catty-corner to the detective on the sofa facing the window.

'Nice view.' Detective Burgess studied the thirty-fifth-floor panorama of midtown Manhattan for a few seconds, then turned back and ran his hands along the polished mahogany arms of the chair.

'I told Detective Bettalini everything I knew.'

He nodded. 'Thought I'd follow up on a few things. This isn't a typical homicide.'

'Why not?'

'Too many things don't add up. Like the fact that her wallet was still on her, full of cash. Like the fact that her face was blown away – what's the point of that? Like the fact that the killer took the time to write some crazy stuff on the wall before he left.'

'He?'

'Sorry. He or she.'

'Do you think the graffiti is connected to the murder?'

'It was painted about the same time the murder took place.

We think the killer was waiting for her, knew her.'

Waiting for her.

Julia told him about coming home from the restaurant, about hearing footsteps, her name. She didn't mention the sleepless night, that faint whisper panting from all corners of her room: *Julia, Julia.*

'The thing is, I'm not sure I actually *heard* my name. It was windy and dark, and after everything that had happened . . .'

The detective's face clouded. His blue eyes were unusually round. There was something oddly trusting and boyish about those eyes. He looked about thirty, maybe thirty-five. Tall, lean, with sandy blond hair and a pale, lightly freckled complexion – probably fried at the beach. Undeniably attractive, but not her type. Too fair . . . too handsome, in a way. Too—

'Would you mind going over what happened Saturday night? The party at your place?'

At least *this* detective was taking her seriously. She recounted the evening's events, which already had the murky, slightly surreal glaze of history. When she finished she was breathing heavily.

'Look, there is not a shred of doubt in my mind that none of my friends did this. You don't know them. They're not—'

'Bettalini's talked to them. They deny knowing the victim.'

'*Deny?*'

Burgess shrugged. When Julia had finally got home the night before, Pamela had given her messages from all of them: Marianne, Jared, Paula and Martin, and Richard.

'What did you tell them?' Julia said. 'How did you explain your interest in them?'

'We kept it pretty general, told them there might be a connection between Jessica Forrester and the party. We left the hypnotism part out of it, and we didn't mention the writing. We're counting on you to do likewise.'

'Well, I haven't—'

'One of your friends stands out,' he said quickly and checked the report on his lap. 'Jared DeSantis.'

'Stands out?'

'No visible means of support.' He glanced around the office. 'The rest of you do pretty well.'

'He doesn't exactly live a life of luxury. Have you seen his . . .' What was the point of being defensive? If he'd interviewed Jared, he'd seen his tiny fifth-floor walk-up in Hell's Kitchen or Clinton or whatever the gentrifiers were calling it these days.

'Anyway, robbery wasn't a motive,' she said.

'What's your take on him?'

'Jared? He's a sweetheart. Handsome, charming . . .'

'A real ladykiller.'

'Look, if you came here to put down my friends, then—'

'Sorry. The fact is, your hypnotism theory, if it's correct, could be a clue to the killer. Or it could make it harder to find the killer.'

Her theory?

'Why?'

'I talked to a staff psychologist this morning. She seems to think that hypnotism might – *might* – have opened up a parallel personality in one of your friends. One side of the killer is absolutely normal, maybe even successful. But this other side is absolutely psychotic. It's been sleeping just under the surface for years – decades, even – until now, when you hypnotized it out.'

'It was a game, a—'

'The problem for us is, there might not be anything about this person to indicate why he would attack and kill a woman the way he did. The two personalities are completely separate.'

'So one of my friends *could* have . . .' Richard, Martin, Jared

73

. . . Julia shuddered. Might as well throw in Gail, Paula and Marianne.

'We can't eliminate them, no matter how *normal* they appear.'

'Then I'm not really sure how I can help you,' Julia said.

'Actually, there is a way. I'm visiting Jessica Forrester's family this evening. I was hoping you could come along.'

'Why?'

Detective Burgess stretched his neck and adjusted his tie. He had on a white shirt and hound's tooth jacket. When had detectives gone preppy?

'There's a connection between Jessica Forrester and your circle – the party, the graffiti, the fact that she lived in your building. Too many intersections for it to be a coincidence.'

'But I didn't really know her.'

'Maybe when we talk to her husband the connection will come out.'

'This will be the second night in a row I leave my daughter with a sitter, but if you think it'll help . . .'

'It could save a life.'

'When you put it like that . . .' Julia shrugged.

'I appreciate it.' His smile brought out tiny squint lines on either side of those round blue eyes. They stood up. He was much taller than she'd realized. At five-eight, she always registered a man's height; Burgess had to be at least six-one.

'I'll meet you at your apartment,' he said. 'Is six-thirty okay?'

She heard her secretary fielding yet another call, promising a quick response. 'Six-thirty is fine,' she said.

Dave McCarty started the car as Ray crossed Park Avenue. He put the two-year-old Buick in drive as Ray got into the front passenger seat and was already merging it into traffic as Ray slammed shut the door.

'So?'

74

'She agreed.'

Dave nodded, focused on Park Avenue. Probably thought he had a poker face, inscrutable. But Ray could read him like a billboard, and not just because they were partners approaching the ten-year mark. McCarty's narrow, creased face was just too damn . . . spare to hide much of anything. He leaked emotions and opinions the way other men perspired.

Right now, what Dave wasn't saying was this: *Hypnotism? Bullshit. If you weren't my partner I'd have made you take the goddamn subway up to interview Miss Advertising Executive.*

'There's a connection,' Ray said. 'Same building. And what about those letters sprayed on the wall?'

'Every homicide brings out the loonies.' Dave turned right, heading for Manhattan North. 'Remember Farley?'

Stu Farley: raped then knifed a jogger in Central Park. An eyewitness – a middle-aged dog walker, Fifth Avenue matron type, blue hair, white poodle – saw a young black man running from the scene. Described him down to the gold pinky ring on his right hand. The Department wasted a lot of manpower trying to find the black youth. They found Stu Farley instead – a Parks Department maintenance worker whose DNA was identified in the rape semen. Farley was as black as Newt Gingrich, and he didn't wear a pinky ring. 'But he *is* black,' the matron said down at the station, staring right into the killer's blue eyes. 'What am I, crazy? Can't you see it? He's black as coal.'

'This isn't like the Farley case,' Ray said. 'Anyway, Breaker authorized this angle.'

'High profile homicide like this, Breaker'd authorize a door-to-door of the entire borough if we had the manpower.'

Dave had a point. Larry Breaker, deputy chief of detectives, was six months from retirement and didn't want a lot of 'pending' notations in his casebook when he headed for the golf course.

'A couple of hours with her tonight, I don't see how that can hurt.'

Dave glanced at him, expressionless: *Things weren't so fucked up at home, you might think twice about wasting your time with Julia Mallet.*

'You want the real reason Breaker authorized this little visit?' Dave said.

'No.'

'Not because he buys the hypnotism bullshit. Uh-uh. He authorized it because he thinks there's a small, very small possibility this Mallet woman could be the perp.'

'Yeah, right. And she told the cops about the writing on that wall because she has a deep, sick need to get caught. More perps like her, we'd be out of jobs.'

'She didn't volunteer squat, Ray. Someone overheard her at the crime scene.' Dave pulled at the elastic of his underpants with his right hand, squirming on the vinyl seat. 'Probably stopped by to admire her handiwork.'

'Christ, Dave, that's—'

'A long shot, okay? If it weren't a long shot we wouldn't be assigned to this angle. We're not exactly the A-team these days, not after—'

'Then put in for reassignment,' Ray said. Dave was thirty-six, only two years older than Ray, but he liked playing the patient, advice-giving older brother, the type who never tires of telling you the facts of life – gets off on telling you, in fact. Ray never had a brother, never especially wanted one. 'Why should you take the heat for something I did over a year ago?'

Dave shook his head, tugged on his jockeys again. 'Not while you're still on active.'

Partners. Cops were always comparing partners to spouses – the intimacy, the loyalty. What they didn't like to talk about was how partners could drive you apeshit like only a wife could.

'You're on borrowed time, my friend.' Another glance at Ray, then back to the crosstown traffic. 'You fuck up once more, there won't be any dispensation. Breaker likes you, but he's on his way out.'

'I'll keep that in mind.'

'You want me to come tonight?' Dave said.

He sounded so unenthusiastic Ray almost laughed. Dave lived in Nyack, up in Rockland Country. The way he talked, it might as well be paradise. Everything perfect, not a single complaint, just counting the days to early retirement. Ray had been there for barbecues over the years, and it hadn't looked like Eden to him. He'd seen Michelle and Dave sniping at each other like every married couple, the children acting up. Still, Dave had a way of sugarcoating everything. He didn't bullshit, he *believed*. Everything tip-top. Hell, the guy had four daughters, named them Randy, Ronnie, Billy, and Nick.

'Better I go alone,' Ray said. 'Make everyone feel more comfortable.'

Dave nodded. 'Be careful, Ray.'

'I know: borrowed time, no more dispensations from—'

'I don't like this Julia Mallet.'

'You never met her. And quit grabbing your shorts, you'll get a rash.'

Dave flashed him a look. 'I read Bettalini's report,' he said. 'And I know the type. Someone gets shot in the neighborhood, someone a lot like her, she needs to be involved. I'm no shrink, but maybe she wants to be punished. Maybe she wishes *she'd* taken the bullet instead of Jessica Forrester.'

'I don't read her that way.'

Dave's face was a study in forced nonchalance. *You've had your problems reading suspects, my friend. Almost got you thrown off the force.* 'Then maybe Breaker's hunch is correct,' he said after a few seconds. 'Maybe she *is* the shooter.'

'Or maybe the hypnotism angle isn't bogus, maybe one of her friends did—'

'Just be careful, Ray, okay? That's all I'm asking.'

7

'Nowadays they say women can't have it all, can't do justice to children and career. Well, Jessica . . .' Roger Forrester got up from his chair and paced the room for a few seconds, then sat down again opposite Julia and Detective Raphael Burgess. 'Jessica was the exception. She was . . .' A child wailed from somewhere in the Forrester apartment. 'Find the guy who did this. I'd like ten minutes alone with him.'

Julia doubted Forrester would do much damage in ten minutes – or ten hours. He was about forty, with watery eyes set in a face that looked collapsed by grief. A research chemist, Burgess had told her, at a pharmaceutical company in New Jersey. Julia only dimly recognized him. Amazing, how two people in the same building could remain strangers for so many years.

'Mr Forrester, are you sure you can't think of any connection between you and Julia, other than this building?'

Julia was trying not to squirm under Forrester's scrutiny when it hit her. *She* was a suspect. She turned to Burgess.

'Are you—'

Burgess raised a finger at her and handed Forrester a list of the six people she'd hypnotized that night.

'Any of these names ring a bell?'

Forrester studied them for at least a minute, forehead creased, squinting, as if he were analyzing some complex new enzyme. Finally he shook his head.

'I'd like to call your wife's secretary, see if she recognizes any of them. Maybe they're business acquaintances.'

Julia glanced over at a framed photo on a bookshelf: Jessica Forrester smiling broadly as she pulls two young boys to her side. The room was the same size as her own living room, filled with beautiful antiques – and a profusion of building blocks, miniature cars, and kids' books.

The wailing had escalated. Forrester started to rise, then fell back. 'Whenever the boys were upset, they always wanted their mommy. Never could calm them down the way she could. Our babysitter isn't much better.' He sniffled, took a deep breath. 'Not that Jessica was a pushover. No sir. She was very strict with them, very firm. *I* was the soft touch. I don't know how I'll keep them in line now.'

Burgess cleared his throat. 'Saturday night, you and your wife were at a party – is that correct, Mr Forrester?'

'In Brooklyn Heights,' he said, practically choking over the last word.

'And you got home at what time?'

'About one-thirty, two. Why?'

'When you came in, do you happen to remember if you saw anyone in the lobby, the elevator?'

Forrester slowly shook his head. 'It was late, we were pretty tired at that—'

'You both had a lot to drink that night, didn't you?'

'It was a party, we didn't get out that—'

'You didn't happen to speak to anyone in front of the building, in the lobby? Maybe you bumped into someone, you picked a fight, you—'

'Hey, what is this? My wife was *killed* two nights ago!'

Ray took a deep breath, let it out slowly. 'Just a few more

questions. You told Detective Bettalini that your wife went to the gym several times a week?'

'After the boys were in bed she'd slip out. It was the only free time she had.'

'Same time every night?'

'They go to bed around eight, eight-thirty. She'd leave a few minutes later.'

'Who else knew about this schedule?' Ray said.

'Who . . . Just me, I guess.'

'Anyone call while she was gone?'

'Nobody that I can—'

'An hour passed between your wife's death and eleven-fifteen, when the police showed up at your door. What were you doing during this period?'

'Watching TV, I guess. I mean, I didn't know that—'

'*What* were you watching on TV, Mr Forrester?'

'Probably hockey or basketball . . . Listen, what are we driving at here?'

Burgess sat back and held up a hand. 'Sometimes you remember things later, details that can help, nothing more.' He pulled a small notebook from his jacket pocket. Julia studied him as he flipped through a few pages. Interesting, the way he pushed Forrester to the brink, then backed off.

'You told Bettalini your wife stayed inside on Sunday except for a trip to the market. Is that right?'

'I took the boys to the Museum of Natural History so she could catch up on work. When we got back she took them out to Fairway on Broadway.'

'We followed up with anyone who paid by check at Fairway – nothing. Is that her usual routine on Sunday?'

'Pretty much. She'd stock up on fruit and things for the week.'

Julia glanced at Jessica's photo again. Sundays at Fairway, negotiating the cramped aisles behind Emily's stroller . . . She and Jessica had shared the same orbit, yet only her murder had brought them into contact.

Burgess stood up and handed a card to Forrester. 'I think your boys need you,' he said. 'Call me if you remember anything that might help.'

Julia waited until the door had closed behind them.

'Tell me something, now. *Am* I a suspect?'

Burgess jabbed the elevator call button.

'Well, *am* I?'

Even through the closed door, she could hear the Forrester children crying, their father's muffled attempts to placate them.

'You were at the party,' Burgess said. 'You knew about the missing letters. You live here, for God's sake.'

The elevator finally arrived.

'This was all a set-up,' Julia said in the elevator. 'Bringing me here, *parading* me in front of Forrester. What were you expecting? "Yes, that's the woman who was stalking my wife"? From a man who's in so much pain?'

'He'll feel better when his wife's killer is caught. Anything I do to expedite that will help him.'

The door opened. She charged into the hallway, stopped and turned. 'And that little game you played with Forrester. One minute you practically accuse him of murder, the next you're his best friend. How can you live with yourself?'

'I needed to see how he'd react under pressure. We never eliminate the husband in a homicide investigation, unless—'

'Well, you're wasting your time. With him *and* me.'

She headed for her door. Her hand was trembling. Had it really been only a day and a half since she'd spotted that photo in the *Post*?

'Let me buy you dinner.'

She froze.

'Look, I know you didn't do anything. But there are procedures to follow in a case like this. As for what I did to Forrester just now, that wasn't easy for me, it never is. You put your humanity on hold for a few minutes, mainly by reminding yourself that what you're doing might save a life down the road. Who knows? Maybe he *did* meet someone in the building Saturday night. He and Jessica got home just when your college friends were leaving your party. Maybe something happened, something he might not even think was important. I have to check every possibility.'

'Still . . .'

'As for dinner, how about a burger, assuming you can still get one around here? I think I read somewhere that red meat's been outlawed in this part of town.'

'I really need to get some work done.' They were both standing outside her door.

'Come on, I'll spend the entire time apologizing. I'll completely humiliate myself in the process.'

She fought back a smile and lost. 'There's a great place for burgers just around the corner,' she said. 'But I need about twenty minutes. Can we meet there?'

He nodded, and she gave him the address of Diane's on Columbus, then watched him head for the elevator.

'Explain again, about loading.'

The black man makes a face, a low groan. He's twitchy, practically dancing on his toes.

'It's a automatic, see? You just—'

'I *know* that. I can't picture how you actually put the bullets in.'

The black man takes the gun back, shakes a couple of .38 caliber bullets from the box, glances up and down the alley.

'You gonna get me busted. Watch.'

He opens the chamber, tries to slide in a .38. But his fingers are trembling; the bullet drops to the packed-dirt ground. 'Shit.' His eyes tell the whole story: five hundred dollars of the customer's cash stuffed in his pants pocket, a few nights' relief, then on to the next deal – who needs this bullshit?

'Here, let me try.'

The black man hands the gun over, the bullets.

'Like this?' The bullet slides in, a perfect, tight fit.

'Right, you got it.' Still toe-dancing, right eye blinking like a camera lens gone berserk. 'I gotta get out—'

'Wait, let me fill it up, okay? Make sure I can close it.'

Click, click, click, click . . . The chamber is full in seconds.

'Just push it back till it snaps.'

Snap.

'Right, now you set. Pleasure doing business, I'll . . . Hey, what the fuck you—'

The bullet hits him just to the right of his nose, sends him crashing against the brick wall. Just a dull, cushiony *pop* – the sound of quality, like closing the door of a Mercedes. The silencer worked. The black man crumples to the ground, eyes wide, still not getting it. Feet really jitterbugging now, arms overhead, like they're surrendering.

A second bullet to his forehead and the dancing stops.

'The pleasure was all mine,' the Wizard says, turns, and walks calmly toward the street.

Diane's was the West Side's last great hamburger joint, a cramped, brick-walled shrine to serum cholesterol. Julia arrived a few minutes later than promised, joined Ray Burgess at a small table, and ordered a cheeseburger, french fries, onion rings, and beer – lite beer.

'You know,' he said, 'the detectives back at Manhattan North, they're pretty skeptical about this hypnotism business.'

'And you?'

He shrugged. 'My first rule as a detective? Taking everything seriously. My partner thinks this is a waste of time.'

'But if you're so sure one of my friends was involved, why not just – I don't know – search their homes for a gun? Tap their phones.'

'I can't go to a judge and say, "Your Honor, I have a hunch that one of these six people may be the killer, I'd like six search warrants." He'd laugh me out of the room.'

They were quiet for a few minutes as they finished their burgers. Ray broke the silence.

'Why'd you go into advertising?'

'I don't know,' she said. 'I was an English major. When I graduated from Madison it was publishing, where I'd start as a secretary, or advertising. An uncle of mine knew someone who knew someone at Todman DiLorenzo, so I started there.'

'And you stayed, what, fifteen years?'

'They kept promoting me.'

'Is that the only reason?'

She rolled her eyes. He was good at opening her up, no question about it. 'I like the game, I guess. We pretend it's all science – why someone chooses Brand X over Brand Y. We throw demographics and psycho-mapping and brand-awareness surveys at the client, but we can't really control what someone buys, let alone what they want. We just make a lot of money pretending we do. It's a game.'

'You have a way of talking about yourself as if you're really describing someone else, an acquaintance.'

Was he interrogating her? She glanced around the small, crowded restaurant. Good-looking West Siders, most of them couples, all of them straining to talk over the din. She and Burgess fit right in, except he was a cop, working on a case, and she was . . .

'Is this part of your investigative procedure – dime-store psychoanalysis?'

'Sorry. My wife—'

'Your wife?' Unfair: no wedding band. Julia picked up a french fry, squeezed it in half, and let the two pieces fall to her plate.

'She always said I read too much into things,' he said. 'I'd tell her there's a motive for everything, she'd say sometimes people just *do* things. No reason, no motive. But cops have to believe in motives, otherwise what do we have? That's what makes me nuts about the Forrester murder. No motive. No *apparent* motive.'

The case again: for a few moments there they had been just two people having dinner.

'Detective, I—'

'Please. Friends call me Ray.'

'Right, well, when you saw my friend Gail Severance, what exactly did you ask her?'

'Where she was Sunday night, did she know Jessica Forrester. She freaked out, right?'

'I don't know if I'd say—'

'Look, I've interviewed maybe a thousand suspects; you get to know real fast which ones are hiding something. Gail Severance is hiding something.'

She doesn't need anyone else. There's nothing really . . . hungry about Gail Severance.

'Doesn't it ever depress you, the work you do? You don't strike me as . . . well, you're not my image of a typical cop.'

'I'm not. I'm a detective first grade, about six promotions up from typical cop.'

'Still, you're more like a . . .' She stopped before coming out with something snobbish and embarrassing, like *professional* or *yuppie*. 'Anyway, I never had dinner with a cop before –

sorry, detective – so I guess I have no basis for comparison.'

She smiled, and he smiled back.

'It's funny. My wife, she thinks she's, like, Queen of Astoria because her husband made detective first grade two years ago. There's only a hundred of them, total, in New York. She thinks I'm important, and sometimes I think so too – you know, now and then, after a good day. Then something happens that puts it in perspective, and . . .'

'I didn't mean to—'

'No, don't apologize. I should be grateful, I guess. I mean, in my little universe I'm top dog, even if in someone else's universe – say someone in advertising or publishing – I'm a miracle just because I mostly avoid double negatives.'

'That's not what I meant.' God, he was infuriating: one minute charming and sensitive, the next treating her like . . . yuppie scum. Or worse, a suspect.

'Most of the people I interrogate look up to cops – unless they've broken the law, and even then there's at least a kind of respect, maybe fear. But with your friends, it's like I'm barely human. I can see it in their eyes when I walk in their apartments. Am I tracking in mud from the street? Are my hands . . . Hey, I didn't mean to upset you.'

Julia wiped tears from her cheeks and shook her head. 'I don't need this,' she said. 'I've been through hell this week. I just visited a man who's practically *dying* from grief; for two nights in a row I have had to leave my daughter with a sitter; and now I'm being attacked as some kind of . . . arrogant snob just because . . .' She rummaged through her purse for a tissue.

He glanced at the check and put some cash on the table. 'Come on, there's something I want to show you.'

Broadway was clogged with post-theater traffic as they drove downtown in Burgess's dark blue, government-issue Buick.

'I wish you'd tell me where we're going,' Julia said.

'Nowhere fast, if this traffic doesn't lighten up.'

He lowered his window, grabbed the flasher from the floor, and placed it on the roof.

Julia stared at him.

'Hey, at least I'm not using the siren.'

There were perks to being a cop – make that detective first grade. The traffic in front of them parted like a zipper as they sailed through red lights after only a moment's hesitation. Detective Burgess – Ray – steered with his left hand, his right resting on his lap, weaving in and out of lanes with uncanny timing.

He turned west on 43rd Street, drove down a dark, warehouse-lined street, and stopped the car at a gate. He left Julia in the car while he opened a large padlock, pushed the barrier to the side, and got back in.

He parked the car at the beginning of a pier that jutted into the Hudson River. They were at the very edge of Manhattan.

'I don't understand. Why—'

'Wait. You'll see.'

He jumped out of the car, circled it, and opened her door. The strong, briny wind blowing off the river felt bracing, not bitter. A thin layer of snow covered the pier. He took her elbow and led her farther out. She started to turn around.

'Not yet, just a few more yards.'

At the very end of the long pier he stopped. 'Okay, you can look now.'

She turned and caught her breath. Manhattan was a glittering wall, at once close and looming yet also reassuringly distant. They were the only two people left in the city – that's how it felt.

'I did a bust here three years ago.' Ray's voice was low. 'I never gave the key back.'

'I can see why.'

'When the shit starts piling up, I come here. I stare back at the city and it looks far away but still close, know what I mean? You stand on top of the World Trade Center, the view makes you feel small. You stand here, you feel bigger, like nothing over there –' he waved an arm – 'nothing bad could happen to you or anybody you care about.'

Julia put her arm through his, wondering what the hell she was doing, but she let it stay. Nothing bad could happen to her here.

After a long and comfortable silence, Ray spoke quietly.

'I should be getting back.'

But they waited several minutes more before heading for the car.

They sailed uptown, through parting traffic, in a companionable silence. He double-parked in front of her building, killed the ignition, and turned to face her.

'Sorry if I was hard on you back in the restaurant.'

'Sorry if I over-reacted.'

They exchanged smiles.

'Aren't you going to tell me not to leave town or anything?'

'Don't leave town. Or anything.'

She got out of the car, closed the door, and bent down to wave goodbye. But Ray was staring straight ahead, his thoughts already elsewhere.

Or were they? Julia entered her building, turned, and saw his car still standing at the curb.

8

The Wizard crouches on the fifth floor of a six-story tenement on East 119th Street. Waiting. Getting into the building was easy, a matter of pushing the intercom buttons until someone buzzed open the front door without asking who was there. Every building has at least one trusting old coot who'll let anybody in.

Yesterday, at seven-thirty, the black woman left her job on East 72nd Street wearing a red beret. She caught the Third Avenue bus uptown, got off at 118th, walked one block north, unlocked the lobby door and disappeared. Home.

She must be working late tonight, or stopping somewhere on the way home. The Wizard's watch says 9:40. The plastic grocery bag feels heavy, reassuring. Any minute now. Any second.

The hallway is preternaturally silent. Overhead, a bare lightbulb sways slightly on its cord. The noise, the voices, are all inside the Wizard's head now, have been for almost a week.

Where is she? What do you mean you don't know? WHAT DO YOU MEAN, YOU DON'T KNOW? Where did you get that . . . that thing? Take off your coat, your boots. You're soaking wet. Is that . . . is that blood? Where is she? WHAT DO YOU MEAN YOU DON'T . . .

Four stories down the lobby door opens, closes. She's home.

Footsteps on the first flight. The Wizard leans over.

A man.

Damn. The Wizard moves to the top of the stairs, prepares to head down if the man comes all the way up. Just another resident of this shithole, on the way out. A *white* resident? Okay, maybe a visitor, then. The monster will live for another day.

The man stops on the third floor, unlocks the door. The Wizard leans against the wall, lets out a long, whistling breath.

Figuring out which floor the woman lives on was easy – yesterday, when the woman entered the building, the Wizard waited across the street until the window on the fifth floor lit up a few minutes later.

'SET THE TRAP.'

The Wizard looks around. 'Who . . . who said that?'

'PREPARE THE SCENE. SET THE TRAP *NOW*.'

There, on the tin ceiling, where the paint is peeling, there, in the intricate pattern of wreaths and rosettes . . . a face.

'DO IT BEFORE SHE COMES. FOR THE ANGELS.'

The face emerges from the pattern, its features severe, almost but not quite human.

'HURRY!'

The voice is deep, authoritative, but not at all harsh. The Wizard hesitates just a moment, then takes out the spray paint. The can hisses as it spits black letters on the grimy wall.

'THE DOLL!'

The Wizard removes the doll from the plastic bag, caresses its fragile, threadbare costume, and places it against the wall, beneath the black letters. The witness. A flick of the switch and the music begins.

'Somewhere . . .'

The Wizard hears nothing but the music, the tinny, precise notes as close and familiar as the Wizard's own breathing. The Wizard sits, admires the scene. A sense of peace returns, just rhythmic breathing and beautiful music, and . . .

Voices. Internal voices this time.

Where is she? You left over an hour ago to play in the snow. What happened?

The Wizard's eyes squeeze shut, but the face trickles into focus behind quivering eyelids – cold, accusing, the mouth distended in rage.

And what's THAT? Whose is it? I've never seen it before. Is it hers? WHERE IS SHE? And what's that splattered all over the . . .

The front door again. Opening, closing. Footsteps. The Wizard peers over the banister, looks down and sees . . .

The red beret.

The black woman starts climbing the steep, uncarpeted staircase. Reaches the second floor, jangles a set of keys. When she gets to the top floor, she stops short and stares at the spray-painted wall, the tiny doll propped against it. The Wizard lets her take it in – *there, behold your fate!* – then steps forward.

The black woman turns. 'Didn't I see you in the—'

'Maybe. I know I saw *you*.'

The woman spots the gun. 'Oh my God, don't, please—'

The first shot hits her in the chest, sends her reeling against the wall.

'My . . . babies, I have three little—'

The second shot explodes in her face. She collapses on to the floor. The Wizard waits a moment, hears nothing. Not even voices.

The voices have stopped.

A few quick steps over to the body, two more shots to her face. *Pop. Pop.* The Wizard puts the gun in the plastic bag, takes out the paint can. Shake, shake, rattle, rattle, spray, spray. Cover the face. Make it go away.

'MAKE IT GO AWAY!'

The Wizard looks up. The face nods once before dissolving into the ceiling pattern. Paint can back in the bag, then the precious doll, the witness. A quick run down four flights. The Wizard peers out on to the street. No one nearby. The only white face for blocks – better not be seen coming out!

The Wizard's stomach lurches at first, but then, safely anonymous on crowded Third Avenue, a feeling of calm takes over. And something else – not the release of tension, not yet, but the promise of release, almost there.

The angels are safe tonight. The monster is dead, obliterated.

Wednesday 1 February

9

Ray stopped the car a few doors away from 221 East 119th Street. Four sawhorses, police-department-blue, blocked the street. A uniformed cop bent over to look in the car window, recognized Ray and Dave McCarty, and dragged one of the sawhorses a few yards to let them through.

'Our shooter's slumming,' Dave said as Ray parked, turned off the engine. 'Assuming this one's connected to Jessica Forrester.'

They both knew it had to be connected; they'd been called because of the signature.

An ambulance was parked out front; the body hadn't yet been moved. Yellow scene-of-the-crime tape was strung across the sidewalk two doors down from 221 on either side. A uniform had been stationed at each end, as well as one across the street. Crowds of spectators, mostly black and Hispanic, swarmed behind the tape, necks craning to glimpse the new arrivals.

'You'd think they'd get used to it,' Dave said. He and Ray paused before entering the building, the focus of a thousand eyes burning with the same questions. Why here? Why now? Why can't we get a closer look?

Ray reached for the front-door handle, stopped, and glanced at the detective standing a few feet away.

'Already dusted, Ray,' he said. Ray nodded and smiled and

97

wished he could remember the guy's name. With each crime scene you piled up a new slate of colleagues – half-familiar faces, names recalled only as *the Fermati double-homicide criminologist* or *the Second Grade from the Nelson rape.*

Ray held open the door for Dave, who checked his watch as he entered the building.

'Must've been a long night,' he said.

It was six-twenty a.m., and the murder had been called in just after midnight. The twenty-fifth precinct had responded, notified homicide at Manhattan North, and Ray got the call at five-fifteen.

They climbed the first flight of the steep, dimly lit stairway.

'Christ,' Ray said. 'Why do they always have to smell like this?' The stink of commercial disinfectant, old cooking, poverty.

'*Eau de crime scene,*' Dave said, already slightly winded from the climb. On the second floor a thin black woman holding a young boy stared hollow-eyed from an open door.

A heavy-set man in a tan raincoat approached them and shook hands. Johnny Flannigan, head of the crime scene unit. A fat, cherubic face – you couldn't help trying to find some reflection in that face of the corpses and bloodied victims and rape survivors Flannigan had seen in his twenty-plus years with the unit. But even at the scene itself, hunched over a warm cadaver, Flannigan would always look like he'd just pinched the cheek of a favorite nephew. Pale blue eyes twinkling, skin preternaturally pink, forehead unlined. Not ghoulish so much as . . . impervious.

'The ME said we can ship her down to the morgue,' Flannigan said as they climbed to the fifth floor. 'We waited so's you could have a look, but she's getting a little gamey. Couple of hours must've passed before it was called in – fifth floor, only one other resident lives up there, he didn't get home till close to midnight.'

'What do we know about her?' Dave asked, panting now. Ray was feeling the climb too; amazing how much effort stairs require when you can't grab the banister, though it had probably been dusted already.

'Alicia Frommer, black woman from Trinidad, works as a babysitter, according to neighbors. We're still trying to locate her employers. Shot point blank. Nothing from ballistics yet, but . . . Stay left, gentlemen.'

Dark blood had flowed from the fifth-floor landing down the linoleum steps, half-way to the fourth floor.

'Striations on the casings. A Ruger, looks like,' Flannigan said.

Ray took a deep breath and held it as he approached the landing. The Wizard had found a new weapon; striations meant a silencer.

'Ray, Dave – meet Alicia Frommer.' Flannigan reached the top of the stairs and swung his hand with a flourish. *Voilà*.

Alicia Frommer was collapsed on the floor against the wall at the top of the stairs. A pool, no, a *lake* of inky blood covered virtually the entire landing. A plank had been placed parallel to the body so the crime scene unit wouldn't have to walk through the gore. A fucking bridge over troubled water. Her face was . . . gone, a glistening, formless mass. Ray searched for a feature in the mass, a vestige, forced himself to look. Found nothing.

'At least two shots to the face. We'll get the exact count after the autopsy.' Flannigan showed all the emotion of a museum guide pointing out brushstrokes on a Rembrandt. Dave McCarty had retreated to the far side of the landing, where he made a show of watching a criminalist place bits of stuff – hair and fiber, ideally, but probably just accumulated dirt and grime – into brown paper bags. *Lunch bags*, Ray always thought. Goddamn school lunch bags. Yes, plastic bags collect moisture, which can contaminate. But did they have to use *lunch* bags?

'Looks like black paint was sprayed on afterwards,' Flannigan was saying. 'Same stuff used on the wall.'

The wall. Ray read the two words, one letter at a time, half hoping an H or a D would be missing. Both were there. 'The Wizard', sprayed in lurid black, the writing somehow the most disturbing part of the whole scene. Imagine doing this to a person, then stopping to leave a signature. Like this monster was proud of what he'd done, wanted the world to know.

'No footprints, fingerprints,' Flannigan was saying as Ray tried to take it all in, memorize the scene before it was dismantled. 'Maybe we should call in a handwriting specialist.' He chuckled, looked at Ray to validate his wit. Ray just shrugged and walked over to Dave.

'Still think the hypnotism angle is bullshit?'

Dave's complexion was the color of fat-free mayonnaise. 'Christ, her face, Ray.' He was staring resolutely at the criminalist, still working his tweezers.

'You want to wait downstairs while I—'

'Two homicides, same MO, different weapon.' Dave cleared his throat, looked up at Ray. 'Where's the hypnotism angle?'

'"The Wizard", Dave, what about that?'

'Serials always leave a signature.'

'But Julia Mallet predicted this.' Ray pointed back at the wall. 'She knew what the missing letters were.'

'I'll call Pat Sajak, let him know.' Dave's eyes darted at the body, the signature, then back to Ray. 'Or maybe we should bring her in for questioning.'

Ray shook his head. 'I'm asking Breaker for permission to handle this part of the investigation myself. She trusts me, she'll—'

'Jesus, Ray – trust? What if she did . . . that?' He pointed over his shoulder at the carnage.

'It's one of her friends, it's got to be.'

100

Dave looked at him a beat, then walked back toward Alicia Frommer, crossed the gangplank, and headed downstairs. Ray followed a moment later, pausing at the top of the stairs.

The thing about homicide scenes, they always looked completely . . . composed. True, no one could predict which way the body would fall, which direction the blood would flow, the exact configuration of limp arms and legs. The futile, last-minute flailing, the desperate lurches, the final slump to the floor – random reactions to a calculated act. Yet they combined to create a still-life that always looked arranged, deliberate, as if an artist had come in and organized everything just so.

Or perhaps it was just the inevitability of the whole thing, that once the first bullet had been fired a chain reaction of gestures and reactions was set off that inescapably led to the crime scene looking a certain way.

Ray studied the body, arms splayed above the head, legs curled fetally. He studied the signature, slashes of black on the jaundice-colored wall. Studied the pressed-tin ceiling: rosettes, floral wreaths, a testament to the building's more luxurious beginnings. Peeling paint now.

A fucking still-life. He might have laughed at the irony of that, but forced himself instead to look at Alicia Frommer's face – what had once been her face.

From under the awning in front of Barney's, Julia watched Paula Freemason emerge from a chauffeur-driven Mercedes at the corner. Silly of Paula to get out at the corner – no one was embarrassed by wealth any more, even if, in the nineties, no one flaunted it. But while Martin was and always would be a product of the eighties, Paula remained very much of the seventies. Which was perhaps why Julia still liked her.

Paula waved and hurried down the sidewalk, her ankle-length

skirt billowing behind her. She looked like an aging flower child, with her frizzy hair, formless blouse, wire-rimmed glasses. Poor Paula. Everyone wanted to make her over – she was a tempting *tabula rasa*, with her big beautiful eyes, wrinkle-free complexion, full lips. No doubt Martin had suggested a makeover and wardrobe more appropriate for a millionaire's wife. But Paula never changed, and there was a kind of integrity in that.

'This is so much fun,' she said after kissing Julia on the cheek. 'I mean, when was the last time we shopped together?'

'We want the fourth floor,' Julia said. She'd scouted the evening-wear department while waiting for Paula.

'I hate these charity benefits,' Paula said as they rode the escalator. 'God forbid I wear the same dress twice. Martin would *die*.'

Julia could tell right away that Barney's was a mistake. Virtually every dress on the fourth floor was black, skimpy, and outrageously expensive. Only the last part didn't faze Paula, who flipped through the racks of clothes with little apparent interest.

'What do you make of this murder investigation?' she said as she held a sequined number in front of her. It barely covered her hips.

'Hard to say. I suppose Bettalini's been to see you.'

Paula nodded. 'And another detective. Can't remember his name, kind of handsome with these really unusual blue eyes.' So Ray was paying follow-up visits. 'They both said it had to do with your party. Was she there, by any chance, the murder victim?'

'It *might* have to do with my party. And no, she wasn't there. I didn't know her.'

'Right. I called around – you know, Gail, Richard, the others. The police interviewed all of us. The same questions . . .' She lowered her voice to a stage growl. '"What were you doing on the night of the fifteenth?"'

Julia laughed as Paula replaced the dress. 'What *were* you doing?'

'Sleeping with Martin, what else?' A moment's silence. 'I mean, sleeping sleeping, not having sex or anything. *That* would have been suspicious.' She laughed at her own little joke and Julia forced a smile. She never knew whether married people who joked about the infrequency of sex were trying to console their single friends or reporting truthfully from the front.

'Martin's attorney has advised us not to agree to questioning unless he's present,' Paula said. 'My feeling is, who needs a lawyer unless you've got something to hide? But Martin hires lawyers as easily as other people hail taxis.'

'In college, were you and Martin a hundred per cent faithful to each other?'

'What a question!'

Julia checked the price on a cocktail suit – $1,350 – and waited.

'Of course we were faithful. I mean, we were committed.' She waved away an approaching sales lady, looked from side to side. 'Martin's my only one,' she whispered. 'My – only – one.'

You poor thing. Martin was probably dependable, aggressive, horny as an adolescent – and very, very quick. Commodity dealers were nothing if not efficient.

'Why do you ask?' Paula ran her right hand along a rack of dresses. 'Don't tell me *you* had an affair with him.'

'I'm just curious,' Julia said. 'Long-term married people fascinate me. You're like a foreign culture.'

'But that's how I feel about you!' Paula winced and touched Julia's arm. 'I didn't mean that negatively. It's just that I was never really single. I can't image it, without Martin and the boys . . .' She shook her head, a gesture that struck Julia as more of a shudder. 'I always forget how great you look dressed for work,' she continued. 'You even manage to look sexy in a suit.' She glanced down at her own loose cotton dress.

'You look wonderful, too, I love that—'

'I always counted on you, Julia.' She was almost whispering. 'When I got pregnant, sophomore year . . .'

It was a weekend Julia would never forget, each hour still vivid as fresh paint. The long drive to the clinic in Syracuse, holding Paula's hand in the waiting room until the doctor was ready, holding her close for two long, sleepless nights. It was at least a week before Paula went back to class, and a month before she'd even talk to Martin.

'I always thought having a child would cancel out the . . . you know, somehow even the score.' Paula took a deep breath. 'What did I know?'

'But you were only—'

'The detective also asked me about the Wizard of Oz.' Paula turned and considered herself in a floor-length mirror. 'Can you think of any reason he'd do that?'

Julia shook her head. 'Anyway, Marianne's the Judy Garland freak.'

'Oh my God, that's right.' Paula turned back to Julia. 'I forgot to mention that. Should I call the detective back?'

They locked eyes for a moment.

'Well, I suppose loving Judy Garland isn't . . . well, it isn't exactly incriminating,' Paula said.

'Of course it isn't.'

'Anyway, I'd never betray Marianne – none of us would. Isn't that right, Julia?' Paula didn't take her eyes off her friend as Julia searched for an answer. 'We stick together, the seven of us,' Paula continued. 'Don't we?'

'I need to use the ladies' room,' Julia said.

When she returned, Paula was modeling a short black dress supported, precariously, by spaghetti straps. She had the legs to pull off the look, and lord knows she had the cash to finance it – but Paula would never look at home in a dress like that, much as Martin might approve. Truth was, he'd left Paula behind in his ascent to the financial stratosphere.

No, she'd *chosen* to stay behind as he took off without her. She'd married a long-haired, dope-smoking Grateful Deadhead, figuring they'd open a bookstore or crafts shop someplace rural and inexpensive. How could she have known that he'd spend the evenings when he stayed home faxing Tokyo or Kuwait? Paula's refusal to make the trip with him would have consequences – if it hadn't already.

'It doesn't say Paula Freemason, somehow,' she said when Julia stepped behind her into the mirror's reflection. 'I think I'll try Lord and Taylor.'

On the sidewalk they kissed. Julia saw the Mercedes idling at the corner and turned to go the other way.

'Julia!'

She turned back.

'Are you sure you don't know why the cops are bothering us about the murder?'

'No idea. Anyway, you were sleeping at the time. Sleeping sleeping.'

Paula laughed and kissed Julia on the cheek. 'Sometimes I wonder what you really think of me, Julia. You know, the Phi Beta Kappa who stays home to raise children.'

'Paula . . .'

'But we all make our peace somehow. Last night Martin and I had dinner with this hot-shot CEO type who insisted that the homeless were good-for-nothings who refuse to work. The worst part was, Martin agreed with him. The guy's sponsoring him for the board of some child abuse hotline charity.'

'Child abuse?'

'Children must be very big this year, otherwise Martin wouldn't bother. Anyway, I sat there all evening biting my tongue like a good little wife. But on the way home from the restaurant I dropped a hundred dollars of Martin's hard-earned money in a homeless man's cup. That's how I slept *last* night. Tonight? Who knows . . .'

Julia laughed. 'That's wonderful.'

'How do you make your peace, then?' Paula said.

'Do I have to?'

'You do if your life is like everybody else's – full of compromises, things we do that run against our nature.'

With that Paula smiled, shrugged, and headed for the corner.

The doorman buzzed at eight-thirty. Julia had just put Emily to bed and was looking forward to an hour or so of reading, a long bath, then an early bedtime.

'Detective Burgess,' the doorman said.

She hurried to the bathroom and brushed her hair – no time to change out of her sweatshirt and jeans. Was there a new development in the case, something involving her? She decided on a shot of lipstick just as the doorbell rang.

'I should have called,' he said when she opened the door. No tie and jacket this time; the green crewneck sweater and khaki pants made him look almost collegiate. 'Mind if I come in?'

They sat in her living room, which he studied for a few moments.

'Nice,' he said. 'It's you.'

Julia glanced at the semi-antique Kirmin, the chintz-covered sofa and love seat, the antique desk, the scattered kid's toys, and wondered how in anybody's mind they added up to 'her'.

'We both need redecorating,' she said with a grin.

'There's been another murder. Last night.'

The grin vanished. 'Here? In—'

'Uptown, East 119th Street. Gunshot to the face – several shots, in fact. Black spray paint covering the whole mess.'

'The Wizard?'

He nodded. 'All letters accounted for this time. The victim was killed in her building, on the way home from her babysitting job. Alicia Frommer, originally from Trinidad. That name mean anything to—'

'Of course it doesn't.' Julia got up and walked over to the windows.

'We're trying to keep the connection to the first murder out of the press,' Ray said. 'We had the wall painted over the minute our crime-site team got through. Anyway, a black woman killed in Harlem isn't exactly front-page news.'

Julia looked at the twinkling landscape, found the Chrysler Building, Citicorp, Empire State – the familiar and reassuring watchtowers of her life, staking the boundaries of her everyday world.

'She worked for a couple on the East Side,' Ray said, 'babysitting their three-year-old. Easton – Hugh and Martha Easton.'

'Never heard of them,' she said without turning from the view.

'Think hard. There's got to be a connection.'

She spun around. 'You mean to me or my friends? There isn't, and you know it.'

'What about the Wizard?'

'You said all the letters were back.'

'And you said that after a few days the – what did you call it, the post-hypnotic suggestion? – that it would fade, disappear.'

He was right. If post-hypnotic suggestions could last forever,

107

there wouldn't be a smoker or overeater left on the planet. She walked to her desk and absently straightened the collection of framed photos – most of them of Emily, two of her parents. She picked up the photo of her brother, aged eight, his last year on earth, and wiped a film of dust off the top edge. She rarely looked at Matthew's picture, and every time she did she felt absurdly surprised that his image hadn't aged. Disappointed, too.

'Why are you here?' she asked quietly. 'This second murder happened in a completely different neighborhood.'

'The victim lived alone; most of her family's down in Trinidad. I doubt any of your crowd knew her.' He sounded bitter.

'Look,' she said, 'I'm sorry about this woman, but—'

'*You're* sorry? I'm the one let it happen.'

'That's ridiculous. How could you know there'd be a second murder?'

'If I'd found the guy after the Forrester killing . . .' he said softly. 'Nobody kills in custody.' Ray's eyes drifted off somewhere, his shoulders slumped, and Julia suddenly felt like walking over and . . .

No. She was through with that. Men who needed her, men who needed saving.

'You haven't answered my question,' she said. 'Why are you here?'

'It's possible that you or one of your friends might know the couple she worked for.'

'I told you, I never heard—'

'I'm heading over there now. I'd like you to come.'

'I just put my daughter to sleep.'

Ray Burgess smiled. 'I keep forgetting you have a daughter.'

'Not the maternal type, right?'

'That's not what I—'

She raised a hand. 'I hear it all the time. If you really think it's worth it, there's a girl down the hall who might be able to sit for a few hours.'

Julia picked up the house phone and asked the doorman to buzz Amy Griffin, who said she'd come right over.

'I just want to check on Emily,' Julia said. She opened her daughter's door and could tell from her even breathing that she was sound asleep. She watched her for a few moments before realizing that Ray was standing next to her.

'She's beautiful,' he said softly. 'Your face and mouth . . . but the blonde hair, where's that from?'

'Emily's sperm donor, I suppose.'

Ray's eyes widened.

'My memory of him isn't exactly vivid,' Julia said.

The doorbell saved her from any further explanation.

10

'The way I see it,' Ray said as they drove crosstown in his car, 'the victim was followed home by the killer. Since she was coming from work, from the Eastons', the killer could be connected to them, or maybe just to their neighborhood.'

Julia raced through a mental address book. Marianne lived in Washington. Gail lived on the East Side, so did Paula and Martin. Richard had just taken a post-separation studio in midtown – East or West Side, she couldn't recall.

'Your friend Marianne Wilson claims she was in Washington.'

'*Claims?*'

'You don't need to give your name when you buy a ticket on the Metroliner or the shuttle. She could even have driven up and back . . .'

'I'd bet my life that Marianne Wilson couldn't—'

'Forget it, you've already bet your life on the other five.'

They reached Park Avenue in minutes, courtesy of Ray's flasher.

'You asked Paula Freemason about the Wizard of Oz yesterday. Why?'

Ray double-parked in front of an elegant pre-war building on East 72nd Street. Immediately the passenger door was opened by a uniformed doorman.

'Just a guess,' Ray said. 'You know many wizards other than the great and powerful Oz?'

They got out of the car, announced themselves to a second doorman, and were escorted to the fifth floor by an elevator attendant.

Both Eastons met them at the door and led them to a book-lined study. 'Refreshments' were offered, without much enthusiasm, and declined.

'This is very upsetting to us,' Martha Easton said with a touch of annoyance, as if blaming them. She was pale and blonde and would probably refer to Julia as a 'career girl'. Her husband, still in a suit and tie, was handsome in a wholesome, square-jawed way that made Julia think 'Republican' – or client.

'She'd been with us since our daughter was born,' Hugh Easton said. 'This is a terrible tragedy.'

Julia winced at the complete lack of emotion in Easton's voice. The real tragedy for Martha and Hugh would be the interruption to their schedules until a replacement was found.

'She had a very special relationship with Sydney,' Martha said. 'Hugh works long hours, and I'm involved in many activities that keep me away from the home for hours at a time.' She lifted both hands and let them drop on her lap. 'We tend to indulge our daughter, spoil her – it's just hard to deny her anything when we're away from home all day. Alicia was much more of a disciplinarian. She kept Sydney to a very strict schedule, made sure she ate her peas, that kind of thing. I don't know how we're going to find someone as good.'

'Have you ever seen Miss Mallet before?' Ray said.

Both Eastons looked at Julia, who scanned the large collection of books, most of them classics, probably bought by the yard. They shook their heads.

'Is she connected to this case?' Hugh Easton said.

'Possibly.'

111

Ray pulled a small piece of paper from his jacket pocket and read the names of her friends.

'We don't know any of them,' Hugh said. 'And I fail to see how *we* are connected to . . .' He looked at his wife.

'To *Alicia's* murder,' she said.

'That's right, to Alicia's murder.'

Julia and Ray got out of there fast.

Ray drove slowly up Third Avenue, retracing the probable route of Alicia Frommer's last commute home.

'I talked to the other sitters she hung out with,' he told Julia. 'A group of three black women, all from Trinidad. None of them remember anything unusual yesterday. We also checked with the Forresters' sitter. Also from Trinidad, but says she never heard of Alicia Frommer.'

At 96th Street the neighborhood changed abruptly from high-rise gentrified to low-rise tenement. Julia never got used to the contrast. 96th Street could be a symbol for all New York, Manhattan's Rubicon.

'Is this a serial killer?' she said.

'Yes and no. Two people were killed by the same person in the same way. No money was taken. In that sense it's a serial.'

'But . . .'

'Other things don't add up. There's usually a sexual angle to serials. The killer gets his rocks off somehow, usually by torturing the victim, maybe having sex, you know, before or after.'

'*His* rocks?'

Ray shrugged. 'Virtually all serials are men in their twenties or thirties.'

'The Wizard's probably a man?'

'We can't rule women out. The weapon, for instance. Serial killers prefer a slow death. They build up a kind of intimacy

112

between themselves and their victims, like foreplay. They drag their prey off like animals, may keep them prisoners for hours, days, even weeks sometimes. With the Wizard, death happens fast. Which could mean the killer isn't strong enough to overpower the victims and needs something quicker than a knife.'

'A woman.'

'There's something else. This shrink I talked to thinks the perp may be getting off *after* the fact. The killing releases some built-up tension, and later . . .' He turned on to 119th Street.

'Later, what?'

'Later he or she finds sexual release, alone or with a partner. The murder frees him to do that, to make sexual contact.'

He stopped the car in front of number 221, a six-story building with a rusty fire escape clinging to the front.

'There are always clues,' Ray said. 'Always. Even the absence of clues – fingerprints, footprints, that kind of thing – can mean something.' He turned to face her. 'The choice of victim tells us something. The location. The weapon. It's all telling us something.'

'And the writing? What does your shrink say about that?'

'A lot of serials leave signatures – mutilated body parts, blood smeared on the wall, that kind of thing. The Wizard's signature, well, it's more literal, obviously.'

He peered up through the windshield. In profile he looked younger, his features softened by the dim light.

'She lived on five, facing the street. It's all in there, everything we need to know.' He paused. 'It was a different weapon this time. *That's* atypical. I haven't seen the ballistics report yet, but the crime-scene crew says the gun used on Alicia Frommer had a silencer. Usually a serial sticks to a pattern.'

'He used a silencer?'

'Technically, a suppressor. You can't really silence the sound

113

of a revolver, you can . . . dampen it, make it sound more like a thud than a gunshot. Anyway, the crime-scene crew noticed horizontal tracings on the cartridges we retrieved, which usually means they traveled through a silencer.'

Julia thought this over, then turned to him. 'It couldn't be one of my friends. I mean, it's hard enough believing one of them's a psychopath, that one of them even owned a gun, much less used it. But there's no way any of them would know how to get a second gun – with a silencer.'

He squinted at her and smiled. Their breath had fogged the windows, cocooning them in the warm car. She wiped a small circle on her window and looked out. The street was dark; half the buildings were boarded up. Too bad they couldn't sit there all night, fogged in together. This was . . . shit, this was as intimate as she'd been with a man in years.

'*Damn.*'

Ray looked at her. 'What's the matter?'

'I was . . . I guess I was thinking about that poor woman,' she said.

'She came here looking for something better than she had. She had three kids back in Trinidad; she was saving up to bring them here. The American dream – work hard, save your money, cash in. This is as far as she got.'

Julia directed Ray to the phone in her bedroom and headed for the kitchen to make coffee. He was still on the phone when she brought two mugs to the living room. She put them down and walked quietly to the hallway, stopping just outside the bedroom.

'. . . dead end. I talked to every goddamn person Jessica Forrester worked with. She was an angel, a paragon – you know how it is. Perfect marriage, perfect kids . . . Nothing on Alicia Frommer either. The Eastons barely remembered her name, I don't think they even knew where she lived. Dave turn up anything from the playground angle? . . . Right. I brought Julia Mallet over to the Eastons . . .'

Julia took a step closer to the door and angled her head to within an inch of the opening.

'They didn't recognize . . . Look, she told us those missing letters added up to the Wizard, how did she know that? I realize it's a different neighborhood, different weapon, but there's a connection, I know it . . . Look, just get me the surveillance I requested, okay? Yes, all of them, the hypnosis bunch . . . I have to get going, I'll . . .'

Julia hurried back to the living room. She noticed Ray's jacket draped over a chair. On the seat itself was his belt, holster and gun. Julia picked up her coffee, sipped, then took a closer look.

'You want to pick it up?'

She started at his voice. 'Not really.'

But she couldn't take her eyes off it.

'It's a Glock automatic, made in Austria. Standard issue nowadays. Sixteen shots, plus one in the chamber.'

'Sixteen . . .'

'Fire until empty. It's one of the first things you learn at the academy.'

'Sometimes I forget you're a cop.'

'Detective first grade.' He smiled. 'Anyway, I need a favor. The Department has a shrink on staff who specializes in hypnosis. I'd like you to see her tomorrow.'

'To hypnotize me?'

'No, just to talk. She might be able to help you remember something about that night, something you've overlooked.'

'If you think it would help, sure. Now, you can do me a favor.'

'What's that?'

'Tell me the truth.'

Ray shrugged, reached for his coffee.

'About *everything*, Ray. Are my friends being watched?'

He looked at her a long moment before answering. 'I've asked for round-the-clock surveillance of every suspect. At the moment, that means your friends.'

'All of them? Gail, Richard . . .'

'The Freemasons. Since we can't let them know they're being watched, there's a limit to how far we can go. We can't follow them into their places of business, for example. But we can keep an eye on them at night, when both crimes took place. And we're counting on you not to talk about this to them, to anyone.'

'Am I being watched?' Julia said.

He looked at her for a moment, then smiled.

'*Officially* watched, dammit.'

'*Officially*, you're a suspect.'

Julia turned away. 'Maybe you should leave now. I invited you up here because . . .'

'Because?'

Because I was scared and lonely and because when you smiled your melancholy smile something snapped inside me, broke free.

'Because this whole Wizard business has me terrified.'

He nodded but she could tell he wasn't buying it.

'Does your wife mind your staying out so much?'

He blinked. 'Why?'

'Does she?'

'Homicide work isn't something you can share with anybody. I never met a woman – or a man, anyone on the outside – who could really understand it, Dolores included. Homicide detectives hang out with each other; we don't have a lot of friends outside the job. Once you're on a case, it's with you twenty-four hours, even while you're at a party or watching a ballgame or asleep. Because the clues are speaking to you, they're pointing the way, and you just have to make sure you're listening to them, always listening. You have any idea what the divorce rate is among homicide detectives?' He'd paced the room, ending up staring out of the window. 'Sometimes I think Dolores and I would still be together if I were in a different line of work.'

'You're divorced?'

'Separated. About three, four months.'

Julia felt something go soft inside.

'I can't blame the job for everything,' Ray continued. 'But it takes a stronger marriage than ours to survive it. In a way Dolores lived through my work, always interrogating me about my cases, talking to the dispatcher about this lead or that suspect. I used to think she wanted to be in the car with me.' He took a breath. 'My partner . . .'

She saw his eyes cloud over and, yet again, had to fight the urge to go to him, comfort him.

How many times had she read to her father when he was blind with pain, tried to distract him with cheerful anecdotes from her school day, most of them invented? None of it made him feel better, but she'd never stopped trying until the day he died.

She was still trying.

'I should check on Emily,' she said.

'I didn't hear anything.'

She went into Emily's room and leaned over the bed. Her daughter had thrown off all her covers, as she did every night. She lay on her back, face to the side, arms straight on the mattress.

Maybe if she just stayed there, with Emily, it would go away, this emptiness that had come over her. Emptiness? Try vacuum, pulling her in. Maybe if she ran through the causes it would go away. Define the problem, then the solution will be obvious — wasn't that how she operated at work?

The problem: two murders, somehow connected to her. No wonder she felt so isolated. Suspicion cast on her oldest, closest friends. Pressure at the office, intensifying every day. Five years without a man.

Big, round eyes, mournful eyes. The eyes of a man who seemed to need her. Gently she stroked Emily's hair, ran the back of her hand along her warm cheek. Maybe he'd leave, just go away. And if he didn't? She'd ask him to leave. This was her apartment, her life. She was in control here.

Perfect job, perfect apartment, perfect daughter. And no husband to complicate things.

She kissed Emily's forehead. 'How much do I love you, Em?'

Julia spread her arms. 'This much,' she whispered, then let her arms fall to her side. She walked down the hall toward the living room but stopped before entering. Ray still faced the window, his back to her. She could ask him to leave. She could ask him and he'd go.

I'd love to be around the day Julia Mallet lets go of her control. That would be worth waiting for.

He turned around as she walked over to him. She saw in his eyes that he knew what was coming. Cop's instinct.

'I have to go,' he said, taking a deep breath as he spoke. 'I'll pick you up at eight-thirty. The appointment with the psychologist shouldn't take more than an hour.'

She stepped closer to him. 'Ray, I—'

He held up a hand, looked at her for several long moments. His eyes clouded as his resistance began to wilt.

'I have to go.' His voice was low and hoarse. He moved toward her, hesitated just a second, then walked around her and left the apartment.

Thursday 2 February

11

Ray greeted Julia with a clipped 'Good morning' when she got in his car the next day at eight-thirty.

'Maybe for you,' she said.

Everything had started out so well: pancakes in the shape of the letter E, drenched in a gallon of maple syrup; a taxi to school, Emily's favorite treat; taking the stairs rather than the elevator up to the classroom, as ordered. But when she'd bent down to kiss Em goodbye – an outburst of tears, frantic clutching at the knees, choking sobs as Robin Lane gently prised her off and carried her into the classroom.

'Maybe your shrink can give me some mothering advice,' she said, then stared out the window for a while. A garbage scow made slow progress up the Hudson, escorted by a tugboat. On the New Jersey side of the river, newly minted high-rises sprouted like huge weeds from the once-beautiful Palisades, as if spawned from seeds blown over from Manhattan.

'You speak to your college friends a lot, don't you?' Ray sounded stiff, formal, awkward.

'I guess so.'

'Well, if one of them should mention anything relevant to the case—'

'You're asking me to *spy* on them?'

He stopped at a light and turned to her. 'One of them might be a killer, Julia. I'm asking you to help find out which one. When you talk to them – on the phone, I don't want you to be alone with these people . . .'

'*These people?* You're talking about my oldest friends.'

'When you talk to them, you could subtly bring up the murders, then pay close attention to their reactions.'

'And report back to Ray Burgess. Or is it Senator McCarthy?'

When the light turned green he accelerated sharply. 'Help me, Julia. Not everybody in the department buys the hypnotism angle, even after Alicia Frommer. *I'm* convinced, but I can't get close to these – to your friends – the way you can. I need your help.'

I need your help. Christ, how she hated those words. 'If one of my friends should happen to confess, I'll let you know, okay?' she said. 'But that's it. Those six people you think of as suspects, they're as much my family as Emily. I won't do anything to hurt them.'

Ray parked in a lot behind the 24th Precinct and led her into a back entrance, through security.

'Ray!' They turned to see a woman hurrying across the linoleum-floored waiting room.

'Dolores, what are you doing here?'

She looked about thirty, with a pale complexion, thin lips, and deep-set eyes. Her long, straight dark hair was a bit tousled, and there were bags under her eyes. Pretty, though, in a delicate, almost jittery way.

'I was doing some shopping in the neighborhood, thought I'd have coffee with Evelyn.'

'Our dispatcher,' Ray said to Julia in a low growl, then turned to Dolores. 'We're kind of busy here lately, I'm not sure Evelyn—'

'That's what she said!' Dolores broke into a big grin. 'But I told her I could run a few errands, be back whenever she was free. We're meeting down the block in twenty minutes.'

'That's great, Dolores, now I have to—'

'I'm Dolores Burgess,' she said, thrusting her right hand at Julia.

'Julia Mallet, nice to meet you.' Dolores's hand felt cold and moist, trembling faintly.

'Those new computers you installed up on three are super,' she said to Ray, eyes still wide. 'The direct link-up to Quantico, fingerprints and personality profiles, and—'

'That's not for public consumption, Dolores. Who showed you how—'

'I'm not *public*, Ray.' Her voice had flattened out. 'I'm a cop's wife.' Ray started to say something when she jumped in. 'Soon to be ex-wife, I know. Anyway, I—'

'Dolores, we have an appointment in—'

'I was checking my calendar this morning, Ray, and guess what? Three years ago today . . .' She looked at her watch. 'At just about an hour from now, we were landing in Jamaica. Do you remember that?'

Ray shook his head, glanced at Julia.

'I think that was the best week of my life. I wish I could have bottled it for later.' Dolores laughed as her eyes drifted off somewhere. 'That little restaurant overlooking Montego Bay, what was it called, Ray?'

'The Dolphin Club,' he said softly.

'Remember that sunset?'

They locked eyes for a few moments, then Ray cleared his throat, started to say something.

'Anyway, I have to run,' Dolores said. 'Nice to meet you, Julia.'

Julia tried to read Ray's expression as he watched his wife

hurry from the building. Wistful? Guilty? Definitely uncomfortable.

'So that's Dolores,' Julia said.

'That's Dolores.'

'Manhattan North detective division is headquartered here in the twenty-fourth,' Ray said as they rode up in an old, sluggish elevator. 'Stella Turner agreed to meet us here as a favor. The psychiatric unit is out in Queens, LeFrak City.'

'Do you work with her a lot?'

'The shrinks are on staff mostly for trauma counseling, not investigations,' he said. 'About ten per cent of all detectives are in therapy.'

They got off the elevator and walked down a long corridor that smelled sharply of disinfectant, making several turns.

'When I first got my badge, my sergeant told me the only way to survive is to go home at night and forget what you saw. The counseling is for the ten per cent who can't do that.'

A woman in a white shirt and black jeans approached them. Mid-twenties, with short, functional hair and no makeup.

'Can I have a word with you, Ray?' She glanced at Julia. 'It's about the case.'

'Can it wait?' Ray said. 'We're late for an appointment.'

'I go on lunch break in fifteen—'

'Fine.' Ray turned to Julia. 'Sorry, I'll be right back.'

The two of them walked several yards down the hallway and turned a corner. Julia leaned against the aqua-tiled wall, glancing up and down the long, empty corridor, then walked quickly down the hall, stopping just short of the spot where Ray had disappeared around the corner.

'. . . the background you requested. Nothing much stands out. Felonies, misdemeanors – zilch.'

'You checked all seven?' Ray said.

'High school, college, employment. Elementary school was a problem, they don't keep records more than ten years. You sure nineteen sixty-three is that important?'

'Keep digging,' Ray said. 'I'll check in this afternoon.'

Julia hurried back to the spot where he'd left her. Ray turned the corner and signalled for her to join him. They continued silently down the hallway.

You checked all seven? Julia didn't have to do the math. Martin, Paula, Richard, Jared, Gail, and Marianne – six 'backgrounds' to check. Easy enough to guess who the seventh was.

Ray knocked on an open door and led her into a conference room. A woman with gray-flecked hair pulled back in a wide barrette sat on the far side of a long table, reviewing a file folder.

'Detective Burgess tells me you're an amateur hypnotist,' she said when Ray introduced them. Stella Turner was generically attractive, with her navy blue suit, white blouse and serious brown eyes. A dark mole clung to the edge of her upper lip, so incongruous on the otherwise unremarkable face that Julia fought the urge to flick it away.

'It's just something we used to do in college,' Julia said. She and Ray took seats across from the doctor. 'I haven't done it since then – until my party.'

'It can be a potent psychological tool. I'm occasionally brought into an investigation to hypnotize witnesses in order to help them recover memories sublimated in their unconscious.'

Julia forced a polite smile. Psychobabble irritated her even more than advertising lingo.

'Why don't you tell me just what happened that night, Julia?'

Dr Turner scribbled on a legal pad as Julia talked.

'You're obviously quite an accomplished hypnotist,' Dr Turner said after a while.

Was she being complimented or reprimanded?

'We used to do this fairly often in college,' Julia said. 'They trust me.'

'Could any of them have been faking it?'

Julia thought for a minute. 'I doubt it. I've seen them all under hypnosis before, so I know what to look for.'

'But one of them might have been faking the hypnotic state back in college, or faking it now, basing his or her performance on what the others were doing.' Her voice was deep, very calm, and vaguely unnerving.

'I guess so,' Julia said. 'But the way they skipped the missing letters without hesitating . . . that's hard to fake.'

'You're probably right.' Dr Turner consulted her notes. 'I would like to focus on your bringing the group back to nineteen sixty-three. You said they all behaved like children. Could you be more specific?'

Julia strained to recall. 'My goal at that point was to get everyone in a position to bring them back to consciousness . . . Let's see, Marianne and Gail argued over a photograph . . . nothing significant. Richard . . . Oh, now I remember. Richard kept pestering me.'

'Pestering?'

'Touching me, nuzzling me. It was annoying.'

'I would assume that he saw you as a mother figure.'

Richard sees *all* women as mother figures, Julia thought. 'He didn't actually call me mother.'

'I would not expect him to. It is possible, even probable, that Richard has very complicated, possibly contradictory feelings toward his mother. He projected these feelings on to you and, depending on the degree of transference, your re-action – you used the term annoyed, I believe – your reaction might have precipitated a profound emotional response in him.'

'Does any of this help?' said Ray, who'd been shifting in

his chair during Dr Turner's lecture.

'If you mean by that, can I tell you which, if any, of these people is your Wizard, then no, of course not. What appears to have happened, however, is that the hypnosis unlocked a drawer of memory inside one of the subjects. Something long buried surfaced, and set off a terrible rage. As you may know, memories of severe trauma can be placed beyond the perimeters of consciousness and later reclaimed.'

'Reclaimed?' Ray said. 'How?'

'A simple gesture has been known to trigger memory retrieval.' She glanced at Julia. 'Hypnosis is more potent.'

'Are you talking about Recovered Memory Syndrome?' Julia said. Keeping up with psych trends was part of her job.

Dr Turner nodded.

'Is that what you think happened at Julia's party?' Ray said. 'Someone recovered a memory from nineteen sixty-three?'

'Possibly. I consulted one study that found that as many as half of all sexual-abuse victims repress memories for a period of time. Even when confronted with medical records, these people have no memory of the events.'

'Incredible,' Ray said.

'But I've been reading about people who recover memories they never had,' Julia said.

'False Memory Syndrome,' said Dr Turner. 'Under hypnosis, and especially under the influence of sodium amytal, subjects often "recover" memories they never had in the first place.'

'But why?' Ray said.

'It's a sure-fire ticket on to the Oprah Winfrey show,' Julia said. 'Make up some juicy stuff about childhood sexual abuse that never—'

'I don't think that's what we're up against here.' Dr Turner smiled primly. 'The murders are very real, unfortunately. But there is nothing in what Ms Mallet has reiterated that pinpoints what memory might have been recovered under hypnosis, or by whom.'

'What about the incident at college?' Ray said. 'I mean when they *thought* they were at college, and Gail came on to Martin. What if Paula – his girlfriend at the time, and now his wife – what if she became jealous, and—'

Dr Turner shook her head. 'The rage driving this killer is much deeper than mere jealousy. It almost certainly goes back to a childhood incident, probably something that happened in nineteen sixty-three, or even earlier. The individual repressed the incident – buried it, you might say – or at the very least buried the pain associated with it. Your hypnosis took the scab off the wound, so to speak.'

Julia felt her chest contract. *She'd* removed the scab that set the Wizard free.

'Still, it's unlikely that the recovered memory alone could trigger the murders. My assumption is that the Wizard was already under some pressure, dealing with something particularly, even extraordinarily stressful. When the child-hood memory came back – *pow*. Everything combined to produce a psychotic rage, which manifested itself in a need to kill.'

'Have any of your friends been under unusual pressure lately?' Ray asked.

'Gail's late with her cookbook,' Julia said.

'Is that unusual?' the doctor asked as she jotted something on the pad.

'As far as I know, she's never missed a deadline. She does seem pretty stressed out lately. Richard . . .'

'What about Richard?'

'This feels like treason.'

'How can saving a life possibly be considered treasonous, Julia?' Dr Turner said.

Julia took a breath. 'Richard's going through a divorce. His wife's idea.'

'Wasn't Richard the individual who –' Dr Turner consulted her notes – 'nuzzled you that evening?'

Julia nodded. Dr Turner made a notation and looked up at her.

'Paula and Martin . . . She's the perfect wife and mother, he's an obscenely successful commodity trader, always under pressure. But who isn't these days? I mean, my job isn't exactly smooth sailing at the moment, but that doesn't mean I kill people in my spare time.'

'When you say "not exactly smooth sailing", what do you mean?'

'I've been under a lot of pressure from a client. They're not especially thrilled with our work lately. Par for the course in advertising, though.'

Stella Turner tapped her pencil against the pad. 'I see.' Another notation, then: 'In nineteen sixty-three, you and your friends were how old?'

'Four,' Julia said.

'Four. It's terribly difficult for most of us to recall with any precision what happened in our fourth year. For instance, what do you recall about *your* fourth year, Ray?'

'Me? Not much. That would be before kindergarten, right? I remember visiting my grandmother in Far Rockaway. She died when I was five, so that must have been—'

'Exactly. Memories are characteristically vague from that period. Julia?'

Julia looked at her and blinked.

'What are your memories from nineteen sixty-three?'

'I remember my nursery school pretty vividly. There was this magnificent dollhouse . . .' She paused and looked at them. 'What's going on here?'

'I'm just trying to demonstrate that memories of early childhood—'

'Bullshit. This whole thing is a setup. You're trying to find out what happened to *me* in nineteen sixty-three, what pressures *I'm* under. That's the real reason I'm here. You and you—'

'That's not it,' Ray said. 'Stella needed to hear your account of the party in your own words.'

'Is that dollhouse your most vivid memory of your fourth year?' Dr Turner said in her calm, deep, infinitely irritating voice.

Julia traced her right index finger along a groove in the table. 'My brother died that year.'

Stella Turner did not make a note. She even put her pencil down.

'He was four years older than me,' Julia said. 'Hit by a car. Died instantly.'

'Were you a witness?'

'No.'

'Did you feel any responsibility?'

She shook her head. 'My mother wouldn't let them bury him. He was in our guest bedroom for days, an open coffin.'

She never buried him, not really.

Dr Turner reached behind her, got a tissue from her shoulder bag and handed it to Julia. 'Often the surviving child feels a sense of responsibility, despite the fact that he or she was in no way involved. Sometimes this feeling is buried, or—'

'Stop it!' Julia made a fist with her left hand. 'Just stop it. I know what you're doing.'

Stella Turner glanced at Ray.

'We didn't mean to upset you,' he said.

'You could have fooled me,' Julia said.

'Ms Mallet. *Julia*. We're only trying to—'

'Can I leave?'

A left hook to the jaw would send the doctor right over the back of her chair.

'Are you familiar with autohypnosis?' Dr Turner asked.

'You mean *self*-hypnosis?'

'Autohypnosis is a widely used therapeutic tool. A hypnotist – a *trained*, *experienced* hypnotist – can actually teach a patient how to induce a hypnotic state in himself or herself. It's a tool with many applications: endogenous, or chemical, depression, or—'

'I didn't hypnotize myself.'

'You didn't *knowingly* hypnotize yourself. But it is possible to induce self-hypnosis unintentionally. One can even—'

'I was awake. Fully conscious – intensely conscious – the whole time. *I* sent them all back to nineteen sixty-three from Madison. How could I have done that if I myself was under hypnosis?'

'It's been documented in the literature. Your subconscious follows your own instructions – in this case, travelling back in time. Your conscious mind remains sufficiently active to control the contemporary situation.'

Julia's hands were trembling. 'Let me see if I've got this straight. I inadvertently hypnotized myself, discovered some deep, hidden event from my past, and then went on a murderous rampage. Is that it?'

Ray put a hand on her arm. 'Julia—'

'IS THAT IT?'

'Nineteen sixty-three was a traumatic year for you,' Dr Turner said. 'And you're under a lot of pressure, as you yourself have pointed—'

'You think I killed these women.' Julia glanced from Ray to the doctor. 'You think *I* did it.'

'We think . . .' Dr Turner looked at Ray. 'I think that you cannot be *eliminated* from the list of suspects. It is possible,

131

even likely, that whoever committed these crimes has no memory of doing so, that his or her memories of these murders are being stored as electromagnetic patterns deep in the brain's—'

'I can't believe I'm hearing this.'

Dr Turner sailed on. 'The hypnosis could well have brought to life an entirely new persona that has no communication whatsoever with the original personality.'

Ray shook his head at Julia, who turned away. 'I didn't know about this,' he said softly. 'I thought we were here to go over the night of your party.'

Julia looked from him to Stella Turner and back to him. 'Can I go now, or do you want to interrogate me some more?'

'I'll drive you to your office,' Ray said.

She stood up. 'No thanks, I'll take my chances in a taxi.'

She left the room, but in seconds Ray caught up with her.

'Julia, let me drive you.'

She stopped, turned to him. 'Afraid I'll kill someone on the way to the office?'

'Julia—'

'Is that why you're spending so much time with me, *Detective* Burgess? Because you think I might let something slip?'

'You know that's not it.'

'Then prove it – let me leave on my own.'

He hesitated just a second before heading back toward the conference room.

Julia turned a corner, then another. Where the fuck were the elevators? She poked her head through an open door to ask directions. The small, windowless room was empty, its walls covered with photographs, maps, charts, all taped to the cinder-block wall. She took a step inside. On the facing wall she saw a hand-lettered sign: WIZARD TASK FORCE. She walked to the center of the room and slowly turned around.

Jessica Forrester smiled vacantly at her from a large color photograph, surrounded by smaller photographs, close-ups of the body slumped against the wall, of the shattered face smeared red and black, of the graffiti-covered wall . . . more shots of the body . . .

Julia spun around, trying not to look.

. . . autopsy photos showing a naked Alicia Frommer, her face red . . . Alicia collapsed in a pool of blood, crumpled, her face a mass of . . .

Black letters sprayed on the wall over her corpse, a signature. *Just get out of here.*
Now.

Julia turned again, and saw . . . Jared. She stopped and cocked her head just long enough to see them all lined up. Jared, Gail, Paula, Martin . . .

She stepped further into the room. Her official agency head-shot – personnel had dozens on file. She looked pretty and happy and thoroughly bland, like . . .

Like Jessica Forrester and Alicia Frommer's head-shots, taped to the other walls. That same insipid, carefree smile, as if the subject's normality invited the crime. Julia stared at herself and felt a crushing sense of inevitability. She whirled around, the gruesome photographs swirling together into an awful montage of body parts, vapid smiles, bloody, nearly obliterated faces. She lurched toward the doorway, stumbled into the corridor, and leaned against the wall for a few seconds.

'Are you all right?' A uniformed cop stood just a few feet away.

She straightened up, took a deep breath. 'Yes, I mean – no, I've managed to lose the elevators.'

He escorted her down the hallway and pressed the call button for her. 'You sure you're okay?'

She nodded and smiled. Radiantly.

12

Richard Portland was waiting in her office when Julia arrived.

'I should have called,' he said, 'but you're always so busy . . .'

They kissed. His beard felt scratchy, and he smelled faintly stale. His marriage had been over for six months and he still looked rumpled and bleary-eyed. He'd put on weight too.

Her secretary appeared in the doorway and gestured helplessly at Richard.

'It's okay, Alison.' Julia turned back to Richard. 'So, tell me what's wrong.'

'Everything's wrong.' He more or less collapsed on to the couch. Julia sat next to him. 'Did you hear about the layoffs at the phone company?'

'It was on the front page. You lost your—'

'I'm basically on life support, but they're bound to pull the plug sooner or later.'

'Sounds awful.'

He let out a long, hissing breath. 'Hey, it's the nineties, right? Companies are downsizing, the government's downsizing. Even Kim's downsizing – one less mouth to feed now that the girls are in school.'

'I gather it's more complicated than that.'

'Everywhere you turn someone's saying we have to atone

for the excesses of the eighties. And I want to say, what excesses? I spent the entire decade trying to pay down a mortgage, not buying RJR Nabisco, for Christ's sake.'

Julia laughed, but wished her office wasn't quite so opulent. Richard was invariably indignant about something. Gail thought him insufferable, but Julia always found his anger admirable. Who *expected* fairness any more? Who even talked about it?

'This detective came to see me. Twice, actually.'

Ah. 'He's been to see all of us,' Julia said.

'He seems to think we're tied in with these women getting killed. I told him about all those girls you poisoned back at Madison . . .' His smile brought out a perfect dimple on his left cheek and a roguish glint in his eyes – the old Richard was still there, thank God. 'Hey, he tortured me, Julia. I had no choice.'

'Very funny.'

'Why is he interested in us?' Richard asked.

'He didn't say.' Julia focused on a jet slicing through the cloudless sky beyond her window. From her angle on the couch, all she could see outside was brilliant blue sky. It was a bit like looking out of an airplane – even the tallest buildings had vanished.

'I mean, all of a sudden I need an *alibi*?' Richard said.

'Well, what *were* you doing when those women were killed?'

He stared at her for a few beats, then laughed bitterly. 'Not very subtle, Julia.' He shook his head, almost a shudder. 'I was alone. I'm always alone.'

Gail's words, almost exactly.

'I was by myself too,' Julia said. 'Emily was sound asleep during both murders; I could have snuck out. That doesn't make me guilty.'

'What were the others doing, I wonder?' Before she could answer he jumped in. 'Marianne was in DC, Paula and Martin were together, of course. Or do you think they might *both* have

135

done it? Some new kind of marriage therapy – you know, the couple that slays together stays together.'

'Richard, are you worried about something specific?'

A vision flashed: Richard spraying black paint across the faces of two dead women. What terrified her was not the image itself but the fact that, in some crazy, edge-of-reality way, the vision stuck. An angry petulance simmered just below Richard's black-humored exterior, a stubborn, almost childish anger that no amount of one-liners could conceal.

'It's the police. I told them I didn't have an alibi. That's true for the first killing, but for the second one . . .' He looked at his lap.

'You have an alibi for Alicia Frommer's murder and you didn't tell Ra— Detective Burgess?'

He looked up at her and chuckled silently. 'It's kind of embarrassing, really. I had the girls with me a couple of weekends ago, and they mentioned that Kim is seeing someone.' He paused to collect himself; separation had been Kim Portland's idea, sprung on Richard out of the blue. 'I can't seem to get any distance from her somehow.' He sounded almost ready to cry. 'I try, but I can't. About the only thing I *have* been able to do since moving out is eat.'

He ran a hand over his newly enlarged stomach, the way Julia used to when she was pregnant, his eyes betraying the same astonishment at what his body had become.

'I've never been into food very much,' he said. 'I mean, I thought *al dente* was one of John Gotti's boys.' He offered a half-hearted smile. 'Now food is all I think about.'

Because food, unlike love, was something he could give himself.

'Your alibi . . .'

'Right. The night that black woman was killed up in Harlem? I was out in Larchmont.'

'With Kim?' Julia felt a weight lifted.

'Not *with* her exactly,' he said. 'I was . . . well, I was watching her. The girls mentioned she had a subscription to this theater series in Mamaroneck, so I called up and drove out to Westchester, and then I . . . I basically waited outside the theater to see who she was with.'

'And?'

'And she was with a man. He used to live down the street from us until his marriage ended. They should call it Divorce Court – sorry. So I followed them back to our house – Kim's house, technically. They went in together and never came out. Well, at least I left by ten and he was still in there.'

'Alicia Frommer was killed around eight, eight-thirty.'

'Exactly!' Richard sat up. 'The play started at seven-thirty. I was there, in Mamaroneck.'

'Did anyone see you? Did Kim?'

'I'd have died if she'd seen me. As for anyone else . . .' He shrugged. 'But I saw them. How else would I know who she was with? And I know where they went after the play – to our . . . her house.'

He had a point, though a weak one.

'But you could have seen them *after* the play. That way—'

'That way I could have killed that woman, driven up to Mamaroneck, and still seen Kim and that man?' He stood up. 'Is that what you're saying?'

He was nearly shouting, but when Alison appeared Julia waved her away. 'Sit down, Richard. I'm trying to help you, dammit.' He sat. 'What did you do between the start of the play and the end?'

'Drove around, mostly. You know, the old neighborhood.'

This was looking worse. 'No one saw you? We're talking two hours.'

'I had coffee and a piece of cake at a diner. Around eight-thirty, I'd guess. The Post Diner.' He glanced at his stomach. 'Chocolate layer cake, with a scoop of vanilla ice cream on the side.'

'Then someone might remember you there.'

Of course, Richard *could* still have killed Alicia Frommer and raced up to the diner in the hopes of establishing an alibi.

Richard studied her for a few moments. 'I came here because I needed advice and I thought I could trust you. My lawyer recommends that I don't have to volunteer anything. In fact he says I *shouldn't* say anything unless—'

'Your lawyer?'

Richard shrugged. 'The police questioned me twice, Julia.'

'Well, my advice is to tell Detective Burgess about that night. Maybe someone at the diner will remember you.'

Although she doubted it. Richard Portland wasn't memorable in most circumstances; at a suburban diner on a week night, sitting at the counter, he'd be practically invisible.

'The children were home that night. She brought him back to the house when the children were there.'

'Talk to the detective, Richard. For your own good.' Julia stood up. 'I've got a meeting in a few—'

'Do you think she slept with him, Julia? Christ, I haven't thought about sex since we split. Every other woman I even look at doesn't measure up somehow. She's still my standard for what a woman should be.'

Julia felt a rush of sympathy for Richard. Kim didn't know what she was giving up. Richard was more Don Rickles than Don Juan, but he was honest and loyal and could be quite funny. Or was living with an adoring disciple harder than it sounded?

He crossed to Julia and kissed her on the cheek. His face felt warm and moist.

'Call Detective Burgess,' Julia said.

Call him and save me from betraying you.

He nodded, started to leave, then turned. 'I always assumed I'd have it figured out by now,' Richard said.

'We all did.'

'I mean, I thought I'd do great things.'

Julia shrugged. He was *never* going to leave.

'Look, Richard, I really—'

'I applied to medical school, did you know that? I didn't get in. Anywhere. I was a good student, but my MCATS were lousy.'

'Well, that's ancient—'

'You know why they were lousy? The night before the exam, I went to bed early. Everything was riding on that exam. I was on full scholarship; no one in my family had gone to college before, let alone medical school. Nothing was more important to me than getting into medical school – except getting stoned, I *really* liked getting stoned.' He closed his eyes for a moment and shook his head. 'About ten, ten-thirty someone knocked at my door. I tried to ignore it, but after a few minutes I got out of bed, opened the door. Remember who it was, Julia?'

Even now she had to stifle a smile at the memory of Richard in flannel pyjamas. 'That was fifteen years ago.'

'Martin, Jared and you. The Three Musketeers, with six-packs and Bolivian hash. And you wouldn't leave; I begged you but you wouldn't leave.'

Julia glanced out the window to avoid his eyes.

'It was my own fault,' Richard said. 'I didn't have to smoke the hash.' He hesitated a moment. 'But you knew I was weak – especially you, Julia. You understand people, you always did. And you knew how important that exam was and you could always control situations like that. I would have done anything you asked me to. You knew how I felt; I was crazy about you from the moment I—'

'Richard, please, not now.'

He raised his arms and let them fall to his side. 'I never slept that night, not one minute. And now . . .' He shook his head.

'I don't think you can pin your entire adult life on one night.'

He stared at her a few moments, dreamy-eyed, as if he were back at Madison again, the pre-med grind mooning at a popular undergraduate, rather generous with her body, who had dimly known how he felt about her and refused to acknowledge it, perhaps the cruelest rejection.

'I guess not,' he said. 'I guess not.' He turned and left.

Julia gathered her papers for the meeting and said a silent prayer that someone at the Post Diner would remember Richard Portland.

She met in her office with the team responsible for Able Brands' Sparkle dishwasher powder.

'The client's moved up the schedule,' she told them. 'We have to get the new concept to them three weeks from Wednesday.'

All four of them groaned in unison. Delivering bad news had become her forte.

'Any ideas?'

'I'm seeing white,' the creative director said, puckering his lips and waving a hand in front of him as if erasing a blackboard. 'Clean, pure.' He paused theatrically, looked each of them in the eye. 'White.'

Julia never knew how seriously to take such conversations. Today, at least, more urgent matters beckoned. Ray and that shrink thought she might have killed those two women. Well, she wasn't going to sit around and wait for them to figure out that she was innocent. She'd do some digging on her own. As for informing on her friends . . . she'd find out what she could and then decide what she would and wouldn't tell Ray.

As her staff debated the merits of white, Julia scribbled on a piece of paper. At the top she wrote 'Alicia Frommer'. Then, skipping a line: 'Richard – in Westchester.' She tapped her pen a few times, added a question mark, and moved on. 'Paula and Martin – together.' Well, at least two of them were accounted for. 'Marianne – Washington.' *Tap, tap, tap.* She added a question mark, then wrote 'Call to confirm.' That left Gail and Jared.

Her mind flashed to Ray, trying to convince her that his . . . reluctance last night had nothing to do with her.

Damn.

'Julia, are you all right?'

All eyes stared at her. She must have cursed out loud.

'I hate these creative reviews, don't you?' she said. 'But I think we're on to something with the white theme.'

The account executive smiled and arched his eyebrows.

'We moved on to blue, actually,' he said.

'Senator Rinaldi's office.'

'Marianne Wilson, please. This is Julia Mallet.'

'I'll see if she's available.'

Even Rinaldi's secretary was rude. How could Marianne have gone to work for the shrew? 'It's about health care,' she'd said, 'nothing else. I'm going into the enemy camp to influence policy.' True, Ruth Rinaldi was on the Senate Finance Committee, but she was an ignoramus on the subject of health care (among others).

'Julia, what a surprise. I've got a hearing in twelve minutes. What's up?'

'It's about the murders. I assume you've talked to Detective Burgess.'

'Several times. And some detective from a local DC unit came by the office. I still don't know what—'

'When did you get back to DC?'

'Monday night. Why?'

Before Alicia Frommer's murder.

'Are you sure?'

'Of course I'm . . . Julia, what are you saying, that you actually think I might have—'

'Of course not,' Julia said. 'But this detective keeps asking questions. I'm getting kind of nervous.'

'*You're* nervous? I work for one of the most powerful senators in Washington. You have any idea what would happen if the press got wind of the fact that homicide cops visited Ruth's office?'

Even murder had its positive side.

'So you were in DC two nights ago?'

A beat. 'Yes, I was.' Marianne sounded petulant, but who could blame her?

'Didn't Rinaldi address a Republican fund-raiser at the Waldorf that—'

'*Senator* Rinaldi was in New York. I wasn't. Is the senator a suspect too?'

No. Rinaldi may have murdered the country's soul, but she probably had nothing to do with the deaths of Jessica Forrester and Alicia Frommer.

'Will you be in New York soon?' Julia asked. 'I'd love to have dinner.'

She pictured Marianne flipping through her bulging Filofax.

'Not till May at the earliest. Do the cops really think the murderer was at your party?'

'I don't know what they think.' Julia sighed; lying to her friends wasn't getting easier. 'I really don't.'

'Call me if you hear anything,' Marianne said. 'Gotta run now.'

Julia hung up and looked at the list of friends. If Marianne had somehow sneaked back into New York on Tuesday, the shuttle service would have a credit card receipt or boarding pass. Ditto Amtrak. Ray would have checked out those possibilities. She could have driven up, of course, but at five hours each way she would have had to have taken the afternoon off in order to arrive in New York by seven.

She crossed out the question mark next to Marianne's name. A minute later she grabbed her coat and hurried to the elevators. At least she'd eliminated Marianne as a suspect – almost eliminated her. But if Marianne was off the list, and Richard and the Freemasons, too, that left only Gail and Jared. Gail couldn't handle raw chicken without getting nauseous.

That left Jared.

The meeting in Larry Breaker's office had been called for noon, two hours after Julia's session with Stella Turner. Ray and Stella arrived together and sat in front of Breaker's gray metal desk, waiting for Breaker to look up from the paperwork in front of him. He moved only to drag on a cigarette, or tap it on the edge of a square glass ash tray.

Ray glanced around the office. The walls were crowded with plaques: commendations from the mayor, the borough president, the commissioner, a variety of US presidents. There were framed photos too: the deputy chief of detectives shaking hands with the mayor, the borough president, the commissioner; toasting some long-forgotten detective at a retirement dinner; brandishing a variety of weapons made notorious from solved homicides.

Breaker stubbed out the cigarette and emptied the ash tray into a trash can under his desk. He grabbed a tissue from a drawer, wiped the ash tray clean, threw out the tissue, and positioned the ash tray in its designated spot on the left side of his desk.

'So?' He looked from Ray to Stella Turner and back again. He had the ruddy complexion, dimpled nose, and overall fleshiness of a drinker, but as far as anyone knew he never indulged.

'She cannot be ruled out as a suspect,' Stella Turner said. 'I believe she is convinced of her innocence, but it's possible that we're dealing with two personalities here.'

Breaker looked at Ray. 'Agree?'

Breaker was a word miser. When he had received his twenty-fifth anniversary badge a while back, a group of detectives had presented him with a leatherbound book inscribed: 'The Sayings of Deputy Chief of Detectives Breaker'. The book was empty. Breaker had scanned the room with beady eyes, generating gallons of perspiration, before saying, simply, 'Thanks.'

'I don't believe she's the perp,' Ray said. 'Everything points to one of her friends.'

'Hypnotized,' said the deputy chief of detectives.

Three whole syllables – Breaker must be warming to the subject. 'There's nothing in her past that makes me think she—'

'What about the brother?' Stella Turner said.

'What about him?'

'He died in nineteen sixty-three. It's quite apparent that Miss Mallet has some unresolved emotions regarding that incident.'

'Ray?' Breaker drummed the thick fingers of his right hand on the top of his desk.

'Her brother died . . . that makes her a killer?'

'But she—'

'We watching her?' Breaker said.

Ray nodded as Stella shifted in her chair, bristling at the interruption. As if Breaker would ever take her side over his.

Ten years before, his detective's shield still shiny, Ray had been assigned to a break-and-enter in a high-rise on Third Avenue. An inside job – they almost always were, in doorman buildings. Ray had tracked the missing jewelry to a pawn shop on Lenox Avenue, nailed the perp that afternoon, and was filing a report at his desk when Breaker summoned him to his office – God reaching down from on high. The jewelry was a gift from a happily married city councilman to his girlfriend, Breaker had said with uncharacteristic verbosity. So be a good little detective and forget the report, okay?

Forget the report and I won't forget you.

'Any connection between the two victims?' Breaker said now.

Ray shook his head. 'We interviewed everyone Jessica Forrester worked with, socialized with, lived near – ditto for Alicia Frommer. No connection.'

'Ballistics.' Breaker took a deep, unhappy breath and exhaled it noisily. Two linked homicides, two different handguns – cops didn't appreciate inconsistency in serial killers. Patterns, not variations, tripped up killers. 'We got two shooters here?'

'With the same signature?' Ray said.

'I don't like this,' Breaker almost whispered. 'We've kept the connection out of the press. Next time, though . . .' He shook his head, glaring at Ray. 'If this hypnotism . . . this hypnotism shit turns out to be a waste of time . . .'

'It won't.'

'We're stretched thin. Nick's got half the force under him.'

Nick Meyer, head of the Wizard Task Force, had a small army of detectives interviewing co-workers, families, going door-to-door at both locations. Breaker drummed his fingers again. 'I hear she's a looker.'

'Quite beautiful,' Stella Turner said.

'Beats knocking on doors,' Breaker said, eyes locked on Ray's.

'What's that supposed—'

'I have a twelve-thirty.' Breaker jabbed his right index finger at the top page of his desk calendar. Stella Turner practically jumped from her seat. Ray hesitated before standing, but decided

145

there was no point in arguing. No need.

He'd gotten his way with Breaker ever since he'd refused to sit on that robbery report. The councilman had resigned, gotten divorced, the mistress had sold her story to the Post for six figures. Breaker had had his ass whipped down at One Police Plaza, then expended a month's allocation of words to chew out Ray in his office. And Ray, for refusing to cave, had secured a godfather in the Manhattan North Detective Bureau for as long as Breaker was in charge.

Which, unfortunately, was only another six months.

13

Julia fought for breath after the five-flight climb to Jared's apartment.

'All that...boxing, you'd think I...could handle a few stairs.'

'Some wine will restore you.' Two giant steps and he was in the kitchen.

Julia looked around. The tiny apartment was even more crowded than she remembered. Jared was a collector – magazines, old bottles, umbrellas, books . . . you name it. The place was a dump, no denying it, on a run-down block in the west Forties. Two small rooms, plus a closet-sized kitchen and moldy bathroom, each opening on to the next, railroad style. But the overall effect was a little like Jared, really; for all the jumble, the contradictions, there was an undeniable charm.

'Here you go, sweetheart.' He handed her a glass of red wine. She ignored a smudge on the edge of the glass and took a sip. Delicious. Jared was always broke, but he never compromised. He sat next to her on the worn sofa.

'I can't believe none of the others have called you about this,' Julia said. 'I've heard from all of them at least once.'

'Why would they call *me*? You're the glue that holds us all together.'

'That's not true.' Not *entirely* true, anyway.

'We never get together except with you. You're the center of the wheel, with spokes going out to each of us on the edge.' He spread the fingers of one hand in front of her face, eyebrows arched. 'The hypnotist.'

'Don't start, Jared.' She cleared a ménage of small plastic wind-up toys from the steamer trunk that served as Jared's coffee table, and put her glass down.

'Anyway,' Jared said, 'as I told these detectives, I have no alibi for either night.' He sighed theatrically and spread his arms out over the top of the sofa. 'I'm afraid it's a lonely life I lead here.'

As if Jared, even in a faded T-shirt and jeans, would ever have a minute's trouble finding female companionship. If in fact he was alone as much as he liked to suggest.

'You mean, both nights—'

The phone rang. Jared jumped to his feet and sprinted across the room as the answering machine – the same model Julia had – picked up. She heard Jared's recorded message, then a beep, then a man's voice: 'This is Max. I'm calling—'

The message stopped abruptly as Jared turned the sound down.

He returned to the sofa and took a big sip of wine. 'Sorry,' he said. 'Now, tell me why the cops are focusing on your party. What's the connection?'

'That's what I can't figure out. None of us knew the victims, although I might have run into Jessica Forrester a few times in the elevator. And neither of them was at the party, and—'

'I think you're bullshitting, Julia.'

'They're questioning me too,' she said.

'But you know why they're interested in us. I'm positive you know.'

There were times when she wished Jared wasn't quite so perceptive.

'What happened that night? You said you couldn't hypnotize

148

us, but we all thought some time had passed.'

'It took a while before I gave up.'

'*Something* happened that night, Julia. What was it?'

'Things got kind of tense between Gail and—'

The phone again. This time Jared didn't get up; with the volume turned down, they heard only a series of clicks.

'Go ahead and answer it, I don't mind.'

'It's probably nothing important. And this is. You said things were tense with Gail . . .'

'When I brought all of you back to nineteen eighty-one – I mean, when I tried to – Gail started coming on to Martin. Apparently they had something going back then. Anyway, Paula got involved, then things got nasty . . .'

'I don't remember any of that,' Jared said. 'Which means I must have been under.'

'I told you before, I was successful with some of you. But when I couldn't—'

'And you didn't let me remember?' he said. 'Very naughty, Julia.'

'I didn't want to hurt anybody. I figured, what's the point of dredging up past history?'

'Gail and Martin?' He shook his head and glanced at the ceiling, as if an image of that unlikely couple were projected there.

'I should never have tried to hypnotize any of you that night. When you're nineteen, twenty, you have no secrets – at least not *dark* secrets. There's time to undo anything that happens. Later you start hiding things, rewriting history, trying to forget. Bringing up the past, it's playing with fire.'

'What are you hiding then?' Jared said.

'I wasn't under hypnosis.'

'That's avoiding the issue.' Jared's eyes burned into her. It wasn't easy refusing him.

149

'That I'm . . .'

He waited for her to finish, almost smiling, eyes fixed. A Roman bust: noble, somehow trustworthy, yet accustomed to compliance.

'That I'm lonely,' she said softly.

'Why—'

'*Sometimes* lonely.'

'Why would you hide that?'

'I . . . well, I guess it feels like a weakness. I have Emily, my career . . .'

'Those are the distractions that keep you from *feeling* lonely.'

'Old friends too – they're like armor; they deflect loneliness.'

But one of them is the Wizard, and I don't know what scares me more; finding out which one is a killer . . . or not knowing.

She got up and walked to the front door. An old-fashioned milk pail was crammed with umbrellas of all shapes and sizes, many with animal heads for handles.

Could she trust anyone now, even Jared? The search for the Wizard, like the hypnosis itself, was going to mean venturing into the furthest corners of friendships that had survived, even flourished, in the dim, cozy shadows that protect long-term relationships.

'Emily's father . . . did you *choose* him?' Jared said.

'Of course not. I slept with this guy once. I hardly remember him.'

'I don't see you just . . . *letting* something like that happen. I can picture you checking into a sperm bank, selecting the perfect donor—'

She turned round to face him. 'He was someone I met at a hotel in Dallas over five years ago. I was monitoring a focus group and—'

'If you had used a sperm bank *I* could be Emily's father.'

Julia started to laugh, but he was serious.

150

'I make regular deposits,' he said. 'About once a month for the past year.'

'For—'

'No, not for money. For immortality, I guess. The genes are good, but I never thought I'd be very successful as a father. Every once in a while, on the bus or subway, I'll see some little guy with blond hair, a certain look on his face, and I'll wonder if he's mine.' Jared smiled and glanced down for a moment before looking back at her. 'You sure you didn't use a bank? Emily's hair is so light, and those curls . . .'

Julia shook her head.

Jared sighed, but a moment later his expression brightened. 'Anyway, it's a good excuse to jerk off once a month, for science.'

The phone rang again, and was picked up immediately by the answering machine.

'Sounds like someone wants to talk to you badly. Are you sure you don't—'

'Do you ever wonder what might have happened if you hadn't called it off between us?'

'*You* were the one . . .'

He shook his head. 'I screwed around. Who didn't back then? But you made it clear we were through after that one night.'

Julia recalled the awkwardness of the first post-coital encounter, the gradual re-establishment of friendship. No heartbreak on either side, no regrets. *Had* she called it off, then blamed the break-up on him to fit some more comfortable image of herself?

'I got the impression you were giving me something that night,' Jared said. 'Like you were, I don't know, saving me. Once I was safe you could move on. I felt like a charity case.'

Damn him.

'I'm leaving,' she said.

'Why are the cops interested in us?'

'After the first murder, they thought they'd found a connection to my party.' She took a deep breath. 'I really don't know what it is.'

Jared joined her at the door. 'Tell me what you know, Julia. I'm your oldest—'

'I just told you, I don't know anything more.' She retrieved her wine glass and took a sip.

He stared at her. 'You don't really trust anybody, do you? No wonder you're lonely.'

'Here we go again. Why can't—'

'Who betrayed you, Julia, way back when?' He placed a hand on her arm and gently stroked. 'Who was it?'

'Nobody *betrayed* me.'

'Someone must have, to leave you so . . . wary.' He cocked his head so their eyes met on the same level. 'Who betrayed you?'

Julia lifted her wine glass to her lips but the words sprang out. 'My mother.'

Jared waited as she finished the wine.

'When I learned how to help my father, with his pain – she never really forgave me for that.'

'Because you *helped* him?'

'And she couldn't.'

'Jesus.'

'That's when I realized she'd never wanted us too close, my father and me. She saw it as a threat, I guess – because deep down, I don't think she ever felt loved by him.'

She blinked and saw herself at nine or ten, wearing a flocked dress and patent-leather shoes, waiting by the front door for her father to take her to his office Christmas party. 'You hate parties,' she heard him whisper in the kitchen. Then her mother's voice: 'Maybe I just want to be invited. Maybe I just want . . . Oh, never mind. What's the point?'

She blinked and saw her father lying in bed, eyes open, his expression vacant but peaceful, free from pain for the first time in days. She had tiptoed from the room to find her mother in front of the kitchen sink. 'Daddy's comfortable.' Her mother spun round, soap foam flying off her hands. 'Comfortable? He's dying. You can't stop *that*, can you, Julia?'

She blinked again, and saw Jared waiting for more. Well, he'd gotten enough out of her already. It was her turn.

'Are you auditioning these days?'

'Now and then.'

'What kind of parts?'

He scratched the back of his neck. 'Parts I don't get, mostly.'

Julia sighed and got her coat. At the door she turned to kiss him, but he took a half-step back.

'I know you, Julia. I know you're telling the cops more than you're telling me.' He looked grim and angry; tiny wrinkles appeared on the edges of his eyes.

'I'm telling you as much as I can.'

'You always have to be in control, even when murder's involved. The hypnotist.'

'Fuck you,' she said.

'Julia, I—'

'For fifteen years now you've walked in and out of my mind like you owned it.'

Which had always been kind of thrilling, in its way – and so what if he remained largely an enigma? He was handsome and charming and his scrutiny felt risky and exciting and incredibly seductive. But the stakes were higher now.

She was two flights down and still hadn't heard him close the door. Then his phone rang again.

'I hope this all works out well for you,' he called down to her.

Something in his voice set her heart pounding. He knew her so well . . .

'I don't understand what you—'

'I hope it works out, that's all.'

Seconds later she heard the door close.

14

Ray was waiting outside Jared's building.

'How did you know I was . . . never mind. I'm being followed, right?'

He took her elbow and guided her to his car. Darkness had fallen since she'd entered Jared's apartment, taking the temperature along with it. Bundled-up pedestrians scurried by on their way to pre-theater dinners.

'Answer my question – am I being followed?'

'We're having Jared watched,' Ray said. 'The cop on surveillance saw you enter and called me.'

Julia stopped and shook off his hand.

'Look at it this way,' he said. 'It's rush hour, you'll never get a cab, and I'm offering you a lift home.'

She looked into his eyes. He met her gaze, unblinking, unsmiling. She got into his car.

'What you did before, with Dr Turner—'

'That wasn't my idea. We were going to talk about hypnosis, period.'

He sounded sincere – or were all cops good liars? In any case, a woman had been murdered three floors down from her, now a second woman had been killed with the same signature. She wasn't eager to be alone.

'You might as well stay for dinner,' she said as

he pulled away from the curb.

He glanced at her.

'Don't worry, Ray, I won't jump your bones or anything. Emily will chaperon.'

He laughed.

'Drop me at Fairway, okay? I need to pick up a few things.'

Fairway was a nightmare. She should have picked a less crowded store, paid a few extra bucks – who cared if the produce wasn't quite as fresh? She elbowed her way through the salad aisles, grabbed a head of lettuce, a green pepper, picked up some fresh pasta and a pint of ice cream.

The checkout line snaked half-way up the vegetable aisle. She watched two shoppers pick through a bin of string beans as if they were sifting for gold. A tug-of-war erupted over a lush head of romaine. A haggard-looking mother yanked a bag of chips from her young daughter's hands, ignoring the resulting sobs, and shoved her into a shopping cart.

Julia turned away from the escalating screams and unloaded her basket. This was where Jessica Forrester had spent her last Sunday with her boys. She reached across her cart to place the pepper on the scale and dropped it on the floor. When she picked it up it was covered with sawdust.

For a few minutes there she'd almost forgotten what was going on.

Emily ran to the door to greet them, Pamela not far behind.

'The police came here again,' Emily said.

Julia glanced from Ray to Pamela and back.

'When I bring Emily back from school,' Pamela said. 'They ask me when you got home the other night.' She looked frightened. Raising two teenage boys on her own in a project in the Bronx, she probably didn't associate police visits with anything nonthreatening.

'They wanted to establish your whereabouts at the time . . .' Ray glanced at Emily. 'Alicia Frommer's time.'

She'd been killed between eight and nine.

'I was here, with Emily,' Julia said.

'Exactly,' Ray said. 'That's all they needed to know.'

'*They*?' Julia said. 'I don't suppose you'd ask yourself.' She headed for the kitchen, where she plunked the Fairway bag on to the counter. Pamela poked her head in a few moments later.

'Is everything all right?'

'Everything's fine,' Julia said. 'I'll see you tomorrow.'

A minute later Julia heard Emily showing Ray her room. She unpacked the bag, slamming its contents on the counter . . . Christ, she really was a suspect! Ray joined her as she was filling a big pot with water.

'I was going to tell you,' he said.

'You actually thought I—'

'In *my* mind you're not a suspect. But *think*, Julia. The department has to check out the alibi of everyone who had anything to do with the killings. And we've – well, *you've* pretty much established that something happened here, in your apartment, on the night of your party. Something related to the two killings.'

'Still . . .'

'Want to play a game?' It was Emily, who'd come in and was tapping Ray on the leg.

Ray looked at Julia, shrugged, and allowed himself to be led from the room.

Julia made dinner while Emily showed Ray how to use the computer. *Emily's* computer. Julia had bought it to write reports and letters, but since she'd added a CD-ROM drive a few months ago, Emily had basically commandeered it.

A half-hour later Ray was back in the kitchen, Emily in tow.

'Smells good,' he said.

'It's what we always have for company,' Emily said.

'Don't give away my secrets, darling,' Julia said. 'Why don't you go wash your hands before dinner?'

Emily ran from the room.

'She's a terrific kid,' Ray said.

'Miracles happen.'

His expression turned serious. 'It might be a good idea to keep away from Jared until this thing is solved.'

Julia smashed a garlic clove. 'Why, is there something about him I should know?'

Ray glanced away. She started to chop the garlic, then stopped.

'Look, you might as well be straight with me,' she said. 'You asked for my help this morning. The more I know, the more I can help.'

'Two nights ago, Jared DeSantis managed to elude the cop we had assigned to him. The night Alicia Frommer was killed.'

'*Elude*? Maybe he just—'

'I checked. The cop on duty is a fifteen-year veteran on the force. No way he'd lose someone unless that person deliberately tried to *be* lost.'

Julia returned to the garlic, chopped a few times, then shoved the knife against the wall.

'You wanted me to be straight with you?' Ray said. 'When we talked to Jared this afternoon, he told us he spent that night in a neighborhood bar. Couldn't remember which one.'

'You talked to Jared today?'

'Didn't he mention it?'

'He may have,' she said. The secrets were spreading like a virus. 'How about the others?'

'The usual. Paula and Martin Freemason were together. Gail

Severance was chopping sassafras or something.'

'Cilantro.'

'Marianne was in Washington – or so she says.'

'And Richard?'

'Alone. You're a strange bunch, the six of you, alone all the time. At least *you* have an alibi for that night. I doubt you'd leave Emily alone, even to act out some deep, dark, homicidal impulse.'

She looked at Ray. He wasn't smiling. 'Do I *need* an alibi?'

He hesitated. 'For me? No. But with the department, it's basically guilty until proven innocent. You have an alibi, so let's leave it at that.'

She stirred the garlic into the saucepan that already contained tomatoes, chopped basil, sautéd onions, lots of fresh pepper, and a dash of most of the spices she had on hand.

'On the other hand . . .' Ray looked at her and smiled weakly.

'I hate the other hand.'

'Stella Turner thinks that you might know something, some detail that you've forgotten that could be significant.'

'I've told you everything I—'

'She wants to hypnotize you.'

'Forget it.'

'She's a trained, experienced therapist, she—'

'*No.*'

'I get it,' Ray said in a tight voice. 'Hypnotism is good enough for your friends. You expected them to trust you completely, you *demanded* trust. But when it comes to turning the tables, you won't budge.'

'Why should I trust Stella Turner? *Doctor* Turner?'

Why should I trust you?

'Just an idea,' Ray said softly.

'A bad idea.' Julia tasted the sauce, then threw two handfuls of linguini into boiling water. A few scalding drops splashed

159

on to her arms. 'Shit,' she said, shaking both arms. 'Dinner's almost ready.'

'This is great,' he said at the table. Emily had eaten earlier and was watching a video in the living room. 'Really excellent. Any Italian in your blood?'

'Pure, homogenized Wasp,' she said. 'About ten years ago I got stoned one night – can I say that to a cop? – and poured every ingredient I had into a pot. You're tasting the result.'

'Did you grow up in New York?' he asked.

'About twenty miles from here, on Long Island,' she said.

'Your parents still live there?'

What exactly was he after?

'My father died when I was in college. My mother moved to the East Side after Emily was born.'

'You mentioned a brother who died?'

'Matthew. Hit by a car when he was eight years old. I was four.'

'That must have been tough on you.'

'The hardest part was that he never really died. For my parents, he kept on living. Not just living but growing. Matthew was this presence in my life, a shadow – no, more than a shadow, closer to a reality. I'd see my mother staring out the kitchen window with this dreamy smile on her face and I would know she was watching Matthew play ball. She hardly ever smiled.'

Julia took a sip of wine. 'When people refer to me as an only child I want to tell them I wasn't, that I had a brother – a perfect angel of a brother who got the best grades, excelled at all sports, was the apple of his mother's . . .' She felt tears on her cheeks. Until today, she hadn't mentioned Matthew in years.

'Are you still competing against an angel?' Ray said.

Julia shrugged. First Jared, now Ray. Who said men only enjoyed talking about themselves?

'My parents never exactly criticized what I did, but they didn't praise either. I was just *there*, on the edges. Their real focus was always Matthew, especially my mother. The only time they sat up and noticed me was when I learned to hypnotize. My father had this degenerative bone disease. The symptoms started appearing when I was in high school, and by the time I was in college he was in almost constant pain. During winter break, freshman year, I hypnotized him out of his misery.'

'How'd you learn?'

'From a psych professor.' Which was all he needed to know about *that*. 'It's incredibly easy. People think it's a special power, but you can learn it from a book, and for the first time in years my father felt some relief. He started calling for me in the middle of the night. He even begged me not to go back to school. He wanted me with him.'

'It must be incredible to have that kind of power over other people.'

'My friends call me a control freak,' she said.

'Are they right?'

'Partly. I mean, what I . . . You're really good at this,' she said.

'Good at what?'

'Getting other people to open up. Must be why you're a detective first class.'

'First grade.'

'Because you're good at interrogations.'

'I wasn't interrogating you, Julia. I think you wanted to talk. Maybe you even needed to.'

She started clearing the table. He was right, of course. The Wizard murders were chipping away at her strongbox of old demons. Talking things out was upsetting, but it helped. And Ray seemed to understand what kind of damage demons could do to a person – from first-hand knowledge, more than likely.

A half-hour later, Emily was face down on the living-room floor, pounding her fists into the carpet.

'Please, Emily, it's past your bedtime and tomorrow is a school—'

'NO!'

'I'm going back into the kitchen, and when I come back I want you in your bed. Do you hear me?'

Julia joined Ray in the kitchen, where he was loading the dishwasher.

'We go through this about once a week, sometimes more.' She leaned against the counter and rested her head against a cabinet. 'Some nights I'll end up dragging her into her bedroom, screaming. I hate ending the day like that. I keep thinking I should be doing something differently.'

'Want me to try?'

It would work, of course. Allowing Ray to put her to bed would offer Emily a face-saving alternative to being dragged into her bedroom. It would also be setting a very bad precedent.

'Sure, give it a shot,' Julia said.

Fifteen minutes later, she could hear him reading *Goodnight Moon*.

'That's the kittens!' Emily's voice rang out. 'That's the mittens.'

It all seemed so idyllic – and absurd. Ray was a detective on a homicide investigation, he just might think she was a psychotic killer, he was seriously fucked up in the sexuality department – and he was doing a masterful job of putting her daughter to bed. Crazy.

'Sing me a song,' Emily said after saying goodnight to the stars, the air, to noises everywhere.

'What song?' Ray said quietly.

'Wainbow.'

'What?'

'*Wainbow.*'

'I'm not sure I know that one.'

'Yes you do.' Emily began to sing. '"Somewhere, over the wainbow . . ."'

'Oh, from *The Wizard of Oz.*'

Julia's stomach lurched.

'Do you like that movie?' Ray asked.

'It's my favorite. I watch it every day.'

'*Every* day?'

'Well, almost every day. Mommy bought me the tape. It's her favorite too.'

When he rejoined Julia in the dining room, she suggested they watch the Knick-Bulls game on MSG. She wasn't ready to be alone. He seemed hesitant.

'Is there a policy against watching basketball with a suspect?' she said.

'You're not a suspect, not in my mind.'

'Then prove it by watching the game with me.'

He looked at her a beat before rolling his eyes. 'Why not?'

His beeper went off in the first quarter. He talked on the kitchen phone for a few minutes.

'Update from the front,' he said when he sat down again. They focused on the game. Julia turned to look at him; he was completely engrossed in the game, yet there was a tightness about his mouth that suggested tension unrelated to basketball. *Update from the front*. She was opening her life to him, and yet she'd bet anything he wouldn't fill her in on the 'update' if she asked.

The beeper went off again in the third quarter, about nine-thirty. He returned the call in the kitchen again. Julia waited a moment before walking to the bedroom and lifting the receiver.

A man's voice: 'We lost Jared DeSantis.'

Ray: 'What? I thought he had twenty-four-hour—'

'He was on foot, Ray. Stopped in a bar, left by the back entrance. Guy's hiding something.'

'I talked to his neighbors, nobody knows how he supports himself.'

'How about Julia Mallet, she know anything? Drugs, maybe?'

Ray waited a beat before answering in a hushed voice. 'She feels very protective about him.' He cleared his throat. 'But I don't think she knows what he does for money.'

'We're putting a lot of manpower behind this hypnotism angle. Don't let her off too easy, understand?'

'See you in the morning.'

Julia waited for Ray to hang up before replacing the receiver. She was heading back to the living room when she heard him talking to someone else.

'I *did* call you back, around three, but you were out,' Ray was saying when she picked up the receiver.

'Where are you, Ray?' A woman's voice, angry.

'I told you, Dolores, I'm with a suspect.'

'Suspect? What's her name?'

'This bullshit was hard enough to take when we were still married, now it's—'

'Who says we're not married?'

'Separated. Why the hell did you call? Your message said urgent.'

'Fuck you, Ray.' The line went dead.

Julia beat Ray back to the living room by less than five seconds. 'Who was that?' she asked.

'Nick Meyer, head of the Wizard task force.'

Julia shuddered; all day, when she closed her eyes for even a moment, those ghastly photos in the task-force room had spun around her mind.

164

Ray looked at her for a long moment. Julia held her breath. Under other circumstances this was the point when he'd reach over, put a hand on her neck, draw her to him.

'I better go,' he said.

'Now? The game's not over.'

Let him go.

She looked into his eyes. He'd been told not to let her off easily, but if she asked him to, he'd stay.

Julia took a deep breath, let it out slowly.

'I'll talk to you tomorrow,' she said.

15

There, it's done, the trap set.

The night is ink-dark, the sky starless, moonless. Dead. But the words shimmer through the gloom as if illuminated by their own significance.

The monster will pass this spot in ten minutes, perhaps sooner. The Wizard has watched her for two nights, trooping down 52nd Street toward Sixth Avenue, waving futilely at cabs already occupied by theater-goers heading home. But the monster has not been at the theater, neither has she been home with her family. She has been at work in a skyscraper just west of Sixth Avenue, toiling until ten o'clock every night this week.

This will be a challenge, no doubt about it. The midtown street is quiet but rarely deserted. Luckily, there is a sliver of unused space between two tall buildings, a narrow alley, just enough room to spray the signature, lay the nest. Eliminate the monster. Timing will be the key. The monster lives in a doorman building on the East Side, takes a cab home every night. It has to be here, near her office.

What are you whining about now? Haven't you caused enough trouble for this family? You've ruined three lives, don't you know that? Mine, your father's, HERS. Stop staring at me that way, you make me—

Footsteps. Sharp, rapid – high-heels. The Wizard looks out

from the narrow alley, sees her. The long, determined stride, the swinging leather briefcase, the ankle-length fur coat. Monster.

This won't be easy, but the Wizard feels energized by the challenge, the risk; head her off just before the alley, shove the silenced gun into her fur-covered gut, force her into the nest. Then the easy part.

The Wizard steps out of the nest, waits for the monster to approach. Pale skin, wide mouth, big, dark-framed glasses. The Wizard squeezes the gun inside the bag, slides it half-way out. Ten more long strides, nine more. Eight.

'Lorraine?'

Another set of footsteps from behind the monster. A woman approaches. The two of them air-kiss as the Wizard watches from several yards ahead, listens. Their breath puffs from their mouths.

'Working late?' The other woman wears mink, carries a briefcase.

'It's this McAnn merger. I can't get out of the office earlier than ten.' The monster's voice is high-pitched, strung out. 'I've barely seen my kids since the weekend. I'm half hoping Andrew will start teething this week so he'll wake up at night and I'll see him.'

The other woman laughs and touches the monster's fur shoulder, then they start talking about the McAnn merger and filing deadlines and SEC guidelines. The Wizard tunes out, lets the gun slide back in the bag. Not tonight.

'DO IT NOW!'

The Wizard looks around, shivers for the first time tonight. Who said that?

'NOW!'

Looks left, right, and finally across the street, three stories up a glass-and-steel skyscraper, in one of the windows – a face, shimmering in the glass, the eyes intent on the Wizard, the mouth

167

moving slowly, just slightly out of sync with the words.

'KILL THE MONSTER!'

The words are harsh, but the voice is curiously unthreatening.

'But the other woman . . .' the Wizard whispers, staring up at the face in the window, the face that *is* the window, a silky fluidity of mouth, nose, eyes.

'SAVE THE ANGELS!'

'But . . .'

'SAVE THEM!'

The Wizard nods, takes out the gun . . .

'NOW!'

. . . raises it, aims . . .

'. . . let an associate handle the pro formas, but the client wants yours truly, so—'

. . . fires. The shot jerks the gun, forcing the Wizard back a step into the dark alley. Just a muffled *pop* as the bullet sails past the monster, lands somewhere across the street.

'Did you hear something?' The monster looks around, eyes glancing right over the Wizard, then turns back to her companion and shrugs. 'Like a champagne cork, only louder,' she says, and they both smile. 'Share a cab?'

The two women head down the street toward Sixth. So close, the Wizard thinks. So close to succeeding; so close to blowing it. Time to cover tracks, destroy the nest. The Wizard takes the can from the plastic bag, sprays the wall, obliterating the signature in a blotch of runny black paint.

The Wizard steps out on to the sidewalk, tries to ignore the voice.

'STOP HER, NOW!'

'I can't, it's too risky.'

'BUT SHE'S A MONSTER!'

The Wizard scurries west, toward Seventh, away from the monster and her friend, away from the voice.

'SAVE THE ANGELS!'

'Not now, *okay*? I can't.'

Running now, starting to pant, the voice growing fainter. There will be other angels to save, other monsters to punish. But not this one, and not tonight.

Friday 3 February

16

Julia took a bite of Paula's chicken and wondered why her friend didn't just hire a cook.

'Delicious,' she said. 'Unusual.'

Martin turned to her, eyebrows arched, but Julia simply smiled and managed a second bite – she wasn't about to conspire against Paula, even if the chicken breast tasted like it had been marinated in furniture polish and baking since Labor Day Weekend.

'Do the police think the two murders are connected?' Paula said. 'Detective Burgess questioned both of us about our whereabouts the night the second woman was killed.'

Julia knew the police were trying hard to ward off any connection between the two killings. Not that the connection was obvious: one victim was an affluent investment manager, the other an immigrant babysitter. And the Wizard's spray-painted signature had been kept from the public.

'They may be connected,' Julia said.

'What I still don't understand . . .' Paula looked from Julia to Martin and back again. 'I still don't understand what their connection is to us, other than that the first woman lived in your building.'

'Join the club,' Julia said, and swallowed a third bite of chicken – penance for the lie.

From the family room at the other end of a long hallway she heard the television droning; the Freemasons' two boys and Emily were watching a video. Julia glanced around the dining room. Say this for Paula, she knew how to put a room together, albeit with a decorator's help and a very lavish budget. The walls were a pale but luminous yellow. *Trompe l'oeil* drapes surrounded the large windows overlooking Park Avenue. Julia had run her fingers along the 'drapes' more than once, just to make sure they weren't fabric. It was all a bit much, really – there was something overreaching about the room; undeniably impressive but . . . straining. Like Martin.

'Do you know if they're closer to catching the killer?' Paula asked. She looked especially pretty in her dining room, as if she'd chosen the fabrics and paint to complement her own coloring. In restaurants or at parties she tended to fade into her surroundings. Here, with her hair pulled back in a simple barrette, wearing a black cashmere turtleneck and black leggings, she looked almost elegant.

'I really don't know,' Julia said.

'What's the connection to your party?' asked Martin, who'd been uncharacteristically silent all evening.

'The police won't say. It could be that my doorman saw someone leaving the building that night . . . Who knows? It could turn out to have nothing—'

'They ought to keep tabs on Jared, if you ask me,' Martin said.

'Jared wouldn't hurt a fly,' Julia said.

'I don't trust him.'

Julia glanced at him. Was he trying to point suspicion at Jared? If so, did he assume that she had an inside track to the police?

'Don't trust anybody,' Paula said. 'Isn't that a commodity dealer's first rule?'

174

'I like Jared, don't get me wrong.' Martin loosened his tie and undid the top button of his white shirt, which had his initials monogrammed in black stitching on the pocket. 'But the guy's a bit of a loser, you can't deny it. He hasn't improved his lifestyle one iota since Madison.'

'That doesn't make him a killer,' Paula said. 'Besides, Jared cares about people. He understands them. At least, he always made me feel . . . understood, somehow. He really knows me.'

'And I don't?' Martin said.

Paula touched one of her silver hoop earrings. 'Jared gets right down to the soul, somehow. Isn't that right, Julia?'

Julia could only nod, and wonder why the fact that Jared worked his magic on Paula – and God knows how many other women – should dismay her.

'How does Mr Understanding support himself? Tell me that,' Martin said.

'These women were killed, they weren't robbed,' Julia said. 'Anyway, I don't have to defend Jared.'

Emily ran into the room and buried her head in Julia's lap. 'Can we go home, Mommy?'

'Aren't you enjoying the tape?'

'I *hate* Power Rangers.'

'Jared's problem?' Martin said. 'He was born too late to really enjoy the sixties. He'd be happier on a commune.'

'I thought that was *my* problem.' Paula turned to Julia. 'Whenever Martin really wants to put me down he calls me a flower child.'

'Don't change the subject,' Martin said.

'Jared is hardly a flower child,' Julia said as Emily climbed on to her lap and reached for a crystal water glass – Baccarat, no doubt, unless something more expensive had come on the market.

'Paula, why don't you get her a paper cup?' Martin said.

'What for?' Paula smiled at Martin and turned to Emily. 'Are you thirsty, sweetheart?'

Emily grabbed the goblet, spilling half the water as she brought it to her lips. Julia extricated it from her hand and placed it in the center of the table.

'Whenever we have Jared up here he looks around at the place with a sneer on his face,' Martin said. 'Like we stole it or something.'

'Jared doesn't sneer,' Julia said, both arms working hard to frustrate Emily's grunting effort to seize the goblet.

Martin poured himself a full glass of red wine without taking his eyes off Emily or the goblet. 'You don't get it, do you, Julia?' he said.

Emily squirmed as Julia held her arms away from the table.

'I think you look down on Jared because he doesn't buy into your whole . . .' Julia stopped and took a deep breath. 'Upwardly mobile philosophy.'

There, that wasn't too offensive.

'*Please* leave the glass alone,' she whispered in Emily's ear.

Emily shook her head and continued her struggle to retake the glass.

'There's ice cream at home,' Julia whispered. 'For good girls.'

'What kind?'

Julia squeezed Emily's thigh.

'What kind of ice cream, Mommy?'

'*Vanilla*.'

'I want chocolate.'

Emily pulled the glass toward her, knocking it against Julia's plate. Martin stood up, circled the table, and jerked the goblet from Emily's hands. Emily buried her face in Julia's shoulder.

'Martin, give her back that glass,' Paula said. '*Now!*'

Martin returned to his seat and plunked the goblet down in front of him. 'She was going to break it,' he said.

'I'm sorry, Julia,' Paula said. 'Emily, would you like a cookie?'

Emily shook her head into Julia's shoulder. 'I want to go home.'

Paula looked down at her plate, the corners of her mouth sagging.

Everyone's life is full of compromises, things we do that run against our nature. It's just a question of finding a way to make peace.

How would Paula make peace tonight? Were her little insults and petty sarcasms enough, or would she seek deeper retribution?

'Jared's jealous,' Martin said, his face as red as the Merlot they were drinking. He'd barely touched his dinner, though that could have more to do with the food than the tension at the table.

'Why is everybody turning against everyone else?' Julia said.

Paula looked up from her plate. '*Everyone*? Has anyone said anything about us?'

Martin shot her a warning glance and addressed Julia. 'Who cares what anyone says about us? We were here, together. A family.'

Julia detected a Quaylesque put-down, but Martin's tone was defensive too. What *was* he afraid of? She covered the last of her chicken with parsley and pronounced herself full.

'Interesting,' Martin said, 'that of all of us, only Paula and I weren't alone.'

'Don't forget, I had company.' Julia hugged Emily. 'You two definitely *were* together, right?'

The Freemasons exchanged glances, then glared at Julia.

'What the hell are you implying?' Martin said.

It hit her, then, with a wave of sadness: their friendship wouldn't survive this mess. Their ties had been woven from familiarity, nostalgia, and the lack of pressure that exists only between people whose lives rarely intersect for any reason other than the occasional social event. The Wizard had given them common ground on which to do battle.

'I wasn't implying anything,' she said.

Just doing my duty.

She was in bed by ten, but the Merlot buzzed her brain, and Martin's bile churned in her stomach. How dare he look down on Jared, who had more class – never mind the Park Avenue co-op, the chauffeur, the fifty-dollar wines.

Martin had always been slightly out of place in the Madison group. They'd all paid at least a little lip service to the pre-1980s, anti-materialistic values then in vogue. But by sophomore year, Martin was already wheeling and dealing as the 'Marijuana Maven', using the proceeds to buy himself leather jackets, a jet-black Camarro, lavish dinners at the one nice restaurant in town. He was likeable enough, with a cynical wit, but the truth was, if he hadn't been virtually attached to Paula from freshman year onward, they probably wouldn't have had anything to do with him.

And now he was putting down Jared, who was the real soul of their group, Julia had always thought.

And why the hell was Paula swallowing her anger like some pre-feminist robot? 'She'd forgive her own murderer,' Gail had once said. Perhaps that was happening now, for Martin was surely murdering her soul, compromise by compromise.

Julia dialed Jared's number. She wouldn't talk about the dinner, she just needed to hear his voice.

His answering machine picked up after two rings. 'I'm not home now, but if you leave a message I'll call you right back. *Beep.*'

Julia hung up. If she left a message he'd more than likely

call back after she was asleep; Jared had a tenuous grasp of the hours kept by working stiffs. She turned off the light and settled into bed.

Fifteen minutes later her head was still buzzing. Damn Martin and his insinuations.

Why had Jared eluded the police? Twice.

She rolled over, buried her face in the pillow. *Buzz. Buzz.*

Who kept calling Jared the day she'd visited? Who was 'Max'?

Buzz. Buzz.

Why had Jared rushed to turn down the volume on the answering machine?

Julia sat up. Jared's machine, like hers, had a 'toll saver' option that took four rings to answer unless there was a message.

She lifted the receiver and dialed his number. When she heard the beep she punched in 24, her retrieval code.

Nothing.

She dialed again and pressed 11 after the beep. Nothing. She pressed 12. Then 13. In seconds she was up to 20. Was she really prepared to go all the way up to 99?

She continued pressing. 29, 30, 31 . . .

Ah. Jared's code was 31.

The message tape rewound with a loud whine. It wasn't too late to hang up. What she was doing was unforgivable, a serious violation of—

'Hello, Brock? This is . . . Pete.'

Brock?

'I saw your ad in *Out There*. I was . . . you know, I was hoping we could get together later. I'm at a hotel, maybe I'll call you back, okay?'

Beep.

'Brock, this is Mario.' A deep voice this time. 'You bullshitting with that description?' Long pause. 'You're for real,

179

maybe we should get together. I got some time tonight, has to be your place. I'd like to know what the one-fifty includes. Call me.' He left a number.

Beep.

'Jared? This is Gail. I was just calling to say hi. Call when you have a chance.'

Beep.

'Brock? Is it true – blonds have more fun? What kind of fun are you having?' This guy was panting as he spoke, with long pauses between words. 'I got eight inches . . . for you, Brock. Ooh, yeah . . . I got—'

Julia slammed down the receiver so hard she missed the cradle and had to do it over. In the bathroom she splashed water over her face and dried off with a towel, but moments later her face was damp with tears. She got back in bed, turned off the light, and lay there on her back, eyes open.

BUZZ. BUZZ.

She knew who Brock was, that was easy enough to figure out.

But who the hell was Jared DeSantis?

Saturday 4 February

17

Julia woke up Saturday morning and knew she had to get away.
Two murders, somehow connected to her oldest friends; the
Jared/Brock phone messages; a persistent desire to talk to, *be*
with Ray Burgess, despite the circumstances, despite his being
all wrong for her . . .

She needed to get away, she needed a good night's sleep –
something that had eluded her since Detective Bettalini had
knocked on her door five long days ago. Above all she needed
the reassurance of an old friend. But who among her old friends
could she trust?

'I'd love to have you,' Marianne said on the phone when
Julia proposed a quick visit: a late-morning shuttle flight, two
nights in DC, then an early flight back to New York Monday
morning. 'But I have to work this morning – the senator's got a
big speech next week.'

Marianne lived two hundred miles from the Wizard's killing
fields. Even if she didn't have alibis for the murders, it was
highly unlikely that she had raced to New York, killed those
women, and raced back to Washington in time for work the
next morning. Besides, Marianne was easily the most
reassuring person Julia knew. If ever she was lonely or
depressed she'd call Gail, whose shoulder was made for crying
on. But if she needed help, she'd call Marianne, who rose to

any occasion with competence and enthusiasm. When Julia got pregnant, she'd called Gail right away, distraught. But Marianne was the friend who'd helped her weigh the pros and cons of having the child, clarifying her thoughts; Marianne had even flown to New York to help Julia set up the nursery and arrange childcare.

'I can't stop you from going,' Ray said when she told him her plans. 'But I have to warn you, Marianne Wilson is a suspect and we can't guarantee your safety in Washington.'

'Have you found any record of her on Amtrak or the shuttle?'

'No, but—'

'Do you really think Marianne drove up here and killed Alicia Frommer, then drove back to DC in time for work the next morning? Come on, Ray . . .'

'All right,' he said after a pause. 'But be careful, okay?'

Emily was restless throughout the forty-five-minute flight to Washington. She seemed to relish provoking the sardine-packed power brokers with little patience for anyone under voting age.

At least she calmed down during the ride from National Airport. They passed the familiar DC monuments, the marble gleaming preternaturally in the early afternoon light, as if irradiated by nothing more complicated than the country's belief in itself. The streets looked clean and orderly and completely safe. An illusion, of course – Washington was, if anything, more dangerous than New York, Marianne liked to point out – but the city put on a good show for tourists, and Julia was happy to be taken in.

Marianne had asked Julia to meet her at her office. They passed through security at the Dirksen Building and found their way, after several wrong turns down endless corridors, to Senator Rinaldi's suite – a series of offices lined up railroad style, one after another. Admission to the sanctum sanctorum meant passing through a succession of chambers whose occupants grew in importance the closer to the senator they sat.

Marianne was but one door away. She hugged Julia and reached for Emily, who buried her head in Julia's skirt.

'She doesn't trust politicians,' Julia said. 'You look wonderful.'

Marianne's short blue dress showed off the small waist and long legs that were her two best features. Her chestnut hair was pulled back in a large black bow – a bit *Town & Country* maybe, but it worked.

'Perfect timing – I just finished going over a new draft of the speech. Want to meet the senator?'

'Well . . .'

'She's a Republican, not a leper,' Marianne said.

Julia closed her eyes, lifted her chin theatrically, and extended a limp hand. 'Take me to her.'

Marianne picked up some papers, rapped on a closed mahogany door and opened it without waiting for a response.

'Senator, I'd like you to meet two of your constituents.'

The thickly carpeted, traditionally furnished office was practically wallpapered with photos of Ruth Rinaldi smiling and shaking hands with assorted political luminaries, not all of them Ronald Reagan. Rinaldi stood up behind an enormous wood desk and beamed a thousand-kilowatt smile. She was younger and better looking than her news photos – about forty-five, tall and fit, with gray-flecked hair and well-defined, TV-friendly features.

'Welcome. Glad to meet you.' She circled the desk, clasped Julia's right hand in both of hers, and smiled at Emily. 'Hello, gorgeous,' she said. 'What beautiful blonde curls you have.'

Emily's right hand blocked the senator's attempt to touch her hair, and Rinaldi's smile dimmed temporarily.

'Julia's with Todman DiLorenzo,' Marianne said. 'She practically runs the place.'

'*Marianne*,' Julia said, 'that's not true at—'

'Is Phil Todman still with the shop?' Rinaldi asked.

'Only on a consulting basis. Do you know him?'

'He handled my opponent's campaign in ninety-two,' Rinaldi said.

Julia had voted for Jack Waxman, of course – she'd have voted for Jack the Ripper over this woman. Rinaldi was famous for coarse language; a paperback compendium of her malapropisms had been on the *Times* bestseller list for months. Feminists in particular felt betrayed by her willingness to let the right-wing use her as some kind of poster-woman for anti-abortion, anti-gun control, anti-welfare legislation. But in person she was undeniably smooth – Julia felt her liberal ramparts crumbling.

Marianne handed over the pages she'd brought with her. 'Here's the new Kids First draft.'

'*Fan*-tastic,' Rinaldi said, then turned to Julia. 'Kids First is a coalition of anti-child abuse organizations, private as well as public. I'm the keynote speaker at their conference next week. Child abuse is very high on my agenda.' She winked at Emily, who clutched Julia's leg and turned away.

'Now, if you ladies will excuse me, I've got to finalize this baby before the word processing unit shuts down for the night. Enjoy your weekend – what's left of it.'

Another smile, another handshake, and they were out of there less than three minutes after entering.

'So how about us *ladies* heading back to your place?' Julia said. 'I need to get out of these shoes.'

'The thing about Ruth,' Marianne said as they got in an elevator to the underground parking garage, 'she's sincere – whether you agree with her or not.'

186

'No one's *that* genial,' Julia said. 'At least, no one outside the Beltway.'

'Ruth is. I'm with her more than her husband, more than anybody. And I've seen so many of the others, the ones who smile for the camera and stab you in the back when nobody's looking.'

'You're talking about the woman who sponsored a school prayer amendment, for God's sake.'

'*Voluntary* school prayer,' Marianne said. 'She also sponsored the most comprehensive child welfare legislation ever introduced at national level, including a very important piece on child abuse that I helped draft.'

'She sure has a way with children,' Julia said. 'Ask Emily.'

'She also introduced legislation that brought over a hundred thousand new jobs to New York State. Maybe they're not high-level advertising jobs, but they support families, communities.'

Her voice had the breathless edge of the convert. Julia knew better than to argue.

'Dan Jessup? Ray Burgess, New York City Police Department.'

'Metroliner Maniac, nineteen ninety-three, right?'

'Of blessed memory.' Four hookers raped and decapitated, one each in New York, Trenton, Wilmington and Washington DC. Turned out the perp hopped the Metroliner to and from each scene. Jessup had been the District liaison with the Department. All aboard.

'What can I do for you?'

'You heard about the Jessica Forrester murder?' Best not to mention Alicia Frommer; the fewer people who knew about the connection between them the better.

'Shot point blank, nice neighborhood, cash in her purse? Yeah, we sent a badge over to the Dirksen Building to talk to a senator's secretary.'

187

'Chief of staff, Marianne Wilson.'

'She turned up clean, far as I know.'

'Yeah, right. The thing is, one of the . . .' No, not suspects. 'One of the people involved in this case is headed down your way. Visiting Wilson, as a matter of fact. I was wondering if you'd keep an eye on her?'

'Suspect?'

'Not really, no.'

'Then why the tail?'

Good question. 'Covering all bases, you know the drill. She's on the shuttle, your guys can probably pick her up at the senator's office.'

'What's her name?'

Ray grabbed up a pen, tapped it a few times on his desk.

'Ray, you there? What's the girl's name?'

'Julia Mallet,' Ray said, so quickly he had to repeat it. He gave a description and his phone number.

'I'll call you when we've got her,' Jessup said.

'The thing you have to keep in mind about Washington is that it's all so . . . ephemeral.' Marianne waved her glass of Chardonnay before taking a sip. She loved to make pronouncements.

'Look at me. I'm chief of staff to one of the most powerful senators in town. But she's up for re-election in less than two years, at which point she could be out on her ass, me along with her. I think this is what makes Washington so intense – everyone knows they only have a limited time to throw their weight around, so they make the most of it.'

Marianne's apartment, in a luxury high-rise near the Washington Cathedral, was like its occupant: well groomed, neat, formal but not stuffy. She and Julia sat on opposite ends of a large sectional sofa covered in pale cream leather. Emily was on the floor, drawing in a coloring book with the markers Julia had packed.

'What if a Republican got into the White House and Rinaldi got a cabinet post? Would you follow her?'

'Probably. She's a remarkable woman.'

'What about abortion, then?'

Julia didn't know why she enjoyed challenging Marianne this way. Who was she to cast stones, after all? Didn't she make her living convincing anxious housewives that their self-esteem hinged on the softness of their laundry?

'What I've learned is that ideology isn't as important as the ability to get things done.'

'Like make the trains run on time?'

'Sure, and make the streets safe and the schools excellent and the world peaceful. What does ideology have to do with any of that?'

'You've become . . . Em! Watch the carpet.'

Emily was scribbling perilously close to the edge of the paper, jeopardizing Marianne's pristine beige carpet.

'They're washable markers,' Julia said. At least she *thought* they were.

'Don't worry about the carpet. You said I've become . . .'

'A cynic.'

Marianne waited a few moments before replying. She'd taken her hair out of the bow; reddish brown, very thick and glossy, it fell across her shoulders, softening her.

'Not cynical so much as disillusioned,' she said. 'I can't relate to what we were fifteen years ago.'

'But at my party you practically begged me to hypnotize you back to nineteen eighty-one.'

'For a lark. God, when I think of the clothes and the books and the music and the politicians we admired – it was all so stupid.'

189

'But we were practically teenagers.'

'The whole country was adolescent in the seventies. Do you remember Fran Leventhal?'

'She was in my dorm freshman year. Wasn't she a painter or something?'

'She has an exhibition at the Whitney. I went to the opening when I was in New York.'

'Fran, at the *Whitney*?'

'That's what I thought. Then I saw the paintings. Black canvases with crude brushstrokes blotched all over. They were so ugly, so adolescent, I didn't know what to say when I talked to her the next day.'

'Someone at the Whitney must have thought Fran was good.'

'That's just it. The whole country is run by adolescents who think glorified finger painting is worthy of a showing at a major museum. That kind of . . . sloppy thinking has infected the whole country, and nowhere more so than here in Washington.'

Julia couldn't help smiling. 'You never even wore a bra at Madison.'

'I was flat-chested,' Marianne said. 'And bubble-brained. Let's go eat.'

Julia stayed awake in Marianne's guest bedroom until well past midnight. Emily was snuggled next to her, snoring. Amazing, the racket a sleeping four-year-old could make.

She flipped through *New York* magazine and tried to figure out why Marianne's conversion to Ruth Rinaldi was so disturbing.

Dinner in Georgetown had been fun, and to Julia's relief the Wizard case wasn't so much as mentioned. Emily had warmed to Marianne as the evening progressed, the two of them finally ganging up on Julia when she tried to squelch Marianne's offer of ice cream cones on the way home.

Visiting Marianne, getting out of New York, had been a good idea. Gail might be a more emphatic confidante, but as Julia got older and her life got more complicated, she was discovering that being able to count on someone for reassurance and advice was often more meaningful than sympathy.

'Ideology isn't as important as the ability to get things done.'

She read a movie review, started the crossword puzzle, thought some more about Marianne. She still felt close to her, still cherished that bracing strength in her life. But Marianne wasn't the same person today as when they'd met at Madison almost twenty years before. She'd always been the first to mock extremist views in others; now she was a zealot. They might kid about their political differences, but Marianne's move to Washington three years ago had been more than geographical, and Julia couldn't help feeling left behind.

She flipped through the listings at the back of the magazine and homed in on the museum section. Fran Leventhal at the Whitney – amazing. That self-consciously eccentric art student, who wore exclusively black long before it had become the uniform of nouveau bohemia . . .? She ran a finger down the list of museums until she came to the Whitney. Sure enough, there was Fran Leventhal, a three-month one-woman show.

Julia couldn't wait to tell Gail. Maybe they'd go together one evening. She checked the show dates: opened on Tuesday, 31 January, closes on . . .

Wait a minute – 31 January?

She counted back several days. 31 January was the night of Alicia Frommer's murder.

Then Marianne had lied to the police about being in Washington. Or she'd lied to Julia about attending Fran's opening.

191

Julia had come to Washington to escape the deception and suspicion that had begun to poison her closest friendships. But the lies were spreading.

Sunday 5 February

18

'Last night was a lot of fun,' Julia said as they drove back to Marianne's apartment from the National Gallery. 'But I have so much to do . . . I needed to get away for a night; two nights would set me back about a month.'

Marianne stopped at a traffic signal. 'Are you seeing someone these days?'

'Why?'

'Jumping ship in the middle of a visit is what women do when they have a boyfriend they thought they could walk away from but couldn't.'

'Well, that's not the reason.'

'I'm sorry it's not,' Marianne said. 'You could use a little romance.'

'So I'm told.'

Julia stared out the side window as Washington gradually turned suburban. Such a clean, civilized city, the poverty cleverly tucked away where you couldn't see it. The day was unusually warm, the cloudless blue sky as immaculate and impervious as all that white marble strewn about the city. Marianne had lied to her – or lied to the police . . . Julia just couldn't buy into the capital's fraud any longer. She crumpled her museum program, waited until Marianne glanced away, and dropped it out the open window. *Take that, Washington Fucking DC.*

'Were you in New York this week?' she asked.

'Not since Monday, when I flew back after your party. Why?'

'Fran's show didn't open until Tuesday.'

Marianne didn't take her eyes off the road. 'I must have attended a preview then.'

'Are you a member of the Whitney?'

'No.'

'Museum previews are usually for members.'

'The senator gets invited to every . . .' Marianne jerked the steering wheel to the right and pulled over to the side of the road. A blue Porsche swerved around them, honking several times, followed almost immediately by a dark-green four-door Chrysler.

'What's this about, anyway?' Marianne put the car in park and killed the engine.

'These murders have me freaked out,' Julia said. 'I don't know who to trust any more.'

'And you think I was in New York last week and *killed* someone?' Marianne stared straight ahead, her face flushed, lips pressed together in a tight frown.

Julia glanced at her friend; Marianne always looked best in profile, strong and resolute. 'I guess you must have attended a preview.'

Marianne's eyes darted over at her, then back at the windshield. 'Why don't I wait in front of my building with Em while you throw your things together? I've got some work to do in the office anyway – and National's just a few minutes out of my way.' She put the car in drive and left the side of the road with a screech of tires. Julia stared out of the passenger window, avoiding Marianne's scrutiny. As they sped through an intersection, several hundred yards ahead Julia noticed a car pull over. No house or store nearby, no blinkers on. The man behind the wheel seemed to be looking in the rear-view mirror.

A dark-green, four-door Chrysler.

Julia called Ray from National Airport and had him paged. He called her back from his place in Queens five minutes later.

'I'm not really sure why I called. I guess I'm feeling pretty confused right now. I don't know . . .'

'You want me to meet you at LaGuardia?'

'I'm on the two o'clock shuttle.'

'Fine, I'll be—'

'Ray, am I being followed?'

She heard him start to answer, then take a breath and hold it.

'Even in Washington, Ray? With my daughter?'

'I'll see you at the gate,' he said, and hung up.

In the airport gift shop, Emily twirled a rack of paperbacks while Julia leafed through a copy of *Out There*. Ten minutes before boarding, she found what she was looking for.

Live out your fantasies with this handsome, blond, well-built, well endowed, straight stud. 6'1", 205 pounds. Safe only. $150 minimum. In/Out. Brock.

The phone number was Jared's.

Ray extended a hand as Julia and Emily approached him at the LaGuardia shuttle terminal. Did he plan to kiss her or just take her bag? He started to lean toward her, stopped himself, then crouched down to face Emily.

'Did you enjoy the flight?'

'I had a soda,' Emily said. 'And peanuts.'

'Lucky girl.' He stood up. 'You're back early,' he said to Julia.

'We need to talk.'

Julia waited until Emily was asleep in the back seat – about ten minutes out of LaGuardia – before telling Ray about Marianne.

'She was here, in New York, the night Alicia Frommer was killed.' Julia felt her voice catch. 'She lied.'

'You mean she *could* have been here,' Ray said.

Glimpsed in the smoggy distance from the Triborough Bridge, the New York skyline, usually so reassuring after a trip, looked grim and impervious. She could ask Ray to turn around, drop them off at an airline that flew to some warm and sunny and safe island, where the word 'goodbye' wasn't in the local patois. If it weren't for her job, Emily's school, the Wizard . . .

'Senator Rinaldi was in New York the night Alicia was killed,' Ray said. 'We found out when we were checking Marianne's alibi. She was staying at the Carlton House, giving a fund-raising speech to a group of real estate bigshots.'

'Did Marianne travel with her?'

'Rinaldi said she was in Washington, as far as she knew. Just got back the day before. But it's something to check into.' He glanced over at her as he pulled on to the FDR Drive. 'You look wired.'

'I thought I could get away from everything. Then I find out Marianne's been lying to me . . . God, I want this to be over.'

Ray nodded, but his expression turned grim.

'What's the matter?' Julia said.

'Are you sure you're going to feel better when you figure out which one of your friends is the Wizard?'

Julia took a deep breath, thought of Jared – Brock. 'At least I'll know I can trust the other five. Right now I . . .' She looked at Ray.

Right now I need . . . I need . . .

'Why don't you come up, have dinner with us? We could

198

order Chinese.' When he didn't answer she said, 'I keep forgetting I'm a suspect.'

'You're not a suspect, just involved in the case.'

'Hey, don't let me force you to do something you don't want to.'

He glanced at her. 'What I *want* to do and what I *should* do are two different things.' He squinted into the setting sun. His hair was beginning to overlap the tops of his ears. What would he do if she reached over and brushed it back?

'Are you and Dolores getting divorced?'

'I guess so . . . I mean, yes – eventually. We're still getting used to the separation. The separation hit her pretty hard. Being a cop's wife was all she ever wanted. She was practically obsessed with my work. When she lost me she lost her life.'

'Do you see her much?'

'She lives a block away, in our old place. I see her some-times, but just to, you know, borrow things, drop off an old bill. Nothing serious.' He gave her a quick look. 'How about you?'

'What about me?'

'I haven't noticed any boyfriends hanging around.'

'Neither have I.'

'Why is that?'

'Is this going to end up in your daily report to the task force?'

He looked at her, then back at the road.

'I'm waiting until Emily's in college to resume dating. Pediatrician's orders.'

He smiled as he shook his head. That first day, in her office, she'd thought him almost too handsome – eyes achingly blue, sandy hair draped perfectly on his forehead, smile slightly lopsided, softening his face. Now she found it hard to look away from him.

She glanced out the window again and outlined a heart with

her finger on the side of her leg. Then she drew a jagged line through it.

'You haven't answered my question,' she said. 'About dinner.'

Ray pulled off the FDR Drive at 71st Street.

'Chinese food it is,' he said.

After one bite of Hunan pork, Julia realized she had no appetite. Emily picked through all the dishes, removing the miniature corn-on-the-cobs and water chestnuts and piling them on her plate. Ray ate quickly, using chopsticks.

'In college we used to eat Chinese four or five times a week. But Dolores always hated the stuff.'

'I didn't know you went to college.'

'Brooklyn College, class of eighty-two. Pre-law.'

'Law school too?'

'One year. Then I had this summer internship at a big Wall Street firm. That was enough.'

'You quit?'

He nodded. 'My father was a cop, so were two of his brothers. They thought being a lawyer was kind of like the next step up the ladder, and I bought into it. But that summer I saw what being a lawyer is all about. You earn your living getting involved in people's arguments. "You said you'd pay up front, not one third." "You said I could have the house, the kids, and a million bucks." "No I didn't". "Yes you did."' Ray paused and shook his head. 'That's the law in a nutshell – "No I didn't." "Yes you did."'

'No I didn't,' Emily said, giggling. 'Yes you did.'

Julia laughed. 'But being a cop, isn't that almost the same?'

'Sometimes, but mostly your disputes are with people who break the law. You put them in handcuffs, you lock them up, you feel like you're making progress, doing the right thing.

Lawyers, they fight with everybody, that's what they get paid for. Guilty or innocent, it doesn't matter to them. Like the Wizard, when—'

'The Wizard of Oz?'

They both looked at Emily.

'A different wizard,' Julia said. 'Em, why don't you go put the *Wizard of Oz* tape on, okay?'

'I already watched a tape, and you said I could only watch—'

'Tonight's special.'

'Why is tonight spec—'

'Because it *is*, okay?'

Julia hadn't meant to raise her voice. 'I'm sorry, honey,' she said in a softer tone. She opened her arms but Emily wouldn't take the bait. 'What do we say when Mommy is cranky with you?' Julia asked.

'Timber, timber.'

Julia smiled. 'Almost. It's temper, temper.'

'Temper, temper.'

'Now, tonight's special because we have company.'

'When we have company I can watch two tapes?'

'Tonight we have company and you can watch two.'

Emily ran from the room.

Ray watched her go, then continued. 'Once the Wizard's locked up, then the lawyers take over, and – who knows? Maybe he'll cop an insanity plea, maybe the cop who nails him will fuck up the Miranda warning and the Wizard will walk. *Lawyers*. But on my end at least it's cut and dried. Find the guilty party, lock him up.'

She looked at him, focusing on his eyes, the bluest, roundest, warmest eyes she'd . . .

He's separated for less than a year, investigating a case in which my closest friends are suspects, and he hasn't

201

exactly invited me to make a move.

Julia stood up. 'You want ice cream? There's a pint of New York Chunk Chip in the freezer. Untouched.'

She left the dining room before he had a chance to answer. He followed her a moment later.

'Julia, I—'

'No.'

'You didn't hear my question.'

She slammed the freezer door. 'I will not be hypnotized.'

'We're grasping at straws here. Anything you might recall, even subconsciously . . .'

'You've been spending too much time with Herr Doktor Turner.'

Ray sighed, shook his head, and left the kitchen.

She put Emily to bed early while Ray made use of the kitchen phone. Later, in the living room, she stood by the window and took in the view that she never tired of – because somehow she never really mastered it. Twenty-seven floors above the sidewalk, the jumpy urban clamor was a benign, muted hum, the myriad lights of midtown Manhattan as beautiful and distant as stars.

'It's peaceful when Emily's sleeping,' Julia said. 'When she stays at my mother's it doesn't feel as quiet somehow.'

Ray joined her at the window, looked at her and smiled. 'I have to go,' he said.

'It's barely eight . . .'

'Look, you have to understand my position. I want to stay, but I can't. You're a beautiful woman, Julia and—'

She placed her hand on his lips.

'Why can't I finish?'

'I hate . . .'

'You hate what?'

'Flattery,' she said softly.

'I was telling you what I thought, what I *honestly* thought.'

She nodded and turned back to the view. But the city had vanished. In its place was a frozen pond full of bundled skaters, her parents huddled on a bench, still points in a whirling, snowy wonderland as she spun around the ice.

Did you see? Did you see me spin around?

You were wonderful, Peaches. Just wonderful.

Did you see me, Mommy?

You didn't keep your arms straight, Julia . . . Well, she didn't, Arthur – no point telling her she was great when . . .

'Thanks for dinner.' Ray headed for the front door.

'Ray . . .'

He stopped and turned.

Tell me I'm beautiful again. Tell me how beautiful I looked spinning on the ice, arms perfectly straight, the earth a whirling wonderland of white, white snow.

Julia shook her head and crossed her arms in front of her chest. After a moment, Ray let himself out of the front door.

The market is crowded, cramped, even at this late hour. Shopping carts collide in the narrow aisles that are the curse of all Manhattan grocery stores. Tempers flare at nighttime, when mothers and fathers working overtime do a food shop before returning home, exhausted, to begin their *other* career as parents.

The Wizard tosses a few items into the cart, lets shoppers with more urgent business pass by. The Wizard has no intention of actually buying anything, but walking through a grocery store without picking up anything would look suspicious.

Nothing catches the Wizard's attention, and this is the second store this evening. Patience, patience . . .

Fairway yielded Jessica Forrester, selecting salad ingredients. Alicia Frommer? Who would have guessed that *their* paths would cross?

When did it become impossible to trust fate to show the way? When did it become necessary to hunt? The need for release, for silence, is a tumor growing inside the Wizard. Is there an ultimate peace, a final silence? Is there an ultimate victim?

No. Not victims. Criminals. They deserve their punishment. They bring it on themselves. The Wizard is but a vehicle, a . . .

Who told you you could play with that? Who told you? Give it to me. Give it! Now, get in the closet. Will you shut up? I'm not interested. You've botched up my life and your father's too – isn't that enough? We can't show our faces in this town any more and all because of you. Now get in there before I . . . Is that how you want it? IS THAT HOW YOU WANT IT? There – how does that feel?

The Wizard cries out in pain, stops the moaning with a fist in the mouth, hopes no one has heard.

The voice keeps coming back, louder and louder and louder . . .

There! Midway down the aisle. A mother with two boys, the youngest about two, sitting in the shopping cart while his brother scampers down the aisle. The older child spots a display of boxed cupcakes, picks up a carton and places it in the cart when the mother isn't looking. They turn toward the dairy section.

Just as the Wizard rounds the corner the older boy starts to wail. The mother leaves the cart, cupcakes in hand, tosses them back on to the rack, and rejoins her children.

'I want cupcakes, I want—'

The plea is abruptly silenced. *Aborted.* How? The Wizard's heart races. A few seconds later the pleading resumes, joined this time by the two-year-old, inarticulate but just as noisy.

'Cakes,' he cries. 'Cub cakes!'

The mother gives the cart a vicious shake. The older boy races back down the aisle toward the cupcakes. The Wizard turns, picks up a quart of milk, pretends to read the label. The mother jerks the cart around and rolls it in pursuit of her older son.

'Sam, come back here. Come back here this instant.'

The mother's voice is thin, grating. Sam pays no heed. He reaches the cupcakes, picks up a box, starts to open it.

'Stop!'

The mother races down the aisle toward her son, still pushing the cart. She slows down before reaching him – but not enough. The cart hits Sam in the back; he stumbles and falls against the metal display rack. The Wizard hears the crack. *Feels* it.

Now he's wailing. Well, what does she expect, keeping the kids up this late? The mother picks him up, bats away the cupcakes, and slams her son into the shopping cart. The younger boy turns around, eyes wide, mouth wider.

The mother lets out a long, hissy breath. 'No crying from you, mister. I mean it, Will.'

The two-year-old opens his mouth, then shuts it. The mother resumes her shopping while Sam's sobbing winds down to a low-pitched whimper.

Let me out let me out let me out.

The Wizard almost sobs, each panting breath a kind of moan.

Clank. *The sound of the kitchen door closing. Listen carefully. It's the car starting. Where are they going? How long will they leave me in here? How long? How long? Darkness, silence, coats hanging at face-level like low-slung branches. Dad? Dad, are you there? Daddy?*

They're all in the checkout line now, the Wizard a few aisles over.

'Damn . . . I'll be right back.' She *leaves them there*.

The Wizard glances down at the cart, then abandons it. Walks to the children, leans over, and whispers: 'I'll make it all better.'

They look up, eyes red-rimmed, cheeks teary. Sam and Will. Two angels.

'Don't worry,' the Wizard says. 'It won't be long now. I'll save you.'

Bucking, writhing, trembling.

The Wizard glances down at tonight's stand-in – eyes closed, body writhing – and holds back a second more, just one second more.

But feels no relief, only sharp, exquisite, very, very focused pain.

'Oh yes, oh yes. Oh!'

The Wizard could call it off right now, simply roll off, get dressed, leave.

'Fuck, oh *fuck.*'

The Wizard rotates a little, in the interests of moving things along. Images flash by – Sam and Will, angels' eyes, red and swollen, the shopping cart ramming the older angel's back. If this is what the mother is capable of in public, imagine . . .

The Wizard bucks, gyrates, eyes squeezed shut to force out these images.

'Oh God, oh God, ooooh.'

Silence then . . .

'You murdering little . . . What do you mean you didn't do it? I wish you had never been born!'

The Wizard cries out, moaning, nearly shrieking.

'Yes, let it happen!'

The Wizard hears this other voice, closer by, urging.

Moaning, thrusting, bucking, yes, closer now, yes, almost, yes . . .

'I wish you had never been born never been born never been . . .'

The Wizard falls on to the bed, gasping for air. 'I wish . . . I had never been born.'

'What's that?'

The Wizard turns away, still sucking air, wipes away warm tears.

'What did you say? Something about . . . being born?'

The Wizard jumps off the bed, still sucking air.

'What's the *matter* with you?'

The Wizard gets dressed quickly.

'Look, if you have a problem with what just happened, I'm sorry, I thought—'

'SHUT THE FUCK UP!'

Silence, dead silence.

At least the Wizard can quiet *some* voices.

Monday 6 February

19

Max didn't even look at her when he gave her the news in his office.

'We're moving you off Able Brands.' He was at the window, looking out. 'New England Air needs a whole new direction. I've already checked with the company's director of—'

'An airline? I don't know the first thing about . . . Wait a minute. You're taking me *off* Able Brands?'

'McGuire thinks we're dragging our heels on the value reposition. We're this close to losing the account.'

Damn. Advertising executives had it easy; whenever the buck needed passing, the client was always waiting in the wings to accept it.

'Didn't you tell him about the new campaign for Sparkle? About what we're planning for the detergents?'

Max sighed and faced her for the first time. 'To the Nephew, you'll always be quality. Right now, he wants value.'

If only she could laugh.

'The eighties were about quality, Julia. The nineties . . .'

'I know, I know, they're about value. What's the New England budget?'

'It's out of my hands.' He turned and straightened one of the plaques on his trophy wall.

'*Max*, what's the budget?'

'Ballpark? Five million. But the company's growing fast, I expect their ad budget to grow along with it.'

Five million wouldn't even cover Sparkle's print budget.

'So what'll I have, an account exec, a writer?' She had twenty people on her staff now.

'And an assistant,' Max said quickly.

Julia waited until she knew she could talk with a steady voice. 'My title?'

'The same.'

Even so, this was a demotion – everyone would see it that way.

'And if I refuse?'

He squinted. 'Refuse?'

'If I turn down the New England Air assignment.'

'We're a team, Julia. And as a team member you—'

'Cut the horseshit, Max.'

'It's New England Air or nothing.'

'I'm fired, you mean.'

'No one's firing you. You have a choice.'

One more word and she'd regret it. If he'd had the decency to warn her, she could have made a case to the Able people. Instead he'd taken the path of least resistance, then blamed it on the client.

Maybe he wanted her out of there; maybe this was punishment for denying him. *Ms High Heels with the illegitimate daughter thinks she can turn me down?*

'That night, after my party—'

'Has nothing to do with it.' Max's eyes bored into her. '*Nothing.*'

She could make things very uncomfortable for Max, and he knew it. But there was the mortgage on the co-op, Emily's nursery school tuition, Emily's clothes, Emily's food . . .

She got up and started to leave.

'Julia?'

She kept walking.

She landed a right uppercut in Carlos's gut, followed by a jab to his left glove. Another uppercut, another jab, a quick feint and a left hook on the way up. Jab, uppercut, jab, uppercut.

Carlos backed off and removed his mouthpiece. 'Jesus, Mary and Joseph, you a crazy woman, Julia. Now I know why they call you the Mallet.'

But he was grinning. So much for his theory about women boxers. 'I never met a girl who put everything behind a punch,' he'd said. 'They always hold back, don't ask me why.'

For two years now she'd done her damnedest to prove him wrong, but some deep-rooted reluctance always kicked in just before she threw a punch, just enough restraint to keep her from doing real damage. So what if Carlos, like her, always wore a chest pad and helmet? She'd never really thrown everything behind a punch before, never could. With the heavy bag, sure. But never with Carlos. Until now.

She spat her mouthpiece into her right glove and sucked air for a few moments.

'Hey, Mallet, you gonna kill somebody today. I'm not your boss, okay?'

Julia smiled for the first time all day. Your sparring partner always understood you better than your spouse or lover – every boxer knew that.

'Another . . . another round.' She still hadn't caught her breath.

'Julia, you been going for fifteen minutes, you gotta—'

'One more, okay? One . . . more.'

They replaced their mouthpieces and assumed the stance. Julia led off with a jab that Carlos easily blocked, followed it with two quick right hooks, also blocked. He countered with a right that she intercepted with her glove – he almost always aimed for her glove, but it felt good to block a punch anyway – and then swung a right hook, which she feinted. She landed a left uppercut in his gut, followed it with a right, then a left as Carlos shuffled back toward the ropes. Her fists were pummeling his midsection; she might as well have been punching a bag at this point.

'Whoa, Julia.'

She stopped and realized that his back was against the ropes. She spat out the mouthpiece, panting.

'Good swinging,' Carlos said. 'But you left your right side open, like always. I wanted to, I could have decked you.'

Julia bounced on the balls of her feet. 'One more round.'

He shook his head. 'I gotta work out with Ramon in five minutes. You had enough anyway.'

'One more.'

'Nope. Sorry, it's no good fighting when you angry. You get careless, you might get hurt.'

She couldn't go back to the office, not today. Didn't want to go home while she was this worked up – why should Emily suffer too?

She'd visit someone. But who? Virtually everyone she knew would be at work. (Paula would be home, more than likely, but she wasn't exactly knowledgeable about office politics.) Jared worked, of course – well, *Brock* did – but Julia couldn't face him, not yet. That left Gail.

'It's a cilantro paella,' Gail said as she stirred a pot in her large, immaculate kitchen. Gleaming white cabinets, white marble countertops, white floor tiles – more laboratory than kitchen, Julia had thought ever since she'd seen the fruits of the major renovation five years ago. Gail's long red sweater and black leggings looked jarring against this arctic backdrop.

'Want a taste?' she said.

Julia shook her head and immediately launched into an account of what had happened that day at the office. Gail listened attentively. Occasionally she'd dip her spoon in the pot, close her eyes and sip, add something, then make a notation on a legal pad.

'So what are you going to do?' Gail asked when the recitation was over.

'If I take the new assignment, I'll essentially be accepting a demotion.' She took a sip of a dense, very heady red wine; Gail always kept the most extraordinary wines around, though she rarely drank. 'If I quit, I figure we can survive financially for about two, maybe three months.'

'You'll find another job.'

'None of the agencies are hiring right now. Anyway, it's not fair. I'm being punished because Able Brands sees its market share slipping and Max needs a scapegoat.'

Gail tasted the paella, frowned. She reached for the wine, sprinkled some into the pot, stirred. 'I think you're being punished because you wouldn't fuck that pig boss of yours.'

That was putting it a bit harshly.

'Even if I won a sexual harassment suit, I'd be forever known as the woman who sued Todman DiLorenzo. Everything else I've accomplished would be irrelevant next to that fact.'

'Then maybe you should stay.'

Julia sighed. She wanted consolation, not advice. 'I'll be right back.'

She headed for the bathroom off Gail's bedroom. After the clinical orderliness of the kitchen, the bedroom was an unexpected disaster. Mounds of clothes covered every horizontal surface, shoes and piles of magazines littered the floor. Julia picked her way through the mess to the bathroom, which was also cluttered, and rather grimy.

'Haven't had time to straighten up lately,' Gail said when Julia returned. 'The cilantro book is driving me up the wall.'

Straighten up? Julia refilled her wine glass. Excavation was more like it.

'You're lucky to have work you really love,' Julia said.

'Work I'm good at, you mean. I'm not sure I love cooking. I've just always had a real feel for flavors. In restaurants I'd ask my mother if she could taste the thyme or rosemary in a dish and she'd shake her head. But they were so sharp and specific for me, the herbs and spices in food.'

Gail blew a loose strand of hair from in front of her face and made a note on her pad. She seemed edgier than usual, almost jumpy – probably the cilantro deadline looming.

Julia took her wine glass into the small living room. It was attractively if unimaginatively furnished. The pastel sofa and oak wall unit could have come from any of the upscale furniture chains around town. A glass coffee table, framed posters on the walls, the obligatory fichus tree – Gail had clearly spent all her creative energy in redoing the kitchen five years ago.

Julia walked to the window that overlooked the front of the building. Across the street a man sat in a dark blue sedan parked in front of a fire hydrant.

'Tell me what you think,' Gail said when Julia returned to the kitchen. She held out a wooden spoon.

Julia sipped. 'Delicious.' The broth was subtly fishy, with an overlay of tartness. 'Is that cilantro, that slightly bitter taste?'

Gail nodded. 'My editor is convinced it's the next great thing – the basil of the nineties. Personally? The stuff gives me heartburn, but it's a living.' She stirred the pot. 'Double, double, boil and trouble . . .'

'It's such a nice, self-contained profession, writing cookbooks,' Julia said.

'And food never denies you a raise.'

'Or pinches your ass. Did your mother ever read one of your cookbooks?'

'I gave her the first one. I don't know whether she ever read it or not.'

'You never really talk about your parents.'

Gail shrugged. 'What's to talk about?'

'I'm sure your mother must have shown the first book to her friends in Florida. You know, "My daughter the writer . . ."'

'My mother had no friends. Never did. We're talking about a woman who made a religion of self-reliance. Getting close to people wasn't part of the ritual.'

Gail resumed chopping an onion. A few deft incisions, then three or four decisive chops – *violà*, a perfect dice, and on to the next one.

'It always takes me five minutes to chop an onion,' Julia said. 'And by the time I'm done, my eyes—'

'*Shit!*' Gail dropped the knife and held her left index finger up for inspection: a droplet of blood clung to the tip.

'I distracted you,' Julia said. 'Want me to get a Band Aid?'

'No.'

'A paper towel?'

'*Forget it, okay?*'

'I never thought you'd . . . Gail, are you okay?'

Her left hand was trembling even as she tried to steady it with her right, almost as if the two hands were struggling against each other.

'I'm . . . fine.'

Her lips barely moved as she spoke. She stared at the wall behind the stove, breathing heavily. A bead of blood plopped on to the white marble countertop.

Julia left the kitchen and waited in the hallway. *What the hell was that all about?* When she returned a minute later the drop of blood was gone and Gail was leaning over the pot.

'What's with the cop?' Gail asked. 'That cute one – is he still asking questions?' Back to normal, no apology for freaking out. Weird.

'Has he called you?' Julia asked.

Gail shook her head. 'But Richard was over here the other night, acting very strange. He kept insisting that he'd run into me last Tuesday night on Third Avenue. It never happened. I was home cooking Tuesday night, as I told the police.'

'Richard wanted you to be his alibi? Why?'

'Maybe he killed those women.' When Julia didn't return Gail's smile, she turned serious. 'He did seem a little desperate. Do the cops really think he did it?'

'I don't know what they think.'

Which was at least partly true. Ray said the Wizard probably had two distinct personalities – one 'normal', the other psychotic. Hypnosis had brought the latter to life – no, *she'd* brought it out. A Chinese wall separated the two, according to the police shrink. There might be some apparent behavior peculiarities, but the Wizard would otherwise appear quite normal. Like Richard, like Gail.

Like all of them. Julia shuddered and drained her wine glass.

'What's wrong?' Gail asked.

'Marianne lied to me,' Julia said.

'She's in politics.'

'She lied about being in New York last Tuesday.'

Gail stopped stirring and turned around. Sauce dripped from the spoon on to the white floor tiles. 'Have you told the police?'

'We're talking about murder. I'd only . . . You're dripping.'

Gail glanced at the floor, then back at Julia. 'I think you should tell them.'

'You don't seriously think—'

'The cops believe there's a connection between your party

and the murders. Marianne was at your party, and she lied about her whereabouts . . .'

'Her *whereabouts*?'

'On the night of the murder. I just think you owe it to the victim to tell the police what you know.'

Gail sounded detached, even for her. Almost clinical.

'This is Marianne we're talking about,' Julia said.

Gail shrugged and resumed stirring. Julia took a paper towel and wiped up the paella sauce from the floor. Gail suddenly seemed completely absorbed by her work, as if the subject of Marianne Wilson had vanished from her mind as suddenly as it had appeared. Talk about a Chinese wall . . .

Double, double, boil and trouble.

20

Julia left Gail's building and took a deep breath. A little cilantro went a long way. She hailed a cab, got in, and rolled down the window, squinting into the cold evening air. Maybe giving up the rat race for a couple of months wouldn't be so bad. She and Emily could take that vacation to the sunny island of no goodbyes. Then she'd work up a résumé, make some calls . . .

The taxi pulled up in front of her building ten minutes later. She paid the driver, got out and was hurrying across the lobby when she heard her name. Julio Gonzalez circled the doorman's podium and approached her.

'I was going to call the police . . . I thought maybe I'd wait until you came—'

'*Police*?' Emily was up in the apartment – with Pamela.

Julia lunged for the elevators.

'Your car . . . the white Toyota? Mrs Levine on five saw it about fifteen minutes ago.'

Julia turned, still holding her breath. 'My car?'

'I don't know when it happened – the garage, it's deserted during the afternoon. Mrs Levine, she tell me first, fifteen minutes ago . . .'

Julia pushed open the door to the garage staircase, raced down a flight and pushed open another door. She sprinted toward her parking space, slowed down about ten yards away, then stopped in her tracks about ten feet away, both hands covering her mouth.

Every window had been punched out – front, back, sides. Myriad shards of bluish glass glistened on the concrete, on the vinyl seats, on the hood and dashboard. She took a step toward the car. The headlights were shattered; there were two big dents in the hood.

Slowly shaking her head, she backed away, then turned and ran for the door.

Ray was there within a half-hour. Julia was sipping Scotch, straight up, trying not to panic. But every time she blinked she saw those glass shards, *felt* them, almost, biting into her arms, legs, her face.

'We have a team downstairs checking for prints.' Ray sat next to her on the living-room couch, grim faced. Emily was drawing a picture for Ray in her bedroom. 'Doesn't look like a burglary.'

'The Wizard?'

'I don't know,' he said. 'Serials stick to patterns. This is definitely *not* a part of the pattern.' Ray shook his head. 'I already checked with our guys watching your college pals . . .'

College pals.

'All accounted for, unless one of them managed to slip out.'

'Jared's building has a back door.' She couldn't afford to protect anyone now.

'We know that. Most buildings have more than one way out. Unfortunately, we're stretched pretty thin as it is, with one man to a suspect. We can't watch all exits, not to mention work locations. Anyway, it's going to be tough nailing down the exact time of the attack. There's not much traffic near your parking space.'

'He could have gotten in at any time,' Julia said. 'When it's

221

raining I've run into the garage after someone's punched in the access code from their car. It's closer to the subway than the front door.'

They talked for a bit, interrupted twice by Ray's beeper. Each time he used the telephone in the kitchen.

'This doesn't make sense,' he said. 'Serial killers are fanatical about routine, they're obsessive – that's why they never vary their ritual. Tonight doesn't fit the Wizard's pattern.'

Julia shuddered. 'Then what was it?'

'The only possible explanation is that the Wizard thinks that you know something that could nail him. If that's the case, then destroying your car is a kind of warning, a message, not part of the pathology.'

Julia shrugged and shook her head. 'But I don't know anything ... well, anything *specific* that points to one person over another.'

'You know a hell of a lot more than the six suspects,' Ray said. 'If one of them even *thinks* you're holding back, it could be enough to trigger a warning.'

Emily ran into the room and handed Ray a piece of paper.

'That's beautiful,' he said. 'What is it?'

Her face clouded as she studied the computer-generated hodgepodge of brightly-colored, overlapping squares and circles.

'It looks like Central Park,' Julia said.

Emily squinted at the picture, then glanced up at her. 'It's Riverside Park, silly.'

'Of course,' Julia said. 'How about making something for me now?'

Emily shook her head. 'I want you to read me a book.'

'A little later, sweetheart. Right now I'm talking with—'

'Read to me *now*.'

'Please, Em, just give me twenty minutes with Detective Burgess.'

'NOW!'

'Don't talk to me like that, *ever*.'

Emily scowled, ran from the room, and slammed her bedroom door. Julia took a few deep breaths, then another gulp of Scotch.

'She always knows when I'm under pressure, picks up on it like magic. Asking me to read her a book – that's just her way of pulling me back, reminding me . . . reminding me that she's the most important . . .' She shook her head. 'I need to be with her – it's bedtime anyway.'

'I should head over to the station, see what's—'

'Stay.'

Their eyes locked for several long moments before he nodded.

Julia read Emily a Babar book, readily agreed to read it a second time, then stroked her forehead as she sang Emily's requested song. '"I once had a girl, or should I say, she once had me . . ."'

He'd leave if she asked him to. He'd stay, too – she'd seen it in his eyes. She knew what *she* wanted – the night would be long and sleepless without him.

'Sound asleep,' she said to Ray in the living room. She walked over to him and placed a hand on his arm. He met her gaze but didn't move.

'You know I want to,' he said. 'What I *should* do is another thing.'

She glanced down, her hand falling to her side. 'What would they do if they found out? The police department, I mean.'

'If I was lucky, they'd take away my shield, boot me back down to beat cop until my pension kicked in after fifteen years. If I wasn't so lucky they'd throw me off the force.'

'You can't risk that, I . . .'

He pulled her close to him, kissing her hard as his hands moved up and down her back. Finally he lifted her, their lips still together, and carried her to the bedroom.

* * *

It was as if she'd known him for years, as if she'd always known him. There were none of the usual first-time compromises, the pleasures forgone in the interests of caution. He covered her face with deep, passionate kisses, nothing held back. Julia was astonished and breathless and, at first, close to frantic. *She'd* started this, and now he was . . . taking over.

He moved down to her neck – he consumed her, devoured her. He shimmied down the bed so that his face was at her breasts. She felt herself evaporate as his hunger swallowed her, as if her soul itself were leaving her body like steam.

But she hardly knew him, hardly knew him at all. Sex, yes – but this?

Her hands tugged at his shoulders, as if trying to pull him off her. *As if*. He moved further down her, his mouth and fingertips conspiring to weaken her.

'Ray, I'm . . . not sure about this.'

He ignored her, or perhaps he hadn't heard her because she hadn't really spoken. Her back arched and she managed to lift her head from the pillow, saw the top of his head, his forehead, then his eyes as they looked up for just a moment. Hungry, desperate.

Her head dropped back, eyes closed. She ran her hands over her damp breasts, her neck, her breasts again, surrendering finally to a wave of pleasure that sent her head flailing to either side. Her neck arched, her teeth clenched until she couldn't hold it any more, then she gave one long, long wavering moan that vibrated through her.

She could hear him panting, almost gasping. He crawled to the head of the bed and fell on to the pillow next to hers. She put an arm over his chest and started to straddle him, but he gently pushed her back.

'I *want* to,' she said.

He shook his head.

224

'Ray, I—'

'No.'

'But I—'

'NO.'

Julia looked away, waiting for her breathing to normalize. She wanted to fuck him not because he'd earned it but because it always felt incomplete otherwise, no matter what the women's magazines and sex therapists preached. And because it had been so long.

'Do you want to talk about it?'

He shook his head.

She watched him for a minute as he stared at the ceiling. It wasn't as if he were impotent – *that* she could understand, deal with. He'd been able . . . but unwilling.

A heavy fatigue came over her. 'Ray, I hate to ask you this, but—'

'You want me to leave,' he said.

'I can't risk Emily finding you here.'

He nodded.

'She's only four, and I—'

'Hey, no problem.' He got out of bed and dressed. She walked with him to the front door.

'Don't let anyone in,' he said. 'Don't go out for any reason. Tomorrow there'll be an escort in front of the building. He'll—'

'Escort?'

'The Wizard won't stop with your car, not if he thinks you know something. We can't take any chances.'

She nodded as he opened the door and left.

Tuesday 7 February

21

She emerges from the small apartment building at seven-forty-five in the morning. Tall, thin, almost gaunt, dark hair gathered in a tight knot, the collar of her long black coat pulled up around her neck.

Sam and Will's mom.

Monster.

She walks swiftly toward the corner. Too bad the sidewalks are so crowded, the morning light so sharp. Perhaps the Wizard could push the woman into a doorwell, ram the silencer into her coat . . . there might even be time for the face.

No. The monster's time will come. It's a question of waiting for the right moment, then doing it right.

The Wizard follows her to the corner, careful not to get too close, watches the way she charges down the street, mouth set in a rigid scowl. Remember the way she shoved the shopping cart so violently . . .

I didn't mean it, Mama. It wasn't my fault. I wasn't even there. I mean, I was there, but I didn't do anything. It's dark in here. Please, it's so dark in here.

The monster enters the subway station at 79th Street, the Wizard close behind, token ready.

Please, it's dark and I have to go so bad. Please?

The Wizard is just a few passengers away from her, the

monster. Too close, but the voices are like magnets, drawing the Wizard closer, closer.

Let me out! Let me out! I hate you, I hate you, I hate you. Let me out. I don't really hate you, I was just saying that. Did you hear me? I don't really hate you.

The Wizard looks at the woman's face, searches the hard features for some physical manifestation of the evil within, the wickedness that would drive a mother to hurt her children.

I hate you, I hate you, I . . .

'. . . hate you, I hate you, I . . .'

Faces turn and look, then look away. It doesn't pay to stare at people who mumble on the subway.

They get off the subway at Times Square, change for the Shuttle, then the Lexington Avenue Local uptown to 50th Street. Now the Wizard keeps as far back as possible. The woman expertly dodges oncoming pedestrians; it's as if she's forcing them from her path with her long stride, her razor-slash lips and brutal eyes.

Saturday, in the park, the Wizard watched from outside the fenced-in playground, bore witness: the monster wrenching Sam from the jungle gym, deaf to his wailing pleas . . . shoving Will into the stroller, holding him down with her elbow while she snapped the buckle.

If this is what goes on in public . . .

She turns into a large glass-and-steel skyscraper on Park Avenue. Heart pounding, the Wizard follows, then slips into the elevator behind her, using two middle-aged businessmen as shields. At the back of the elevator, the Wizard smiles when the woman gets off on the third floor.

Sam and Will's mom will be the Wizard's third . . . the Wizard's third rescue. Third floor, third rescue.

A sign.

The Wizard rides up to six, gets off, takes another elevator down to three. Nods at the distracted receptionist, walks down a long corridor before spotting the monster in a corner office, head bent over a legal pad, writing. The Wizard glances at the nameplate outside the office: N. Venucci. So focused, so controlled – but the Wizard has seen her other face.

22

The twenty-yard walk from the elevator to Julia's office seemed to take twenty minutes. Conversations ceased as she approached, people either greeted her with too much enthusiasm or ducked into offices with cursory hellos. The attack on her car the night before hadn't made the news, not surprisingly – she was guilty only of the crime of demotion.

She sat down at her desk, arranged to have her car repaired, and tried to focus on her work. But a scene played over and over in her mind: a sledge-hammer crashing down on a windshield, headlights . . . on her own arms as she reached out to defend herself. At such moments there didn't seem to be enough oxygen in the air.

Ray called a few minutes later.

'How'd it go this morning?' he said. All business.

'With the escort? I had to beg him not to come into Emily's classroom with us. Is he really going to wait outside my office building all day?'

'Until we find out who attacked your car yesterday.' Ray cleared his throat. 'I did some digging in Jared's neighborhood first thing this morning, including a visit to the local check-cashing office.'

'What for?'

'People who don't file tax returns usually don't have checking accounts either. Sure enough, he stops by the place all the time to pay Con Ed, telephone, get a money order for his rent. He also wires money every month.'

'*What?*'

'One thousand dollars. The clerk I talked to didn't remember who the money went to, just that this same guy shows up on the first of every month and buys a money order for two grand.'

'But why?'

'It'll take time to trace the money. Meanwhile, we're trying to figure out how an out-of-work actor gets that kind of money.'

Live out your fantasies with Brock.

'I have to go,' she said and hung up.

She eyed the growing mountain of paperwork on her desk. Max had asked her twice now to call Frank McGuire at Able Brands and say something gracious about team players and long-term relationships. She started to dial his number and hung up. She'd probably lose it and tell the Nephew what a liver-bellied asshole he really was, and McGuire was a bridge she couldn't afford to burn right now.

She dialed Ray's number. *I know why Jared slips by the police at night.* She hung up when he answered and called Jared. His machine picked up after four rings.

'Jared? Are you there? It's Julia. Listen, please pick up the phone if you're there because I think you're in big trouble with the police. Jared?'

She waited.

'Will you pick up if I call you Brock? Are you—'

A piercing screech, then Jared, sounding tired. 'Hello, Julia.'

'Jared, we . . .' The sound of his voice brought her close to tears. 'We need to talk.'

'How did you know about—'

'Can you meet me in an hour?'

'I'll make coffee.'

'Well . . . look, I don't have all that much time. Could we meet in between, in the Rockefeller Center someplace?'

He hesitated before suggesting the northwest corner of the patio overlooking the skating rink. Had he heard the fear in her voice? She hung up, wishing she knew just what she was going to say to him.

She left the building through the underground parking lot to avoid her escort, who for all she knew might have instructions not to let her see Jared. Who needed an escort, anyway? She felt safe on the crowded midtown streets.

They met at the designated corner, both a few minutes early. He gave her a big hug, which she did her best to reciprocate.

'I figured out how to tap into your answering machine,' she said. They both leaned on the railing and watched the skaters circle the rink below them, accompanied by tinny pop music. A glorious sight, but Julia felt completely detached from the scene, isolated by fear and anger. 'We always wondered how you supported yourself.'

Jared glanced at her, then back at the center of the rink, where a young woman in a white blouse and skirt was skating with near-professional proficiency. He shook his head and smiled as she executed a perfect double axel.

'Tell me about Brock,' Julia said.

'That part of my life has nothing to do with you.'

'Everything about you—'

'*No.*' His lips were white, eyes narrow.

'I guess your best role turned out to be playing it straight,' she said. 'You really had me fooled.'

'I never played it straight.'

'No? Then who's Brock?'

He shook his head.

'This is me, remember?' Julia said. 'You can trust me.'

234

'Remember when I used to wait on tables?' he said after a long pause. 'I did that for five, six years, auditioning in between. I hated it, but I was convinced that any day I'd get a part. I never did. Casting directors said I was too pretty for the kind of roles being written back then, in the early eighties. Then, in the late eighties, they said I was too Waspy – everyone wanted ethnic types.'

He interrupted the monologue to watch a male skater in a black leather jacket complete a dazzling figure eight.

'You got some parts,' Julia said. 'Remember when we all went to that theater off St Mark's Place to see you? What was that play?'

'*Rent Control.*'

'You played the landlord's son. You were terrific.'

'I had ten lines, Julia. I was the ditzy son of the greedy capitalist. And that was the pinnacle of my career.'

Julia sighed. That had been a wonderful, giddy evening, sharing Jared's big break. They'd all felt elevated by the prospect of his imminent – inevitable – success.

'So, one night I was bartending at a restaurant in the theater district. There was this guy who'd been there all night, in his forties, balding, with a wedding ring. He'd made some small talk, but mostly I didn't pay much attention. Gradually everyone else left except him. He said he was staying at a hotel in the neighborhood, asked me if I wanted to come up to his room.'

Jared looked around the exterior of the rink, at the hundreds of flags fluttering in the chilly winter wind.

'I'm used to guys coming on to me, you know. I don't think, I look gay . . .' He seemed unwilling to continue until Julia confirmed this.

'Whatever "looking gay" means,' she said.

'But I have something gays are attracted to, always have

235

had. Anyway, that night in the bar I said no thanks, told him I was straight. Instead of this putting him off, he offered me money. A hundred dollars. I said no, but then he offered another fifty, said all he wanted was to see me without clothes on. All I could think of was that I was dead tired after six hours behind the bar and I had made less than half of what this guy was offering me to show a little flesh. AIDS was already in full bloom then, but I knew I wasn't going to do anything unsafe.'

'So you agreed.'

Jared shrugged. 'It was pretty sordid, actually. I went up to his room, he gave me a drink from the mini-bar, I took off my clothes, flexed a little, let him touch me. He told me about *Out There* magazine, said I could make a fortune running an ad. Then he jerked off in maybe three minutes flat, after which he practically pushed me out the door. Probably felt guilty about the wife and kids back in Podunk or wherever.'

Jared joined the other bystanders in applause as the leather-jacketed skater leapt from the ice and landed, spinning fast, arms gradually folding to his chest. 'I went home to sleep right away. I didn't want to think about what had happened. But you know something? When I woke up the next day I felt fine. I didn't feel like I had done anything wrong, I didn't feel dirty. That afternoon I placed the ad in *Out There*, and it's been running once a month ever since.'

'You seem so matter-of-fact about it all,' Julia said.

'It's a living.' The smile he flashed her sent a shiver down her back. 'A good living.'

'All they want to do is . . . look?'

'Look and touch, one-fifty.' Jared craned his neck at the GE building looming over them.

'I don't believe you,' Julia said.

Their eyes met.

'Sometimes they want more. For an extra fifty I let them get

236

me off, and that's the limit, I swear. They're married guys, most of them, out-of-towners.'

Julia couldn't even look at him now.

'It's completely safe,' he said. 'I always use a condom, and half the guys insist on two. It's called double bagging. Me and the A and P.'

A tear ran down Julia's cheek.

'I wish you didn't have to know about this,' he said softly. 'Our friendship means everything to me. This other thing, it's just a job, a small part of my life.'

'How can you say that? When was the last time you had a relationship with a woman? When was the last time you auditioned for a part? It *is* your life, Jared, the only one you've got. Have you really convinced yourself that you do it just for money?'

'I'm not gay. I mean, you have personal knowledge of my sexual—'

'No!' Julia took off a glove and ran her fingers through her hair. 'I think it must really satisfy you in some deep way, humiliating those pathetic men.'

'I give them pleasure, Julia.'

'You're like some kind of god to them, aren't you?'

'It's not like that,' he said.

'No? Then what *is* it like?'

He waited a moment. 'You of all people should know,' he said finally. 'It's about control. These men, some of them are successful businessmen. I've had politicians, actors. Over the years I've recognized quite a few of them, and it's like a game we play, my pretending not to know who they are. They pay me big money, they set the terms – where, when, how long – but it's my show all the way. Because I have something they want, desperately want, and all I have to do is show up.'

'No auditioning, no rejection.'

He smiled. 'And I'm the star. Christ, half the time I can't even, you know, get off for them, especially on a busy day. Or when I've made a deposit.' He grinned. 'And you know what? They blame themselves.'

'Doesn't it depress you? Aren't you ever lonely for genuine human contact?'

'Sometimes. But none of this changes how I feel about you.'

'I can't say the same,' she said. 'I feel betrayed.'

He put a hand on hers. 'Please try to work it through,' he said gently. 'I need you, Julia. I need what we have together.'

She glanced down at their hands. She would work it through eventually. Only Emily was more a part of her, had more power to hurt her. But first she had to get over the betrayal.

'You need an alibi for last Tuesday.' She took a step back and put her glove back on.

'An alibi? Why?'

But she was ten yards away. After a few more feet she turned and saw him, staring not at the skaters now, but into space, so beautiful, so flawed, and inextricably wound up in her life, once and forever.

Please have an alibi, Jared. Please.

In the small vestibule of the apartment building the monster calls home, the nameplate reads: 'Venucci/Thompson'.

The inside door opens at two-fifteen and the Wizard sees them – Sam and Will, with a Hispanic-looking babysitter.

Do they remember the promise whispered in the market? Will's eyes are red around the edges, as if he's been crying, and Sam has gray-brown circles under his eyes. Even the sitter looks grim.

The Wizard holds the door open as the sitter maneuvers the double stroller through.

The sitter squints – *Do you live here?* – then pushes the

stroller toward Riverside Park. The two children peer around the edges of the stroller, wide-eyed. The Wizard starts to follow.

'SET THE TRAP *NOW*, DON'T LET HER HURT THE ANGELS.'

The Wizard stops, glances around. 'Who—'

'DON'T LET HER GET AWAY WITH IT. SAVE THEM! SAVE THE CHILDREN!' *This* voice is loud but somehow gentle. Encouraging.

'SET THE TRAP *NOW*.'

There! Across the street, carved in plaster on the front of that large apartment building, a gargoyle-like creature above the front door . . .

'DO IT FOR THE CHILDREN.'

Its mouth moves, its eyes blaze with life. Yet the voice is tender.

'YOU KNOW WHAT YOU HAVE TO DO. WHAT YOU HAVE TO SAVE THEM FROM.'

'The monster,' the Wizard says.

The gargoyle nods once . . . and freezes back into stone.

The Wizard walks down the street a few yards, then darts into a small patio-like area formed by the two steep staircases of adjoining brownstones. Private, no light fixture, and situated between the monster's building and the 79th Street subway station.

The Wizard removes a can of paint from a plastic bag and sprays the wall. With both words formed, the Wizard steps back, almost panting. Preparing the nest is a good idea, brilliant. Now it *will* happen, it must. This time there will be no backing off.

The paint drips in a few places, a nice, sinister touch. This is where it will happen, right here! First the wall, and then the face.

The Wizard presses the paint can between both legs, rolls it, using two hands. The black signature catches the late-morning light, glistens. Oh, God, this is where it will happen . . . The Wizard presses the can more firmly, feels something warm and electric shoot upwards . . . Oh, God, yes. OhmyGod, this is where . . .

Footsteps approaching. The Wizard straightens up, jams the paint can back into the bag, and waits, breathing heavily, for the footsteps to pass. Moments later, the Wizard emerges from the hidden patio and glances across the street before heading for the corner.

'SOON.' The carved lips stretch to a half-smile. 'YOU'LL BE BACK SOON.'

23

Julia slipped back into her office building through the garage, and spent the afternoon trying to figure a way to get through the next few weeks on the job. Even as a lame duck there was much for her to do, and it was work that required a level of enthusiasm she didn't have and couldn't fake.

She could blow it off, spend the days sparring with Carlos or running errands. But she had never walked away from an obligation. Take away the job title, the corner office, the responsibility, and what was left? Mother? Yes, of course, but that title didn't tell the whole story and never would. Without her work she'd feel cut off from the world outside her daughter – and how would *that* help Emily?

So she'd tackle the media schedules, the budgets, the creative reviews, one task at a time, concentrating on the chore at hand rather than the big, depressing picture. And when the shattered glass flickered, the sledge-hammer loomed, she'd dig in all the more intensely.

Yes, one task at a time. She fished through her in-box, found a focus group report on Sparkle, and plunged in.

When she left the building at six, Ray was waiting.

'Your escort, Madame.' He bowed with a sweep of his arm.

'Any progress?' she said as they drove uptown.

'None whatsoever. Not a good day.'

She studied him for a while, then shook her head. 'Come on. I just spent three hours going over media budgets; Emily's staying at my mother's for the night – I could use a distraction.'

He shrugged. 'I wish I had something for you.'

'Ray, you asked me to help you. How can I help when you don't keep me informed?'

He glanced at her and sighed. 'Nothing's making sense. The MO's the same for the two killings – the bullets in the face, the paint. The victims are both women. But beyond that they have nothing in common. One solidly middle class, with two children – your neighbor. The other, Alicia Frommer, lived in a tenement . . .'

'Both were on their way home.'

'In two very different neighborhoods,' Ray said. 'All *that* tells me is that the Wizard didn't have a way to get into their apartments. He or she had to intercept them.'

'So the Wizard probably doesn't know the victims.'

'But they were chosen somehow. The Wizard knew them, even if they didn't know the Wizard.'

They were silent for several blocks, then Ray spoke again.

'It's like the Wizard is punishing them.'

'For what?'

'We have this guy on the task force, he spent a year down at the FBI's Behavioral Science Services Unit in Quantico. He specializes in profiling serial killers.'

'Lovely,' she said. After a career spent profiling detergent buyers she was something of an expert in mapping the human mind. 'I wonder if they have any openings.'

Ray shot her a look. 'Usually with a serial there's a sexual element, the killer's getting off in some way. This behavioral specialist, he doesn't see that here. He believes the killer is punishing these women, mutilating them with the bullets and the paint. If there's a sexual angle, it probably has to do with release. The compulsion to punish builds up like a sexual need, then it's released by the act itself. Maybe the perp gets off later, by himself, but—'

'Why do these women need to be punished? You still think it's connected to my party?'

'After I saw your car yesterday, I'm almost positive. Remember what Stella Turner said? The Wizard may have two distinct personalities – one relatively normal, the other one . . .'

The other one *she'd* brought to life.

He pulled up in front of her building, put the car in park, and glanced at her.

'Can I come up?'

'Not tonight, I'm trying to catch up with work.'

'You said Emily's with your mother, I thought—'

'We need to talk about last night,' she said.

'You mean, *you* need to talk.'

She started to get out, then turned back. 'Ray . . .'

He looked at her, waiting.

'I can't . . . be with you unless you're completely open with me. You're not telling me everything.'

'What is it I've been doing for the past—'

'Not about the Wizard. About *you*. Last night . . .'

Their eyes locked for a moment before he turned away.

'Talking about it might help,' she said. 'I need to know why.'

'Don't you mean, why *not*?'

'Forget it.' She opened the car door and got out.

'Julia?'

She closed the door but heard his shout through the window.

'I'm not your problem, Julia.'

She started walking.

'Remember that!' he shouted after her. 'I'm not your problem.'

Julia got in the elevator and hit the close-door button twice. Ray was bad news. Very bad news. She jabbed the button again and the doors finally shut. He was bad news and *damn it*, why didn't that turn her off? Her entire fucking life was falling apart and she was falling for a cop with sexual hangups.

Her life was a mess? Impossible. The beautiful daughter, the steadily ascending career track, the tight circle of old and beloved and dependable friends. The only constant in her life was Emily, and even Em was beginning to pick up on the tension, Julia's growing sense of terror since that first visit by the police just over a week ago.

How had it all collapsed?

She got off the elevator on the twenty-seventh floor and fished through her pocketbook for her keys as she walked down the long corridor. She should never have agreed to let Emily sleep over at her mother's – a hug and a cuddle would have helped a lot.

She opened the door to the apartment and could already feel the weight of the long evening stretching ahead of her. She flicked on the light, placed her purse on the table in the foyer, and was about to head for her bedroom when she noticed a light on in the living room.

Strange, she never left a light on when . . .

'Hello, Julia.'

She spun around, making a fist as she drew back her right hand.

Someone was there, just a few yards away, coming at her from the living room.

'I hope I didn't—'

She planted a right jab on the intruder's nose.

'JESUS!' A woman's voice. She went reeling back into the living room, almost toppling over, one hand covering her nose. 'Christ, I'm bleeding.'

The adrenalin rush was giving way to a powerful instinct to retreat. Ray had said that they couldn't rule women out. Julia turned and headed for the front door.

'Wait – Julia! Don't . . . don't you recognize me?'

The voice *was* familiar, and the face . . .

She turned. 'Senator Rinaldi?'

Ruth Rinaldi fished a crumpled tissue from her pocketbook and dabbed her bloody nose. A few drops had fallen on to a lapel of her navy suit jacket.

'You throw quite a punch.'

'What the *hell* are you doing here?'

'I hope to God it's not broken. What would I tell them at the emergency room?'

'I asked a question.'

'Marianne has a key to your apartment,' she said. 'I let myself in.'

Julia would *kill* the doorman for letting her up. So what if Rinaldi was a senator? No one had the right to enter the building unannounced, much less enter her apartment uninvited.

'May I sit down?' she said.

'Maybe you'd like a drink, a little dinner while we're at it.'

Rinaldi smiled for the camera, walked unsteadily into the living room, sat on the sofa, and crossed her legs. Julia chose the wing chair across the room. Her pulse was almost back to normal. At least Rinaldi couldn't be the Wizard – she hadn't been at the party.

'Marianne was opposed to my coming here.' She touched a nostril with the tissue, which she inspected before replacing it in her purse. 'But I insisted, and she gave me the key.'

'I'd like it back.'

She took the key from her pocketbook and tossed it on to the coffee table. How long had it been since they'd all exchanged keys? Ten years? Longer? Gail, Marianne, Paula – *shit*, Jared still had a key from that time he watered her plants.

'You could have waited downstairs.'

Rinaldi smiled again and shook her head, jiggling her rigidly coiffed hair, the type of restrained bouffant favored by First Ladies and corporate wives – and, apparently, middle-aged feminist apostates. 'A senator waiting in the lobby of a building in her constituency is bound to be recognized. I couldn't take that chance – especially when there's been a murder on the premises.' She seemed at once uncomfortable and condescending, as if she wasn't really nervous about being there, just annoyed.

'This is about the killings,' Julia said.

'After you left on Sunday, Marianne called me, almost frantic. Apparently you'd found out she was in New York the night of one of the murders.'

'She mentioned an art opening—'

'And you checked the dates.'

'I didn't *check* them. The painter was a friend of ours and I wanted to—'

'Forget it. The truth is, she was with me the entire day.' The senator took a deep breath, let it out slowly. 'And night.'

Julia covered her mouth to stifle a gasp. All the evidence had been there right in front of her – while she had puzzled over Marianne's apparent lack of a romantic life, her fervent defense of Ruth Rinaldi's right-wing policies . . .

'You're lovers.'

Ruth Rinaldi nodded solemnly as Julia fought back a wave of shock and anger. Another secret added to the growing pile of betrayal.

'But Marianne—'

'I'm her first woman, if that's what you're worried about.' Rinaldi's half-smile brought out a relief map of tiny wrinkles in her makeup. 'I don't think I was part of her five-year plan, however. It just happened.'

Julia shook her head and tried to imagine what Marianne saw in Ruth Rinaldi. She was attractive in a conservative, unselfconscious way, not especially feminine but not at all masculine – and about as sexy as a pair of Bass Weejuns. But Marianne had always gone for *cute* rather than handsome – cute *men*.

'Does your husband know?'

'Does he *care*, you mean. He has a girlfriend too – we have a lot in common, you see.'

Rick and Ruth Rinaldi – the quintessential power couple of a thousand fawning profiles, one a senator, the other a high-ticket Washington lawyer, with no children to complicate their busy lives.

'I travel to New York frequently,' Rinaldi was saying. 'It's all part of representing the state. It's also a good opportunity to spend time with Marianne. But for obvious reasons Marianne travels . . . incognito. She books the shuttle flights using my secretary's credit card. And of course I register at the hotel under my name only.'

'You'd better tell the police—'

'Why the hell do you think I'm here? Marianne has an alibi – she was with me. There's no need whatsoever to involve the police.' She leaned forward. 'This child welfare bill I'm sponsoring – with Marianne's help – I've pulled every string I have to get it out of committee.'

'It ought to be a real image-booster,' Julia said. 'The penny-pinching Republican actually cares about children.'

'Motives are for psychiatrists. In politics, only results count. This bill is my chance to show another side of Ruth Rinaldi, the caring side. You think my colleagues in the Senate give a damn about child abuse? Forget it, children don't vote. Any

247

hint of scandal and the bill's dead.'

'I wish you luck, then.'

'Don't *you* care about children, Julia? Marianne said you had one of your own.'

'Why are you here, Senator?'

Rinaldi had picked up a sofa pillow and was absently kneading it with both hands. Marianne had crocheted that pillow at Madison and given it to Julia for her twenty-first birthday.

Julia closed her eyes for a moment to fight back the tears.

'I need to know if you've mentioned Marianne's New York visit to the police.'

Julia nodded.

'Shit.' Ruth Rinaldi punched the pillow. 'Do you have any idea what this could mean?'

'There's no law against having an affair.' Julia got up, took the pillow from her, and sat down again. 'And if your husband already knows . . .'

'My husband? He's the least of it. It's not about the voters, either.'

'I don't get . . . Wait a minute. You've been charging Marianne's trips to the government.'

'If the Federal Election Committee ever found out . . .' Rinaldi let out a long sigh through clenched teeth. 'Do you think for one minute I'd have a prayer of re-election next fall?'

'Not even a school prayer.'

She shot Julia a glance. 'You're all so clever.'

'*All*?' Julia smiled sweetly. 'Who exactly do you mean?'

Rinaldi went to the window and gazed out over the constituency. 'I was a joke six years ago when I announced for the Senate. "Ms Goombah Goes to Washington". People like your friend Marianne looked down their Ivy League noses at me, the "Guidos from Gotham", they called me and Rick. Well, maybe I went to a state college, and maybe I never lost the

Brooklyn accent. But I got on the right committees, worked twice as hard as anyone else, and never forgot who it was I represented. Not Marianne Wilson and her ilk. Not you, either. My constituency is real people with real problems.'

'Like unwanted pregnancies and the need to pray in school.'

Rinaldi spun around, grinning. 'I'm still a joke to people like you. But I'm also the second or third most powerful senator in Washington. Someday I'll be the most powerful. And the people who count? They take me seriously, don't kid yourself. Even Marianne.'

'Now that you're sleeping with her.' She might be a US senator, and the lover of one of her oldest friends, but Ruth Rinaldi had broken into her apartment, scared her to death. 'That's the real turn-on, isn't it, *Senator*? Scoring with a prep-school co-ed who used to think you were a feminist joke, and charging it to the taxpayer. Isn't that what gets you off?'

Rinaldi crossed the room in three long strides, stopping just two feet from Julia. 'You and your little love child, it's all so . . . *tidy*, isn't it? Easy for you to thumb your nose at family values; you don't need a man to raise a child, you can be mother *and* father. Families are for the little people, right? Not for a hotshot executive who can *pay* someone to raise her kid while she sets Madison Avenue on fire. What were you thinking when you had your daughter, Julia? Were you thinking of the child – or were you thinking how nice it would be to add this . . . this *accessory* to your glamorous life?'

'Get out of here or I'll show you the real damage this hot-shot can do with a right jab.' Julia took a deep breath, holding it for a moment as Rinaldi watched her. The woman was head of the Senate Finance Committee, for God's sake.

Finally the senator started for the hallway. 'Here's a message for you and your detective friend.' She stopped just a foot away from Julia.

'He's not—'

Rinaldi thrust a finger at her. 'Marianne was with me, and that's all you two lovebirds need to know. Poke around where you shouldn't and you'll find out what *real* influence can do.'

'You can't threaten me,' Julia said.

'But I just did, Julia. I just did.'

With that she left the room and let herself out of the apartment.

It builds slowly inside, inexorable as a yawn until the Wizard can no longer keep silent. Release is a hair-trigger away. Panting yields to a deep, guttural moan.

On the bottom tonight, relaxed – and why not, given that deliverance is only a day or two away? – the Wizard's pelvis jerks in small, involuntary spasms.

'Ooooh, ooooh,' cries the Wizard's partner, but the moans fall on deaf ears, for the Wizard hears nothing and, eyes pinched shut, sees only black. Who is this person, writhing, bucking, occasionally remembering to stroke the Wizard in the appropriate places? Did they even introduce themselves earlier, in the bar? Who cares?

Almost there, almost! The Wizard takes on final breath, girds for the moment, so long denied, holds it in, sees the black signature on the small patio wall, electrified by sunlight, inhales even deeper, just one more . . .

A sudden light, eyes open to a silhouetted figure looming in the closet door. Mama, is that you?

The Wizard exhales. Slowly . . . perhaps it's not too late, if the voice doesn't resurface.

The Wizard's arm squeezes the warm, damp body. Another deep breath, almost there, almost. The Wizard's stomach arches, head thrown back, grabbing, pulling the body on to . . .

Get up to your room, NOW.

But Mama, I didn't—

Did you hear me? Get up there now, and I don't want to hear from you until I call you. NOW!

The Wizard's head jerks from side to side, a desperate attempt to shake off the voice. N. Venucci's face jerks into focus. The face must be covered, destroyed.

The Wizard grips harder, pulling with every ounce of strength.

'Jesus Christ, what the fuck are you doing?'

But the Wizard can't hear, won't hear. Pulling, grasping, *tearing*, the Wizard inhales and doesn't, *won't* let the air out, can't even feel the dizziness. Almost there, almost, almost . . .

'You're *sick*. Let go of me!'

A slap on the face . . .

. . . and it happens. The Wizard's howl escapes like rushing steam.

'Get the hell out of here, now.'

But the Wizard hears only the silence.

'Did you hear me? *Get out!* Christ, my arms – I'm going to have bruises. Get out of . . . Oh, my God, there's blood.'

Footsteps leaving the room, a light flicked on, water running in a sink. These sounds gradually come into focus as the Wizard gets out of bed, picks up the crumpled sweater and pants, starts to get dressed.

In less than a minute the Wizard is in the hallway, waiting for the elevator. From inside the apartment, a muffled cry: 'Jesus Christ, I may need stitches . . .'

The Wizard squeezes the plastic bag with the big gun and the paint, feels their reassuring weight.

The angels will be saved. The voices silenced.

Wednesday 8 February

24

The phone was ringing as Julia entered her office the next morning. It had been a long, mostly sleepless night. Marianne's betrayal, her deceit, her inexplicable lack of trust, had inflicted a crushing sense of isolation. She picked up the phone, half hoping it was Marianne: '*The senator was only kidding, Julia. It's all a big joke.*'

'It's Martin. I'm trying to get everyone together tonight to celebrate Paula's thirty-fifth.'

Julia sighed. Bringing them all together was no doubt Martin's way of collecting information. The cops were turning up the heat on everyone she'd hypnotized. Information is power, he'd once told her. The commodity trader's first principle.

'I'll have to check with my sitter to find out if—'

'Look, you had *your* party,' he said.

'I didn't wait till the day of the party to invite the guests,' she said. 'Anyway, I'm not saying I won't come.'

'It's just the six of us, at La Sorgue.'

Leave it to Martin: La Sorgue was barely a month old and already the hottest French restaurant in town. At least with all six of them together, New York's Finest would have a breather.

First things first: a meeting in one hour with the account supervisor in charge of the New England Air business. Charles

Devon would not appreciate reporting to her after years of relative autonomy. A notorious lunchtime boozer – and you really had to work at acquiring a drinker's reputation in advertising – he was probably sticking pins in a Julia Mallet doll already.

She wasn't even close to deciding whether to accept the 'lateral transfer', or risk the stress of unemployment. But focusing on the tasks at hand would at least keep her mind off Marianne, the attack on her car, the fact that one of her oldest friends might be . . .

Julia swallowed and reached for the stack of mail in her in-box. Her hands trembled as she sorted through several days' worth of memos and letters and reports, trying with little success to concentrate.

An escort had its advantages. She never had to worry about finding a cab during rush hour, for one thing. The city provided the transportation gratis, no small matter when facing possible unemployment. And she was pretty much safe from the Wizard – another plus.

Her morning escort was back waiting for her that evening. Lou LaVigna, part of the Wizard task force, was tall and thin, with a blond crewcut and a prominent Adam's apple.

'Do you do a lot of work with Detective Burgess?' she asked as they drove uptown.

'This is my second assignment with him, ma'am.'

Ma'am? LaVigna looked about twenty-five.

'Please, call me . . .' Ms Mallet? Almost as bad. 'Call me Julia.'

'Yes, ma'am – sorry.' He blushed. 'I did some footwork on the Prescott case, our paths crossed once or twice back then.'

'The Prescott case?'

'Gordon Prescott, a big case a few years back. Half the force was working on that one.' He doubled parked in front of the restaurant.

'You don't have to stick around,' she said. 'This may take a while.'

'That's okay, ma'am.' He took a deep breath. 'Julia.'

Gail, Richard, Jared, Marianne, Martin and Paula were already at the table at six o'clock. Probably ravenous – but for information, not food. She smiled back at their collective gaze as she approached the table, and took the one empty seat, between Martin and Richard.

Desperate to avoid eye contact with Marianne and Jared, she glanced around the room: country antiques, dried flower arrangements, colorful china. All that was missing were truffle-sniffing boars and grumpy Provençal peasants.

'What's everyone drinking?' Julia said.

The conversation seemed forced that evening, probably because nobody was so much as mentioning what they all really wanted to talk about. A half-hour into the dinner Julia still couldn't bring herself even to look at Marianne, sitting directly opposite her. What did she expect to see, a scarlet L on Marianne's blouse? She also avoided looking at Jared, two seats to her right and half-way through a double Martini.

The small talk petered out after a while, leaving in its wake a brief, depressing silence. Normally there'd be two or three overlapping conversations humming at once as they raced to catch up. But the Wizard had settled on their friendship like a chilling frost. They focused on the menus for a while, passed around the thick wine list, and, finally, got down to the real reason for the dinner.

It was Martin who broke the ice. 'Do they actually think one of us is killing these women?'

He threw the question out to the entire table, but all eyes turned to Julia.

'They think there's a connection to my party.'

'But *what* connection?' Gail said,

'They haven't talked to any of the other guests, have they?' Paula said. 'I mean, there were a dozen people from your agency at the party.'

'They may have,' Julia said. She needed a hefty infusion of wine, but even lifting her glass at this point might be misconstrued.

'You might as well know – we've consulted our attorney about this,' Martin said. 'I suggest the rest of you do likewise.'

'I already have,' Richard said. 'He basically told me to keep my mouth shut. That bit of brilliance cost me two-fifty.'

'I've talked to a lawyer,' Gail said.

Julia glanced at her.

'I didn't actually *hire* a lawyer,' Gail added quickly. 'I called Pete Simon, who helped negotiate my last book deal. A little friendly advice never hurt.'

'What I can't figure out is why these two murders haven't been covered in the media,' Marianne said.

'They were articles about both of them,' Julia said.

'But there was no mention of a connection,' Gail said. 'Yet the police keep questioning us about *both* killings.'

'And that Raphael Burgess?' Paula leaned across the table. 'He implied that if we breathed a word of this to the press we'd be in serious trouble, though I can't imagine what he could really do to us, since we're not exactly—'

'Tell us what you know, Julia,' Richard said.

Julia looked not at his face but at his wrinkled shirt and stained tie.

'We're all convinced you know more than you've been letting on,' Martin said.

She glanced around the table. Only Marianne and Jared weren't participating.

'It's not so much that the police think that . . . one of you actually killed anyone.' Julia took a sip of wine – to hell with what they thought. 'It's more that they think you might know something. Something you may not even realize you know.'

She looked around the table. No one seemed happy with her response. Gail spoke first.

'Well, what *were* we all doing the night . . . What was her name? Alice Frommer? What were we all doing the night Alice – no, Alicia – was murdered?'

'This is ghoulish,' Paula said.

The waiter appeared with their appetizers, deposited them amid a tense silence, and left.

'It's only ghoulish if one of us actually did it.' Gail leaned over her appetizer – two immense, gleaming scallops surrounded by exotic greens – prodded it with a fork, took a sniff, shrugged, and tasted a sliver of scallop. Everyone else silently, solemnly observed the ritual. Only when she'd declared the appetizer 'interesting' did the conversation resume.

'Paula and I were together, at home, last Tuesday,' Martin said. He glanced at his wife. 'Tell them, Paula.'

'As I told the police this morning,' Paula said without looking up from her soup. 'We were together, at home.' She was festooned with jewelry – sapphire earrings, a diamond pendant and ring, gold watch – all trotted out at Martin's insistence, no doubt. But with her untamable hair, makeup-free face and vaguely ethnic dress, she still looked like she'd just driven down from Woodstock – with a pit stop at Tiffany's.

'I was home alone,' Gail said. 'So I could have done it, I suppose. Though my aim has never been good.'

'They were shot at point-blank range,' Richard said in a mournful voice.

This killed the conversation for a few moments.

'Have you had much target practice?' Marianne asked Gail, who looked puzzled. 'You mentioned that your aim wasn't very good.'

'Just a joke,' Gail said. 'Where were you that night?'

'In Washington.' Marianne glanced briefly at Julia. 'I took the Metroliner from DC this morning.'

Julia stared at Marianne, now calmly poking at her salad. 'Did you speak to the police in the past few days?' she asked.

'The police? No. Why, did they contact the rest of you?'

Everyone nodded.

'Senatorial privilege,' Julia muttered.

'What was that?' Marianne said.

'I told the police I was at the movies,' Richard said. 'I even described the plot. They seemed satisfied.' He looked around the table. 'Do you really think we need . . . *alibis*?'

'You could have read a review,' Martin said.

'Oh, Christ, Martin.' Paula's soup-spoon clanged against the rim of the bowl. 'You don't have to accuse everyone else just to prove you didn't do it.'

'I wasn't accusing anyone. And I certainly don't need to prove—'

'Then why bring up the review?' Paula's face was flushed, her voice quaking.

'Simply to point out that—'

'Could we stop this?' Julia spoke louder than she'd intended, attracting the attention of diners at nearby tables. 'This is a birthday celebration.'

Martin lifted his wine glass. 'A toast. To Paula – and old friends.'

All six lifted their glasses, but Martin's toast seemed so ludicrously ironic that the mood remained leaden through the arrival and consumption of their main courses. As the plates were being cleared, Gail asked Jared why he'd been so quiet all evening.

'Have I?' he said. Looking at him, Julia tried to remember when she'd last seen him dressed up. Tweed jacket, narrow wool tie – Mr Chips as stud. She sighed. Living a double life ought to take its toll in some visible way, yet Jared looked gorgeous.

'So where were you on the evil evening?' Martin asked him.

'*Martin*,' Paul said.

'Hey, Gail brought up the whole issue of alibis,' he said.

'I was home.' Jared smiled and glanced at Julia, who looked away. 'Alone.'

Dessert menus, then dessert itself and coffee distracted them.

'Did everybody get the brochure about the fifteenth reunion?' Paula asked.

The rest of them looked at her as if she'd announced she had rabies.

'Well, did you or didn't you? I'm on the reunion committee, so if you didn't, I—'

'I got one,' Julia said.

The others nodded gloomily.

'Is everyone planning to go?' Paula asked.

Coffee cups were lifted, dessert plates scraped, but no one said a word.

'So, we're going to let this ridiculous murder thing break up the greatest friendships in our lives?' Paula's face was red again.

'It's not ridiculous,' Julia said. 'Two women were killed.'

'But not by one of us,' Paula said. 'We didn't do it – we couldn't have.'

'You talk about *us* like we're a solid block, Paula,' said Gail. 'We're six individuals.'

'I'm with Paula,' Jared said. 'We *are* a solid block. We've known each other almost twenty years, good times and bad . . .'

261

'Oh, Lord,' Marianne said.

'We've always looked out for each other, always. Back at Madison we were practically a campus institution, the way we stuck together.'

'The Madison Seven,' Paula said.

'Exactly,' Jared said. 'There was even a picture of us in the *Campus Times* with that nickname in the caption. Everyone knew there was something special about what we had together. We can't let these suspicions come between us.'

'Remember how we came to Martin's rescue when he stole those T-shirts from the bookstore?' Gail said.

Martin leaned toward Gail, dragging the tip of his Hermès tie through a puddle of raspberry sauce on the tablecloth. 'Why the hell are you bringing that up?'

'Because we stood by you then.' Gail smiled primly.

'She's right,' Jared said. 'Character witnesses before the student senate. God, I was so stoned that afternoon I could barely talk.'

'You were always stoned in the afternoons,' Marianne said.

'Well, they never found me guilty,' Martin said. 'Where's the waiter? I'd like some more decaf.'

'I was on the student senate,' Marianne said. 'I argued like hell for you, Martin. If it weren't for me, you'd have served a hundred hours in the cafeteria, cleaning dishes.'

Paula giggled. 'What a thought!'

'Where the hell is the waiter?' Martin spotted their waiter and waved.

'I don't know, Martin, they say all criminals start small,' Gail said. 'A few T-shirts in college, commodities scams later on, then serial killing . . .'

'Makes perfect sense to me,' Jared said.

'Someone call the police,' Marianne said.

262

Martin glared at Gail. 'This is . . . What do you mean, commodities scams?'

'Did I strike a nerve?'

'Fuck you. Fuck all of you.' Martin stood up and stalked across the restaurant. He took out his wallet and thrust a credit card at their waiter. A moment later Paula got up and joined him.

'Happy birthday,' Jared called after her.

25

They stepped from cozy Provence into frigid February. The air at eight-thirty was stinging cold; New Yorkers scurried by the restaurant, gloved hands in pockets, heads bowed against the wind, chins tucked into scarves, all flesh concealed save for desperate, watery eyes.

Martin and Paula got into the back seat of a waiting Mercedes. Gail hailed a cab and offered to drop off Marianne at her hotel. Richard set off on foot for his apartment.

That left Julia and Jared. Lou LaVigna dozed in the front seat of the dark blue sedan a few yards away. She wouldn't point out the escort to Jared since she couldn't discuss the reason for it. Ray had told her not to mention the car incident to any of the Madison bunch.

'Detective Burgess questioned me at Manhattan North this morning,' Jared said. 'They found something at the second murder scene.'

'What?'

'Some hairs, blond hairs.'

'Oh God.'

'They're not mine, Julia. I wasn't there, I didn't do these things. I couldn't.'

She nodded, but her heart was racing.

'The thing is, they want to do a DNA test on the hair. They

need a sample from me – which I don't have to give them, at least not without a court order.'

'Why wouldn't you? If you weren't there, the hairs can't be yours.'

'Because what if they *are* mine? What if someone planted them there?'

'That's absurd, you—'

'This whole thing is absurd, Julia. I mean, do you really see me as capable of killing those women?'

None of them was capable . . . and yet she was beginning to think that the Wizard was inside each of them, aching to satisfy a chronic hunger, bristling just beneath the civilized surface, biding time until the moment of release when old scores would be settled.

'Well, *do* you?' Jared said.

'No,' she whispered.

'The crazy thing is, I *wasn't* alone that night.'

Julia sighed. 'Brock?'

'I was with a guy most of the night, at the Waldorf. That's why I slipped past my *guard* that night, I had an appointment.'

'Then you have to find him, ask him to—'

'I don't even know his name. I called the hotel, gave his room number, but he'd already checked out the next morning. The switchboard wouldn't tell me who'd been in that room.'

'They'd have to give his name to the police.'

'I can't get the cops involved in this . . . this part of my life.'

'You may not have a choice. If you have an alibi you have to—'

'I didn't do these things.' His voice sounded an octave higher than normal. He shoved his hands in his coat pocket and hunched toward her.

'What if I talked to Detective Burgess?' she said.

'You?' Still bent slightly, he looked at her face through tear-ridged eyes.

'I . . . well, I've been pretty involved in this case. If I explained things to him, maybe he'd agree to track down your alibi, the Waldorf man, and not, you know, look into things any deeper than he has to.'

'You'd do that for me?'

Julia nodded but looked away. The radiant smile, the focused energy, the compelling light from his eyes – all were gone. She couldn't bear to see Jared looking pathetic.

He cupped her chin and gently turned her face to his. 'Since we had coffee I've been sick with the thought that I'd lost you.'

He was talking as if they were lovers – which in a way they were, though they'd *made* love just that once, over fifteen years ago. He'd claimed part of her, back at Madison, and never let go.

She smiled and kissed his cheek. Now, how was she going to get into the car without his noticing?

'I forgot something inside the restaurant,' she said.

'What is it? I'll go—'

'No, it's my brush, in the ladies' room.'

Now I'm the one who's lying. Oh, Jared!

'I'll wait . . .'

'Please, it's freezing. Go home and get warm. I'll call you tomorrow.'

She watched him walk to the corner – the familiar, easy lope, arms swinging slightly. She could call him back, tell him she still hadn't forgiven him but loved him anyway, always would.

Instead she waited until he had turned the corner, then woke LaVigna with a rap on the car window.

26

N. Venucci hurries west from the subway, lugging a packed briefcase, heading home. She walks quickly, high heels striking the sidewalk in a fixed, angry rhythm.

The Wizard is five yards behind. It is eight-forty-five, and the cold air lashes the Wizard's face, penetrating the lungs. The farther west the monster walks, toward Riverside Drive, the more deserted the street becomes. On the last block before the Hudson River, the street will be empty. And if it isn't? The nest is prepared. The Wizard will find a way.

It has to be now. The voice has been too persistent lately, sleep too difficult, the waking hours a trial. Following this woman, so close to stopping her yet forced to wait . . . It has to be now. The nest is ready.

The Wizard closes the distance. Four yards. Three. N. Venucci – Sam and Will's mom – turns, smiles at the Wizard, continues walking.

Nothing to be afraid of, sweetheart. It's only me.

A pretty woman, *Ms Venucci*, with an intelligent face, big compassionate eyes, two adoring children and a husband with a different name . . .

Don't they see? Why can't they see? The face tells the story – the mouth, the eyes. That face must vanish.

Two yards. Five feet. The Wizard passes her, close enough

267

to sniff a tangy cologne, hurries down the block and disappears into . . . the nest. One hand twists its way into the plastic bag, feels the cold steel of the gun, finds the trigger, strokes it.

Footsteps approaching. Wait, *wait*. Not yet. Deep breaths . . . inhale the knife-cold air, hold it, hold it, exhale . . . slowly.

'Nancy? How *are* you?'

The Wizard peers out of the nest. The monster and another woman are ten yards away.

'Running late, as usual. Sam and Will get so crazed when I come home this close to bedtime.'

'I'm sure they'll forgive you.'

'Sam's birthday party is on Saturday. I'm taking tomorrow afternoon off so we can bake the cake together. Will says he wants to break the eggs.'

Both women laugh as the Wizard's right hand grips the gun. That voice – gentle, sweet, *false*.

'Anyway, my brood awaits me.'

The Wizard hears the monster's footsteps approaching, removes the doll, turns the switch, and bends down to place it against the wall. The footsteps are closer, louder.

Now.

The Wizard steps out on to the sidewalk, a few feet in front of the quarry. Nancy Venucci looks puzzled: *Didn't you pass me just a minute ago?*

The music drifts from the small patio, sharp, distinct notes. 'Somewhere, over the . . .'

The Wizard's right hand is in the bag, gripping the gun. When the woman turns to face the music – ha! – the Wizard knows the monster is trapped.

'What's that?' the woman says.

She turns and takes a few steps toward the patio. Sees the doll, takes another step into the shadows.

'Is someone here?'

The Wizard stifles a groan of pleasure. The monster has lured *herself* here. The monster is the agent of her own destruction.

Nancy Venucci sees the writing, glances from the big black letters back to the doll and up again. Shrugs, turns . . .

Sees the gun.

Her mouth opens but only to pant: 'Uh, uh, uh . . .' She steps back, flattens herself against the side of the staircase, clutches her pocketbook to her chest.

The Wizard aims the gun at her mouth.

I won't tell them about Daddy, I promise I won't. Just let me out, please? I didn't do anything, I didn't, and I won't tell, I won't tell . . .

'Please don't . . . I . . . I'll give you everything. Here.' She thrusts out her pocketbook. 'Please, my children . . .'

The Wizard hesitates, the gun trembling at arm's length.

Something moves on the side of the building across the street.

'DO IT. SHE HURT THOSE LITTLE BOYS, YOU SAW IT WITH YOUR OWN EYES.'

The gargoyle's angry eyes are on fire now, but the voice is still calm, reassuring.

'You hurt them,' the Wizard says.

'I don't know what you . . . They're waiting at home . . .'

'SHE'S A MONSTER. KILL HER. DO IT NOW.'

'Hurting little boys . . . it's wrong,' the Wizard says.

'Please, it's my son's birthday—'

'And Will wants to break the eggs.'

The first bullet glances off the monster's left shoulder, shattering the glass in the door behind her. Damn. The monster starts to scream, tries to run around the Wizard. The second shot hits the woman's face. The monster crumples to the ground, leaving blood behind her on the wall and door.

I didn't do anything wrong, Daddy. Please stop, please don't do . . .

269

The Wizard takes a step forward, positions the gun directly over the monster's heart and fires. The body jerks, hits the sidewalk with a thud. Another bullet to the face . . .

The face is gone.

'COVER HER FACE. COVER IT NOW.'

The Wizard moves back, replaces the gun, takes out the can, sprays the monster's face. Now even the irises are black, but still the Wizard sprays . . .

I didn't do anything I didn't do anything I DIDN'T DO ANYTHING.

. . . and sprays.

Black paint drips off the monster's face, mixing with her blood to form a mottled pool on the concrete. The fumes make breathing almost impossible, but the Wizard keeps spraying until the can is empty.

I didn't do anything. I . . .

'. . . didn't do anything.'

The Wizard's words reverberate in the small patio. Time to leave. A quick glance at the crumpled body, at Sam and Will's mom, silent, faceless. *Harmless.* The Wizard puts the can back in the bag, pauses again to take in the scene, hears . . .

Nothing.

The Wizard looks across the street. The gargoyle nods once, then hardens back to stone. After a quick glance up and down the street the Wizard calmly steps on to the sidewalk and heads east.

This time will be easy, the Wizard thinks as their torsos create a delicious friction, here in the stranger's bed, another stranger. This one produced cocaine, an offer almost quaint but not refused. And now the powder is doing its magic, focusing desire, intensifying it.

This time will be easy because Sam and Will are safe, the voices silenced.

But for how long? The Wizard imagines tossing the gun into the Hudson river, pictures it sinking slowly, its job done, joining countless other weapons at the bottom. Acquiring the gun wasn't difficult, a few inquiries uptown, the hastily arranged meeting with the dealer. An idiot – thank God – who handed over the gun, showed the Wizard how to load it, then served as its first target.

The Wizard tries to concentrate on the present. Eyes closed, only moans breaking the silence, the blessed silence. One set of hands kneading breasts, toying with hard nipples, another set stroking the cock, long and rigid. Expert fingers find the clitoris, make it hum. Sweat pours from both bodies. Stroke the cock, strum the clit. Strangers forging intimacy when it counts, where it counts. The Wizard on top at first, now on the bottom. On top again. In control.

Yes, the Wizard likes control, needs it, demands it. And they're always happy to give it away, in bed, no matter what they say.

Both of them are groaning now, panting. No voices. No voices, *please*? Yes, yes. OhmyGodohmyGod. The voices have retreated to where they came from; Sam and Will are safe. The angels are safe tonight.

Oh my God. Oh – MY – GOD.

The Wizard's shriek fills the room. The accomplice comes at the same moment, body shaking violently, eyes suddenly wide with . . . terror.

The Wizard falls off, rolls over. It never felt like that before, never. Had the pain kept such pleasure at bay, all these years? Locked it up like a jewel, beyond reach? Maybe the Wizard should be grateful for the hypnosis. Maybe bringing the pain to the surface – and giving the Wizard the chance to exorcise it – has made intensity like this possible.

The Wizard rolls back to face the stranger, lying on the pillow, panting, eyes wide, haunted, sheet pulled neck-high. After a moment's hesitation the Wizard reaches under the sheet.

'What are you doing?'

The Wizard's fingers start their magic again.

'I *said*, what are you doing?'

The Wizard looks up, says nothing.

'Oh, no, really, no more. That was . . .' Groping for words. 'That was intense. Too intense. Wild. Like . . . an animal. We just met a few hours ago. That was . . .'

The Wizard works faster to kindle a response, but the stranger rolls over, gets out of bed.

'Would you mind leaving now?' the stranger says. 'It's been a long day.'

The Wizard pounds the mattress, fights for breath.

'I mean it. Please leave now.'

The Wizard stands up, grabs pants and sweater. Perhaps another bar, another stranger. It isn't even eleven yet; plenty of time. Not for relief this time, but for pleasure. A more profound . . . satisfaction. The monster is gone, and relief has given way to pleasure. The angels are safe tonight.

Thursday 9 February

27

Nancy Venucci's husband, William Thompson, sobbed into his open hands. Julia focused on the marble fireplace across the living room, the framed photographs lined up on the baby grand piano, the botanical prints above the mantel – anything to avoid facing Thompson himself. This scene was becoming all too familiar, and harder to play each time. She turned to Ray: had visiting the families of the newly-murdered become old hat to him?

'Mr Venucci – excuse me, Mr Thompson . . .' Ray said. 'We have reason to connect your wife's murder to two others that occurred recently in Manhattan. I'm going to ask you to keep this confidential, but I'd like to know if—'

'Two other murders?' William Thompson stared at Ray with his mouth open, his face damp with tears. 'Two *other* murders?'

'It's important that you keep this information confidential.'

Thompson looked dazed, bewildered, but he nodded.

'The other victims were Jessica Forrester and Alicia Frommer.' Ray's voice thickened slightly as he recited the names.

'Never heard of either of them.'

'Are you sure? Think carefully: Jessica Forrester and Alicia Frommer.'

'The police have Nan's . . .' He took a deep breath. 'They

have her address book. You can check for yourself, but I doubt you'll find either name.'

'And you're sure you don't know Ms Mallet.'

Thompson turned and looked at Julia, who forced herself to return his gaze. He shook his head.

'In the police report you said your wife was coming from work.'

'That's right,' Thompson said. 'She usually works . . . she usually worked until around seven.'

Ray had told Julia that Nancy Venucci worked for an accounting firm on Park Avenue. William Thompson was a lawyer with a large midtown firm.

'Did she often stop on the way home from the office?'

'Sure, at the market, the pharmacy. Once she got here there wasn't a free moment to . . .' Again his face disappeared into his hands. Julia glanced at Ray, who nodded back at her.

'We won't keep you any longer,' Ray said.

A second later Thompson looked up. 'It's selfish, it's incredibly selfish, but you know what I'm thinking? I'm thinking how the hell am I going to deal with everything? The children, the apartment, everything. Right now Nan's parents are with Sam and Will, but they aren't staying forever. Christ, Sam has . . . he had a birthday party this week. How am I going to deal with it all?'

Ray stood up. 'For what it's worth, you're probably better off not making any decisions until you've had time to sort things out.'

Thompson nodded. 'She always said I spoiled the kids.' He shook his head slowly. 'I guess I just didn't have the patience for discipline, it usually seemed easiest just to let them have their way.'

'How old are your children?' Julia asked.

'Will's two, Sam's four.'

Emily's age. If Julia were gone there'd be no surviving father to take over, however anxiously. She swallowed and fought back tears. Her love for Em, her solemn commitment, had been reduced – diminished – by a maniac to one simple obligation: stay alive.

'How . . . how are the children doing?' she said.

'I don't think it's really sunk in for them. Maybe for me, either. Nan . . . she was special. Loving and warm, but firm too. Kids at this age can be hard to handle, especially boys. Nan didn't let them get away with much. I used to get on her case for being too hard on them – you know, sometimes she'd lose it, but only when they were acting up. And she was right . . .' He took a deep breath. 'She was right. I was just plain lazy about discipline. I guess I'll have to be stronger now.'

'He's going to be a problem,' Ray said as they drove back to Julia's building. 'I could see it in his expression when I told him about the other two murders. Once the shock wears off he's going to start asking why we didn't publicize the fact that we had a serial killer in Manhattan. He'll need to try to blame this on someone.'

'You can understand his point.'

'Think, Julia. What would have been the purpose of publicizing the connection between the first two murders?'

'I don't—'

'We had no way to narrow down the potential universe of victims. We still don't. If the Wizard was hitting on prostitutes, or NYU students, or off-duty cops, fine, we'd probably go public with what we had.'

'I'm sure you did the right thing, Ray.'

'For all the good it did us.' He punched the steering wheel. 'Once the press gets hold of this . . .'

The city looked grim as they drove the short distance to Julia's building. Store lights and street lamps harshly illuminated people scampering along the filthy sidewalks in the non-darkness, stooping and squinting against the wind like bundled moles. New York was dead. The Wizard had killed it for her.

'Ray, who's Gordon Prescott?'

His expression hardened. 'Why?'

'I was just wondering. This policeman—'

'Why the hell would you bring that up now?'

'I'm sorry. It's an old case I heard about, I didn't know it . . .'

She didn't know *anything*.

Ray stopped the car in front of her building and Julia got out.

'I'm opening up my whole life to you,' she said before closing the door. 'So are my friends. I guess it's asking too much for you to reciprocate.'

'Julia, I—'

'You know something? I can't wait for this case to be over so I won't have to see you any more.'

Julia thanked Pamela for working late, locked the door behind her, and went into Emily's room. She slid a hand under her daughter's head and gently lifted it a few inches from the pillow. She never got used to how soundly Emily slept, nor how much heat she radiated at night. But above all she never got used to that weight, the compact, pressurized, life-affirming solidity that was her daughter. She held Emily's head until her arm ached, then gently let her down.

She heard the gentle rapping on her front door as she headed for the kitchen to pour a drink. She looked through the peephole.

'I was afraid the doorbell would wake up Emily,' Ray said when she opened the door. They'd parted just fifteen minutes earlier.

'I'm tired,' she said. 'What do you want?'

'This.' He pulled her to him but she pressed a hand against his chest before he could kiss her. He grabbed her wrist and forced it down, pulling them close enough for their lips to connect.

In bed a while later she caressed the back of his head, ran her hands along his chest, his back, his legs.

'What's this?' Her finger circled a small, perfectly round scar on Ray's left thigh.

'Bullet wound.'

She ran her finger over the scar, pressed it gently. 'Tell me about it.'

He shook his head and buried his face in her neck. She closed her eyes and heard his breathing quicken, felt him harden against her leg. His hands played across her shoulders, her breasts.

She opened her eyes and tugged at his arms. He glanced up at her.

'What's the matter?'

His eyes were so plaintive, so earnest, she almost said nothing.

'I don't want . . . this to be like the other time.'

'But I thought . . .'

She pulled him on top of her, clenched her hands behind his lower back. When he entered her she squeezed her eyes shut and moaned. He put his tongue in her ear, ran it down her neck and began thrusting, slowly at first, then faster. She came with an intensity that astonished her.

'Come inside me,' she whispered in his ear as he continued thrusting. She ran her hands along his damp shoulders, his back, grasped his buttocks and pulled him deeper in. 'Come inside me.'

But *she* came instead, a second time, with even greater intensity, calling out his name as she fought the air. Her toes curled, her whole body felt . . .

He rolled off her on to his back, eyes staring at the ceiling.

'Ray, what's the . . . Why didn't you . . .'

'Forget it, okay?'

Still breathing heavily, she touched his chest, ran her hand down towards his stomach, but he picked up her hand and moved it to her side.

'Please. Tell me what's wrong.'

'Wrong? You sounded pretty content just now.'

She rolled over, away from his anger. 'I need to . . . give you something. I . . .'

I don't deserve you.

'You have to believe me, Julia. I'm okay with this.'

'I'm not.' She stood up and put on a robe. 'You're holding something back,' she said. 'Why are you like this? Why is it that I can *feel* you wanting me, and . . . you won't?'

He got up and began buttoning his shirt.

'Is it because you're still technically married? Everything's okay as long as you don't actually come?'

'Stop it, Julia.'

'*Answer me.*'

'Our sex life, mine and Dolores's, wasn't exactly magical. She's seeing a shrink, all right? This wasn't easy for her either. Is that what you wanted to know?'

'I . . .'

'I'm falling in love with you, Julia.'

She grabbed on to a chair back.

'Dolores wanted to start a family. We even talked to a therapist, since I wasn't sure I was ready – I wasn't sure the two of us were going to make it, which is why I don't . . . Well, that's the prevailing theory.'

'Which you don't buy.'

'Right.'

'Then *what*?'

'Can't we drop it?' He put on his coat and walked to the door.

Might as well let him go – she was long past kidding herself that all this man or that man needed was the right word from her, the soothing gesture, the heartening response. 'You should wear a sign,' Gail had told her years ago, back when she still had a sex life. 'Mercy fucks on the house.' Well, for almost five years she'd put everything into saving herself and her daughter. There just wasn't any room left over for Ray Burgess.

'Do you trust me?' she asked.

He turned to look at her.

'Do you?'

'Of course.'

'Because maybe Dr Turner's right, maybe I am the Wizard. Is that what's scaring you, Ray? That once you really let yourself go with me I'll blow your face away?'

The front door slammed shut.

It was just ten o'clock, and she felt light years away from sleeping. In the kitchen she made herself a Scotch and water, took one sip, and poured the rest down the sink. She watched the local news report on television, then went to her bedroom. She was unbuttoning her blouse when Emily walked in.

'Sweetie, what's the matter?'

'I had a bad dream.'

Emily never had nightmares. Julia sat on the side of the bed and lifted her daughter on to her lap.

'What was it about, Em?'

Emily buried her face in Julia's shoulder. 'I couldn't find you, Mommy.'

Julia squeezed her tight. 'I'll always be here when—'

'But I looked everywhere. And I called your name.'

'Well . . .' A vision of shattered glass, hands fending off a plunging hammer. Julia fought to keep it together. 'You must have woken up before you found me. Now, tomorrow's a school day . . .'

Emily was practically asleep a few minutes later when Julia lowered her on to her bed. She changed into shorts and a T-shirt, dragged a chair across her bedroom, stood on it and removed a philodendron from a ceiling hook. She got the small punching bag from the closet, stood up on the chair again, and fastened it to the swivel hook. A minute later she flexed both hands – the cloth wraps felt snug, not too tight – got back on the chair, and began firing punches.

She attacked the bag with the heel of her hand, left then right then left then right. The bag clattered in a steady beat as it bounced off her fists and hit the ceiling. *Rap-ap-ap, rap-ap-ap, rap-ap-ap*. Faster now, and harder. Good thing the two bedrooms didn't share a wall. Emily loved to dance around the room, trying to keep pace with the popping rhythm, but she needed her sleep.

'*I couldn't find you, Mommy*.' She wouldn't let the Wizard, her job problems, poison Emily's life any longer. She owed her at least that.

She felt better now, stronger – working out with the bag was always better than alcohol. Strange, to feel restless now. Ray's . . . reluctance had left her wired. What the hell was she doing with him?

Rap-ap-ap, rap-ap-ap, rap-ap-ap.

A minute later a faceless image of the Wizard penetrated the high. Shit. She hit faster, still in rhythm, the bag a dark blur. How could anyone she knew be . . .

Rap-ap-ap, rap-ap-ap, rap-ap-ap.

And yet the Wizard was inside each of them, waiting, hungry. Martin's Wizard craved money. Paula's craved . . . peace, the easy camaraderie that had united them all back at Madison, a

lifetime away from Park Avenue. Marianne's craved power –
she thrived on it, even fucked it. Richard's was starving for
love and stuffing himself with food. Gail? Her Wizard craved
connection, desperately craved it, a genuine yet always elusive
human contact beyond the herbs and spices she obsessed herself
with. Jared used his physical beauty to humiliate pathetic,
desperate men. Was it power he craved, or revenge?

Rap-ap-ap, rap-ap-ap, rap-ap-ap.

What does your Wizard crave, Julia? Money . . . peace . . .
power . . . love . . . connection . . . revenge? All six, perhaps?

Rap-ap-ap, rap-ap-ap, rap-ap-ap.

Think of the victims. The Thompson children, Sam and Will.
Those wailing Forrester kids – how long would she hear their
howling? Motherless children, all four of them. Two bereaved
husbands, neither of them up to coping with single parenthood.
Both seemed frantic at the prospect. Then there were the Eastons,
panicking at the loss of the no-nonsense Alicia Frommer.

Rap-ap-ap, rap-ap-ap, rap-ap-ap.

Cold sweat glazed her forehead. Her hands worked the bag
on their own. *Rap-ap-ap, rap-ap-ap, rap-ap-ap.*

Images floated by, faces, eyes. She hit faster, harder. And
still saw the faces, the eyes. Not the victims – though she'd
seen their photos often enough in newspapers, on television, in
silver frames on bookcases, pianos, end tables.

The faces belonged to the two husbands, their grief all but
consumed by panic at being left behind. The real strength in
those families had been the three dead women, the tough ones.

Rap-ap-ap, rap-ap . . .

Jessica Forrester in the elevator, ground floor, Julia pressing
the open-door button. One son in Jessica's arms, the other
refusing to get on. 'Get in here this instant.' An embarrassed
smile for Julia. 'Get in here now.' A step forward, freehand
grabbing the boy, yanking him into the elevator, his head grazing

the edge of the cab. Instant wailing. 'Will you press twelve, please?' to Julia, voice trembling.

Rap-ap-ap, rap-ap . . .

She dropped her hands. 'Oh my God.'

The bag stuttered on its own for a few seconds before coming to rest.

How had they missed it?

She jumped off the chair and fumbled through her purse for Ray's home number – she'd unwrap her hands later. He answered on the second ring.

'I figured it out,' Julia said. 'I know what the three victims had in common.'

28

'Remember how the husbands described their wives?' Julia said. 'Strict disciplinarians, no-nonsense types.'

'So?'

'Remember Hugh and Martha Easton describing Alicia Frommer as strict? All three women were tough on their children.'

'Is that so unusual?'

'It's practically the only thing they mentioned about the women, that they were tough on the kids. I mean, these two husbands are in the depth of grief – don't you think it's odd for both of them to mention something like that? Both husbands, and the Eastons, said that they weren't nearly as hard on the kids as the three victims.'

'So what you're saying is, the Wizard's knocking off strict women?'

She was *right* about this, never mind his sarcasm.

'Didn't you say that the Wizard seems to be punishing his victims? I think he's punishing them for what they did to the children.'

A long pause.

'Ray, I know I'm on to something. Since Jessica Forrester was killed I've had this nagging suspicion that I know something about her. Just now I remembered.' She told him about the

285

incident she'd recalled while working out, the way Jessica had practically yanked her son's arm out.

'But killing these women because they were disciplinarians seems kind of a stretch.'

'If you dig around a little bit more you might find that it goes deeper than just discipline.'

'Abuse?'

'Maybe.' She hated to defame the women, victims themselves. But the bullets in the face, the black paint – the Wizard hadn't just killed those women, he'd *punished* them.

'I don't know,' Ray said. 'It makes sense in a way, but there's still something missing. Assuming you're right, how did the Wizard find out that all three women were child abusers? None of your friends works in a family service clinic, anything like that.'

It always came back to her friends. Sometimes she managed to forget that learning the identity of the Wizard might be more painful than not knowing.

'So maybe the Wizard just *suspects* these women,' she said. 'Sees something that raises suspicion of abuse. We're not talking about somebody who's sane and logical, after all. If the Wizard was abused as a child . . .'

'I'll ask around, see if there were any complaints about physical abuse involving the women. It still doesn't explain the attack on your car.'

His voice on the phone was deep but somehow hollow, as if they were speaking over a great distance. A map of the city formed in her mind: Ray out in Queens, Emily asleep, here on the West Side, her mother across town, the Wizard . . .

'Remember what I told you about Marianne?' Julia said. 'About her being in New York for that gallery show?'

'I looked into it.'

'Well, it turns out she was in New York the night—'

'. . . Alicia Frommer was killed. She was traveling under the senator's secretary's name. Working overtime.'

Julia sat on the edge of the bed and rested her elbows on her knees. 'Wait a minute, you *knew* that already?'

'Her alibi's not water-tight – Alicia was killed while Ruth Rinaldi was on the way to a fund-raising dinner. Your friend was alone.'

Your friend. To hell with mentioning Ruth Rinaldi's visit. Julia could have secrets, too.

'We have to treat this delicately, given who she is,' Ray said. 'We know they were in New York on Tuesday and Wednesday night. We had Marianne watched while she was in town. She's in the clear for Nancy Venucci's murder – unless she slipped away while we thought she was still in the hotel. It's a big hotel; there are ways to get in and out without anyone noticing.'

It was bad enough being betrayed by Marianne. But couldn't Ray have told her about the affair, so she wouldn't have had to hear about it from the senator?

'You asked me to help you,' she said quietly. 'But you lie to me—'

'I never lied to you.'

Withheld information, then. And there could be only one explanation for *that*. 'You still think I might be the Wizard.'

'That's ridiculous.'

'Why else would you deliberately keep me in the dark, when I'm in the best position to help you find the killer?'

She walked with the portable phone to her bedroom window, pressed her face to the glass to get a look at the street below. A black four-door sedan was parked across from the front entrance of the building.

'Is someone watching me?'

'An escort—'

'I'm not going anywhere tonight. You knew that.'

'Julia, I'm not in charge of this investigation, I'm on a task force of—'

'There *is* someone following me.' She waited a moment to collect herself. 'Do you really think I could have done those things?'

'No, Julia, of course I—'

She hung up and sat, motionless. Her safety was threatened, her privacy invaded. Even if Ray trusted her, nothing she said or did seemed to convince the police that she wasn't a killer. Only finding the Wizard would do that.

She picked up the phone, pressed redial. Ray answered on the first ring.

'I'll do it,' she said. 'I'll let Stella Turner hypnotize me.'

Friday 10 February

29

'Are you relaxed, Julia?'

She almost laughed in Stella Turner's face. Relaxed? In a windowless conference room on the third floor of the Manhattan Bureau, about to be hypnotized by a virtual stranger, her life and privacy on the line? Relaxed?

'Completely,' she said, glancing at Ray, sitting to the right and slightly behind her. He smiled weakly. They'd talked little in the car ride from her office that afternoon.

'I trust the chair is comfortable?' Turner said. 'We dragged it in from the waiting room downstairs.'

The upholstery was lumpy and damp, the burgundy fabric badly frayed. Worse, sitting in it, Julia's chin barely cleared the top of the table – hardly conducive to the sense of trust that was so vital to a successful hypnosis. Still, they might as well get started, get it over with. She rested her head on the chair back, closed her eyes, crossed her legs at the ankles.

'Fire away.'

Stella Turner coughed. 'Yes, well . . . I want to reaffirm that we will only ask you about the events of the night in question. We will not deviate from that, you have our firm—'

'I understand.'

'And, of course, I will allow you to recall everything that happens while you're in the hypnotic state.'

Julia nodded, eyes still closed. 'I'm feeling my legs relax. I'm feeling the tension leave my legs, the relaxation traveling up my body . . .'

'Sarcasm is *not* conducive to an atmosphere of mutual trust,' Stella Turner said.

'I thought it's called auto-hypnosis.'

'Julia, please, try to work with Dr Turner.' With her eyes closed, Ray's voice sounded distant and thin.

Julia shifted on the chair, digging in.

'I want you to . . .' Another shallow cough from Dr Turner. '. . . feel yourself relax . . . feel the tension drifting away. Listen only to my voice, nothing else, as your legs begin to relax, the tension begins . . .'

The identical technique. There were half-a-dozen induction methods; why the hell did Herr Doktor Turner have to choose this one?

'. . . Relax your arms now, feel the tension drift away as you focus on my voice, my voice alone, your arms are . . .'

Christ, it was working. Her legs felt like they were evaporating, her arms heavy, tired – but somehow weightless. She'd always assumed she'd be impervious. The control freak.

'. . . Listen to your own breathing, slowly breathe in, breathe out, clear your mind of all thoughts but the sound of your breathing. Breathe in, breathe . . .'

The tidal whoosh of breathing . . . the doctor's voice like a low, soothing hum . . . head wobbly, listing to the side . . . sensibility leaving her mind and body in a long, slow sigh . . .

'Is she under?' Ray whispered.

'Let's see. Julia, when I clap my hands your arms will rise in front of you. They will be like steel, completely rigid; no matter how hard I push them down you will not be able to lower them until I clap a second time. Do you understand?'

Julia nodded. Stella Turner clapped, Julia's arms levitated to a horizontal plane.

'Ray, perhaps you'd like to do the honors.'

He stood and crossed the room, then hesitated. He'd touched her before, God knows he'd touched her before – but this simple act, pushing down her arms, felt wrong, a violation.

'Ray?'

He pressed on her arms. 'They're completely rigid.'

'Try again.'

He pressed – any harder and her arms would snap.

'Fine,' Stella Turner said with a tiny grin of satisfaction. 'Julia, I want to take you back to the night of your thirty-fifth birthday party. When I clap my hands you will be back at your party, in your apartment. I want you to tell me everything that is happening, leaving nothing out, omitting not one detail.'

When Stella Turner clapped Julia opened her eyes, but didn't speak right away; for a moment Ray thought she wasn't going to talk at all. Then her voice emerged, faint and monotone, barely hers.

'Paula and Martin . . . first ones. A bottle of wine, Bordeaux, Pauillac, very expensive . . .'

And so it went, for almost an hour, Julia reciting the events of the evening in that droning voice, squinting now and then as if watching a videotape of the event. New details emerged – that they'd all gotten stoned, that Marianne and Gail had fought over the framed photograph of the seven of them. But nothing that seemed to point to one person's guilt.

'Now, Julia, I want to ask you about the night *after* your party.'

Ray looked at Turner and shook his head. They'd promised Julia there'd be no excursions beyond Saturday night. The doctor's expression remained resolute as she pressed on.

'What did you do on the Sunday evening after your party?'

'I was home,' Julia said. 'With Emily. We watched a video.'

'Are you sure you stayed home the entire night?'

'Stella, we promised her we weren't going to—'

'We watched *The Wizard of Oz*,' Julia said.

'The Wizard?' Stella glanced at Ray, eyebrows arched, then back at Julia. 'Is that a favorite of yours?'

An almost childish grin formed on Julia's lips as she nodded.

'Julia, tell me what you know about Jessica Forrester.'

'She lives in my building, two boys. She's dead.'

'Before she died, what did you know about her?'

'Her boys were very difficult.' Ray heard an uncharacteristic primness in Julia's voice.

'In what *way* difficult?'

'You know, noisy, wild. Emily was afraid of them. Once the little boy . . .'

'What about the boy, Julia?'

'He . . . he pushed Emily away, in the elevator; she wanted to press the buttons but he wouldn't let her.'

'That must have been very upsetting to Emily.'

Julia nodded.

'Upsetting to you too, Julia?'

Julia didn't respond.

'Did the little boy's pushing Emily upset you, Julia?'

'A little, I guess,' Julia said.

'Just a little?'

'I don't like it when people hurt Emily.'

'Did you want to punish the little boy, Julia? Because of what he did?'

Julia waited a moment to respond. Ray leaned toward her, held his breath. Finally, she shook her head.

'Discipline is good for a child.' The prim voice again.

'What *kind* of discipline, Julia?'

Julia shook her head, slowly at first, then more emphatically.

Stella Turner frowned. 'I see. What about Alicia Frommer? Did you ever meet Alicia Frommer?'

Julia looked at Stella Turner as if puzzled by the question.

'Julia, did you ever meet Alicia—'

'She's . . .'

'She's what, Julia?'

'She's dead.'

Ray saw a tear escape one eye. 'Stella, let's stop here.' He put a hand on Julia's shoulder.

'Why are you crying, Julia?'

Julia shook her head quickly.

'Why are you crying? Do you feel responsible for Alicia's death?'

'No! I . . . I . . .' Her head flailed from side to side. 'I didn't do anything, I—'

'Julia, did you kill Alicia Frommer? DID YOU?'

'No, no, no, NO!'

'I insist that you be completely honest with me, Julia. Did you kill—'

'I DIDN'T DO ANYTHING!' Julia was clutching the arms of the chair as if afraid of being hurled from it.

Stella Turner looked at Ray, a glint of panic in her eyes. 'This has gone far enough,' she said. 'Julia!' Turner clapped her hands. 'Julia, when I clap my hands again you—'

'I didn't *do* anything I didn't *do* anything I didn't—'

'Julia, when I clap my hands again you will close your eyes and fall into a deep sleep.'

Stella Turner grabbed Julia's shoulders, shook her, then let go and clapped her hands sharply. Julia's eyes closed, her body slowly relaxed, became stationary.

Turner took a deep breath. 'I'm going to count back from ten to one. When I reach one . . .'

* * *

Julia squinted into the sharp light, stretched her neck, and gradually found Ray, then Stella Turner, both watching her.

'Did I . . . did it . . .?'

Turner nodded. 'You were a perfect subject, Julia.'

'We talked . . .' Julia cleared her throat, sat up. 'We talked about that night.'

'You provided new details,' Ray said. He sounded stiff, nervous, his eyes avoiding hers. 'Nothing earth-shattering.'

'You asked about the night after the party, about Jessica Forrester, about Alicia . . .'

'For background,' Ray said quickly. 'In case there was a connection you weren't aware of.'

'*Consciously* aware of,' Stella Turner added.

Julia stared at Ray a few moments. 'That wasn't part of the deal, Ray. And you know it.' She stood up and grabbed the conference table while a wave of dizziness washed over her.

'Did I kill them?' She glanced at Stella Turner, then back to Ray. 'Well, *did I*?'

At least they had the decency not to answer. Julia grabbed her purse and briefcase and left the room.

She saw the boxy blue four-door sedan parked in front of Manhattan North – they might as well paint 'Undercover Police Cruiser' on the side.

Lou LaVigna quickly turned off the radio when she got into the passenger seat.

'I should have said something before . . .' LaVigna's face was bright red. 'You're supposed to be in the back.'

'Does it matter?'

Lou flinched at the edge in her voice. And they said hypnosis was supposed to relax you.

'Well, I guess not,' he said. 'Are you going home?'

Not yet. She needed to work off steam, lots of it. She gave

him the address of an aerobics studio in her neighborhood. Carlos couldn't take her until seven, and she wanted to spend the evening with Emily.

He pulled into the early rush-hour traffic.

'How'd you end up with this assignment, Lou?' Trying to lose the anger, focus on someone else's life for a change.

'New kid on the block. Protective custody isn't exactly what I had in mind when I got my detective's shield.' He glanced at her. 'Not that I'm complaining.'

'I suppose they told you I'm also a suspect. Apparently I destroyed my own car in some sort of rage.'

LaVigna fought back a grin. 'I wouldn't be here if *someone* didn't believe you.'

'Not only that, but I have these blackouts. I murder women, blow their brains out, and can't even remember I did it. Three women in less than two weeks. What do you think of that, Lou?'

'My orders are to protect you,' he said without looking at her.

'How old are you?'

'Twenty-six.'

'Married?'

He shook his head.

'Girlfriend?'

His eyes flicked at her. 'No.'

'Live by yourself?'

'With my mom and dad. How come you're asking me so many questions?'

'Shouldn't I get to know the guy who's supposed to be saving my life?'

He glanced at her and smiled nervously. Julia looked out of the window at Amsterdam Avenue sailing by, an unwinding reel of familiar stores and restaurants. How long would it be before she felt safe on these streets again?

'Do the police have a lot of people working on this case, Lou?'

'There's about twenty, twenty-five guys on the task force.'

'Detective Burgess is a senior detective, right?'

'Detective first grade.'

'Why did they assign him to me then? I mean, out of twenty-five cops, why him?'

LaVigna shrugged and changed lanes.

'Lou, don't tell me *you* think I'm a murderer.'

'Oh, no, I—'

'Then tell me why Detective Burgess was assigned to me.'

'Well . . . you see, a lot of the guys, some of the senior detectives, even Dave McCarty, Ray's partner, they don't really buy the hypnotism angle. Some of them are pissed off, working twenty-four-hour coverage on your friends and all. Someone gets killed, like that woman in your building, neighbors come out of the woodwork with theories. Not that *I'm* pissed off.' He glanced at her. 'Just some of the detectives on the squad.'

'Wait a minute, what does their not believing my angle have to do with my being assigned Detective Burgess?'

He stared resolutely ahead.

'Please tell me, Lou. It's important to me.'

'Burgess had some . . . problems a while ago.'

'Gordon Prescott?'

'I really can't talk about it, ma'am.'

Back to ma'am again.

'Was Detective Burgess assigned to me as a kind of punishment?'

'Someone had to talk to you, cover the hypnotism angle. No one at North wanted to do it, is all. Burgess hadn't been on any big cases since Gordon Prescott. So they gave you to him.'

Because they don't believe me . . . and they no longer trust him.

'Shit.'

'Ma'am?'

Julia banged a fist against the door.

'I mean – Julia?'

The Forresters' babysitter let Ray and Dave McCarty into the apartment. Cynthia Maynard was twenty-five: tall, angular, dark brown skin. She wore a white sweater and tight blue jeans, her hair corn-rowed flat against her head, gold and silver beads at the tips.

'Mr Forrester is not here,' she said in a lilting Caribbean accent. Ray heard a television set from somewhere in the apartment, two boys arguing about something.

'We checked with him at the office,' Dave said. 'He told us we could ask you a few questions.'

She looked worried but stepped aside to let them in.

'Our report says you're from Trinidad,' Ray said after she'd closed the door. She'd given a statement the morning after Jessica Forrester was murdered.

She nodded, almost imperceptibly, took a step back. The report also indicated no green card.

'Did you know a woman named Alicia Frommer, also from Trinidad?'

She looked from one detective to another, shook her head.

'Positive?' Ray said. He handed her a photo of Alicia. She stared at it a few moments before giving it back.

'I don't know her. Is she—'

'Take another look.'

She complied, shook her head a moment later.

Ray studied her a beat as she kneaded her hands in front of her chest, eyes glancing everywhere but at the two cops. Nervous, high-strung – but probably telling the truth. There were tens of thousands of Trinidadians in New York; and Alicia had lived in Manhattan, Cynthia in Queens. Later, they'd talk to her neighbors, interview friends, see if any of *them* remembered seeing her with Alicia Frommer. He doubted they would. Still, Trinidad was the one connection between the two victims, however tenuous.

The hypnosis session with Julia had been a bust – though Stella Turner couldn't stop talking about Julia's apparent guilt over Alicia Frommer's death.

'You ever run into Julia Mallet, lives upstairs in this building?' Ray said.

She shook her head slowly. 'I keep to myself, me and the boys, we—'

'She has a five-year-old daughter, Emily,' Dave said.

'Four-year-old,' Ray said. Dave shot him a look.

'Maybe I see her in the elevator, I don't—'

'She ever been in this apartment?' Dave said. 'Maybe she had a playdate with the Forrester kids.'

'I don't think so.'

'Mind if we take a look around?' Ray said.

'I should call Mr Forrester, see if it's okay.'

But Ray and Dave were already in the living room. Opening drawers might get them in trouble, looking around probably wouldn't. Cynthia Maynard hovered in the doorway, still kneading her hands.

'Let's go,' Dave said. 'This is a goddamn waste of time.' He checked his watch.

'The first victim is always—'

'I know, I know – the richest source of clues. It's the first victim gets the serial started, whets his appetite. But this case doesn't follow the rules, Ray.' Dave took a breath. 'And neither do you.'

'What's that supposed to mean?'

Dave glanced back at Cynthia Maynard, lowered his voice.

'You and Julia Mallet – you think I'm blind?'

Ray continued to pace the room, not really looking for anything now. Dave grabbed his shoulder, stopping him.

'We're partners, Ray. You betray the force, you betray me. Our job is to—'

'No sermons, okay?'

'Stop fucking her, Ray. She's not worth it.'

'I'm not fucking her,' he said softly. *At least, technically I'm not.*

Dave looked at him a long while, his face so full of disappointment and hurt that Ray had an urge to hug the guy. After he decked him.

Dave checked his watch again. 'Let's get out of here.'

Ray held up a hand. The guy probably couldn't wait to get back to paradise, his perfect wife, four girls: Randolph, Ronald, William, and Nicholas.

'There's nothing here,' Dave said as he left the room.

But Ray had already given up looking for clues – the apartment had been picked over the morning after the murder. Right now he was looking for something askew, some reassuring testament to the absence of Jessica Forrester. They walked to the kitchen, glanced into the boys' room, into the master bedroom, where the kids were watching television. Beds made, toys picked up, dishes clean. Perhaps no parent was indispensable, provided they had the right 'help' on board. No wonder the Eastons had panicked at losing Alicia Frommer.

'Kind of creepy, how together it looks,' Dave said as they crossed the lobby. The doorman nodded at Ray; with the Forresters and Julia Mallet living here the building was practically Ray's second home.

'Worse than the crime scene,' Ray said. Victims' houses always were, a week, a month after the murder. Like looking out from inside a funeral limo – you couldn't believe how the world went on spinning.

'I'll take the subway home,' Ray said on the sidewalk. 'You go on home in the car.'

'You sure? I could—'

'Ray!'

They both turned.

'Shit,' Ray muttered. Dolores jogged towards them, waving.

'Hello, Dolores,' Dave said. She kissed him on the cheek, stepped toward Ray, then fell back a few feet.

'What are you doing here?' Ray said as evenly as he could.

'I found a new apartment, out on Gerald Street, but the landlord wants you to co-sign the lease, on account of I—'

'Who told you I was here?'

She dug into her pocketbook and fished out a crumpled piece of paper. 'Here it is! All you have to do is sign, Ray, at the bottom. Near the X.'

'Who told you, Dolores?'

'I have my sources.' She arched her eyebrows.

'But—'

'I need somewhere to live, Ray. Our old place is too big for one person. Too expensive. Here's a pen.'

'This could have waited.' He found the X on the lease, signed his name.

'You're looking good, Dave,' Dolores said, touching his elbow. 'How are your beautiful girls?'

She sounded breathless, as if she were putting an exclamation point after every sentence. She seemed never to blink, and her face was flushed. Some of the anti-depressives she'd been on for the past year made her sluggish, saggy around the mouth. Not this latest one.

'They're great, the girls are great,' Dave said, his hand groping behind him for the door handle. 'I'll give them your regards.' He turned, opened the door, and almost dived into his car.

'Shall we share a subway, Ray?' Dolores said as Dave pulled away.

Shall we?

'Dolores, I . . .' He hesitated, saw the hungry expectation on her face, caught a glimpse of the prettier, happier – genuinely happier – girl he'd married right out of college, and felt a giant sob of regret welling up. Oh, Dolores.

'I'm heading downtown, actually.'

'Oh! Really!' As if he'd said he was heading for Los Angeles. Or Mars.

The separation had been her idea as much as his – he forced himself to remember that fact whenever Dolores seemed especially fragile. But she'd moved in with him directly from her parents' house, never really learned how to survive independently. Being a cop's wife was her career, she hungered for the details, exulted in his every promotion. She hadn't asked to get back together, but she had a way of . . . showing up all the time, as if to reassure herself that he was still part of her life, and she his. And maybe if things hadn't fallen apart sexually, maybe they would still be together, working things out. Though he doubted it.

'Why don't we ride together for a few stops, then?' she said.

'I have an errand to run first,' he said. 'Around the corner.'

'I see.' No exclamation point this time. 'Fine. Take care, Ray.' An edge of anger bubbled through the chemical screen. 'I'll be in touch.' She turned and walked away, heels clicking on the sidewalk.

'Dolores?'

She stopped, spun around.

'You need help moving or anything, call me, okay?'

She stared at him. Her face had fallen, like makeup washing

303

off in the rain. She looked older than her thirty years, tired but not quite defeated. Ray met her gaze and forced a smile. *The separation was your idea as much as mine, Dolores.* For a moment he thought she was going to return the smile, but she merely turned and disappeared around the corner. He let out a long, slow breath.

30

Julia glanced through the large picture window between the aerobics studio and the waiting area and saw Paula, a towel wrapped around her neck, heading for the locker room. With luck she'd be showered and out of there by the time the class was over. The birthday dinner had left a nasty aftertaste.

Forty minutes later Julia was in the steam room. She sat on the tile platform, a club towel wrapped around her torso. After a few minutes the steam thinned out.

'Paula, is that you?'

Paula started. 'Oh, Julia.'

Had Paula been in the steam room all this time – thirty minutes at least?

'What are you doing here so late in the day?' Julia said.

'Couldn't find the time earlier.' Her voice sounded weak.

'Are you all right?'

'Just a little tired. I've probably been in here too long.'

The valve jet hissed out a torrent of hot steam that made conversation temporarily impossible. When it ended the room was opaque.

'I feel awful about the other night,' Paula said through the fog. 'Do you think things will ever be the same for us, once they find out who this killer is?'

'Everybody's so tense right now,' Julia said, 'having to explain our whereabouts.'

'You're probably right. I mean, how many lives can stand up to close scrutiny?'

'Yours would,' Julia said.

'Mine? I'm a housewife, for God's sake.'

'But you never sold out. If you told me back at Madison that I'd make my living pitching fabric softener I'd have moved to Antarctica. Marianne used to be a socialist. Now she works for Ruth Rinaldi. Richard wanted to be a doctor; Jared was going to win an Academy Award; Gail—'

'What about me?'

'You're still . . . you, Paula. That's what makes you special.'

'Just because I won't have my hair permed and talk about homeless shelters at charity dinners?'

Julia laughed. 'Just because you never got sucked into the whole Park Avenue charity-circuit bullshit.' *Even though that's exactly what Martin wants you to do*. 'You may not be editing *Ms* magazine, but you're not being photographed for *Town and Country*, either. That counts for a lot in my book.'

Paula wiped sweat from her forehead and stood up. Even through the steam Julia saw her wobble.

'I think I've had enough.' She opened the door and stepped into the bright light of the shower room.

Julia followed her a minute later and finished showering as Paula was drying off. Two pregnancies had left not a trace – why did Paula hide her shape in baggy sweaters and loose dresses? She smiled nervously at Julia, turned, and wrapped a towel around her torso. She was avoiding eye-contact, but Julia caught her reflection in a mirror as she walked away.

'My God, Paula! What happened to your eye?'

Paula sighed and turned around, giving Julia time to size up the hideous purple half-moon under her left eye.

'I was hoping the steam would soften it a little before I saw the boys at dinner.'

A woman joined them in the shower area. Julia took Paula's arm and led her back to the locker room.

'Who did this to you?' Julia asked.

'What makes you think it was a person?' Paula calmly spun the dial of her combination lock, opened it and started dressing. 'I might have fallen, or walked into something.'

'Like a fist. Was it Martin?'

Paula stared into her locker. It *was* him, Julia thought.

'Why did he do this to you?'

'He's never done it before, Julia. You have to believe me. I couldn't stand it if you thought of me as one of those women who tolerates . . . this.'

Oh, Lord.

'I've known you over fifteen years,' Julia said. 'You wouldn't put up with something like that.'

Probably wouldn't: Paula had made so many sacrifices over the years at the altar of marital stability.

Paula nodded and resumed dressing. 'He's having an affair,' she said. 'Martin is having an affair.'

'I can't believe . . .' Julia stopped herself. *Of course* she believed it. 'How do you know?'

'I guess I've known for a long time. He works late a lot, always has. But the past few years . . .'

'*Years?*'

'The business has gotten so big, the money's been *pouring* in. I just assumed the more he made, the harder he had to work for it.'

'You never confronted him?'

She shrugged, walked to a sink, and began raking a brush through her hair. Julia followed her.

'At some point I decided I didn't want to know. But about

three years ago he hired this Wharton MBA to be his second-in-command. Maybe you remember her from our party last June. Darla Stuyvesant?'

Julia nodded. Darla was about five-ten, very young, very blonde . . .

'She's smart too,' Paula said. 'Martin says she's indispensable to the business, and I believe him. Our income has quadrupled since she came on board. So my husband's mistress may be responsible for putting our children through college.'

She looked into the mirror and touched the bruise gently.

'The detective's visits brought it all out into the open,' she said. 'Except for . . .' She turned to Julia. 'Can you keep a secret?'

Julia sighed and nodded. She was hauling around too many confidences as it was, and could easily guess what was coming.

'The nights of the killings? Martin wasn't home – at least, not until very late. So I . . .' She put a hand in front of her mouth. 'What am I saying?'

'That you lied to the police.'

'He asked me to,' Paula said softly. 'That's when I finally confronted him, after the first murder. It all came out. I even asked him to fire her. *Darla*. He said he couldn't, she was too valuable to the firm.'

She finished applying concealer under her eye and stuffed her gym gear into the locker. 'Tell me something, Julia. What are the chances that Martin will stop sleeping with her while she's still working for him? Long legs, perfect tits . . .'

Julia shrugged. *Not a chance*. 'Why did he hit you?'

'He hasn't stopped coming home late; it's almost like he's rubbing it in my face. I was awake when he got in this morning. After two.' Paula shook her head slowly, as if Martin had walked in with his pants around his ankles. 'I told him that if he didn't fire Darla I'd tell the police he wasn't at home when the murders happened. He said he couldn't fire her. I picked up the phone, said I was calling that detective. He grabbed it from me.' Tears slipped down her cheeks. 'He hit me with it.'

She coughed a few times, then the coughs dissolved into sobs. Julia put her arms around her. She seemed oblivious to the two other women in the locker room, trying with no success to keep their eyes off the scene.

'Why do you think Martin's so worried about your calling the police?' Julia said. 'I mean, if he was with Darla the whole time, and you already know about the affair, what difference does it make?'

Paula pulled away, found a Kleenex in her locker, and blew her nose. 'He says he want to protect her. *Darla*. God, think of it – my husband is having an affair with someone named Darla. A Wharton MBA, no less.'

Martin liked his women smart. Smart and compliant.

'Are you going to leave him?'

'Oh, Julia, you *would* say something like that.'

'But he *hit* you.'

'You have no idea, the compromises people make to stay together. Maybe that's why you never married, because you refused to compromise. You think it's tough raising a daughter on your own? Try living with someone like Martin. But leave him . . .?' She shrugged. 'Where would we live?'

'I was talking figuratively. You could throw him out.'

'He won't leave. He says he's very happy with our life. Anyway, I have a plan. I'm calling the police, that Detective Burgess, first thing tomorrow morning.'

'You don't seriously think Martin—'

'He fucks women, Julia, he doesn't kill them. Anyway, I'm not interested in getting Martin in trouble. I'm hoping to spook Darla Stuyvesant.'

'Spook her?'

'Let the police interrogate her for a little while, then we'll see how interested in Martin she really is. And how interested *he* is.'

'Aren't you afraid of what Martin will do?'

Paula grabbed her purse and headed for the exit. 'I can't afford to be afraid any more, Julia. My marriage, my entire life is at stake.'

Emily spent the evening dashing from the easel in her bedroom to her blocks on the living-room floor to her doll collection arrayed on Julia's bed, repeating the circuit every fifteen minutes or so. By eight o'clock the apartment looked like a toy store after an earthquake, and Emily was still going strong.

At eight-thirty Julia initiated the bedtime ritual with a silent prayer to the god of sleep. She hoisted Emily on to the closed toilet seat so she could brush her teeth facing the mirror. She read her a Curious George book in the living room, then carried her to bed.

'Can I have some apple juice?' Emily said.

'You've had a gallon already today. Anyway, drinking juice in bed is bad for your teeth.'

'I'll get . . . what are they called, Mommy?'

'Cavities.'

Emily nodded solemnly. 'Can I see?'

Julia opened her mouth and let Emily examine the fillings.

'Still want apple juice?' Julia said.

'No way, Jose.'

Julia kissed her, left the room, and wasn't at all surprised when her daughter called out a few minutes later.

'I'm not tired, Mommy.'

It was going to be a long night.

She sat on the edge of Emily's bed and sang two of their

favorites: 'P.S. I Love You' and 'All My Loving'. Emily's eyes were almost closed when the phone rang.

Damn. Julia ran to the kitchen and lifted the receiver during the second ring.

'Hello?'

Click. The line went dead.

Julia slammed down the receiver and practically tripped over Emily in the hallway outside her room.

'Em, I thought—'

'But I'm *not tired*.'

Why fight it? She put *Aladdin* on the VCR and left Emily in the living room.

She finally had time for something she'd been wanting to do all day. She turned on the computer in her bedroom, plugged the phone line into the back of the unit, typed a few simple commands, and entered her password. A high-pitched squeal several seconds later admitted her to the Nexus data base, paid for by Todman DiLorenzo – at least this privilege hadn't been taken away.

She typed 'Gordon Prescott' and waited a few seconds.

'Two matches,' the computer responded, both from the *New York Times*. She clicked the mouse on the first entry, from two years ago, 22 May.

POLICE ARREST MANHATTAN SUPERINTENDENT SUSPECTED IN MULTIPLE SLAYINGS

Manhattan police stumbled on to the scene of a grotesque murder-in-progress, arresting the perpetrator who is suspected in at least three other slayings – but not before he'd killed his latest victim.

Gordon Prescott, 45, resident superintendent at a luxury Manhattan apartment building, had just killed his latest victim, Joyce Shin, 25, of Flushing, Queens, when police stormed his workshop beneath the thirty-story building. Manhattan detective Raphael Burgess, who apparently happened upon the scene earlier, was incapacitated by a bullet wound.

Three prior murders of young oriental women over the past two years have been the focus . . .

Julia clicked the mouse on the 'Done' button and the story vanished. She'd had enough blood and gore lately. She clicked on the second story, which the *Times* had run the following day. It added some details, covered Prescott's arraignment – but didn't mention Ray at all.

She took the cord from the computer's modem jack and snapped it back into the phone.

Did Ray think it was even remotely possible that she was leading two lives: one conscious, normal, the other subconscious, psychotic? Her alibi was a sleeping four-year-old. Still, she had no gun, no black spray paint. No homicidal impulses . . .

Emily was sleeping in front of the television. Julia carried her into her bedroom, gently lowered her on to the bed, and kissed her forehead. She was heading for the kitchen to make a cup of tea when she heard a soft but insistent tapping from the foyer. She stopped a few feet from the front door and listened. Someone was knocking on the door.

'Who's . . .' She cleared her throat and took a breath. 'Who's there?'

'It's Jared.'

'How did you get up here?' she said through the closed door.

'I told the doorman that buzzing you would wake up Emily. Can I come in?'

She felt a powerful reluctance to let him in.

'Julia?'

She unlocked the door, opened it just a foot or so.

He looked dreadful. Two days' worth of beard, bloodshot eyes, and a shirt that looked like it had been slept – no, wrestled in.

'Jared, what's the matter?'

'Aren't you going to let me in?'

Julia hesitated just a second before nodding.

'I'll try not to kill you.' His smile at the black humor was pathetic.

She poured a Scotch for Jared, decided against tea for herself, and led him to the living room.

'Remember the man at the Waldorf?' Jared said. 'He denies ever meeting me. The cops brought me down to the Manhattan North again this morning. They had photos of the guy faxed in from St Louis. Harry something – I forget his last name.' Jared took a swig of Scotch. 'He told me it was Harold. They always make something up.'

'Was it the guy you met?'

'Even on a fax I couldn't miss him. Kind of chubby, with a dimple. He's a lawyer, married with three kids, served a term in the Missouri Senate. Fixated on my armpits, he kept—'

'*Jared.*'

'Sorry.' He drained the glass and held it out to her for a refill. 'He admits to being in New York that night – the hotel gave the cops his name – but says he was alone. He refused to come to New York to make a statement, threatened a lawsuit.'

'Do the police believe him?'

'I don't think so. I mean, where would I have gotten his name? How would I have known he was in New York that night?'

'Why are you so upset, then?'

'Because even if he's lying, even if the cops *believe* he's lying, it still doesn't clear me.'

'Why not?'

'Look, I was with him for three hours that night. He paid triple – four-fifty – wanted to talk, asked me a lot of questions about the other . . . you know, the other guys I see.'

'Three hours,' Julia said.

'Three hours, during which time the woman was killed. And even if the cops believe I was with him, how do they know it wasn't a fifteen-minute quickie? Most guys, once they get off, they start getting shy, maybe a little guilty, they're out of there like—'

'How did you leave it with the police?'

'They let me go,' Jared said with a shrug. 'But they're still having me watched. I told you about the hair they found at the crime scene.'

Julia nodded and looked away.

'At least they aren't pressing me about a hair sample. My lawyer says there's no way I have to give them one. In fact, he thinks they may be bluffing. Anyway, one of the cops started to get kind of tough with me. Not physically, he just threatened to make life difficult, given how I've been making my living.'

He flashed the Jared smile, chilling without the energy behind it. 'When this is all over,' he said, 'I think I might leave New York for a while. I've got a lot of money saved up, and I need to get away from this place.'

'New York isn't the problem.'

'It is for me. I've been in Manhattan fifteen years – every time I turn a corner I run up against some version of myself I can't stomach any longer.'

'As long as you stop . . .'

'Hustling? Might as well call it what it is.'

'Are you thinking of going back to Chicago?'

'My parents have been in Arizona for almost five years. I don't know anyone in Chicago any more.'

'Your sister?'

'She's there, but we don't have much in common. Her husband's a civil engineer, whatever the hell that is. Two cars, three kids, one golden retriever.'

'Still, family—'

'Please, Julia, no lectures on the importance of the family. I had the picture-perfect childhood, so I know what *that's* all about. If I'd gone to law school like my father, maybe we'd still be one big happy family unit. But I chose acting, and he's never gotten over it.'

He took a sip of Scotch and twirled the ice in his glass. 'You know what the worst part of what I do is? I look at someone like my old man and I start to feel sick.'

'Jared . . .'

'No, wait. These men that pay me? Most of them are married. They're fathers, grandfathers some of them, like Harry or Harold or whoever the fuck he is. Pillars of the community, only they get off on licking other men's toes or jerking off while—'

'*Please.*'

'My father looks down on me because I didn't choose to live his kind of life, but after all these years of hustling I know what that life is all about. It's not real, Julia. Nothing is.'

Bitterness had changed his face, revealing a hard, angry core beneath the boyish veneer.

'You see the worst side of mankind, Jared. It's not necessarily representative.'

'No? How the hell would you know? Your whole business is about lying.'

'That's enough.' She walked to the front hallway and began thumbing through several days' worth of unopened mail.

Jared joined her a moment later. 'Look, you don't know what

315

I've seen. A couple of months ago I went to this guy's apartment on the East Side – I remember thinking the place was kind of big for one person. Maybe ten minutes into the session the bedroom door opens and there's this . . . this little girl, standing there, taking it all in.'

'Oh God.'

'Men like that guy on the East Side, like Harold-slash-Harry, they're real scum because they set themselves up in this position where they can look down on everyone else, make everyone else in their life feel like shit, when all the while they—'

'Jared, you're frightening me.'

Sweat lined his forehead. His hand shook, jangling the ice in his glass. 'You know who I really feel sorry for? The children.'

Julia swallowed hard. 'Children?'

'Because they'll always try to live up to something that's not real, never was. I keep picturing that little girl's face as she tried to wrap her little mind around what she was witnessing. I could see the innocence just *draining* out of her.'

'Thinking about children makes you . . . angry,' she said. 'I'm surprised.'

He put down his drink on the hall table. 'I'm full of surprises.'

Julia tried to smile.

'Better get back,' he said. 'Before I'm missed. The idiots watching me haven't caught on – there's a back door to my building that leads to a kind of courtyard. All I have to do is hop a fence, cross another courtyard, and I'm out on the street.'

Julia stepped back. Their faces were just a few inches apart. He smelled of liquor and perspiration and rage.

'If the police really thought you'd killed someone they'd subpoena that guy in St Louis, make him take a lie detector test or something.'

'You're probably right.'

She took his empty glass. All she could think about was his

unexpected and rather fierce concern for children, and the back door to his building.

He leaned over and kissed her gently on the cheek. She closed her eyes and held her breath.

'Thanks for being here,' he said as she showed him out. 'I feel a lot better.'

At least one of them did. She double-locked the door behind him and leaned against it until her breathing was back to normal. She walked to her bedroom, undressed, padded to the bathroom and stared at herself in the mirror for a while. She'd always measured herself against those around her – colleagues, family, but especially her oldest and closest friends, her touchstones. If she were the tree falling on the island, the Madison crowd had always been there to hear the crash. Now it turned out she'd never really known them. Especially Jared. She squinted at her reflection, pulled her hair back into a ponytail. If she didn't really know her closest friends, did she really know herself?

She let her hair fall loose on her shoulders, shivered, and went back to her bedroom. Illuminated only by the small bedside lamp, the room felt isolated and eerie, anything but cozy. She pulled back the bedspread and blanket, and was reaching to turn off the lamp when her heart all but stopped.

Her sheets . . . her white sheets with the pale blue pinstripes . . . her sheets were black, a deep, glossy, wet-looking black. Julia bent over and touched the topsheet, examined the smudge on her fingertip, fought hard for breath. The sheets were still tacky.

She stood there, unable to take her eyes off the bed, groping behind her for the phone, knocking her lamp and a book off the bedside table before she found it.

Someone had been in her apartment, her bedroom. Someone had painted – *spray-painted* – her sheets.

317

31

'You probably think tax law is incredibly dull.'

The Wizard takes a sip of club soda and fumbles for a convincing response. 'It's . . . it's highly intellectual, I always thought.'

The lawyer's eyes widen. 'Almost an art form, in a way – which might explain why it attracts as many women as men these days. I didn't think anyone really understood that, anyone who wasn't a tax attorney. Those of us in the profession, well, we chose it because . . .'

The Wizard tunes out. It's been a long evening. Singles bars aren't what they used to be, what with AIDS and teetotaling health nuts and serial killers . . .

Hah!

There aren't many such places left; the Wizard never hung out in bars anyway. This one, on Second Avenue in the sixties, has been around for years. The clientele looks desperate, like it's been around for *decades*. The Wizard had almost given up when the tax lawyer walked in – attractive, glossy brown hair and eyes, pouty lips. The Wizard likes big, pouty lips.

After the last one, Sam and Will's mom, the impulse to . . . to rescue isn't nearly as strong. Only this morning the Wizard saw a woman on the subway practically yank a little boy's arm out of its socket when he tried to move away from her. A flash of rage, a powerful urge to follow the woman and the boy when they got off at the next stop . . .

But the Wizard remained seated, let the monster and her son walk away.

So why is the Wizard here, tonight, at this has-been fern bar full of has-beens on the make? Because another urge was awakened that night at the party, two weeks and a lifetime ago. Not the need itself – that never completely vanished – but the ability to satisfy that need. Like an itch in the upper back, always there, but inaccessible. And now someone has handed the Wizard a back-scratcher.

'. . . a purity that goes beyond filling out returns. It's almost mathematical, really. You could spot the tax majors in law school, you know. We were the intellectual ones, I always thought, I'm—'

'Are you ready to leave?'

The lawyer looks confused.

'It's just that I'm kind of tired,' the Wizard says. 'I thought maybe we could continue this discussion back at your place. Do you live nearby?'

The lawyer looks tempted but worried. People don't cut to the chase like this any more – men or women.

'Two blocks away.'

The Wizard drinks down the rest of the club soda.

'Let's go.'

It isn't happening. The Wizard gasps for air, both bodies bucking and shimmying on the lawyer's queen-size bed, and inside, deep inside, the Wizard feels . . . nothing. It isn't a question of *coming*. That's inevitable now. It's a question of release, of how the Wizard will feel later. It's a question of silence.

You think that hurt? Try this on for size.

The Wizard feels panic germinating. The voice is back. *Her* voice. And the face, those angry eyes, those thin, flat red lips. Why does the voice always return when the Wizard is so close, so close to . . .

Physical pain is nothing compared to what you put me through. I can't even show my face in public without them whispering. Some of them don't even try to hide it, you know. And you whining here about a tap on the arm. About your father touching . . . Don't you run away from me, GET BACK HERE!

The Wizard reaches over and jerks the belt from the trousers lying on the floor. Leather mesh – nice and supple. The lawyer doesn't even notice, eyes squeezed shut, moaning blissfully. The Wizard is good, no question. Good at pleasuring *other* people.

Stop it, please? That hurts and I . . .

The belt is around the Wizard's neck. Crisscrossing the two ends, the Wizard places the buckle in the lawyer's right hand.

'What the . . .'

The Wizard puts the other end in the lawyer's left hand.

'Pull,' the Wizard says.

'You must be—'

'PULL!'

The lawyer freezes.

Please stop please stop please . . .

The Wizard grabs the belt from the lawyer's hands and yanks both ends, feels it dig in, cutting off air.

'You're sick . . . this is sick.'

The lawyer starts to get up from the bed. Eyes closed, the Wizard senses the movement and locks both legs around the lawyer's lower back. Pulling harder and harder as the belt squeezes the neck, a flash of light behind both eyelids, grasping for air, sucking, sucking, but pulling on the belt at the same time, dimly aware of a gargling sound from the throat.

The lawyer struggles to break free, but the Wizard's legs are locked, rigid.

That hurts, Mommy. That . . .

Silence.

Silence washes over the Wizard with a deep shudder that begins down below and works its way up. Silence. The voice can't reach the Wizard now. Body trembling, back arching, pushing the lawyer up with it, the flashes of light dissolving into a deep, steady wash of purply-black. The Wizard knows, in some vestigially rational part of the mind, that it's time to release the belt. The lawyer has managed to get free, is standing next to the bed, moaning something unintelligible.

Release the belt, *now*.

But still the Wizard pulls on the two ends, lost in a silence that feels pure and timeless.

'Jesus, your face . . . it's white as . . . You're going to . . . give me that . . .'

The Wizard feels the lawyer tugging at the belt. No, no – just a minute more.

'. . . arms like steel . . . give me the belt, now.'

The Wizard feels the belt loosen . . . a surge of light-headedness, a big gasp as air rushes in. 'No, no, not yet . . .' Trying to grab the belt, light flashing across both eyes.

'You need help, serious help!'

Wheezing, panting, coughing. And through it all a realization. The voice will never go away. Those eyes, those lips, that voice – back for good.

'Here, take your clothes and get out of here.'

The Wizard manages to sit up, waits for the dizziness to dissipate, starts to dress, feels a tear escape from one eye.

You should have died, not the other one. Not the angel.

The voice is back. Perhaps it never left. The Wizard's work will continue.

Monday 13 February

32

Julia had spent the entire weekend in her apartment with Emily, three brand-new locks between them and the rest of the world. She hadn't answered the phone, hadn't dared even to order in food. For Emily's sake she'd refused to break down, give in to the powerful sense of terror, or violation. They drew together, watched TV, ate leftovers. By Sunday night she felt as if she'd reclaimed her apartment, if not her life.

She'd called Ray as soon as her fingers were steady enough to push the buttons. He'd arrived twenty minutes later, followed by a phalanx of cops. They'd questioned her for almost an hour – had she told anyone about the Wizard's spray-painted signature? (No.) When had the apartment been empty that day? (At least several hours in the morning and afternoon.) Later they grilled the night doorman, contacted the day man – neither recalled letting anyone up to Julia's apartment, except Jared, of course, and he'd never left Julia's sight. Ray inspected her front door, said her lock might have been picked, but had probably been opened by someone with a key. Who has a key to your apartment, Julia? She'd waited a moment before answering: they all do, she'd said, then ran to her bathroom and slammed the door, wanting to be alone when she lost it completely.

They all do.

She got to the office at ten on Monday morning, having slept at most two or three hours the night before. Lou LaVigna had taken her and Emily to the school, then driven her to the office. Later, he'd take Pamela to pick up Emily, deposit them safely at home. Julia had arranged for Pamela to take Emily to her grandmother's for dinner; Lou would escort them there too.

She stormed past Alison, desperate to be in her office, yet another door shut between her and the world outside.

'You have a visitor,' Alison said meekly from her desk, just as Julia noticed Richard Portland in one of her guest chairs.

Julia sat down in the chair behind her desk, across the room from Richard. He stood up and started across the room, then stopped.

'I need to talk to you. I was afraid if I called . . .' He took a step forward. 'I understand that you and Detective Burgess are . . . friendly.'

'Who—'

'Marianne, actually. We were discussing the case. The papers are having a field day with the story about the Venucci woman; they're even speculating about a connection between her and the first murder. Marianne happened to mention that you and Burgess are . . . seeing each other.'

Julia tapped a pencil point against the desk. How had Marianne figured out that she and Ray . . .? Of course. Ruth Rinaldi no doubt had contacts up and down the police department.

'I didn't realize you and Marianne were close.'

'We're old friends, like you and me.' Another step closer; his fingertips brushed her desk. Richard's shirt had been ironed, his tie was unblemished, and the dark circles under his eyes had lightened. He couldn't have lost more than a pound or two since the birthday dinner, but he looked trimmer. 'I need to talk to you before I talk to Detective Burgess. My lawyer thinks I should just keep my mouth shut. Ever notice how lawyers always tell *you* to shut up, and they never do? Anyway, I thought I'd see what you think.'

'About what?'

'Well, during the most recent attack – murder, actually – I wasn't alone. I was with Kim. We're getting back together.'

Julia let the pencil drop. 'You *are*?'

'In a way, I have this murderer to thank. I've been worried about being alone so much. It makes me a suspect, though none of us understands why in the world anyone even thinks we're involved. You haven't really been forthcoming about that, Julia.'

'Hold on, Richard. Kim's getting back with you so you'll have an *alibi*?'

'Of course not. But the murders, the suspicion, it's all made me realize that I can't stand being alone. I'm not good at it.'

'And Kim? What about the man she—'

'Over. It was never serious.'

Julia noticed a plain white envelope on her desk. No name, no postmark. She tore it open and saw a newspaper clipping inside. 'But you haven't explained why you're here,' she said as she pulled out the article and glanced at the headline: 'Cop Blunder Called Honest Mistake'.

'When Detective Burgess questioned me,' Richard said, 'I didn't mention being with Kim.'

'Why the hell not?'

The article was from the *New York Post*, of 30 May, two years ago.

'Well, you see, Kim and I talked things over, and agreed to get back together . . . eventually. She was meeting a friend that night, at her health club, so I left around six, six-thirty.'

'Then you weren't with her when the murder occurred. Richard, I . . .'

She saw his name, midway down the article.

Detective First Grade Raphael Burgess, who was injured in the incident, proceeded without authorization, the Internal Affairs report states. However, the investigation concluded that waiting for backup would not have resulted in a 'materially different outcome'. The victim, Joyce Shin, died from strangulation before officers from the 20th precinct arrived.

'But I *was* with Kim. She told me it was over with this other person – but Kim's idea of exercise is running the food processor on high speed. Sorry. So I followed her.'

'Did you put this on my desk?' She held up the envelope and clipping.

He shook his head. 'I *said*, I followed her.'

'Oh, Richard.'

'No, you don't understand. She *did* go to the health club. She met a woman there.'

'Did she see you?'

'At the health club?' He shook his head.

'Then you really don't have an alibi.'

She put the clipping back in the envelope. The *Post* wasn't on the Nexus data base, and the *Times* hadn't mentioned an Internal Affairs investigation. Who wanted her to know about it?

'Was this on my desk when you got here?'

He shrugged. 'Your detective friend keeps asking questions about Kim, about our marriage.'

'Just because you're divorced—'

'Separated.'

'Doesn't mean you killed anyone.'

Alison leaned in from the hallway. 'There's a Steve Franklin on the phone for you. From the *Daily News*.'

'Send him to media,' Julia said.

'He said it's personal.'

'Tell him I'll call back. Oh, Alison? Did you see who left this envelope?'

'It was on your desk when I got here at eight-thirty.'

'Everything's going great again,' Richard said. 'I thought I'd lost Kim for good – men were swarming around her, she's a beautiful woman, as you know.'

Attractive, perhaps even pretty. Beautiful? Maybe on a very good day.

'But now I'm being questioned about these killings . . . I don't want to blow it, Julia. What do you think? Should I do what my lawyer says and keep quiet – or tell the police about my alibi?'

Near-alibi.

'I'd tell Detective Burgess what happened. But if your lawyer thinks otherwise . . .'

He stood up, leaned over her desk. 'You could talk to Burgess. You're sleeping with him, aren't you? That's what Marianne said. He'll listen to you, Julia, he'll believe you if you tell him what I told you, including the part about following Kim to the health club.'

Sleeping with him? Rinaldi's spies might have seen Ray entering her building, but they couldn't know she was sleeping with him. And 'sleeping with' might be technically correct, but it was hardly an accurate description of their relationship.

'I have an appointment.' Julia checked her watch. 'In five minutes.'

'You'll talk to him?' Richard said.

Julia sighed and stood up. 'Just call him, Richard, tell him exactly what you told me.'

Richard started for the door, then stopped and turned. 'You're no friend to any of us,' he said. 'You know what happened at your party that's setting them on us and you're not saying.'

As soon as he was gone Julia called the reporter.

'My contacts at Manhattan North tell me there may be a serial at work,' Steve Franklin said. 'Nothing concrete yet, but your name keeps coming up. What gives?'

'Good question,' Julia said. 'Only I don't know the answer.'

'Who is the Wizard?'

'What—'

'I keep hearing about some wizard.'

'I don't – I haven't the slightest idea what you're talking about, okay?'

'Who is the Wizard, Julia?'

She hung up.

Lou LaVigna was leaning against the side of his car when she left the building at five. She gave him Gail's address as she got in the front seat. She had to tell someone about Richard's visit, Martin's affair, the ever-expanding soap opera she seemed to be at the heart of. She'd been too distracted all day by ad business to deal with the terror that was growing like a tumor inside her. Maybe she didn't *want* to deal with it.

'Mind if I ask who you're visiting?'

'A friend.'

'Mind if I—'

'Yes, I do mind,' she said softly.

She saw his face redden from the neck up.

'Sorry, Lou, but I don't have a lot of privacy lately.' Even her bedroom had been contaminated.

They reached Park Avenue and headed uptown.

'How old's your daughter?' he asked her after a few blocks of silence.

'Four.'

'I guessed three and a half. My sister has a three-year-old girl.'

'I figured you had some experience with little girls. Emily likes you.' She smiled for the first time that day.

'Are you divorced?' he asked.

'Never married.'

He stared resolutely ahead, but the telltale blush was back. She'd have to invite him the next time she played poker.

'Do you follow basketball, Lou?'

They stopped for a light.

'Sure.'

'I get season tickets to the Knicks, through the agency. When this is all over, how would you like two courtside seats?'

He looked over at her and the redness deepened.

'For you and a friend, Lou.'

He exhaled audibly. 'That would be great.'

Ten minutes later she was drinking Chardonnay in Gail's living room.

'Kim will never take him back,' Gail said. 'She's in love.'

Julia groaned.

'You really didn't know?' Gail said. 'It's some guy who used to live on their street. He and his wife separated last year.'

'How did you find out?'

'I stopped by their house in Larchmont a year or so ago, on my way back from shopping at Stu Leonard's in Norwalk. I always liked Kim – she never seemed overwhelmed by the six of us, and God knows she did wonders with Richard. Remember his beard!'

'Rasputin with glasses.'

'Oh, God, those nerdy horn-rims? Anyway, I stopped by, and this other guy was there. In the middle of the day. Kim answered the door in a bathrobe. I nearly died of embarrassment. If you ask me, he went up there to beg for another chance. If he thinks she'll lie to save his ass he's dead wrong. More wine?'

Julia nodded and headed for the bathroom, picking her way around the piles of clothes, the stacks of magazines, the shoes of every color and style.

'Sorry about the mess,' Gail said when they were back in the living room. 'My editor's threatened *in writing* to cancel my contract if I haven't delivered the manuscript in two weeks.'

'It's not like you to be this late.'

Gail sighed. 'My heart's not in it any more, I guess. I mean, what's the point?'

Julia glanced at the wall unit across from the sofa. Seven or eight Mrs G books were lined up on a shelf. On the same shelf, in a brass frame, was the original cover artwork for the basil volume – plump, bespectacled Mrs G, snipping a sprig with kitchen shears. Julia looked back at Gail, thin and stylish in a big hand-knit sweater and black leggings, and couldn't help smiling.

'You should be proud of what you've done,' she said.

'Proud of *recipes*? Think about it, Julia. The world is falling apart all around us, and I spend days and nights cooking.'

'The world isn't falling apart,' Julia said.

'No? Well, maybe it should be. I was in London when the IRA was putting bombs in mailboxes and left luggage compartments. You never knew when the next one was going to detonate, or where. God, that was amazing.'

Gail's smile was almost blissful, her eyes unblinking. 'I have this recurring fantasy about leaving bombs all over the city, then waiting for them to go off, like planting tulip bulbs in the fall. *POW, POW, POW* – uptown, East Side, midtown. Think about it—'

'Stop it, Gail. I don't *want* to think about it.'

'Why, because *innocent people* would die? When was the last time you met an *innocent* person?'

'Emily,' Julia said softly.

Gail looked at her a moment and nodded. 'I didn't say I *wanted* bombs going off, just that I think about it sometimes. Sometimes I don't even set the bombs, I'm just there when they go off. And then everything . . . ends.' She waved a hand in front of her face. 'The crooked politicians and the murderers and the child abusers and the pornographers and—'

'Gail!'

'And not just them, either. The smelly cab drivers who slam on the brakes just to make you nauseous, and the beggars who open the door for you at the cash machines and wish you a nice day as if they really cared, and the bicycle messengers who try to run you down when you—'

'Gail, you're crying.'

'Everything . . . It all just . . . *ends*.' She ran from the room and returned a minute later with a tissue balled in her hand.

'It gets dark so early this time of year,' she said as she sat on the sofa.

Julia looked at her for a moment, at the gray circles under her eyes, the sudden paleness of her lips, then dutifully glanced out of the window, where the cloudless sky lingered on the purple threshold of total darkness. Visiting Gail had been a mistake – but who else was left?

'Did you ever sleep with Martin?' Julia asked.

'Where did *that* come from?'

She told Gail everything about the hypnotism, except for the alphabet test and the subsequent spray-painted message with the missing letters. She described the tension in 1981, her bringing them back to 1963.

'So, did you sleep with him?' she said when she finished.

Gail rolled her eyes. 'Once, at Madison, after a party. Paula was studying, naturally, and Martin and I were pretty drunk. Actually, it was a disaster, as I recall. Martin was *very* drunk, and—'

'Just that once?'

'Trust me, he didn't leave me begging for more.'

'The police think I unlocked some deep dark secret one of you was hiding.'

'From nineteen sixty-three?'

Julia nodded.

'That's it. That's the entire reason the police think one of us did it?'

'Well, that and the fact that the first murder took place in my building,' Julia said. 'What *were* you up to in 1963?'

'Let's see . . . I was four. I guess I was in nursery school.'

'Nothing traumatic?'

'Nothing that would make me kill three women.'

Julia tried to smile but couldn't. *I have this recurring fantasy about leaving bombs all over the city . . . like planting tulip bulbs in the fall.*

'Did you ever run into Jessica Forrester, when you visited me?'

Gail looked at her a moment before answering. 'I may have. Why?'

The doorbell saved Julia from responding. Gail went to answer it.

'There's a Detective LaVigna for you.'

He stepped into Gail's foyer, looking very uncomfortable. 'I . . . ah, phoned in your location to the station,' he said. 'Detective Burgess blew a gasket when I told him where I dropped you off, said I had to come up and get you.'

Julia glanced at Gail. 'Detective Burgess thinks I may be in danger. He's given me an escort.'

'But how could you be in danger here, with . . .' She looked at Lou, then back at Julia. 'They think *I* might hurt you?'

'They don't want me alone with anybody unless I have a police escort,' Julia said quickly. 'Anyway, I need to get going.'

334

She turned to LaVigna. 'Let me just check my phone messages. Could you wait by the elevators?'

He hesitated.

'You want to handcuff me while she calls?' Gail said.

LaVigna blushed and left the apartment.

Julia dialed her number from the phone in Gail's kitchen. As it rang she scanned the list of speed-dial numbers: fire, police, ambulance, and one mystery – 'EC'.

She retrieved two messages, one from the *Daily News* reporter, the other from her mother: 'Do you have a cold? You sound nasal. I bought Emily a sweater at the Gap this afternoon; that jacket she had on was a little flimsy. Anyway, she and I are off to the coffee shop for dinner. She wanted to say hello before we left. We'll call later. I can't believe you're still working, don't you ever . . .'

Julia cut short the message by punching a two-digit code, then pressed the switch hook for a few seconds before hitting the 'EC' speed-dial key. After two rings the call was answered by a recording.

'You have reached the offices of Excell Commodities. Our office hours are—'

Julia hung up, took several deep breaths, kissed Gail goodbye, and left.

In the elevator, she hit the Lobby button and leaned against the back wall.

'Everything okay?' LaVigna asked.

She nodded without looking at him. What the hell was the number for Martin Freemason's company doing on Gail's speed-dial?

33

The 79th Street transverse through Central Park was as dark as a tunnel. The West Side didn't look much more appealing. Julia's spirits sank even further as LaVigna turned on to her block.

'*You have reached the offices of Excell Commodities. Our office hours . . .*'

Someone had invaded her apartment, her own bedroom. Even with the locks changed, the doormen on heightened alert, she wasn't ready to face being alone there.

'Lou?'

He flinched. 'Ma'am? I mean miss . . .' He rolled his eyes. '*Julia.*'

'How late are you working tonight?'

'Another couple of hours.'

'I was thinking of stopping by my mother's, on the East Side, to see Emily. But I need to run up to the apartment first and get some things for her. You mind waiting?'

'No problem.'

'Some job, babysitting a thirty-five-year-old,' she said.

'Oh, I don't know, some of the guys on the squad . . .'

'What about them?'

'Nothing.'

'*Lou!*'

'Well, the guys who saw you when you came in that time

with Burgess, to see the shrink? They think I pulled a real sweet assignment . . . you know, watching you.'

Her gloom went into instant remission.

'I shouldn't have said anything.' He pulled in front of her building.

'I'm glad you did,' Julia said. 'I'll be right down.'

Not five minutes later she was back at the car. She opened the rear door to deposit Emily's stuffed bear, and smelled something sharp, metallic.

'Lou, my mother lives on . . .'

Shattered glass covered the front seat . . .

Lou was slumped forward, head on the steering wheel . . .

Blood ran down his . . .

Oh, Christ.

She jerked up, smacking her head on the doorframe. She took a step back from the car, mouth open to scream, one hand on the back of her head where she'd whacked it on the car.

An explosion from behind, a sizzling sound just overhead, then the windshield erupted.

Julia screamed and spun in the direction of the shot. The street was deserted. She ran around the car and back into the lobby. 'Call the police,' she yelled at the doorman.

The lobby was too exposed. The front wall was all glass; anyone could come in. She ran to the staff bathroom, locked the door behind her, and leaned on the sink, breathing hard. She gaped at the mirror but saw a stranger, a thirty-five-year-old woman with hollow, beseeching eyes, pale, thin lips, disheveled hair, staring out from a newspaper photo – grainy, heavily shadowed, only the caption distinct: 'Manhattan Mother Killed . . .'

She didn't recognize this person; this was happening to some other woman, some other Manhattan mother at some other . . .

She heard a woman's scream a minute later, then sirens. She

337

splashed cold water on her face, then glanced at the mirror again: Julia Mallet. A deep breath, then she opened the door and returned to the lobby. Through the closed door she could hear shouts from the sidewalk, more sirens.

Finally the front door opened. She more or less ran into Ray's arms.

'He's dead, isn't he?'

Ray nodded. 'Shot, once, in the head. Close range.'

He'd called her ma'am, then miss . . .

'Who did it? Do you know, did you find anything?'

'We were kind of hoping you'd seen someone.'

'I didn't even realize it was a shot at first, it was almost like a . . . crack. When I finally turned round, nobody was there.'

'Could you handle a look at the car? Sometimes people remember things at the actual scene.'

She stared at him for a few seconds. 'Don't leave me tonight,' she said.

He nodded, took her arm, and led her outside.

The police had already cordoned off the sidewalk with scene-of-crime tape. A platoon of police cars lined the street, along with an ambulance. She saw uniformed cops questioning some of her neighbors. One shot, one victim, and half the city, it seemed, had sprung into action. Strange, then, given her starring role in this tragedy, to feel suddenly small and insignificant, the swarm of police and neighbors making her feel more vulnerable, not less so. She gripped Ray's arm as they approached the car.

'You heard the shot from back there?' Ray asked her.

'I was standing by the back door of the car.'

He nodded. 'It must have missed you by an inch or less, judging by the hole in the windshield. When you turned round, the sidewalk was empty?'

She closed her eyes, tried to recapture the moment. *'Yes,*

338

ma'am. Yes, ma'am, ma'am ma'am ma'am.' She shook her head and opened her eyes.

'There was nobody there,' she said as a man walked up to them.

'Julia, this is Detective Flannigan,' Ray said, 'from the crime scene unit.'

'Sorry, but I need to take a look at your hands.' Johnny Flannigan hiked his trousers over his copious midsection.

'My *hands*?'

'Evidence of gunpowder – standard operating procedure.'

'Gunpow . . . You think *I* shot him?' She turned to Ray. 'The shot was meant for me. *For me.*'

'Look, Johnny, is this really necessary?'

'You know it is,' he said 'Standard operating—'

'I know.' Ray turned to Julia. 'They have to do it. I'm sorry.'

She waved an arm at the bystanders. 'You aren't checking *their* hands.'

'You're involved in another investigation, miss,' Flannigan said. His voice, his expression, were unnervingly composed, almost matter-of-fact, as if he were giving her directions to a subway stop, as if there wasn't a dead man slumped over the steering wheel just a few feet away. 'A woman was killed in your building.'

'I don't seem to have a gun, or haven't you noticed?'

'It's procedure, Julia. The department—'

'Fuck the department.' She thrust out her right hand. Flannigan waved over his shoulder. A meek-looking man in a suit and tie approached with a small plastic kit.

'Mark Laster, pleased to meet you,' he said as he took Julia's hand and turned it back and forth. He leaned forward, sniffed, looked at Flannigan, shook his head. 'No odor.'

He handed the kit to Flannigan, who held it as Laster removed a vial of liquid, opened it and inserted a swab.

'Diluted nitric acid,' he said. 'Won't harm you.'

Laster swabbed the liquid on to her right fingers and palm, frowning when he noticed Julia wiping tears from her eyes with her left hand.

'We'll need the other hand, too. Preferably dry.' Laster placed the swab in a plastic container in the kit, and repeated the process with Julia's left hand. When he was done he handed her a paper towel.

'I'll take this back to the lab for an NAA,' Laster said. 'Neutron activation analysis,' he told Julia with a tight smile, and walked off.

'I have to get out of here,' Julia said. 'An hour ago I was attacked, now I'm being accused. I can't take any more of this.'

She ran into her building.

Dave McCarty approached Ray as Julia disappeared into the lobby.

'Was all that necessary?' Ray said. 'After what she'd just been through?'

'Our role is not the care and feeding of Julia Mallet,' Dave said. 'Our role is to catch a serial killer before he strikes again.' He arched his eyebrows. 'He or she.'

Dave glanced over Ray's shoulder, where two white-jacketed morgue attendants were easing Lou LaVigna's body from the car.

'You're letting your dick get in the way of an investigation.' Dave sounded so earnest and disapproving, Ray felt something foul fill his mouth. He turned and headed into the building.

'A police officer has been killed, Ray,' Dave called after him. 'Remember that.'

Ray poured Julia a Scotch and made some phone calls from her kitchen.

340

'You're going to be in the papers tomorrow,' he told her when he'd finished. 'Someone released your name. We're trying to keep out the connection to the Wizard killings.'

He stood next to her. They were both leaning on a counter top. Ice jingled in the Scotch glass as Julia tried to keep her hands steady. She told him about the call from the *Daily News*.

'They'll make the connection soon enough,' she said. 'But what *is* the connection? Why me? Oh, Ray, he called me ma'am and he blushed every time I even looked at him, and he'd be alive if somebody hadn't tried to kill me. *Why*, Ray? You said serial killers stick to a pattern.'

'I don't know. This doesn't fit, unless the Wizard thinks you know something. That might explain the spray-painted sheets, and the attack this evening. All of your friends were accounted for, although they might have gotten by our surveillance. With just one man on each suspect . . . Maybe now they'll take your story seriously, put some more manpower behind this part of the investigation.'

Julia finished the drink and considered a refill. But more Scotch would offer at best only temporary amnesia – and a giant headache in the morning. She needed to *remember*, to think clearly, starting now. Someone had broken into her apartment, shot at her, had killed Lou LaVigna. A breakdown would be a luxury now.

'I want you to stay with me tonight, Ray.'

'I said I would, and—'

'But only if you trust me.'

Ray let out a loud sigh. 'How many times do I have to tell you I know you didn't do any of these things?'

'I'm not talking murder, I'm talking trust. I need you to tell me about Gordon Prescott.'

'That's got nothing to do with—'

'It has everything to do with *us*.' She almost told him about the clipping left on her desk, then decided to hold off. He had to tell her about Gordon Prescott on his own, because he trusted her, not because it might further the investigation.

'I've opened my whole life to you, Ray. I've had to lie to my best friends. I've been shot at, I've been accused—'

'Nobody's accused you of anything.'

'All I'm asking is for you to be open with me. I need to feel close to you, Ray, I need to feel safe and connected.'

She got up, walked into the living room, and sat down on the sofa. Ray joined her a minute later, hesitating in the doorway before crossing the room and sitting next to her.

'It happened almost two years ago, in May . . .'

34

'He was a super at a luxury high-rise on Second Avenue. There'd been a series of murders in the city, strangulations – one in Queens, two in Manhattan. All women, all oriental, all in their twenties, all of them raped . . .' Ray shook his head and closed his eyes for a moment. 'After he killed them.'

'Oh God.'

'We were hard up for leads,' he said, 'so I was grabbing at just about anything. The last victim was Korean, worked for a nail salon down in Murray Hill. Turned out she'd given manicures to an old woman, a shut-in, who lived in this East Side high-rise. I checked it out. The woman had to be ninety, but she liked to have her nails done every week by this Korean. Another dead end.'

He took a deep breath, let it out slowly.

'On my way out I asked the doorman if he'd ever noticed anyone following the Korean woman out of the building – never hurts to ask, right? The doorman's Puerto Rican, late twenties. He tells me no, nobody has followed the girl, but he wouldn't blame them if they had; she was a looker. You like oriental girls? I ask him – maybe there's a little threat in there, it's been a long day, a long case . . . He says no, he don't like no slant eyes, but the super . . .? You should see the super's office, he says, wallpapered with pin-ups of Chinese, Japanese, Koreans . . .'

Ray was quiet so long that Julia prodded him.

'What happened?'

'I headed down to the super's office in the basement, knocked on the door. No answer, and it's locked. I knock again. I'm about to turn away when I hear something. A moan. Sounds like a woman is in pain. I knock again, I throw myself against the door, finally I shoot open the lock. First thing I see is this girl on a table in the middle of a workshop, tied up, gagged, but squirming. Joyce Shin. Then there's a shot.'

Julia touched Ray's thigh, where she'd seen the scar. She felt cramping in her stomach.

'The shot went right through my leg. I guess I collapsed; maybe I blacked out for a moment. Anyway, he got my gun, I don't even remember how – I was an asshole any way you look at it, walking into a situation like that without backup. Next thing I know, he has his gun on me. He was short and hairy and panting hard. I could smell his sweat. He made me crouch by a radiator pipe, then threw a pair of handcuffs at me, told me to cuff both my wrists around the pipe. When I said no he backed over to the girl and . . . hit her face with the gun. So I handcuffed myself to the pipe.'

'Didn't anyone hear the shot?'

He shook his head. 'The workshop was at the end of a long hallway, next to the boiler room. On the other side of the boilers was the laundry room, with half a dozen washers and dryers going full blast.'

Julia's hand was still on his leg; it felt tense as steel.

'This animal, this Gordon Prescott, he takes a rag and ties it around my head, gagging me. "I never had no one watch before," he says, this big grin on his face. "Enjoy the show." I start to yell but you can't make a lot of noise with a rag in your mouth. Prescott walks around to the far end of the table . . . You want me to stop?'

Julia shook her head.

'He takes off his pants, then grabs an extension cord, same as he used on the other girls. He gets up on the table, pushing the girl's legs apart, wraps it around her neck. She's squealing, but she's gagged and tied pretty tight. She didn't make much noise.' Ray's voice was a hoarse whisper. 'He had this look in his eyes – excitement, and something else, an intense . . . focus, as if he had to get this right, exactly right. That's the picture I can't shake out of my mind. He looked like a surgeon about to do something . . . delicate.'

A long pause. Then: 'I think he needed for her to die at the very moment he came.'

'Oh, no.'

'I don't know why I watched. For two years I keep thinking, if only I'd closed my eyes, just kept them closed. But I watched, pulling so hard against the handcuffs I took skin off.'

He placed a hand, palm up, in front of her. Just below the wrist she saw a patch of paler skin with faint red striations through it.

'How did you get out of there?'

'How do you think? Through shrewd detective work and incredible bravery.' He laughed bitterly. 'I got lucky. The doorman noticed that I'd been down there a long time. He looked out front and saw my car still there, decided to call the local precinct. A couple of beat cops arrived just as Prescott was getting down from the table. I, of course, was still cuffed to the radiator.' He hadn't looked at her since she sat down. Now he stood up, still not facing her, and walked back to the window.

'Do you blame yourself for what happened? Because it wasn't—'

'Blame myself? Every fucking minute of every fucking day. Internal affairs ran an inquiry, said I acted improperly – no backup, not even my partner – but that the outcome . . . that it

345

wouldn't have mattered what the fuck I did.'

He gazed out of the window. 'I need to make a call.'

'That's not the whole story, Ray.'

He hesitated, shook his head, then sat down. 'Whenever I even think about making love, I see that animal.'

He turned to face her. 'You know how some memories keep coming back as images, like photographs, that you see for a moment, maybe a little blurred, then they evaporate?'

Julia nodded.

'This is different. It's like an entire movie playing in my head, in color even; and I see it all at once, his face, his . . .' Ray shook his head. 'I see *her* face, her eyes bugging out, mouth twisting, knowing what's happening, what's going to happen.' He took a deep breath. 'And when I even think about sex with a woman my head feels like it's going to blow apart, like this movie is running inside me and it's filling me up and pressing and pressing . . .' His hands massaged the sides of his head and squeezed his eyes shut.

'The other night, with you, I was almost there . . . and then it happens again, this movie inside my head.'

'Have you talked to anyone about this?'

He opened his eyes. 'It's SOP to see a shrink after you've been in a traumatic situation. Mandatory, even. I saw this guy out in Queens for about three months. We figured it out easily enough – my guilt prevents me from consummating my physical desires with a woman. Simple. Problem was, we never got beyond that.'

'Beyond the guilt?'

He waited a beat. 'Because I *was* guilty,' he whispered.

'Ray . . .'

'Don't, please. I've been through it so many times.'

'But I can help you,' she whispered. 'I can make you forget – no, not forget – I can help you make peace with what happened.

Through hypnosis. Like with my father, I can take away the pain.'

He stared at her. 'Hypnosis is what got you in this mess in the first place.'

'This is different.'

He shook his head.

'You still don't trust me,' she said. 'I can help you, but you won't let me because you don't trust me. I don't know why. Unless you think I'll shoot you once I have you in my power, is that it?'

'You know it's not. I wouldn't be here if I thought that.'

'Then let me do—'

'NO!' The round blue eyes were glittering. 'You can't save everybody; you weren't put on this earth to rescue tortured souls.'

But I can save you.

'Let me hypnotize you,' she said. 'You've got nothing to lose.'

I NEED to help you.

'I don't see it that way, Julia. It's playing with fire.'

Your father's dying. You can't stop THAT, can you, Julia?

She ran into her bedroom and slammed the door behind her. A few minutes later she heard the front door open and close.

Tuesday 14 February

35

The story made the front page of the *Times*' Metro section: 'Police Officer Slain as Manhattan Woman Eludes Attack'. At least they hadn't managed to find a photo of her. Lou LaVigna was there, though, on the front page, in hat and uniform, looking a few years younger, the innocence in his eyes shining through the stiff official photograph. She stared at him for a while, trying to memorize his face, those eyes, until a tear-drop fell on the photo, spread across his face . . . the way blood would race across cheeks whenever he felt embarrassed by something she . . .

Julia threw aside the paper and called her mother.

'Do you want to talk to Emily? We were just getting ready for school.'

She hadn't read the paper yet.

'There's something I have to tell you, Mother.' Julia took a deep breath. Terror was a low rumbling just beneath the surface of her mind. She felt it, always, but had to keep it there, buried, until she was safe. Otherwise it would destroy her. 'Someone tried to . . . attack me last night.'

'*What*?'

Julia filled her in, dodging as many questions as she answered, trying to sound cool, unafraid. She talked for a few minutes to Emily, then hung up. The phone rang immediately.

'I'm okay, Mother, really. It was—'

'It's Ellen Friedman, from the *Post*. I'm looking into the possible connection between a series of recent killings and the attack on you. What—'

'No comment.' Julia hung up, and the phone immediately rang again. She deactivated the ringer and let the machine pick it up.

'Julia, it's Steve Franklin from the *Daily News*. We talked yesterday about—'

She turned down the volume and reread the article, avoiding the photograph this time. Her building was described as a luxury high-rise; Julia was an attractive single mother, an advertising executive, a quiet woman who didn't go out much – according to neighbors, all anonymously quoted. No one knew why such a person would be 'stalked' (the *Times*' word). The target herself was 'unavailable for comment'.

The answering machine took another call. They'd be talking about her at the agency today, the Madison crowd would be checking in. She left a message on Alison's voicemail saying she wouldn't be in all day.

When Ray arrived at eight o'clock she was still in her robe.

'I'm sorry I ran out last night,' he said. 'You were so determined about the hypnosis and, well, I didn't see any middle ground . . .'

'I pushed too hard.' She rolled her eyes and felt a glimmer of sadness. 'God, we sound like an old married couple.'

'Take it from me, old married couples don't talk this reasonably. Anyway, there's something I have to ask you.'

'What?'

She saw him swallow. 'If you hypnotized them all again, and—'

'God, no.'

'Dr Turner would supervise. She feels that if you brought

them all back to nineteen sixty-three again, we'd have a clearer idea of what happened back then and might see what the connection is to these killings.'

'But if one of them *is* the killer, he – or she – would hardly agree to this.'

'I'd say the killer couldn't afford to refuse.'

'Why not ask Dr Turner to do it?'

'She thinks it should be you, and you should do it here, to replicate as closely as possible what happened at your party.'

'Just the thought of bringing them all back here . . .'

'It might save somebody's life, Julia.'

Saving people was her specialty, after all. 'I guess I have no choice, then.' The Wizard was calling the shots in her life.

She crossed the living room, opened a window and inhaled the sharp, cold air. She visualized the scene – all her friends gathered in her apartment again for what would probably be the last time. One more betrayal. She'd already withheld critical information from them, now she was being asked to fuck around with their minds again.

It might save somebody's life, Julia.

The police couldn't get a warrant to search her friends' homes – that would be an infringement of their Constitutional rights – but she could search the deepest recesses of their minds, and she didn't need any judge's permission to do it.

Ray put his arms around her waist, but Julia backed away.

'If you won't let me help you, then we should keep things strictly business, okay?'

He nodded and took a step back.

'Jared told me his alibi fell through,' she said.

'The guy denies seeing him, but he could be lying to protect himself. The St Louis cops are working him over. They'll offer him a deal if he cooperates – you know, no publicity, no charges.'

'He was here the other night,' Julia said.

353

'You shouldn't have let him in.'

'He started talking about children, about how they suffer for their parents' hypocrisy, especially their fathers'. He was so intense . . . almost violent about it.'

'That fits with something else I learned about Jared yesterday. The money he wires every month? We traced it to a children's hospital in Chicago. The checks have been arriving on the first of every month for the past two years. No indication of the sender, no return address, nothing. There was a note with the first one, telling the hospital to use the money any way it wanted, so long as it directly benefited the children. After that, just the money, every month, like clockwork.'

'He sends them . . .?'

'Twelve thousand a year, and doesn't even get to deduct it.'

A children's hospital? A thousand dollars a month. She knew how he earned that money, and what it cost him.

'We've been following up your abuse angle. Two detectives on the task force checked out the local psychiatric hospitals, clinics, social service agencies. None of the victims was registered. If any of these women hit their kids, they never got caught.'

'Oh yes they did.'

'You mean the Wizard caught them. Anyway, I interviewed the three families again, raised the issue of discipline. You were right – they all harped on about the fact that the women were very strict, no-nonsense types, not averse to gentle spanking or other punishments if circumstances warranted.'

'Maybe the Wizard saw them being spanked in public, then.'

'Stella Turner thinks your theory makes sense. The Wizard witnesses some form of discipline – a spanking in public, say – and something inside goes off, something's triggered. These women may not have been true abusers, but the Wizard *thinks* they are – and the "abuse" provokes a psychotic reaction.'

She told him about Gail's speed-dial.

'I talked with Martin's deputy yesterday,' Ray said. 'She denies having an affair with him.'

'But Paula told me—'

'Darla's hired a lawyer, says she'll sue Martin and the police department if we pursue this.'

'Do you believe her?'

'Why not? If she *is* having an affair, she's got nothing to lose by admitting it. The wife already knows. I think she's telling the truth.'

'Paula was convinced he was sleeping with someone. If it's not Darla . . .'

She has the look of someone whose needs are being met.

'It's Gail,' Julia said. 'She admitted to that one night at Madison – do you think it's possible they never stopped having sex?'

'If so, at least she's got an alibi.' He sighed. 'I need to talk to both of them today.'

She told him about the clipping left on her desk. His head dropped, and she heard him take several deep breaths.

'Why would anyone do that?' she said.

He shook his head, looked at her. 'Someone wants you to doubt me, I'd say.'

'Another cop?'

'Doesn't make sense. Do you still have the envelope and the clipping?'

'At my office.'

'I'll send someone over to pick it up. Could be fingerprints, though I doubt it.'

'I could run downtown later and get it.'

'Forget it. That attack last night was desperate, not rational. It could happen again, any time. You're safe as long as you stay inside and don't let anyone in.'

'I'm a prisoner then.'

A quiet woman who doesn't go out much.

'For the moment, yes. Call your friends, invite them over this evening, tell them it's about the case but don't mention hypnosis. And don't leave the apartment for anything.'

Ray headed for the front door. 'Oh, Julia?' He looked at her and smiled a bit sadly. 'Happy Valentine's Day.'

36

Julia called her six Madison friends and asked them to come over that evening at seven. She followed Ray's instructions and said nothing about hypnosis, only that she had information about the serial killer and that the information concerned them personally. They all mentioned the *Times* article right away, asked if she'd seen the *Post*.

'We'll talk tonight,' she told all of them, fighting to keep the terror out of her voice but still faltering in those long, panicky moments when her chest felt too constricted to accommodate enough oxygen.

Paula agreed right away, Jared was suspicious but said he'd be there, Richard was also reluctant but ultimately gave in. Marianne was the hardest sell; she consented to take the shuttle up only when Julia explained that the police would view anyone's refusal to come as suspicious.

'The senator's already pissed that the cops are snooping around,' Marianne said. 'I guess I'd better come.' Nothing about her affair with Ruth Rinaldi, nothing about the betrayal. Julia left a message on Gail's machine.

The calls made, Julia resolved to keep busy despite being grounded. She tried paying bills but lost patience, tried writing long-overdue thank-you notes for Emily's birthday presents, but lost interest. She tuned into the daytime talk shows, but nothing she saw – the incest survivors, the devil worshippers, the transsexuals – could distract her from her own situation.

Was Ray right? Did the Wizard think Julia knew something that could lead to his or her identity? Was that why he or she had tried to kill her?

She opened a novel but kept rereading the same paragraphs. What had happened yesterday to trigger an attack? Richard had visited her office, she'd stopped by Gail's. Had either of them let something slip? Had Paula, earlier that week? She'd also seen Jared, talked to Marianne. What had she missed?

Once, the idea that one of her college friends was a killer had struck her as absurd. Now it was a question of which friend and why.

She picked up the house phone and asked her doorman if he had a copy of the *New York Post*.

'I'm not sure, I—'

'Come on, Reinaldo. I've seen you reading it practically every morning for four years.'

'I'm looking, I'm looking . . . Oh, here it is.'

The article must be godawful.

'I'll be right down,' she said.

'Cop Takes Bullet for Single Mom'.

Julia read the front-page headline while walking back toward the elevator, and felt her legs buckle. Lou's innocent eyes bore into her from the half-page photo, following her as she tossed the paper back on to the doorman's podium and ran into the elevator.

They think I pulled a real sweet assignment . . . you know, watching you.

The phone was ringing when she got back to her apartment. She'd turned up the ringer ten minutes ago, after running through a dozen or more messages – all three New York newspapers, two frantic calls from her mother, the Madison crowd. She wanted to pick up the next time her mother called.

'Julia Mallet? Doug Marshall, *New York Post*.'

'I have nothing to—'

'One question, Julia. Who's Emily's father? Just his name.'

'*What*?'

'The girl's father. I've been trying to track him down – background piece, you know? Single mom, swanky address, mysterious stalker. Maybe the father is—'

Julia slammed down the receiver, caught her breath, and set up the punching bag. Ten minutes into her workout the intercom buzzed.

'Miss Severance to see you, Miss Mallet,' Reinaldo said. 'Send her up?'

No way she was letting Gail up to her apartment. Even if Gail did have an alibi, she'd lied to Julia all those years.

'Tell her I'll be right down,' Julia said.

'The apartment's a wreck,' she told Gail as she crossed the lobby from the elevator. 'Do you mind if we talk down here?' She gestured to a seating area across from the doorman's station.

'In the lobby? What's wrong?'

Gail wore a shearling coat dyed a deep green and mid-calf boots. She looked stylish but tired.

'I've been home all morning,' Julia said. 'I really need to get out of the apartment.' She walked to the facing sofas and sat down. Gail hesitated, then sat next to her.

'I haven't been completely honest with you,' Gail said. Julia noticed that her hands were shaking. 'About an hour ago Detective Burgess came by. He accused me of having an affair with Martin, if "accuse" is the right word.' She looked down at her lap. 'The thing is, I am. I wanted to tell you, Julia, but Martin insisted we keep it quiet, especially from the Madison

359

crowd. With all these killings, I've wanted to talk about it – at least I'd have an alibi. But Martin insisted.'

Goddamn her.

'How long?' Julia asked.

'On and off . . . fifteen years.'

Since college? Through the birth of Martin and Paula's two sons?

'Sometimes we don't see each other for months – once it was a whole year,' Gail said. 'I get so disgusted with myself, socializing with Paula . . .' She wiped away a few tears. 'Even with you and everyone else, it's been so hard to keep it all inside. No one knew, no one.'

'It started back in Madison?'

'Just that one time.'

The incident that had been reenacted under hypnosis. Julia tried hard to keep the anger out of her voice. 'I never thought you liked Martin all that much.'

'Who says I liked him?' She laughed, the cynical wheeze Julia was used to. 'Sometimes I think I hate him, if you want to know the truth. But I've never been able to break it off. I'm that way with a lot of things. Whenever I try dating men who are actually available, I realize what I've been missing all these years. And then Martin calls after a long break and we start all over.'

'Were you with him the nights the women were killed?'

Gail nodded. 'The last month or so has been one of our intense periods. We're together almost every night.' She raised her eyebrows and shrugged. 'Well, week nights, anyway. But the thing is, every time we're together lately, all he wants to talk about is . . . ending it.'

'But you said you've been seeing him a lot.'

'I've been under so much pressure lately. The book is way overdue – I can't seem to catch up. And Martin threatening to . . .' Gail smiled as her voice broke. 'I almost said leave me – as if we've ever been really together. See, I couldn't let him go, not at this point in my life.'

'How would you stop him?'

'I guess he . . . I suppose he thinks that if he broke off, I'd, you know, make a fuss.'

'You mean tell Paula?'

Gail nodded. 'Sounds like blackmail, right? It wasn't quite that simple, really. I never *said* I'd tell Paula. But I think Martin thinks I've been a little unsteady lately, what with the deadline looming.'

'Did you tell the detective any of this?'

'He'd already been to see Martin, who spilled the beans, apparently. He's probably telling Paula right now. Oh, Julia, how am I ever going to face her?'

'It's a little late for guilt. You could do her a favor and never see either of them again.'

You could do her a favor by leaving town and never coming back.

'Maybe this is the catalyst I need to finally get rid of him,' Gail said.

'Murder?' Julia said.

Gail looked at her for a beat. 'Wait a minute, you don't really think I—'

'Of course not.' Having an affair with a married man was such a nice, ordinary, *non-psychotic* thing to do. So if Gail and Martin were together, that left Richard, Marianne, and Jared. But if Jared really was with the St Louis attorney when he said he was . . .

'Can you forgive me?' Gail said. 'I never wanted to lie to you.'

'Fifteen years, Gail. I told you everything, and you kept the most important part of your life a secret.'

'Please, Julia,' Gail said. 'I need you to forgive me.'

Their friendship was over. Julia owed nothing to Gail, and yet . . .

'Of course,' she said. 'I'll see you tonight.'

'I'm doing a little shopping nearby,' Gail said. 'Cilantro may be the basil of the nineties, but it's hard to find on the East Side. You want to come along?'

Julia turned and headed for the elevator. 'Some other time.' Some other century was more like it.

As the elevator closed she saw Gail walking toward the exit, elegant and self-possessed in her shearling coat and suede boots. Then she thought of Gail's bedroom, the jumble of clothes and shoes and papers. And Gail's secret dream: planting 'tulip bulbs' all over New York, waiting for them to explode. She thought of Gail and Martin, deceiving Paula – all of them, really – for fifteen years . . .

And then she thought of having to face them all that night, one last time.

37

'Feel the tension leaving your legs, feel it floating . . .'

It was so much like that other night, when it all began, that she could hardly bear to look at her five friends, let alone hypnotize them. Paula, Gail, Marianne, Richard, Jared. She hadn't known them – really known them – then. She realized that now. But did she know them today?

She'd asked Pamela to take Emily to a pizzeria for dinner and not return until eight-thirty at the earliest, even if it meant buying time at an ice cream parlor. Pamela had been full of questions about the shootings, Julia full of assurances that she and Emily were in no danger.

'So what's the news we had to hear in person?' Martin had asked once they'd pumped her about the shootings. He'd been glancing at his watch since arriving promptly at seven.

'You didn't mention that we'd *all* be here,' Marianne said.

'This is so Agatha Christie,' Gail said. 'Are you going to tell us who done it?'

Saved by the doorbell. Ray came in with Stella Turner and an apology for being late. He wore a knit tie and houndstooth sports jacket; Dr Turner was in a dark burgundy suit over a white blouse buttoned to the neck.

'What's *he* doing here?' Gail asked.

Julia could tell from their eyes, their glances, their opened mouths, that they knew they'd been set up. Ray stood with Dr Turner at the entrance to the room.

'You've all met me,' he said. 'I'm Ray Burgess, Manhattan North Detective Bureau. This is Dr Stella Turner, a police department psychiatrist.'

'Oh Lord,' Jared said.

'The six of you were hypnotized at the birthday party here,' Ray said. 'Subsequent to that event, a series of murders has taken place. We believe there may be a connection between those murders and Ms Mallet's party.'

Julia saw Paula appraising Ray with approving eyes. He seemed completely comfortable in front of the group, cool and decisive.

'What connection?' Martin said.

'We're not sure,' Ray said. 'That's why we've asked all of you here tonight.'

'*Julia* asked us,' Gail said.

The sting found its target. Julia moved from Ray's side to a chair closer to her friends. Friends? She glanced at the Tiffany-framed photo of the Madison group in front of Lenox Hill. Had they changed so much since that enchanted afternoon, herself included? Or were all seven smiles hiding something even then?

'How can we help?' Paula said. 'We've told you what happened that night at the party. Several times.'

Dr Turner stepped all the way into the room. 'We'd like Ms Mallet to hypnotize you again,' she said.

All six muttered their objections, to which Stella Turner raised a hand.

'The entire affair will be closely supervised by me and Detective Burgess. I am a board-certified practitioner with—'

'What if we refuse?' Jared said.

'You are not required to participate,' Ray said. He paused for a few moments. 'Of course, I'll be interested in the reason for refusing, given the fact that you were all willing subjects at Julia's party.'

'This is outrageous,' Martin said.

'What exactly will you be looking for?' Paula asked. Martin glared at her.

'That night at the party, Julia took you back, under hypnosis, to nineteen sixty-three,' Dr Turner said.

Julia felt six pairs of angry eyes turn to her.

'I thought you never managed to hypnotize us,' Marianne said.

'You always said . . . you always *promised* you'd let us remember what happened under hypnosis,' Paula said.

Julia opened her mouth to reply, but Dr Turner jumped in.

'It is our belief that something happened to one of you in nineteen sixty-three, an event of some kind so painful that the conscious mind kept it buried for years in the subconscious.'

'You mean we forgot it completely?' Gail asked.

'Not necessarily. You – by which I mean *one* of you – might remember the event itself but not the pain it caused. It's the *pain* that resurfaced that night at the party, and it's the pain, and the rage associated with it, that may be prompting one of you—'

'We don't believe for certain that one of you is a killer.' Ray looked at Dr Turner, his eyes warning her. 'But we do believe there's a connection.'

'So you want to take us back to nineteen sixty-three, see what happens?' Martin said.

'Exactly,' said Dr Turner.

Martin stood up. 'Count me out. If my attorney found out I was even considering this he'd have a fit.' He turned and extended a hand for Paula.

'I'm staying,' she said. 'I have nothing to hide.'

'What's that supposed to mean?' He glanced around the

room. 'You're all going through with this?'

'If we refuse, we're prime suspects – right, Detective Burgess?' Jared said.

'Not necessarily, though we'll be interested in—'

'But do we have your word that you'll stick to nineteen sixty-three?' Jared said.

'Guaranteed,' Ray said.

'Absolutely,' Dr Turner said.

Jared sat back and spread out his arms on the sofa back. 'Let 'er rip,' he said.

Again Martin extended his hand. 'Paula, let's go.'

Again she said, 'I have nothing to hide, Martin.' Then added, 'Do you?'

He balled both hands into fists and stormed from the room, slamming the front door.

'The stock market must have been down in nineteen sixty-three,' Gail said without cracking a smile. 'You can understand his reluctance to relive that particular year.'

Paula looked at Gail, seemed about to say something, but instead sat back on the sofa. This was the first time they'd met since Gail's affair with Martin had surfaced. Gail struck Julia as being nonchalant about everything, Paula nervous and fragile.

'We'll talk to Martin later,' Ray said. 'Now, if you're all ready . . . Julia?'

She stood up and gripped a chair back. 'First, I want to say how sorry I am that I haven't been totally honest with you.'

'*Totally* honest?' Jared said.

'I said I was sorry, this wasn't my—'

'I think you should get started,' Dr Turner said quietly.

Julia nodded. 'Are you all comfortable?'

'That's a laugh,' Richard said. That was the first time he'd spoken, and they all glanced at him for a few seconds.

'I think I'll turn off some lights,' Dr Turner said. A few

minutes later the room was lit only by a faint glow from the hall ceiling fixture.

And so she started, beating back a suffocating reluctance to play with fire a second time.

They were remarkably good subjects. Stella Turner had warned her that the pressure of the situation might make it difficult to establish hypnotic control, but they went under as quickly as ever. Perhaps a residue of trustworthiness still clung to her, even after all that had happened. She watched them for a few moments, arms levitated in front of them as ordered, eyes closed, five people she'd betrayed who nevertheless consigned themselves to her authority.

'Let your arms relax,' she said. She turned to Stella Turner. 'Should I bring them back to nineteen sixty-three now?'

'Follow the same procedure as last time.'

'The alphabet thing?'

Dr Turner nodded.

'I want you to forget the letters . . . C and G,' Julia said. 'I want these letters to vanish from your minds, so that . . .'

She tested them, one by one. Jared, Paula, and Richard skipped over the letters without hesitation. Gail and Marianne faltered very, very slightly, requiring another dose of hypnotic induction. Marianne passed the test the second time, but Gail still paused as she skimmed over the missing letters. Julia quickly talked her through the induction again, and when asked to recite the alphabet a third time, she smoothly skipped over the letters C and G.

Or had she? Again Julia asked her to repeat the exercise. Again Gail jumped over the two letters without pausing.

'She's under,' Dr Turner whispered.

Julia looked closely at her friend. Gail's eyes were closed, her expression blank, her breathing slow and regular.

'They're all under,' she said.

'Take them back,' Dr Turner said.

Julia gave the commands, clapped her hands, and watched them open their eyes to 1963.

She turned to Dr Turner. 'Now what?'

'Introduce the Wizard,' the doctor said.

Julia faced her friends. 'Does anyone know this song? "We're Off to See the Wizard"?'

Smiles appeared on several of the faces.

'Sing it for me,' Julia said.

Jared started. Within moments he was joined by everyone except Marianne, whose face bore the defiant expression of a pouty four-year-old. None of them knew all the lyrics, but they pressed forward with the melody, humming when they couldn't remember words. Paula got up and started skipping around the living room.

'Ask Marianne why she's not singing,' Stella Turner whispered in Julia's ear.

'Why aren't you singing, Marianne?'

'Don't want to.' She folded her arms in front of her.

'Insist that she join in,' the doctor said.

'Marianne, I want you to sing with the others.'

'NO.' Marianne turned to face the wall.

Gail and Jared were following Paula around the room, singing 'Because of the wonderful things he does . . . because of the wonderful . . .' over and over again. Richard was still cross-legged on the floor, singing softly.

'Don't you like this song, Marianne?' Julia said.

She shook her head.

'Did your mommy and daddy ever sing it to you? Did you ever see the movie on TV? *The Wizard of Oz*?'

'No.'

Julia turned back to the doctor and shrugged.

'Ask them to sit down,' Dr Turner said.

'Sit down, everyone. Enough singing.'

Jared and Paula obeyed, but Gail kept skipping around the room.

'Gail, I asked you to sit down,' Julia said in her sternest, most maternal voice.

Gail slowed down, seemed to consider whether or not to obey, and finally sat next to Jared on the floor.

'Ask them to describe the worst thing that happened to them,' Dr Turner said.

'They're only four,' Julia said.

The doctor sighed. 'Introducing the Wizard didn't provoke anything. Perhaps a more direct approach will work.'

Julia turned back to the group. 'I want you to tell me the worst thing that ever happened to you. Think hard – what's the worst, the most awful, most horrible, scariest thing that ever happened to you?'

Five blank faces.

'When I was your age,' Julia said, 'my brother was killed by a car. I loved him very much, so did my . . .' Julia took a deep breath. 'So did my parents . . . and that was the worst thing that ever happened to me.'

'I fell off my bicycle without training wheels.' Paula pointed to a small scar on her right knee. 'I needed *eleven* stitches – right here.'

'Thank you, Paula. That must have been terrible.'

'I got chicken-pox,' Gail said. 'And I didn't scratch, even though it itched like the dickens.'

'That was very grown-up of—'

'My mother had a baby but she lost it,' Richard said.

Julia saw Dr Turner and Ray exchange glances.

'How did she lose it?' Julia asked.

Richard looked blank for a moment.

'How did your mother lose the baby, Richard?'

369

'At the hospital,' he said. 'She lost it at the hospital.'

'How did you feel about that?'

Richard shrugged. 'Sad. Mommy cried, too. She was *real* sad.'

Julia looked at Dr Turner.

'Ask Marianne,' she said.

'Marianne, what was the worst thing that happened to you?'

'I'm not telling,' she said, her face bright with mischief.

'Marianne, I want you to—'

'Jared!'

Emily bolted into the room, ran over to Jared and hugged him. Emily enjoyed all her mother's friends, especially Jared and Gail, the two she saw most often. Jared responded with a look of complete confusion – little boys didn't always appreciate hugs from little girls. Emily next headed for Gail and threw her arms round her.

Julia turned to Pamela, standing in the living-room doorway. 'It's only seven forty-five.'

'She have to go to the bathroom,' Pamela said. 'We already leave the restaurant, and I—'

'Fine, Pamela, take her into the bathroom, then keep her out of here until we're done. She can watch a video in my room.'

Emily left Gail and grabbed her mother's legs as Pamela crossed the room.

'Come on now, Emily,' Pamela said. 'You wanted to go to the bathroom.'

'No,' Emily said. 'I want to stay with my mommy.'

Marianne and Jared giggled.

'Emily, I'm very busy now and I need you to go with Pamela.' She nodded at Pamela, who prised Emily from Julia's legs and carried her kicking and shrieking from the room.

Julia took a deep breath. 'Marianne, what was the worst thing to happen to you?'

'Who was that?' Marianne said.

Julia looked back at Dr Turner, who nodded.

'That was my daughter,' Julia said.

'What's her name?' Gail asked.

'Emily. Now, Marianne, I want you to tell me the—'

'Mommy, Mommy!' Emily ran across the living room and collided with her mother's legs, wailing.

'Emily, I told you to stay in your room.'

'I want to stay with you,' Emily said in between sobs.

'Not now. Pamela!'

Pamela reappeared; Emily wrapped her arms around Julia's legs.

'Pamela, maybe you can take her for a walk?' Julia said.

'But it's cold out,' Emily said, tightening her grip.

Pamela walked into the room and leaned over for Emily, now flailing with both arms.

'NO.'

Emily grabbed Julia's legs again; Pamela took a reflexive step back.

'You can play in the lobby for a little while.' With trembling fingers Julia tried very gently to prise Emily off her.

'NO!'

Emily still clung to Julia's legs. Jared had gotten up and was rapping at the window. Marianne was bouncing on the sofa. Gail and Richard were staring at Julia open-mouthed, as if she were Cruella DeVil come to life, and Emily a helpless Dalmatian about to be slaughtered.

'Emily, I want you to go with Pamela. *Now.*'

'NO! NO! NO!'

Richard covered his ears with his hands. Paula buried her face in a sofa pillow.

Marianne was starting to hyperventilate. 'I want my mommy,' she said between gasps. 'I want my mommy.'

Julia leaned over and grabbed both of Emily's hands, which were still clamped around her legs. It took all her strength to force them apart – they felt as tense as steel. When she'd finally managed to unclench them Emily fell backward, away from her. Her head hit the side of the glass coffee table with a sharp *thwack*.

Instant hysteria – convulsive sobs, arms lashing at Julia, legs flailing. Some of the other 'children' began to cry.

Julia managed to pick Emily up and inspect her head. A small red welt was faintly visible just to the side of her right eye. Nothing serious, though there might be a bruise later. She longed to comfort Emily, hold her until the shock of the fall wore off, but under the circumstances she had to settle for kissing the spot and handing her sobbing daughter to Pamela.

Emily's sobs escalated to howls as she was carried from the room. Julia wiped tears from her own eyes and tried to ignore the wailing from outside the front door. Finally the elevator arrived, and the screaming faded.

She managed to get her five subjects back on the floor, assured them that everything was all right, then tried again to coax Marianne into revealing the worst thing that had ever happened to her. Marianne preened under all the attention but refused to say anything other than 'no'. Julia looked at Dr Turner, who sighed and shook her head.

'You might as well bring them out.' She turned to Ray. 'Nothing significant. I think you need to talk to Martin Freemason as soon as possible.'

38

'So, end the suspense.' Jared rubbed his eyes and stretched. 'Who done it?'

'What deep, dark secrets am I hiding?' Richard said.

This time Julia had let them remember what went on under hypnosis when they emerged from their trances, vaguely confused and angry.

'I'm afraid the . . . experiment was inconclusive,' Stella Turner said.

'That leaves Martin, then,' Paula said. 'Dare I go home to that monster?' She stole a quick glance at Gail, who met her gaze without flinching.

Julia retrieved their coats and managed to avoid one-on-one conversations as she ushered all of them except Ray out of the front door.

Ray looked miserable.

'Well, it never sounded very scientific anyway,' Julia said.

'Stella's pretty certain that if something *had* happened in sixty-three, it would have come out.'

Julia began collecting glasses from around the living room.

'I'm going to request added surveillance on Martin Freemason,' Ray said. 'If none of the five here tonight is involved, that leaves him.'

'It's not Martin,' Julia said. 'It can't be.'

'You've said that about all of them at one point or another.'

Julia walked to the kitchen and set the glasses on a counter.

Ray followed a few seconds later. 'What's the matter?' he asked.

'Nothing.'

'Tell me.'

'That was very difficult for me,' she said, her back to him as she loaded glasses into the dishwasher.

'You were terrific,' he said.

'Right, some performance.'

'What you did was try to save lives, including your own.'

She spun around. 'What I did was betray five of my best friends,' she said. 'Since that party I've lied to all of them . . . I can't do it any more.'

'They haven't been honest with you these past fifteen years, either.'

Julia shook her head. 'And the way I snapped at Emily – if she'd hit the table any harder . . .'

Ray put his arms around her. 'Let me make a call, maybe I can stay longer.'

She pulled away. 'Those five people . . . they put themselves in my hands, even after my lies and half-truths and evasions. But you? You don't trust me enough to let me help you.'

'Why can't you accept me for who I am?'

'I don't *know* who you are.'

'I'm—'

She held up a hand. 'Anyway, I need to be with Emily tonight. Just the two of us.'

He said nothing, then got his coat from the hall closet.

'I'll call you tomorrow.'

He opened the front door and let it slam shut behind him.

'I'm sorry about what happened, Em,' Julia said. 'Remember

what we say when Mommy gets angry?'

'Timber timber.' Emily shook a finger at her.

'That's right – temper, temper.'

'I hurt my head, Mommy.'

They were in the kitchen, Emily sitting on a counter, Julia stroking her forehead. There was a little swelling, but no sign of a bruise as yet.

'I'm under a lot of pressure lately.'

'What's pressure?'

'It's when you have too much to do, too many things to think about.'

'What kinds of things?'

'Well, my job, paying bills, all sorts of things.'

'Me, Mommy?'

'I *like* thinking about you, silly.'

Emily smiled. 'Your *friends* looked silly,' she said.

'They did, didn't they?'

Emily jumped down from the counter and pulled on the refrigerator door.

'What's an angel?' She took out a half-empty juice pack.

'Let's see. An angel is like a fairy, a perfect little creature who flies around us. Why?'

'Because Gail said I was her angel,' Emily said.

'She . . . When did she say that?'

'Before.'

'In the living room? Tonight?'

Emily nodded. 'She whispered in my ear when I gave her a hug. It tickled.'

'What did she whisper, Em?'

Emily took a long swallow of apple juice. 'It felt like a feather tickling my—'

'What did she whisper to you?'

'"You're my perfect angel".'

'You're sure she said that tonight, in the living room?'

'Sure. Mommy, can I be an angel on Halloween?'

'Of course, Em.'

'When is it Halloween again?'

'What? Oh, not for a long time. It's way past bedtime, Em. How about a story?'

Julia tried to keep her voice steady as she made her way through *Sleeping Beauty*. It wasn't easy. *You're my perfect angel.* A four-year-old would never say that. And Emily had run into the living room *after* Julia had taken them all back to 1963. Gail had hesitated over the skipped letters on the first alphabet test, then slid right over them the third time.

Or had she? Julia tried to recall Gail's voice reciting the alphabet. She'd been so eager to get the hypnosis over with . . . perhaps she'd overlooked a split-second hesitation.

She closed the book and kissed Emily, then went into her bedroom and sat on a chair by the window.

You're my perfect angel.

Even as her mind moved inexorably toward the truth she cast about for alternative explanations. Four-year-old Gail was parroting something she'd heard? Unlikely. Emily had made it up? No, Julia knew when her daughter was telling stories.

That left only one conclusion. She picked up the phone to call Ray.

I sometimes fantasize about leaving bombs all over the city, then waiting for them to go off, like planting tulip bulbs in the fall.

Gail Severance had been faking.

39

The Wizard's right hand moves in slow, rhythmic strokes. Eyes pinched shut, back arched, left hand gripping the sheets. No visit to a bar tonight, no accomplice. Is going solo the answer?

Don't you go whining about what your father does or doesn't do. You of all people, complaining. Let me tell you one thing – whatever happens to you in life you got coming to you, understand? You brought it on yourself.

The Wizard stops for a moment. The picture is so vivid now: the hours in the closet, the beatings, Daddy's thick, chapped fingers doing what even a very young child knew they shouldn't. Where have the memories been all the years, waiting to re-emerge? And why does the Wizard reserve the deepest, bitterest hatred not for him but for her?

She was a little angel, that one. Not you, you're filthy. I suppose there's logic in there somewhere – damned if I can find it. But I know one thing, whatever your father does with you, and I'm not saying I believe you, whatever he does it's no worse than what you've done to him. I'm not saying it's right, only that . . . Don't go crying on me now, I used up all my pity on that little angel, flattened like a pancake she was, and your father, cheated out of a promotion on account of the shame we all bear, thanks to . . .

The Wizard lets out a howl and all but levitates from the

bed, right hand moving faster, harder. Turns over, draws up both knees, forearm aching, face buried in the pillow, teeth tearing at the pillowcase.

He's gone, GONE. Are you happy? Isn't that what you WANTED?

The Wizard collapses on to the bed, panting.

After he left, everything changed. No more nights in the closet, no more beatings – nothing ever said by anybody about anything that happened back then. The Wizard forgot about it too, the whole thing. An entire childhood escaped from the memory like steam from a teapot.

Until now.

The Wizard sits up and shivers with frustration; every patch of flesh feels swollen with blocked desire. That awful moment earlier today scrolls across the Wizard's mind once more – Emily falling backwards, her head striking the glass coffee table. *Thwack*. The Wizard puts a hand over each ear.

Thwack. Thwack. Thwack.

How could she do that to a child? How could any mother treat an angel so cruelly? To toss her aside like unwanted merchandise, never mind her feelings . . . She needs to be saved, little Emily.

Angel.

The Wizard falls back on the pillow, right hand moving in a familiar rhythm.

You've ruined three lives – first that poor angel's, then your father's, and now . . .

NO. The Wizard conjures a new image. A face. Attractive, sophisticated, but with devil's eyes that betray its true character. The Wizard imagines the bullet sailing into the face, starting the process, then a second bullet, obliterating it. Black paint to cover it, *erase* it.

The Wizard's hand works with ferocious speed, back and

forth, up and down, the mattress vibrating as the Wizard jerks up and down, back and forth, up and down. Closer, closer . . . Yes, oh Christ, yessss.

The Wizard lets out a hissing steam of breath, mouth stretching into a smile. The voices are silent. All the Wizard sees behind closed eyelids is that black void, that harmless vacuum, where once there was a face.

Julia's face.

40

Ray returned at ten that evening, thirty minutes after Julia called him.

'Gail was faking a trance,' she said before he'd taken his coat off.

'How do you know?'

She told him, trying to keep her voice steady. She felt jittery with fear and sorrow and . . . something else, a heady sense of discovery pushing through the panicky surface.

'You're right,' he said, 'it's not something a four-year-old would say. But even if she was faking it, that doesn't necessarily mean she's the Wizard.'

'It means she has something to hide.'

'Maybe she was afraid her affair with Martin would surface in front of all of them – it came out the last time you hypnotized her.'

Julia started picking up Emily's blocks and tossing them into a large shopping bag.

'I'll talk to Stella about this in the morning,' Ray said.

'Ah, the great and powerful Stella.' Julia threw a block at the bag but missed the opening. A moment later Ray's hands were on her shoulders.

'I'm sure you're right about Gail,' he said. 'You've been right about everything else so far.'

He turned her around and leaned forward to kiss her.

'No, Ray.'

'But—'

'If you won't let me help you there's no point in going on together. You might as well go back to Dolores and keep on torturing yourself about Gordon Prescott and Joyce Shin and the others. Just leave me out of it.'

'Hypnotism is what got this whole thing started.'

'I know that, Ray. I think about that every minute of the day, asking myself how I could have let this happen.'

'Don't start blaming yourself.'

'Let me help you, then. I want to do something positive with hypnosis, something *good*. I need to. What happened earlier, with my friends — it felt ugly and deceitful. If I could help you . . .'

He looked at her for a long moment.

'What have you got to lose?'

A smile slowly kindled. 'You, I guess, if I don't let you do it.'

'You mean . . .?'

'Let's get started.'

Julia got two candles from the dining-room table and placed them on either side of her bed. She lowered the blinds, lit the candles, and turned off the overhead light. The room, illuminated by the flickering candles, felt insulated, safe.

She undressed him slowly, massaging his chest, his arms, his legs. When she noticed him beginning to respond she walked away from the bed.

'Lie down on your back.' She sat in a chair across the room. 'Now close your eyes,' she said in a soft, even voice.

Just before he complied she saw something flash in his eyes, a final reluctance, a withholding. She stared back at him without moving or speaking. He had to find the trust inside himself; she couldn't give it to him.

Finally, he closed his eyes.

'Now take a deep breath, hold it in . . . hold it. Okay, let it out slowly, very slowly . . .'

She watched his chest rise and fall as she talked him under, her voice deep and slow and steady, his body relaxing until he became completely still.

'. . . Now your arms, let them rest on the bed as you relax . . .'

The words poured out of her like syrup. Ray's naked body glowed in the candlelight as his breathing slowed to an even tempo. How beautiful he looked, eyes closed, features untouched by his distortions of true sleep. Even her father's pain-twisted face and body had achieved a kind of dignity under hypnosis. There had been times, before she'd learned to induce him, when she had had to force herself to look at him.

'. . . Your whole body is relaxed, your eyes are heavy . . .'

She felt closer to Ray now, at this moment, than ever before. Was this intimacy, for her? Control?

'. . . From ten to one, and as I do I want you to lift your arms, slowly, slowly . . . By the time I reach the number one your arms will be straight up. I'm going to begin counting now. Here I go. Ten. Nine. Eight . . .'

His arms were perpendicular when she finished counting.

'. . . And when I reach ten your arms will be back by your side . . .'

She stopped talking when his arms were once again on the bed. The room was utterly silent, his chest rising and falling slowly, almost imperceptibly.

Julia stood up and watched him for a few moments. Was it wrong, what she as about to do? She ran a finger along his chest, down his abdomen. She studied his skin close up, slid a fingernail over the faint cross-hatching of wrinkles, the fine, golden brown hairs that ran up the center of his stomach. She'd never felt anything like this before. His body seemed warm, almost feverish. Like hers. She took a step back from the bed, watched, waited.

He was hers.

'When I clap my hands . . .' Her voice was shaky. She swallowed her reluctance, took a few breaths. 'When I clap my hands, you will be back in the superintendent's workshop. You are tied to the radiator; you've been shot in the leg. The monster, Gordon Prescott, is on the table with the girl. He's raping her, killing her as you watch. You will hear my voice the entire time, Ray. As you watch the monster you will hear my voice. Nod your head if you understand.'

He nodded.

'When I clap my hands a second time you will leave the workshop and return to sleep. Listen carefully: on the second clap, you will leave the workshop and go back to sleep. Nod your head if you understand.'

He nodded.

Julia took a deep breath and clapped her hands. For a moment Ray lay motionless, breathing slowly and evenly. Suddenly, his head moved from side to side, as if he were watching something, though his eyes were still closed. After a few seconds he began rubbing the scar on his right thigh. His breathing accelerated.

'What do you see, Ray? Tell me what you see.'

His mouth opened, closed, opened again. 'He . . . he has her tied to the table . . . He's on top of her. He's fucking her . . . He's . . . oh God, no . . .' Ray turned his head to the side, eyes squeezed shut. 'I can't look . . . watch.'

'You must look, Ray. You have to watch. Now tell me what you see.'

'He . . . he's hurting her. Her mouth is stuffed with something, with a rag, but she's squealing, squirming underneath him . . .

383

Her arms are pinned down, he's thrusting . . . grunting . . . Now what's he . . . Shit. The cord, like the others, the extension cord – NO!'

Ray 'looked' away. Julia brushed tears from her face. He had to confront it – pity wouldn't help him.

'Ray, you have to look at what he's doing, do you understand? You have to watch.'

Facing forward again, eyes still closed, Ray resumed talking. 'He's slipping the cord under her . . . under her neck, not thrusting any more but still inside her, panting like an animal . . . Her head is flailing back and forth . . .'

His mouth opened and closed, but no more words came.

'What is it, Ray, what do you see?'

'He's pumping again – hard, the table's rocking. She's squealing, louder, higher. He keeps pumping, thrusting, grunting, now the grunts are closer together, the thrusts faster and faster . . . Now he pulls on the cord, both ends. Her head lifts off the table; her eyes, her mouth, she knows what's happening, she *knows* . . .'

Ray's left hand jerked on the bed as if he were pulling against a restraint. His feet slid up and down the bed. He was gasping for air.

'Tell me what you see, Ray.'

'Her neck arches, head thrown back, eyes popping . . . I'm pulling against the cuffs, harder and harder, trying to get loose . . . Come on. Pull harder, *pull* . . . Prescott groans louder, much louder, he screams, his mouth is open, his tongue is hanging out . . .' Ray's voice dropped. 'He collapses on top of her.'

Ray rubbed his right wrist, twitching in spasms.

'Why don't you stop him, Ray?' Julia kept her voice stern. 'Why don't you stop it?'

'Because I can't, because I'm cuffed to the radiator.'

'Why are you cuffed?'

'He shot me. Prescott shot me in the leg.'

'Why did you let him shoot you, Ray? Why did you let that happen?'

'I didn't let . . . I couldn't stop it, I was alone, I went into the workshop alone, I didn't know he'd be there.' Tears streamed down his face. 'I didn't know he was there.'

'Look at that girl on the table, Ray. Is she dead?'

He nodded slowly.

'What if you had waited to call for help, what if you had waited upstairs in the lobby for backup? Would that have saved her?'

He didn't reply.

'What if you had waited for backup, Ray?'

His head started to shake slowly. 'No . . . She was already tied up when I got down there . . . If I had waited for help it would have been too late.'

'Are you sure about that, Ray? Are you positive you couldn't have saved her?'

'It would have been too late. Much too late.'

'I want you to look at her, look at the woman on the table. Tell me what you see.'

'She's just . . . lying there, not moving. He's on top of her, breathing, rubbing her . . .'

'Is she dead?'

'Yes.' Tears were slipping down his cheeks again.

'Could you have saved her, Ray? *Could you have saved her?*'

He held his breath for a moment, then answered in a long, slow exhalation: 'No.'

'Listen to me, Ray. Are you still looking at them, on the table in the workshop?'

'Yes.'

'I want you to imagine what you're looking at as a

photograph. You're looking at a photograph of a woman lying under a man. The woman in this photograph is the victim of a violent rape and murder. But it's just a *photograph*, nothing more than that. You can look at the photograph any time you want, Ray. But you can also put the photograph *aside*. You can put the photograph aside any time you want. Do you understand?'

Ray nodded.

'When you're making love to a woman, Ray, this image may enter your mind, this vision of violence and rape and murder. But now you have learned that it's a photograph – that this image is a photograph and you can put the photograph aside, you can stop looking at it any time you want. You are not responsible for what happened in this photograph, you can put it aside and make love without looking at it, without thinking of it. Do you understand?'

'Yes.'

'Making love to a woman has nothing to do with this photograph, Ray. Making love to a woman is beautiful, gentle, pleasurable. The photograph is violent and ugly. You can put it aside whenever you want, but especially when you are making love to a woman. The photograph cannot come between you and a woman when you are making love because you *control* the photograph, Ray. You determine when to look at it and when to put it aside.'

His breathing had subsided; he'd stopped rubbing his wrist.

'Who killed the woman, Ray?'

'He did, Prescott.'

'Could you have stopped it?'

He shook his head.

'Whenever you see this photograph of the woman and the man on the table in the superintendent's workshop, Ray, you must always tell yourself: I couldn't prevent this, I couldn't save her, it wasn't my fault. You will never feel any guilt or responsibility when you look at this *photograph*, and you can always put it aside, especially when you are making love to a woman. Do you understand, Ray?'

'Yes.'

'Good. Now, when I clap my hands you will leave the superintendent's workshop and wake up. You will remember what I told you about what happened there – that it wasn't your fault, that you can see it as a photograph, and put it aside at any time – but you won't remember that it was I who told you this. You will feel this naturally, by itself, just as I said.'

Julia let a few seconds pass, watching Ray. Her skill as a hypnotist had never been tested in quite so personal a way before, but her reluctance to put an end to Ray's trance went deeper than mere anxiety. When she clapped her hands she'd be relinquishing something important, something profoundly fulfilling.

Control.

'When I clap my hands you will leave the superintendent's workshop and wake up. You will leave your sense of responsibility behind. And you will remember, always, that this is a photograph that you can put aside at any time. You will not remember that it was I who told you this, it will occur to you naturally, on its own. But you will always remember . . .'

She closed her eyes and fought to keep the rest of the sentence to herself.

'You will always remember . . . that I love you.'

She clapped her hands.

Ray blinked, blinked again, and smiled groggily.

'Did I . . . did you . . .?'

Julia got on to the bed and lay down next to him. 'How do you feel?'

'Sleepy. I was really under?'

She smiled. 'Tell me what you remember?'

He closed his eyes. 'I remember being in the super's workshop, watching . . .' His eyes opened, and then, gradually, a smile broke out. 'Something's different. I don't feel it . . . here.' He pushed a fist into his stomach, then put an arm around her.

'Ray, it's important to wait before—'

'Oh, no. After all that?'

'It's the only way to be sure that the post-hypnotic suggestion is working. Trying it out too soon . . .' She couldn't help smiling. 'Well, it could undo everything that just happened.'

'I can't believe you're going to make me wait.'

'Anyway, Emily had a rough evening, I wouldn't be surprised if she climbed into bed tonight. I don't want her to find you here.'

'Not fair, bringing Emily into it.' He shook his head, but he was still smiling. 'I guess I don't have a choice, do I?'

He got out of bed and started to get dressed.

'But you do have something to look forward to,' Julia said. 'We both do.'

Wednesday 15 February

41

Julia left her building through the garage the next morning at eight, holding Emily's hand. Her escort introduced himself as Joe O'Hearn and pointed to his car. Even in the garage with an escort she felt vulnerable, watched. Should she hold Emily protectively close, or stay as far from her as possible?

'Where's Lou?' Emily asked.

O'Hearn glanced at Julia.

'He's . . . he couldn't come today,' Julia said.

They got in the back seat and she gave him the address of Emily's school. As they left the garage Julia saw a crowd in front of her building. A few people held cameras. *Shit*, reporters.

A *Times* piece that morning had connected Lou LaVigna's death to the three murders. The article raised more questions than it answered, but it placed Julia squarely at the center of the entire mess. The first victim had lived three floors below her, after all.

As O'Hearn drove off she tried not to think of Lou LaVigna. *They think I pulled a sweet assignment . . . you know, watching you.* Lou's funeral was in two days – maybe Ray would go with her.

'You planning on going out this morning, Ms Mallet?' O'Hearn asked after Julia had dropped off Emily.

'Don't you read the papers? I'm the quiet woman who doesn't

391

go out much.' Julia sighed. No point in alienating . . . What was his name? Joe something. 'I've been told to stay inside,' she said quietly.

He smiled nervously at the rearview mirror.

She was back in her apartment by nine. Reporters from half-a-dozen newspapers and several local television stations had left messages. She called her office.

'Are you okay?' Alison asked.

I'm scared shitless.

'I'll survive. But I won't be in today.'

You're my perfect angel.

Gail's words were cloyingly sinister, somehow. Emily was no angel, thank God – no child was. Why had Gail faked hypnosis? What was she hiding?

Something from 1963, it had to be – even though Ray said the background check had turned up nothing unusual. 'No one in New Jefferson remembered Gail Severance,' he'd told her. 'And high schools keep records for ten, fifteen years at most.'

Gail had once told Julia that her mother made a religion of self-reliance. Getting close to people wasn't part of the ritual.

Still, *someone* must remember her. Everyone left a mark, and if something awful had happened in 1963, somebody would remember it.

She called Alison again. 'Do me a favor? Run down to Media, get the CD-ROM disk with all the phone books, and call me back.'

Alison called back five minutes later. 'There are two CDs. One's eleven million businesses, the other is seventy million households.'

'Can you messenger me the households CD right away?'

When she went down to get the envelope an hour later, one of the reporters out front spotted her and began banging on the large window next to the revolving door. Soon several people were pounding, calling out questions.

'Julia, what's the connection to Jessica Forrester?'

'Julia, who took a shot at you?'

'Julia, is it true you're a suspect in three murders?'

Julio Gonzalez held the elevator door open until she was inside. 'Don't worry, I won't let nobody in.'

Back in her apartment, the front door triple-locked, she booted up her computer and inserted the disk. She worked through a few menu screens, typing in 'Gail Severance' at the prompt. The computer searched through all 70 million entries – every phone book in America, according to the CD's marketing notes – and came up with one match: Gail Severance, East 78th Street, Manhattan.

Pretty impressive. Julia next typed 'Severance'. The computer found forty-two matches, none of them in New Jefferson. She'd concentrate on the Severances in the New England and Middle Atlantic states – most Madison students were from the northeast. The computer narrowed the list to ten matches.

She began by calling Arnold Severance in Great Neck, on Long Island. A woman answered on the second ring.

'Hello, I'm doing a credit check on a Gail Severance, who has applied—'

'Don't know her.' *Click.*

She tried the next name on the list: Herbert Severance, in Albany. Herbert was nicer – he listened to her entire spiel – but he'd never heard of a Gail Severance.

She called Ruth Severance in Treemont, New York.

'Hello, I'm doing a credit check on Gail Severance,' she said. 'Miss Severance has applied for—'

'Is this some kind of sick joke?'

'Not at all. I'm with First City Bank; we're reviewing a mortgage application for Gail Severance.' Julia held her breath.

'I don't know any such person. Goodbye.'

'Wait. You asked if I was joking.'

Long pause. 'I had a niece named Gail. My brother's child.'

'*Had*?'

'She died many years ago, in an accident. The year President Kennedy was shot.'

'Nineteen sixty-three.' Julia swallowed hard. 'What . . . kind of accident?'

'You need this information for a *mortgage* application?'

'Actually, no. It's personal. I'm looking for background on Gail Severance – probably not the same Gail you're talking about, but it's very important that I have as much information as possible. You mentioned an accident?'

'She was hit by a train, killed instantly.'

'*Gail* Severance?'

'My niece, yes. She and a friend were playing in a field behind Gail's house. The Hudson Line ran right through the field, still does. There was a fence between my brother-in-law's backyard and the field, of course, but there was a hole. The girls slipped through . . . It was a double tragedy, really.'

'Why is that?'

'I don't think Gail's friend – Rachel Meriwether, they were inseparable – ever got over the accident. She was a peculiar child, a loner even as a little girl. Especially after the accident. She was bright, a good student, but she never seemed interested in any of the other students.'

'The accident happened in Treemont?'

'That's correct, across from . . . I still don't understand why you need to know all this.'

'It's complicated, but very, very important. Do Gail's parents still live there?'

'Both passed away several years back.'

'And Rachel Meriwether?'

A long, exasperated sigh. 'She graduated, left – can't recall where to. Her father left them, Rachel and her mother, a few years after the accident. Her mother moved away soon after Rachel graduated, maybe to be closer to her, wherever she ended up. Neither parent ever had much to do with the community anyway. A bit like their daughter in that respect.'

'You sound as though you didn't like them very much.'

'Do I? I'm not sure I have *any* feelings for the Meriwethers. This is all ancient history, don't forget. And certainly I've never heard of a Gail Severance other than my niece. My husband and I attend the Severance family reunion every August, right here in Treemont. If there was another Gail in the family, I'd know about it.'

Julia thanked Ruth Severance, hung up, and tried to make sense out of what she'd just learned. The train accident in 1963 had killed a Gail Severance who was four years old – the exact age of the Gail Severance who had faked a hypnotic trance that would have regressed her to the age of four.

Sharing the name of a dead girl was hardly evidence of psychosis. But the coincidence was mind-boggling.

Gail Severance: *My parents never had any friends. Neither did I, as long as I lived with them.*

Ruth Severance: *The parents never had much to do with the community anyway. A bit like their daughter in that respect.*

Julia's Gail Severance had always said she grew up in New Jefferson, but no one there remembered anyone by that name. Perhaps the answer lay in Treemont, just a few miles from New Jefferson and only an hour north of Manhattan. If there was a connection, she'd find it. She turned off the computer.

I sometimes fantasize about leaving bombs all over the city, then waiting for them to go off, like planting tulip bulbs in the fall.

Julia grabbed her purse and left the apartment, entering the parking garage directly from the elevator. Her car was in its usual spot, the windows replaced. She drove right by the crowd of reporters in front of her building. They were standing in the spot where Lou . . .

They think I pulled a sweet assignment . . . you know, watching you.

Julia wasn't going to wait around for a second attempt.

42

The drive to Treemont was unexpectedly calming. She felt safe in the locked car, cocooned. But then anything was better than being cooped up in an apartment with the entire New York press corps camped out front, the Wizard out there somewhere, waiting. If it weren't for Emily she'd keep driving and driving . . .

Treemont retained a veneer of country charm – quaint farmhouses, a cozy downtown area free of chain stores, clapboard churches with white spires gleaming against a cloudless blue sky. She imagined living there with Emily: the center-hall colonial, the golden retriever, the yellow school bus taking Emily safely to . . .

Hell, they probably stoned unwed mothers at the border.

Treemont's high school fit right in: ivy-covered red brick, large double-hung windows, neatly tended shrubs. Julia parked in front and entered the building through the main door. It was just after twelve, lunchtime, and the hallways were nearly empty.

She found the library, went in, and looked around her. The rows of polished mahogany bookshelves, the yellowed window shades, the musty scent, the strained hush of students crouched over wooden tables – this could have been *her* high-school library, on Long Island not Westchester. Only the half-dozen computer terminals tucked away in a corner suggested the passage of nearly twenty years.

The young woman at the main desk greeted Julia with a puzzled expression and an offer of help.

'I'm looking for information on . . . Actually, I was looking for old yearbooks.'

The woman's features relaxed into a smile. 'Did you graduate from Treemont?'

'Well, no, but a friend of mine . . .' Better not use the name Gail Severance. '. . . Rachel Meriwether attended the school, back in the early seventies.'

'You're in luck, then.' She turned and called through an open doorway. 'Mrs Angermeyer?'

An elderly, heavy-set woman stepped through the door.

'This woman is looking for information on Rachel Meriwether,' the librarian said. 'You've been here since the early sixties, so I—'

'Rachel is a friend of yours?'

The reading glasses perched on the end of Mrs Angermeyer's nose were attached to a beaded necklace that hung loosely on either side of her face.

'She's not exactly a friend, but I *was* hoping to find a yearbook photo of her. She's a relative, a cousin . . .' Julia had never been much of an actress. 'I haven't seen her in years, but she's mentioned in . . . a will, her uncle's will, and I need to track her down.'

The older woman gave her a penetrating look. 'I'll show you the yearbooks.' She led Julia across the large room, leaning on chairs and tables as they went. 'I remember your cousin. She wasn't very popular here in Treemont, but then I guess you know why.'

'The train accident?'

'I'd just started working here when it happened. The Severances were about the most respected family in town. Hugh Severance was the town counsel, his wife was on the library board . . . No one could believe what happened. Still, it wasn't fair, the way people blamed Rachel for little Gail Severance's death. Then again, she *was* there when it happened.'

'Wait a minute, people *blamed* her?' Julia thought of Ruth Severance's disapproving reticence on the subject of Rachel Meriwether.

'Maybe blame's too harsh a word,' the librarian said, 'but it was like Rachel was . . . tainted. You have to understand what the Severances meant to a town like Treemont. Burton Severance's great-grandfather founded the—'

'I'm sure they're very important people,' Julia said. 'But how can a five-year-old be tainted by another little girl's death?'

'That's just the way it was,' the old woman said. 'Every time you looked at Rachel Meriwether you couldn't help thinking, Why is she alive and the other one dead? The Severance girl was so darn pretty. I remember her even now. There was a kind of glow about her.'

'An angel.'

'Yes, an angel. But the other – Rachel – well, of course she couldn't help being so heavy and plain, but still you couldn't help wondering what God had in mind when he let the one girl live and the other die.'

They had reached a far corner of the room, with dozens of identically bound yearbooks neatly aligned on a low shelf. Julia crouched down and found the 1977 volume of the Treemont 'Reminiscences'. The librarian hovered just behind her as Julia turned the pages.

The yearbook, like the library itself, could have been her own. Unmistakably mid-seventies: boys and girls with long, straight hair parted down the middle, below each name a quote, presumably chosen by the student to represent his or her true, inevitably anguished soul. Only the dreamy smiles and half-drape yearbook poses were timeless.

'Sometimes I think even her parents blamed her,' the librarian said as Julia flipped through the senior class section.

'*What*?'

She shrugged. 'You hear things, working in this place all these years. Not that I'm one to gossip.' She clasped her hands in front of her. 'Rachel's parents never made it to any of the parents' nights, the class plays – not that Rachel was ever anything but a backstage gofer. Still, they should have come. Of course, the father left them, and then . . . well, there was talk, too.'

Julia stopped flipping pages and looked at her.

'Idle gossip, really,' the old woman said.

Which you, of course, would have no part of.

'What kind of talk?'

'Mind you, this was before people even whispered about, you know . . .' She looked down and shook her head. 'My daughter was a class ahead of her at the elementary school, and this is a small town . . .'

'Before they whispered about *what*?'

'Hurting them,' she said.

'Hurting *children*?'

The librarian looked up and put an index finger to her lips.

'Rachel's parents *hurt* her?' Damned if she was going to lower her voice.

'Who's to say? But she had this cast on her arm, back in grammar school. Two times, in fact.' Her head dropped again. 'Maybe three.'

'Oh, no.'

'She was an awkward girl, nervous, always tripping over her own feet – right through high school. At least, that's what people said.'

'And no one looked into it, no one spoke to her parents?'

'It wasn't like today, with your movie stars competing

400

with each other on the television to tell the world how their parents hit them.'

Julia returned to the yearbook. A few more pages and she found Rachel Meriwether.

'Back then we left child-rearing up to the parents, we left the parents alone.'

'Oh my God.'

The girl in the photo was holding a doll. Small, obviously dog-eared, with a pointed cap and a thin rod in its hand . . . a wand.

'The Wizard,' Julia said.

'Yes, it does look like a wizard,' the librarian said over Julia's shoulder. 'Probably the closest friend she had here. I remember she carried it with her a lot. Even had it with her when she worked in the principal's office after school. I think she preferred working to going home. She made quite a stink about being photographed with that doll.'

Julia peered at the photo. Long, slightly frizzy hair, fleshy face, wire-framed granny glasses . . . Could it possibly . . . ?

She held the book at arm's length and squinted. The cheekbones. The deep-set eyes . . .

She blinked and Gail appeared: almost twenty years older, hair stylishly short now, face leaner, more angular, much more attractive. She blinked again and the eighteen-year-old Rachel Meriwether reappeared. Another blink, Gail was back.

'Can I . . .' Julia took a deep breath. 'I want to make sure I have this straight. Gail Severance was run over by a train. Rachel Meriwether, who was with her at the time of the accident, graduated from this high school.'

'And just disappeared. Her mother moved away – to Florida, I think. We never heard from Rachel again.'

Julia turned back to the photo. Gail – or Rachel – held the doll, the wizard, in the crook of her arm, like she might hold an actual child. An eerie image, this spurned teenager cosseting a homely little doll as if it were the most precious thing on earth.

She started to close the book, then flipped back to read Gail/Rachel's motto: 'I'll bide my time, but don't you worry. I'll get you, my pretty. And your little dog too!'

Julia slammed shut the book and handed it back to the librarian. 'I need . . . I have to get back to the city. Thanks for your help.'

I'll get you, my pretty.

'Are you all right?'

But Julia was already jogging toward the library exit.

43

She cruised at sixty-five on the twisty Saw Mill River Parkway, slamming on the brakes at the occasional traffic light. She'd paged Ray from a pay-phone at the high school, but when he hadn't called back after five minutes she got into the car and headed for the city.

So many questions. How had Rachel changed her identity to Gail, starting when she enrolled at Madison? And why? The murders at least made sense: Gail/Rachel was acting out some sort of revenge fantasy. '*I'll get you, my pretty.*' Dormant for thirty years, the compulsion had been revived under hypnosis just two weeks ago.

She'd revived it by playing God. And the Wizard – Gail – thought she knew something, tried to warn her off with the attack on the car, the spray-painted sheets, the attempt on her life.

Now she pressed the accelerator past seventy and pondered the one question that loomed above all others. How was it possible that Gail Severance, whatever her real name, was a killer? Stalking those women, shooting them, spraying their faces with black paint . . . If Gail really had been with Martin all those nights, she couldn't have . . .

No. Gail *was* the Wizard. Everything pointed to that. Including the pressure she'd been under lately – the cookbook deadline, and Martin's threatening to end their affair. Dr Turner had gotten *that* right. *Hypnotically retrieved memory, combined with other, ongoing pressures, could trigger a psychotic reaction.* And the person could otherwise appear completely normal . . .

Julia pulled off the West Side Highway at 79th Street, found a phone booth on Broadway, and tried Ray again.

'He's in with the deputy chief of detectives,' the dispatcher told her once she'd introduced herself

'But this is important,' Julia said. 'It's about the murders, the serial—'

'What do you think he's talking to the chief about? You want me to give him a message when he gets out?'

'Just tell him I called,' Julia said and hung up. After a moment's thought she got back in the car and headed for midtown.

'We know you're fucking her.'

Deputy Chief of Detectives Larry Breaker stubbed out a cigarette and emptied the ash tray in the garbage can under his desk. No one in the room moved a muscle – not Breaker, Dave McCarty, Stella Turner.

Ray felt his body go clammy and decided to do what the cleverest suspects always did: shift the focus to the details, trip them up on the nits – and avoid the big picture, the issue of guilt and innocence, at all costs. 'You bugging her apartment?' he said.

'Nope.' Breaker's lips didn't move.

'Her phones?'

'*No.*'

'Because *you* assigned me to cover her. I didn't ask for it, you know. Spending time with her is part of the—'

'If the press finds out you're fucking her you're on your own.'

Breaker wiped a fleck of ash from his blotter with the side of his pinky. 'I can't save you.'

Fucking her. Ray might have smiled under different circumstances. Technically, at least, he was still innocent. 'I want to know who told you this,' he said. A sudden thought: they were guessing, grabbing at straws. He glanced at Dave, who turned away. 'I have a right to know my accusers.'

'You *have* no rights, my friend,' Breaker growled. Three women killed, Julia attacked – all part of the job. A cop killed? Now it was family. Ray Burgess's petty problems counted for squat.

'Look, I've spent a lot of time with her, that's part—'

'Task force meeting, fifteen minutes.' Breaker lit a cigarette, blew out the first puff of smoke in a long, thin stream. 'Bring me up to date on the LaVigna investigation.'

Julia got off the elevator on the thirty-third floor and walked quickly to the receptionist.

'Martin Freemason, please.'

The receptionist eyed Julia's baggy sweater and blue jeans. 'Do you have an appointment?'

'Just tell him it's Julia Mallet.'

A minute later she was being shown to Martin's office by his very tall, very beautiful secretary. They navigated a maze of cubicles and desks. Excell Commodities occupied the entire thirty-third floor. Traders hunched over computer screens and barked into multi-line telephones. Styrofoam coffee cups occupied every horizontal surface not already covered by reports, printouts, crumpled phone messages.

'Julia, what a surprise.' But Martin looked more worried than surprised as he stood up behind his enormous desk. 'Please close the door,' he told his secretary.

Julia walked right up to the desk, placed her hands on it, and leaned toward Martin. 'I need the truth,' she said. 'Was Gail with you the nights the women were murdered?'

'I told the cops, we—'

'*The truth.*'

He sat down. Julia remained standing in front of the desk.

'Haven't you caused enough trouble?' he said. 'The cops were here this morning – most of the morning, in fact. Wanted to know why the hell I wouldn't let you do that voodoo stuff on me.'

'What did you tell them?'

'I didn't *tell* them anything because I didn't have to. Christ, when my lawyer heard about what you did last night, he nearly hit the ceiling.'

'You were afraid I'd ask about Gail. And maybe there were other women?'

'Fuck you, Julia.'

'Look, I don't know what the police think, and I know you didn't kill those women. But it's important that we . . .' She didn't have time for the whole story, not that she owed him the truth anyway. 'It's important that we establish where Gail was those nights.'

'Gail? You mean—'

'Were you with her?'

He glanced down at his desk. 'It's possible I left early enough . . .'

'But you told the police you were with her until after the murders.'

'They were *accusing* me, Julia.' He looked up at her with those hungry, jittery eyes, and she caught a glimpse of the pre-Park Avenue Martin, the Marijuana Maven, always hawking something, trying to score. 'It seemed easiest for all concerned to just . . .'

'Lie?'

'Look, I'm not really sure what time I left Gail's. But it's possible I left early enough those nights for her . . .' He shook his head. 'This is unreal.'

She had what she'd come for and was almost out the door when he called her name.

'I never meant to hurt anyone, Julia.'

'All those years? Lying to Paula, to everyone?'

'It was a strange fucking affair,' Martin said. 'I never understood what Gail got out of it. She never seemed to enjoy the sex much. I don't think she ever once had an orgasm during the entire time we—'

'Then why did you continue seeing her?'

Martin turned to face the window.

'*Why*, Martin?'

He looked back at Julia, a shadow across his face. 'She was totally focused on me,' he said. 'I mean, she didn't seem to enjoy a single thing *I* did, but Christ, she knew how to turn me on. I've never experienced anything like it with anyone else. She wanted nothing from me except . . . to enjoy myself.'

'That's so selfish.' And sick.

'It was like she was playing me, like I was some sort of instrument she was perfecting.'

Or a recipe. Gail didn't talk about sex much – at least, not about her own behavior.

'And it never really felt intimate,' Martin continued. 'I never felt close to her – not emotionally, anyway. That's why I didn't feel like I was betraying Paula, not emotionally betraying—'

'The nights of the murders, did you have sex?'

'Not the last time, no. As for the other times, I'm not really sure. The fact is, I was trying to break it off. It was just so . . . sick, and Gail seemed to be getting even more strange lately, almost desperate, trying new things, new ways to please me.'

'Gee, that must have been real hard on you.'

Martin scowled at her. 'But every time I mentioned breaking off, Gail went crazy, screaming and threatening me. I couldn't figure out how to end it – she hasn't been herself lately.'

Jesus.

'How's Paula doing?'

'We're trying to work things out. I am, at any rate.' He glanced out of the window, eyes fixed on some distant point. 'After these murders stop, she wants me to move out.'

He looked back at her, his expression inviting pity or at least encouragement. He got neither.

The gathering of reporters, photographers, and cameramen in front of Julia's building had become a crowd. She slowed her car just enough to avoid actually running over any of them and pulled into the parking garage. She entered the lobby from the garage, careful to keep her back to the front door.

'Miss Mallet?' Reinaldo, the afternoon doorman. He probably saw her from the rear more than anybody.

'Yes?' She didn't turn around.

'Your sitter has Emily in the park, she ask me to tell you. I told one of the porters to let them out the service door.'

'Thank you, I really appreciate every—'

'Julia, wait!'

She turned to find the revolving door spitting reporters and cameramen into the lobby.

'Julia, are you connected to the gunshot killings of the . . .'

She lunged into the elevator and jabbed at the close-door button.

'Miss Mallet, there's something else . . .'

'Julia, isn't it true you're a suspect in the . . .'

The elevator shut.

Julia downed a finger of Scotch, no ice, and tried Ray again. He was still in with the chief of detectives.

'Tell him to call me right away.' Julia hesitated. 'And give him this message. Are you writing this down? Tell him . . . tell him that it's Gail.'

'It's Gail?'

'Just give him the message – shit, what's that?'

'Excuse me?'

'A noise, I . . . Never mind, just make sure he gets the message.'

Julia hung up and walked from the windowless kitchen into the living room. The noise was even louder there – a rhythmic throbbing, like an amplified heartbeat. She crossed the room to the window.

A helicopter hovered less than fifty yards from her building, the video camera held just outside its right hatch aimed at her.

She took a step back, then another, then tripped over her coffee table and fell to the floor. She rubbed the back of her leg where she'd hit the table. The phone rang, picked up after two rings by her machine.

'Julia, Frederica Samuels, New York *Newsday*. We understand you're a prime suspect in the recent murders of three Manhattan women. But you're also a victim of an assassination attempt. If you'd like your side of the story told for a change, give me a call. I'm keeping an open mind.'

Julia's sobs erupted without warning. She'd kept it together until then, she'd had to. But now, sprawled on the floor, she let two weeks' worth of fear and rage pour out. Maybe a lifetime's.

The noise from the helicopter sounded as close as her own heartbeat. Or was the throbbing noise her own heart? Time to get off the floor, get moving, get it together again. Regain control.

Regain control? She would have laughed if she hadn't been crying, sobbing, without the control to get up off the floor.

Is this what they wanted, her oldest and dearest friends?

One day I want to see Julia Mallet let go of the control.

That would be worth waiting for.

Fuck you, Jared. Fuck all of you.

She crawled across the living room, away from the window, careful to stay out of camera range. In the windowless foyer she stood up, grabbed her coat and keys. She'd find Emily in the park, take her across town to her mother's – no, the media would find them there. They'd have to check into a hotel until this whole mess was over.

In Hong Kong.

She opened the front door. She'd use the service entrance to avoid the reporters in front of the building. Reinaldo was doing his best to keep them out, but if they saw her crossing the lobby for the garage there might be a stampede.

Reinaldo. Something he'd said earlier, as the reporters were streaming into the lobby . . .

Miss Mallet, there's something else.

She crossed the foyer and buzzed the lobby. 'It's Julia Mallet. You said there was something else.'

'I wanted to tell you, your friend was here before . . .'

Friend. Her stomach clenched at the word.

'Which friend do—'

'Miss Severance. Gail. About ten minutes before you come back.'

'What . . . what did she want?'

'She ask for you, I tell her you go out. Then she ask for Emily, so I tell her Emily in the park with—'

'You told her where Emily was?'

'I see Miss Severance many times, she is a good friend, I didn't see nothing the matter with—'

Julia dropped the house phone and ran for the elevator. A minute later she left the building through the service door. A quick glance in both directions – no reporters, no cameras – then she turned right and sprinted toward Central Park.

410

Gail had asked where Emily was . . . *Why?*

She ran the entire way, ignoring the fatigue that began to cramp her legs after several blocks.

You're my perfect angel. Gail was planning to rescue Emily. Her angel.

She entered the park at 67th Street. Emily's favorite playground was a block north, just off Central Park West. Traffic thundered along the main park drive, joggers hugged the outer perimeter, nannies wheeled their charges in prams and strollers. Julia ran even faster, gasping for air but feeling nothing but determination. Emily was close. In a minute she'd grab her and get the hell away from there.

She left the sidewalk and cut across a grassy area, crashing into several low branches as she ran. Just fifty yards more to the fenced-in playground. She squinted and tried to make out Pamela and Emily, but something else caught her eye, something on the dark stone wall separating the park and the street.

She slowed down to a walk, stepped a few feet closer.

Oh, Christ, *no!*

The black letters glistened, luridly fresh on the dusky gray stones of the wall.

Get away, go find Emily and get the hell out of . . .

But she couldn't tear her eyes from the glossy black words. *The Wizard*, its D dripping black paint, as if the letter itself were melting. It must have been painted a few minutes ago.

The music – a succession of tinny, muted notes – made her glance to the right. There it was: a tattered doll, propped against the wall, its pointed cap drooping to the side, a ghastly red smile the only feature not yet worn away. But the tune it sang was vivid enough. 'Somewhere, over the . . .'

'Hello, Julia.'

She spun around, gasped.

'I've been waiting for you.'

44

'Gail, is that *you*?'

She had on an ill-fitting, cheap blonde wig, oversized sunglasses that obscured half her face, lips smeared with red lipstick like . . . the Wizard.

'What are you *doing* here?'

'Waiting for you.' She waved a hand at the graffiti, like a hostess pointing to an elegantly set table, then took off the sunglasses and glanced over at the playground.

'Emily's favorite place in the whole wide world.'

Her eyes were glazed but jumpy, as if she were having trouble focusing. Her right hand held a large plastic bag. A flash of red as she shifted weight drew Julia's attention to her feet. Red shoes, preternaturally bright, as if they'd been polished over and over.

Ruby slippers.

Julia started to back away. 'I have to get Emily.'

'No, you don't.'

The gun Gail jerked from the bag was aimed squarely at Julia. The long silencer put it only a few inches from her face.

'Gail, whatever this is about . . .'

Gail waved the gun toward the stone wall just a few feet behind them. The darkening sky, the height of the wall, and the thick trunks of two large trees a few feet away, would at least partially conceal them in shadow. Someone might notice them – but not necessarily spot the gun.

'Let's go back to my—'

'NOW.'

She looked tattered and frayed – as shabby and worn as the Wizard doll she'd cared for all those years. Only her voice evoked the old Gail, strong and insistent, with a new-found edge of icy rage.

Julia walked to the wall, Gail right behind her. At least they weren't heading closer to the playground, and Emily. At the wall, Julia turned around. Gail had the gun leveled directly at her face.

'Gail, don't.'

'You're a monster,' Gail said.

'I'm your oldest—'

'Listen!' Gail said.

'I don't hear—'

'Listen, it's telling me what to do.'

Julia glanced behind her. 'It's just a wall, I don't—'

'No, listen! It's that face. It says . . . it says you threw her, you flung her like a piece of trash.'

'*Who*? Who did I . . . You mean yesterday, when Emily came in?'

'She's an angel.'

'She lost her balance, Gail. I—'

'You *threw* her! I saw the red patch, next to her eye, you could have *blinded* her.'

'You know me too well to think I'd harm Emily.'

Gail's lips quivered as she slowly shook her head. 'You had me fooled, all these years. I loved you, Julia, and now I know the truth. You're a monster, like the others, and . . .' She glanced over Julia's shoulder and nodded, as if in response to a command. 'And you must be stopped.'

413

'Is that why you killed them, Gail? To save the children?'

'Angels.' Her eyes drifted off somewhere; her lips gathered into a smile that lasted a second or two at most before flattening to a cold, hard grimace. Eyes now locked on Julia's, she spoke in a low, frigid monotone. 'I saw what was happening to them. I had no choice.' She took a step toward Julia, poked the gun at her cheek. 'I have no choice now.'

She pulled the trigger.

Ray pushed his way through a crowd of reporters and cameramen and entered Julia's lobby.

'She's not here,' the doorman said. 'She go out, about fifteen minutes ago, maybe twenty. She use the service exit. I see her in the monitor.' He pointed to the three black-and-white screens built into his desk.

Damn her. She was under orders not to leave the building.

'Any idea where she went?'

'Earlier, when she come back, I tell her Emily and the sitter, they go to the park. I think she went to get them. Too noisy around here for her.' He glanced at the media swarm outside the front door. 'For everybody. Try that playground inside the Park at Sixty-seventh Street. Like I told her friend earlier, that's where all the kids in the building go.'

'Her friend?'

'Sure – Miss Severance. She come by an hour ago looking for them.'

'And you told her where Emily was?'

The doorman cleared his throat, straightened his jacket. 'She here all the time, Miss Severance. Gail Severance. I wouldn't tell a stranger, but she—'

'An hour ago?'

Ray ran across the lobby, shoved his way through the throng of reporters, trying to absorb it all: Gail had faked hypnosis,

414

had called Emily an angel. *A perfect angel.* Gail, Emily and Julia were in the park together.

He got into the front passenger seat of his car. Dave McCarty had the engine running.

'Central Park at 67th Street,' he told Dave. 'Fast.'

'*Rachel, NO!*'

Gail flinched as the gun fired with a muted pop. Julia heard the bullet hiss past her left ear.

'I – I know who you are.' Julia fought for breath, her nose burning from a sharp, sulphury smell. 'I know . . . you didn't harm little Gail in nineteen sixty-three. It was an accident.'

Gail stared at her, mouth open.

'You were blamed for Gail's death, but you were innocent.'

'They all thought I should have died. Fat, plain, no blonde curls, no blue eyes . . . Gail had everything, toys and dolls and parents who loved her.'

'No child deserves to die.'

'She had this one doll, with the most beautiful little satin suit . . .' Gail glanced at the Wizard propped against the wall. 'She had so much and she wouldn't let me have this one thing. I tried to take it away from her and she fell . . . I heard the whistle . . . I heard it but I didn't know she would roll under . . .' She looked down at the ground. 'I kept the Wizard, after.'

'You were innocent, Gail.'

'Everyone turned on me. My own parents. And my father . . .' Gail's eyes drifted for a moment, then refocused on Julia's face. 'At first it was punishment, that's what he *said*, but later it was . . . it was something else.' She sniffled as her free hand massaged her chest. 'When I tried to tell my mother about it she locked me in a closet for hours and hours, and sometimes—'

'Give me the gun,' Julia said. 'Emily needs me, Gail. I'm all she has, and if—'

415

'DON'T YOU THINK I KNOW THAT?'

Gail's voice was so shrill, her face so livid, that Julia stopped as if taking a physical blow.

'You're all she has – and you're a monster. I saw what you did. You thought you'd hypnotized me like the last time, but you hadn't.'

'But you were hypnotized the first time – at the party?'

'You made me feel it all over again that night. I'd forgotten . . . No, I never forgot what happened, but I'd forgotten how it *felt*. You brought the voices back.' Gail raked the end of the gun along the side of Julia's head, digging it into her.

'Put the gun down, you're hurting me,' Julia said. 'Put it down, *Rachel*.'

Gail shook her head violently. 'Rachel's gone.'

The fading light of dusk made them less visible to the rest of the park. She could scream for help, but the gun was still pressed into her face. Gail was so jumpy, she'd probably fire at any sudden sound or movement.

'I didn't deserve to live. *She* did. Rachel had to die so that Gail could come back.'

Julia saw her finger tighten on the trigger, saw a deepening of rage and pain in her eyes. She closed her eyes and waited for the shot.

'Mommy!'

Julia opened her eyes and saw Emily running toward them, Pamela in pursuit.

'Emily, no!' Julia tried to shout but her voice was hoarse. 'Pamela, stop her!'

Emily kept running toward them, too fast for Pamela to catch up.

'I'm going to save you, angel,' Gail said when Emily reached them. 'I'm going to save you like I saved the others. You'll see . . .'

'I'm not a monster,' Julia said softly. 'I'm Emily's mom, that's all.'

Emily wrapped her arms around Julia's legs and stared up at Gail, who was smiling blissfully as if at a vision. *An angel.* Pamela was slowly walking backward.

'Don't hurt my mommy!'

The gun lowered an inch or so.

'It's only me, angel.' Gail flung off the wig.

'Gail?' Emily squinted at her, smiling.

'Mommy is mean to you, angel. She punishes you for things you didn't do.'

'Friday is parents' day at my school, Mommy promised she was coming.'

Julia felt the gun slide from cheek to neck, then down to her chest. 'I'll . . . be there,' she said. 'Mommy will be there.'

'We're making cookies for it,' Emily said. 'Chocolate chippety cookies.'

Gail took another step toward Emily and Julia, the gun aimed at Julia's heart. Pamela began running to the park entrance at 67th Street.

'Your mommy fools you by making you cookies and taking you places.' Gail knelt down to eye level with Emily.

Julia fought the urge to lunge at her. She might get in a good kick to Gail's side, but she was so close to Emily, the gun just a few inches from her back . . .

'You don't realize it yet, my angel, but someday you will,' Gail was saying. 'What she does to you is bad. Very bad. She—'

'When Mommy's bad we say timber timber.' Emily looked up at Julia. 'Right, Mommy?'

'Temper, temper – that's right, darling.'

Emily let go of Julia's legs and moved closer to Gail. 'Say it,' she said. 'Say temper tem . . .'

Gail grabbed Emily with her left arm and tried to lift her.

'Rachel, don't hurt her,' Julia said.

Gail stood up. Her left arm now cradled Emily against her chest; her right hand still held the gun. 'Hurt her? I'm saving her.' She took a step back, still clutching Emily, and pointed the gun squarely at Julia's face – away from Emily. Julia heard Pamela from Central Park West, shouting for the police.

But she couldn't afford to wait for the cops to get there.

Julia held her breath. She'd be lucky to get in one decent jab. Both fists clenched, she swallowed, drew back her right arm . . .

'I never met a girl who really put everything behind a punch. They always hold back, don't ask me why.'

. . . and swung out as if to hurl her arm itself at Gail. Her fist powered into Gail's jaw. The gun fired into the air. Emily went sprawling to the ground, screaming. Gail staggered back a few feet, still clutching the gun, then seemed to regain her balance. She took a step forward, raised the gun and fired.

Julia felt her left arm catch fire, felt the heat shoot through her body as she pulled back her right arm and let loose a hook that landed just to the side of Gail's nose with a sickening crunch. Gail staggered backward for a moment, then steadied the gun.

'MOMMY!' Emily got up and ran toward Julia.

'No, Emily, stay back!' Julia charged at Gail and threw a right jab under Gail's chin. Gail teetered a moment, eyes wide, almost incredulous, and then crumpled to the ground.

Julia pulled Emily to her and squeezed her hard as she looked at her left arm. Blood was soaking through the coat, the burning sensation had intensified.

Emily was safe.

'Julia!' A man's voice. She turned and saw Ray getting out of his car. He ran toward them, followed by another man, as several patrol cars pulled up on to the lawn. Pamela was running back toward them.

Julia heard something and turned around.

'All I wanted . . . was to save you, my angel,' Gail whispered. Her head fell back to the ground.

Julia handed Emily to Pamela, knelt, and bent over Gail. She gently stroked her forehead.

'I never wanted to hurt you, Julia,' Gail whispered. 'But you brought Rachel back . . .'

Julia smoothed back Gail's hair and thought of the three murdered women, of Lou LaVigna.

'When I left your apartment, after your party?' Gail's eyes were closed, the lids quivering. 'I saw Jessica Forrester and her husband, coming back from a party, I guess. Sloppy drunk, she was laughing like an idiot, pawing her husband – but I'd seen a different Jessica a few weeks earlier.'

'Oh, God.'

'In your lobby . . . I was on my way to see you when she slapped that little boy of hers. Broad daylight. I put it out of my mind at the time, but after your party, seeing her drunk, laughing like . . . like nothing mattered, all I could think of was how she hurt her children, her angels. I knew that night I had to protect them.'

She opened her eyes and looked at Julia. 'Emily's innocent,' she said, the words barely audible. 'Innocent . . .'

Julia touched Gail's forehead, brushing back a lock of hair. 'So are you, Rachel,' she said. 'So are you.'

Thursday 16 February

45

Emily slept in Julia's bed Wednesday night. Julia kept running the past twelve hours – no, the past twenty years – through her mind, while Emily rolled over every few minutes, thrashing with her hands and legs. Just before midnight, Julia gave her a spoonful of cough medicine, which made her drowsy. A half-hour later she was asleep. It would have taken a lot more than cough medicine to knock Julia out that night. Her arm had been stitched up at Roosevelt Hospital, and she'd taken the pain killer the doctor had prescribed. The surface injury had stopped throbbing not long afterwards. But not the deeper wounds.

In the morning Emily was full of energy and eager to go to school. But she was almost too enthusiastic, too restless, eating little of her breakfast, unable to sit still for more than a few moments. She didn't mention the incident in the park, and when Julia gently raised the issue, hoping to gauge her emotions, she changed the subject immediately. At eight, they left through the service entrance, to avoid the reporters.

'How about a *big* hug?' Julia said at the classroom door.

Emily complied and skipped into the room. Tears would have been more comforting to Julia at that moment: Emily seemed to be blocking out the previous day, but she couldn't erase it completely. Eventually the horror would rise to the surface, and would need to be dealt with. You couldn't bury the past completely – Julia had seen evidence enough of that lately.

She fielded calls all day – from her mother, the Madison . . . five, other friends and colleagues. Two cops from the Wizard Task Force stopped by with still more questions. She spent the late afternoon and all evening with Emily, painting, reading together, watching television. Ray stopped by at eight-thirty, as promised.

'How's she doing?'

'At the moment, sleeping.'

'And you?'

'One day down, the rest of my life to go.' Julia hesitated a beat. 'How is Gail?'

'She's under heavy sedation at Bellevue. We've been trying to question her but so far she's basically incoherent. We'll get the details from her eventually.'

Julia felt tears running down her face. Ray put his arm around her.

'Two days ago you said you wanted to do something positive with your hypnosis skills,' he said. 'Think it's time to test your expertise?'

'Ray, I can't, not after what—'

'You *can*, Julia. *We* can. The investigation's over, we're free. I'm just an ordinary cop . . . in love with a civilian. Nothing wrong with that, is there?'

'After everything that's happened it *feels* wrong.'

'Let's see how it feels.' He picked her up and carried her to the bedroom, where they undressed slowly, watching each other. They kissed for a while before settling on to the bed, where all restraint ended.

'Don't expect a miracle, Ray,' she whispered in his ear. 'Just do what feels right.'

He lifted her off the mattress, turned her on her back, and rolled on top of her. As he entered her he touched his mouth to her ear and whispered, '*This* feels right.'

Friday 17 February

46

Julia walked into Max Altman's office on Friday morning without the slightest idea of what she was going to say.

Ray had urged her to take the day off, give herself time to process what had happened. Process it? She'd be happy if she could forget the past three weeks altogether. Except for last night.

Ray had left before Emily woke up, but would be coming over tonight. The Knicks were playing the Bulls. They'd order in Chinese, and later, after Emily was asleep, they'd make love again and again.

She plopped three file folders on Max Altman's desk and sat down.

'I'm sorry about what happened,' Max said.

'I'd rather not talk about it,' Julia said.

'Amazing how she changed her identity, took on a whole new persona.'

The *Times* had dug up Gail/Rachel's past – how she'd worked in the principal's office in high school, used a little white-out to change the name on her transcript, taken the SATs as Gail Severance and been admitted to Madison under the new identity. Several Madison alumni dimly recalled for the *Times* how a chubby freshman had become svelte by Christmas break – Rachel *becoming* Gail. Julia had turned down all interview requests.

429

'You did good in the park, Julia, you really—'

'Max – please . . . ?'

'Sorry.'

'This is my analysis of New England Air's seasonal market share.' She patted one folder, then another. 'This is the report from the media department, which I've annotated. And this is a strategy memo I put together – very preliminary, but a good enough starting point.'

Julia watched Max open a folder and realized that she felt not the slightest twinge of anxiety. Who cared what he thought of her report? What, for that matter, did she care? Just how important *was* New England Air's seasonal market share?

Hell, all over the city parents beat children, grown-ups beat each other, people beat back memories that threatened to consume them from the inside out. And Julia Mallet earned her living convincing all of them that softer laundry and more legroom would make them happy. *Shit*.

Julia was watching Max as he pored over the report – nodding here, making a notation there – when it hit her: if she wasn't interested in her performance or his opinion of it, she had no business working for Todman DiLorenzo.

'I'm leaving, Max.'

He looked up. 'Fine. I'll stop by when I've been through these. Looks good.'

'I mean, I'm leaving the agency. Resigning.'

Max gripped the arm-rests of his chair. 'But this is good stuff.'

She stood up. 'I'm sure there are plenty of people here who'll be happy to take credit for it.'

She turned and left.

Ray called Dolores at her house – their former house – and let the phone ring six times to make sure she wasn't there. She was moving out in a week and had asked him to come by and pick up a few things. With the afternoon off, and the coast clear, he decided to get it over with.

He walked the six blocks from his apartment to Dolores's place, trying to keep the events of the previous day out of his mind. Trying, but failing. He'd filed his report that morning, shrugging off the congratulations and high-fives: *The cop-killer is in custody. She'll give a statement as soon as she can string two sentences together, then she'll stay locked up for good. Nice work, Ray.*

Shit.

The three-bedroom cape – white shingles, black shutters, lace curtains in the front-facing windows – had once seemed like the end of the rainbow to him, the first and last house he'd ever buy. Now the prospect of a five-minute visit felt like a jail sentence. He unlocked the front door and stepped in.

Dolores hadn't changed a thing since he'd moved out. His softball trophies still gleamed from the top of the bookshelf in the living room. Freshly-polished silver frames held photos of their wedding, their honeymoon, their married life. A fucking shrine to their marriage. He shivered and hurried from the living room. The place had the eerily pristine pallor of a victim's home a week after the murder.

He found a carton in the basement, brought it up to the living room and began filling it. A couple of college textbooks, the trophies, the family photos. He carried the box to the dining room, then the kitchen, opening cabinets and drawers and closets but taking nothing. Ten years of marriage and everything he owned, apart from clothing, could fit in a single carton. He inspected a plate from their floral-patterned dinnerware set, put it back on the stack and closed the cabinet door. Had he really been so uninvolved in assembling the life they'd shared? Was there nothing accumulated during those years that he wanted to hold on to?

Things would be different with him and Julia. *Life* would be different.

Upstairs, in the master bedroom, he opened the bottom drawer of what had been his dresser and took out a sheaf of yellowed clippings of old cases, his high school and college diplomas, his first police-issue gun, a graduation certificate from the academy, an old pick set from his days as a beat cop – how many cars had he broken into for owners who'd locked their keys inside? He stuffed them in the carton, still only half full. Half empty.

Raphael Burgess, this is your life. Was your life.

He stood up and reached over to lift the box – and felt his chest seize up. He glanced down at the carton and took a step back, shaking his head.

'Oh, no. Please, God, no.'

But the smell told the whole story. He went to the bathroom off the second-floor landing, grabbed a hand towel, walked back to the bedroom, and reached into the carton. With the towel covering his fingers he took out the gun, pressed the nozzle to his nose, inhaled.

Fresh powder. The sharp, metallic odor filled his nostrils – filled in the missing pieces. He hadn't fired the Smith & Wesson in at least three years, not since the department issued the Glock automatics. He should have turned it in, but hadn't.

He could take the gun and toss it into the East River. Gail Severance was in custody; Julia was alive – case closed. He opened the chamber: three bullets left. He could put the gun to his head, pull the trigger. Case closed.

He heard the front door open and close, sat down on the bed and waited. A minute or two later she found him there.

'Ray! I didn't know you were here!'

The exclamation points were back, the perfectly made-up face, the tight blouse and pressed jeans.

'I came back to pick up my old things.'

'You should have called, I would have helped you with—'

'Including this.' He raised the gun, dropped it on the bed.

'You want some lunch, Ray?'

'Why, Dolores?'

'I have some tuna made, some—'

'*Why*?'

She stared at him, slowly shaking her head. 'I don't know what you're—'

'You killed a police officer, Dolores. With this.' He pointed to the gun.

'Ray, I haven't the—'

'You tried to kill Julia Mallet. And you killed a cop. A *cop*, Dolores. We recovered the bullets; they'll be traced directly to this gun.'

She stared at him, frozen, but her face was mutating to something harder, older, her lips and cheeks turning white, eyes darkening. 'I should have killed you,' she said, her voice low and growly. 'All those nights when you told me to be patient, to understand. You had problems, big problems after Gordon Prescott. I tried to understand, Ray, I really did. But then *you* stopped trying . . . and I didn't see why we should be married any more.'

'You knew I—'

'Then I find out you're fucking someone else. Here I was, thinking it was you who had a problem, then I find out it was *me* that was the problem. Gordon Prescott, he was just an excuse. It was *me* you didn't want to fuck.'

Tears streamed down her face, but her body remained rigid in the bedroom doorway.

'Dolores . . .' *Shift the focus to the details, avoid the big*

433

picture, the issue of guilt and innocence, at all costs. 'Julia Mallet was involved in an investigation. She was even a suspect at one point.'

'All those nights I . . . *begged* you, Ray, and you said you couldn't. You said be patient, try to understand.'

'You followed me to Julia's . . . you were watching me whenever—'

'I'm, like, full up to here with medication.' She ran the edge of her right hand along her throat. 'My shrink tells me I have a tendency to blame myself on account of all this childhood shit. And then . . . then I find out I *am* to blame. Your cock works just fine – it's me you won't fuck.'

He could remind her that the marriage had gone flat long before Gordon Prescott robbed them of the one thing they still shared. He could tell her about Julia hypnotising him, curing him. He could tell her it wasn't *about* her, not really. But none of that mattered any more.

'So you tried to kill her.' And killed Lou LaVigna instead.

She waited a long beat before answering, her eyes narrowing to angry slits. 'It should have been you, Ray.' She walked toward him. 'It should have been you.'

Part of him knew he should reach for the gun; the other part said, Let her have it. She'd kill herself, kill him – either way he'd be off the hook.

But he grabbed the gun as she sat next to him on the edge of the bed, resting her head on his shoulder. He grabbed the gun and saw a lifetime's commitment open up ahead of him.

It's you and me, Dolores. Just like you always wanted it.

Ray arrived shortly after Julia put Emily to bed.

'Why so late?' she asked.

He stood in the foyer, coat still on. His hair was a mess, his eyes bloodshot, avoiding her.

434

'We searched Gail's apartment last night, and again this morning,' he said. 'We never found the Smith and Wesson thirty-eight used on Lou LaVigna.'

'Gail must have thrown it away.'

Ray looked at her for a few moments, then slowly shook his head. 'This afternoon I went over to Dolores's. I needed to pack up some papers, a couple of books. My old gun . . .' He rubbed his face with both hands.

'Oh, God.' Julia moved a step toward him.

'I smelled the fresh powder the minute I picked it up.' He put his hands in his coat pockets. 'Dolores made a statement a few hours ago. About how she followed me here . . .'

'The car, the newspaper clipping, the sheets . . .'

He nodded. 'She found out about the spray-paint hanging around the department. We think the dispatcher let it slip. We knew for a fact that she was inside the task force room. She could have seen the spray-painted faces there, in the photos. We figure that's also where she got your home and office addresses, your license-plate number. She used my old pick set to get into your place.' Ray made a fist with his right hand and pounded his left palm. 'We were never too comfortable with the attack on you, the warnings. It never fit the pattern. But with Gail in custody, too fucking crazy to give a coherent statement . . . we figured we'd work out the details eventually.'

'Why, Ray?'

'We hadn't had sex since Gordon Prescott. At least with you, I . . .' He took a deep breath. 'Anyway, the marriage wasn't solid before Prescott. Dolores had been on and off medication for mood disorder for years. But when she found out we were spending time together she flipped out. I had a hunch she was following me – no, more than a hunch. Apparently she saw me come up here a few times at night.'

Julia shuddered.

'I'd blamed my problem with sex on Prescott. Seeing us together made me look like a liar, like *she* was my problem.'

She touched his arm. 'Ray, I'm—'

'They booked her at the Fortieth Precinct. She's in Bellevue now, for observation.' He laughed mirthlessly. 'With Gail Severance.'

Julia put her arms around him, felt him trembling.

'These past two years have been hell on her. I should have seen it, all the evidence was there.' A sob got through and she let him work it out in silence, holding him close while she stroked his back.

'Sit down, Ray,' she said after a while. 'I'll get you some—'

He pulled away. 'I'm really not sure how to say this.'

She looked into his eyes and would have cried herself if she had any tears left. 'Let me help,' she said. '*It's over.*'

He closed his eyes for a moment, nodded almost imperceptibly. 'She's been through so much, Julia, a lot of it my fault. I can't let her face this alone.'

Julia turned and walked into the living room.

'What about me?' she said when he followed her. 'Who says *I* can face everything alone?'

He put his hands on her shoulders, but she flinched and he backed off.

'It wouldn't feel right, Julia. I need to give one hundred per cent to Dolores, at least until she and I are able to talk it out, work it out. Maybe then . . .'

'Maybe then *what*? You'll give me a ring, see if I'm still *available*?'

He closed his eyes for a beat. 'I owe you everything,' he said. 'Everything.'

'Damn straight,' she said, anger bubbling up, rescuing her.

'I'm sorry.' He took her shoulders again, turned her around. Again she pulled away from him.

'I have to be there for Dolores,' he said. 'I need to make sure she gets through this. I owe her that much.' He reached to touch her shoulder but she pulled away. 'You and I, we—'

'What about us?'

'What we've been through . . . what we have together, it can't be erased. I hope we can work it out . . .' He shook his head. 'I *know* we can. Eventually. But I need time.'

'And I'm supposed to wait around?'

'I can't ask you to,' he almost whispered. 'But I—'

'I know what I'm going to do,' she said. 'I'm going to hypnotize myself. It's something I'm good at, right? I'm going to order myself to think of you as a photograph, a beautiful photograph that I can put in my pocket and forget about.'

'*I'll* never forget,' he said. 'Someday, after I've straightened things out with Dolores . . .'

She held up her hand, palm out. 'I can take out the photograph any time I want. But I'll always know that I can put it away again, too.'

He reached out a hand but pulled back just before touching her cheek.

'At the count of ten you'll be a photograph in my mind, a beautiful photograph I can look at or put away any time I want.'

'Julia, if I—'

'Ten, nine, eight . . .'

He looked at her for a second, then kissed her forehead and turned to go.

'. . . five, four, three . . .'

The door closed when she reached one.

She walked to the living-room window and looked out over the night-filled city. She had no job, no lover, no best friend. But she saw lights flickering on in apartments, streetlights flashing, even a star or two sparkling in the dense black sky, and she felt something inside her light up.

She couldn't control other people's lives, certainly not Ray's – she was done playing God. But she'd at least taken charge of her own life. She wouldn't sit around waiting for Ray to clean up his life so he could rejoin hers. But he'd be back eventually. They both knew it.

Manhattan glittered splendidly beyond her window, waiting for her. She went into Emily's room and stood over her daughter's bed until her eyes adjusted to the darkness and she could make out Emily's sleeping figure.

She'd keep Emily out of school tomorrow, they'd spend the whole day together, just the two of them, and the next day after that. No more goodbyes, ever.

A selection of bestsellers from Headline

STRAIT	Kit Craig	£5.99	☐
DON'T TALK TO STRANGERS	Bethany Campbell	£5.99	☐
HARVEST	Tess Gerritsen	£5.99	☐
SORTED	Jeff Gulvin	£5.99	☐
INHERITANCE	Keith Baker	£5.99	☐
PRAYERS FOR THE DEAD	Faye Kellerman	£5.99	☐
UNDONE	Michael Kimball	£5.99	☐
THE VIG	John Lescroart	£5.99	☐
ACQUIRED MOTIVE	Sarah Lovett	£5.99	☐
THE JUDGE	Steve Martini	£5.99	☐
BODY BLOW	Dianne Pugh	£5.99	☐
BLOOD RELATIONS	Barbara Parker	£5.99	☐

All Headline books are available at your local bookshop or newsagent, or can be ordered direct from the publisher. Just tick the titles you want and fill in the form below. Prices and availability subject to change without notice.

Headline Book Publishing, Cash Sales Department, Bookpoint, 39 Milton Park, Abingdon, OXON, OX14 4TD, UK. If you have a credit card you may order by telephone – 01235 400400.

Please enclose a cheque or postal order made payable to Bookpoint Ltd to the value of the cover price and allow the following for postage and packing:

UK & BFPO: £1.00 for the first book, 50p for the second book and 30p for each additional book ordered up to a maximum charge of £3.00.

OVERSEAS & EIRE: £2.00 for the first book, £1.00 for the second book and 50p for each additional book.

Name ....

Address ....

....

....

If you would prefer to pay by credit card, please complete:
Please debit my Visa/Access/Diner's Card/American Express (delete as applicable) card no:

Signature .... Expiry Date ....